With-Me High系列

108課綱、全民英檢

U0052800

核心英文字彙力

2001~4500

隨身讀

三民英語編輯小組 彙整

📱 APP　🎧 音檔

三民書局

序

英語 Make Me High 系列的理想在於超越，在於創新。
這是時代的精神，也是我們出版的動力；
這是教育的目的，也是我們進步的執著。

針對英語的全球化與未來的升學趨勢，
我們設計了一系列適合普高、技高學生的英語學習書籍。

面對英語，不會徬徨不再迷惘，學習的心徹底沸騰，
心情好 High！
實戰模擬，掌握先機知己知彼，百戰不殆決勝未來，
分數更 High！

選擇優質的英語學習書籍，才能激發學習的強烈動機；
興趣盎然便不會畏懼艱難，自信心要自己大聲說出來。
本書如良師指引循循善誘，如益友相互鼓勵攜手成長。
展書輕閱，你將發現……
學習英語原來也可以這麼 High！

使用説明 ▶▶▶

符號表

符號	意義
[同]	同義詞
[反]	反義詞
～	代替整個主單字
-	代替部分主單字
<>	該字義的相關搭配詞
( )	單字的相關補充資訊
▲	符合 108 課綱的情境例句
💡	更多相關補充用法
__ / __	不同語意的替換用法
__ / __	相同語意的替換用法

略語表

1. adj. 形容詞
2. adv. 副詞
3. art. 冠詞
4. aux. 助動詞
5. conj. 連接詞
6. n. 名詞
   [C] 可數
   [U] 不可數
   [pl.] 複數形
   [sing.] 單數形
7. prep. 介系詞
8. pron. 代名詞
9. v. 動詞
10. usu. pl. 常用複數
11. usu. sing. 常用單數
12. abbr. 縮寫

圖片來源：Shutterstock

電子朗讀音檔下載方式

請先輸入網址或掃描 QR code 進入「三民・東大音檔網」。

https://elearning.sanmin.com.tw/Voice/

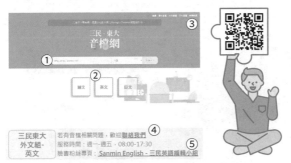

① 輸入本書書名即可找到音檔。請再依提示下載音檔。

② 也可點擊「英文」進入英文專區查找音檔後下載。

③ 若無法順利下載音檔,可至「常見問題」查看相關問題。

④ 若有音檔相關問題,請點擊「聯絡我們」,將盡快為你處理。

⑤ 更多英文新知都在臉書粉絲專頁。

英文三民誌 2.0 APP

掃描下方 QR code，即可下載 APP。

Android

iOS

開啟 APP 後，請點擊進入「英文學習叢書」，
尋找《核心英文字彙力 2001~4500》。

使用祕訣

① 利用「我的最愛」功能，輕鬆複習不熟的單字。

② 開啟 APP 後，請點擊進入「三民 / 東大單字測驗」用「單
機測驗」功能，讓你自行檢測單字熟練度。

目次

嗨!你今天學習了嗎?
一起使用進度檢核表吧!
學習完一個回次後,你可以在該回次的◯打勾。
一起培養核心英文字彙力吧!

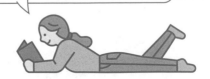

我的進度檢核表，
學習完成就打勾✅！

Level 3	①②③④⑤⑥⑦⑧⑨⑩ ⑪⑫⑬⑭⑮⑯⑰⑱⑲⑳ ㉑㉒㉓㉔㉕㉖㉗㉘㉙㉚ ㉛㉜㉝㉞㉟㊱㊲㊳㊴㊵
Level 4	①②③④⑤⑥⑦⑧⑨⑩ ⑪⑫⑬⑭⑮⑯⑰⑱⑲⑳ ㉑㉒㉓㉔㉕㉖㉗㉘㉙㉚ ㉛㉜㉝㉞㉟㊱㊲㊳㊴㊵
Level 5-1	①②③④⑤⑥⑦⑧⑨⑩ ⑪⑫⑬⑭⑮⑯⑰⑱⑲⑳

Unit 1

1. **award** [ə`wɔrd] n. [C] 獎項 <for>
   - ▲ Emma has won many awards for swimming.
     Emma 得了許多游泳的獎項。
   - **award** [ə`wɔrd] v. 授與，頒發
   - ▲ They awarded the athlete a gold medal for her excellent performance.
     由於這運動員的絕佳表現，他們頒發給她一面金牌。

2. **bubble** [`bʌbl] n. [C] 泡沫，氣泡
   - ▲ It is relaxing to take a bubble bath after a long day of work. 工作一整天後洗個泡泡浴讓人放鬆。
   - ♥ burst sb's bubble 打破…的希望 | bubble (milk) tea 珍珠奶茶

3. **cave** [kev] n. [C] 洞穴
   - ▲ There are many bats living in that cave.
     有很多蝙蝠住在那個洞穴裡。
   - **cave** [kev] v. 坍塌 <in>；讓步，妥協 <in>
   - ▲ Because of the chemical factory explosion, the roofs of the nearby houses all caved in.
     因為化學工廠爆炸，附近房屋的屋頂都坍塌了。

4. **communicate** [kə`mjunə,ket] v. 溝通 <with>
   - ▲ Many parents find it hard to communicate with their children. 很多父母發覺與孩子溝通很困難。

5. **county** [ˋkaʊntɪ] n. [C] 縣，郡 (abbr. Co.)
   ▲ The Tropic of Cancer goes through Chiayi County.
   北回歸線通過嘉義縣。

6. **dine** [daɪn] v. 用餐 <with>
   ▲ The Smiths invited me to dine with them.
   Smith 一家人邀請我和他們一起用餐。
   💡 dine on sth 正餐吃… | dine out/in 在外 / 在家用餐

7. **enable** [ɪnˋebl] v. 使能夠 [同] allow
   ▲ The new treatment enabled the patient to recover
   very soon. 新療法使病人能夠迅速復原。

8. **hollow** [ˋhɑlo] adj. 中空的，空心的；空洞的，虛偽的
   ▲ The squirrel hid in a big hollow tree.
   這松鼠躲在大樹的中空洞裡。

   hollow [ˋhɑlo] n. [C] 坑洞
   ▲ The government should do something about the
   hollows in the streets.
   政府該對街上的坑洞採取一些行動。

   hollow [ˋhɑlo] v. 挖空，挖洞 <out>
   ▲ The green activists were angry at hollowing out a
   tunnel in the mountain.
   環保人士對在山上開挖隧道感到憤怒。

9. **inform** [ɪnˋfɔrm] v. 通知，告知 <of, about>
   ▲ The leader held a meeting to inform everyone of the
   new sales figures.

領導人舉辦會議以告知大家最新的銷售數據。

10. **knit** [nɪt] **v.** 編織 (knitted, knit | knitted, knit | knitting)

   ▲ The grandmother is knitting a sweater for her grandson. 這位祖母正在幫她的孫子編織毛衣。

   knit [nɪt] **n.** [C] 針織衫，毛衣 (usu. pl.)

   ▲ The latest winter knits were snapped up within a few days. 最新款的冬裝針織衫在幾天內就被搶購一空。

11. **mostly** [ˋmostlɪ] **adv.** 通常 [同] mainly

   ▲ The customers of that store are mostly women.
   那家商店的顧客主要都是女性。

12. **ownership** [ˋonɚˏʃɪp] **n.** [U] 所有權

   ▲ The ownership of the restaurant has changed.
   這家餐廳的所有權已經換人了。

   ♥ private/public ownership 私人 / 公共所有權

13. **passage** [ˋpæsɪdʒ] **n.** [C] 通道 <through>；(文章的) 段落

   ▲ The reporter forced a passage through the crowd.
   這名記者在人群中擠出一條路前進。

14. **patience** [ˋpeʃəns] **n.** [U] 耐心，耐性 <with> [反] impatience

   ▲ The teacher always has a lot of patience with her students. 該老師對學生總是很有耐心。

   ♥ require/lose patience 需要 / 失去耐性

15. **persuade** [pɚˋswed] v. 使相信，使信服 [同] convince；說服，勸服

▲ The manager has persuaded his boss that the project is a good investment.
經理已經讓他的老闆相信這個專案很值得投資。

16. **poverty** [ˋpɑvɚtɪ] n. [U] 貧窮

▲ Unable to earn a living, the old woman lived in poverty. 這老太太因為無法賺錢謀生，所以生活貧困。

💡 a poverty of sth 缺乏…

17. **replace** [rɪˋples] v. 取代，代替 <with>

▲ For the sake of health, many people nowadays replace butter with olive oil in cooking. 為了健康的緣故，現今許多人烹飪時用橄欖油取代奶油。

replacement [rɪˋplesmənt] n. [C][U] 替代 (物)

▲ In some factories, the replacement of human workers by robots has become common.
在一些工廠，用機器人取代工人已經很普遍。

18. **risk** [rɪsk] n. [C][U] 冒險，風險

▲ Andy ran the risk of losing all his savings when he invested in the stock market.
Andy 冒著損失所有存款的風險投資股市。

💡 at your own risk 風險自負

risk [rɪsk] v. 冒…的危險

▲ You should not risk your health by smoking.

你不該抽菸來讓自己的健康承擔風險。

19. **rough** [rʌf] adj. 粗糙的 [反] smooth
▲ The man's hands are very rough. 男子的手非常粗糙。
rough [rʌf] adv. 粗魯地
▲ The player played rough so she was shown a yellow card. 那位球員踢球粗魯，所以她被舉了黃牌。
💡 live/sleep rough 餐風宿露
rough [rʌf] n. [C] 草稿，草圖
▲ The speaker did several roughs of the important speech. 講者擬了幾份這次重要演講的草稿。
💡 in rough 粗略地，大致上

20. **sticky** [ˋstɪkɪ] adj. 黏性的；棘手的 (stickier | stickiest)
▲ The glue left my fingers sticky.
膠水使我的手指黏黏的。

21. **stomach** [ˋstʌmək] n. [C] 胃，下腹 (pl. stomachs)
▲ Don't swim on a full stomach. 吃飽時不要游泳。
💡 an upset stomach 腸胃不舒服 | have a weak/strong stomach 易 / 不易反胃；忍耐力差 / 好

22. **temporary** [ˋtɛmpə͵rɛrɪ] adj. 暫時的 [反] permanent
▲ Gary's house collapsed in the earthquake, so he and his family are living in a temporary shelter.
Gary 的房子在地震中倒塌，所以他和家人現在正住在暫時的避難所。
💡 temporary measure/solution 暫時的措施 / 解決辦法

23. **van** [væn] n. [C] 廂型車
  ▲ As there are six of us traveling together, we have to rent a van instead of a car. 因為我們有六個人一起旅行，我們必須租廂型車而不是小轎車。

24. **vanish** [ˋvænɪʃ] v. 突然消失 [同] disappear
  ▲ When Betty heard the bad news, her smile vanished immediately.
  當 Betty 聽到這個壞消息時，她的笑容瞬間消失了。
  💡 vanish in a puff of smoke/into thin air 消失得無影無蹤

25. **weekly** [ˋwiklɪ] adj. 每週的
  ▲ Sam pays a weekly visit to his parents in Taichung.
  Sam 每週去臺中探望父母一次。
  weekly [ˋwiklɪ] adv. 每週地
  ▲ The factory workers are paid weekly.
  這工廠的工人領週薪。
  weekly [ˋwiklɪ] n. [C] 週刊
  ▲ *The Economist* is a weekly, focusing on political, technological, and business news worldwide.
  《經濟學人》是一份週刊，專門報導世界各地政治、科技和經濟新聞。

Unit 2

1. **bamboo** [bæmˋbu] n. [C][U] 竹 (pl. bamboos)
  ▲ Bamboo shoots are very delicious. 竹筍相當美味。

2. **bucket** [ˋbʌkɪt] n. [C] 水桶 [同] pail

▲ Mrs. Chen carried a bucket and a mop to clean the balcony. 陳太太提著水桶和拖把去清理陽臺。

💡 in buckets 大量

3. **cheek** [tʃik] n. [C] 臉頰

▲ My mother kissed me on the cheek and said "Good night." 媽媽親吻我的臉頰後道聲晚安。

4. **connect** [kəˋnɛkt] v. 連接 <to>；和…有關聯 <with> [同] associate

▲ The United Kingdom is connected to France by the Channel Tunnel. 英國和法國由海底隧道連接起來。

5. **dairy** [ˋdɛrɪ] n. [U] 乳製品

▲ Since Elena has an allergy to milk, the doctor asks her to avoid dairy.
由於 Elena 對牛奶過敏，醫生要求她要避免乳製品。

6. **dinosaur** [ˋdaɪnə͵sɔr] n. [C] 恐龍

▲ The museum houses several dinosaur fossils.
這間博物館收藏了一些恐龍化石。

7. **erase** [ɪˋres] v. 擦掉，去除；(從腦海中) 清除 <from>

▲ The teacher asked Ella to erase the words on the blackboard. 老師要 Ella 擦掉黑板上的字。

8. **imagination** [ɪ͵mædʒəˋneʃən] n. [C][U] 想像力

▲ The poet has a vivid imagination.

這名詩人有生動的想像力。

💡 capture/catch sb's imagination 引起…的興趣

---

9. **intelligent** [ɪn`tɛlədʒənt] adj. 聰明的 [反] unintelligent

▲ Life becomes easier with the application of the intelligent devices like computers and smartphones.
生活因為使用智慧型裝置如電腦和智慧型手機而變得更輕鬆。

---

10. **leak** [lik] n. [C] 漏洞;漏出物

▲ Roger found a leak in the roof of his house.
Roger 發現房子屋頂有一處漏洞。

leak [lik] v. (液體或氣體) 漏出 <into, from, out> [同] seep;洩漏 (機密) <to> [同] disclose

▲ There is some water leaking from the pipe.
有一些水從管子中滲漏出來。

---

11. **opportunity** [ˌɑpə`tjunətɪ] n. [C][U] 機會 [同] chance (pl. opportunities)

▲ The attendees have the opportunity to win a free concert ticket.
出席活動者有機會贏得免費的音樂會門票。

💡 seize/grasp an opportunity 抓緊機會 | miss/lose an opportunity 錯失機會

---

12. **passion** [`pæʃən] n. [C][U] 強烈的情感;[C] 熱愛 <for>

▲ The councilor spoke with passion about what she would do to help the people in need.

這位市議員激動地述說她要如何幫助需要幫助的人民。

---

13. **pile** [paɪl] n. [C] 堆

▲ There is a pile of dirty clothes in the corner.
角落有一堆髒衣服。

💡 make a pile 賺很多錢

pile [paɪl] v. 堆積

▲ The professor piled his teaching materials on the desk. 教授把教材堆在書桌上。

---

14. **practical** [ˋpræktɪkl] adj. 實際的 [反] impractical；實用的

▲ Your plan is not very practical. I am afraid it won't be put into practice.
你的計畫不大實際。它恐怕不會被實行。

💡 for (all) practical purposes 其實，事實上

practically [ˋpræktɪklɪ] adv. 實際上

▲ Practically speaking, there is no rule without an exception. 實際上來說，所有規則都有例外。

---

15. **process** [ˋprɑsɛs] n. [C] 過程 (pl. processes)

▲ My company is in the process of merging with another firm. 我的公司正在與其他公司合併的過程中。

process [ˋprɑsɛs] v. 加工處理；審核文件

▲ The pork is processed into sausage.
豬肉被加工處理成香腸。

---

16. **puppet** [ˋpʌpɪt] n. [C] 木偶；傀儡

▲ Children like to go to puppet shows.
小孩喜歡看木偶劇。

17. **situation** [ˌsɪtʃʊˋeʃən] n. [C] 情況

▲ Frank still stays positive in such a difficult situation.
在如此艱難的情況下，Frank 仍然保持樂觀。

18. **stool** [stul] n. [C] (無椅背) 凳子

▲ Curious about what we were talking about, Susan pulled up a stool to sit beside us. 由於好奇我們談論的內容，Susan 拉了張凳子來坐在我們旁邊。

19. **strategy** [ˋstrætədʒɪ] n. [C][U] 策略 <for> (pl. strategies)

▲ The government should work out an effective strategy for fighting crime.
政府應制定有效打擊犯罪的策略。

♥ economic/political strategy 經濟 / 政治策略 | adopt/develop a strategy 實行 / 發想策略

20. **tablet** [ˋtæblɪt] n. [C] 藥片 [同] pill

▲ Take three tablets a day after meals.
每日服用三片，三餐飯後服用。

♥ vitamin/sleeping/indigestion tablet 維他命片 / 安眠藥 / 胃藥

21. **threat** [θrɛt] n. [C][U] 威脅

▲ Reckless driving poses a serious threat to pedestrians. 魯莽的駕駛對行人造成嚴重的威脅。

● be under threat of sth 受到…的威脅

22. **tourist** [`tʊrɪst] n. [C] 觀光客
▲ Tourist attractions are always crowded with tourists in high season. 觀光景點在旺季總是擠滿觀光客。
● tourist industry 旅遊業

23. **vision** [`vɪʒən] n. [U] 視力 [同] eyesight；遠見 [同] foresight
▲ The boxer lost vision in one of his eyes.
這位拳擊手的一隻眼睛失明了。
● good/poor/normal vision 視力好 / 差 / 正常

24. **volume** [`vɑljəm] n. [C][U] 容積；[U] 音量
▲ What is the volume of that container?
那個容器的容積有多大？
● turn the volume up/down 調高 / 低音量

25. **yearly** [`jɪrlɪ] adj. 一年的，每年的
▲ Frank's yearly income is US$60,000.
Frank 的年收入是六萬美元。
● on a yearly basis 按年的
yearly [`jɪrlɪ] adv. 每年地
▲ The interest on my savings account is paid twice yearly. 我存款帳戶的利息一年給兩次。
● grow/increase/rise yearly 逐年增加

Unit 3

1. **achieve** [ə`tʃiv] **v.** 達到，實現 [同] attain, accomplish
   ▲ Jimmy achieved great exam results through studying hard. Jimmy 透過認真學習得到很好的考試成績。

   achievement [ə`tʃivmənt] **n.** [C] 成績，表現；[U] 成就
   ▲ It is an impressive achievement for a beginner.
   這對一名初學者來說是很出色的成績。

2. **appeal** [ə`pil] **n.** [C] 懇求，呼籲；[U] 吸引力
   ▲ The president made an appeal to the international community for help after the earthquake.
   總統在地震後向國際社會懇求救援。

   appeal [ə`pil] **v.** 懇求 <to> [同] plead；吸引 <to> [同] attract
   ▲ Being sentenced to death, the prisoner appealed to the judge for mercy.
   當被判死刑時，這囚犯懇求法官開恩。

   appealing [ə`pilɪŋ] **adj.** 有魅力的
   ▲ The voice actor has a very unique and appealing voice. 這位配音員有很獨特且富有魅力的嗓音。

3. **attract** [ə`trækt] **v.** 吸引
   ▲ What attracts me to the job is that I can always learn something new.
   這項工作吸引我的地方是我總可以學新事物。
   ♥ be attracted by/to sb/sth 被…吸引

4. **bride** [braɪd] n. [C] 新娘
   ▲ At the wedding reception, Mr. Chen stood up and proposed a toast to the bride and groom.
   在婚宴上，陳先生站起來，為新娘和新郎舉杯祝福。

5. **cabin** [ˋkæbɪn] n. [C] 小木屋；(船或飛機的) 客艙
   ▲ There is a log cabin in the forest.
   森林裡有一棟原木小屋。

6. **cheerful** [ˋtʃɪrfəl] adj. 開心的，快樂的
   ▲ May really enjoys Richard's company because he is always cheerful.
   May 真的很喜歡 Richard 的陪伴，因為他總是很開心。

7. **conclusion** [kənˋkluʒən] n. [C] 結論
   ▲ Gary and Lisa finally reached the conclusion that they would have their wedding in June.
   Gary 和 Lisa 終於得到要在六月舉行婚禮的結論。
   💡 in conclusion 最後，總之｜draw/reach/come to a conclusion 得到結論｜jump/leap to conclusions 草率下結論

8. **considerable** [kənˋsɪdərəbl] adj. 相當大的，相當多的
   [同] significant
   ▲ Social media has a considerable influence on the way people interact with each other.
   社群媒體對人與人之間的互動方式有相當大的影響。

9. **definition** [͵dɛfəˋnɪʃən] n. [C] 定義，解釋

▲ A dictionary gives the definitions of words.
字典說明字的定義。

💡 by definition 按照定義

10. **dip** [dɪp] v. 浸，蘸 <in, into> [同] dunk (dipped | dipped | dipping)

▲ The boy dipped his biscuit in the milk.
這男孩把餅乾蘸一下牛奶。

dip [dɪp] n. [C] (短時間) 游泳，玩水；[C][U] 調味醬

▲ We took a dip in the lake. 我們在湖裡游泳。

11. **explode** [ɪk`splod] v. 爆炸 [同] blow up ；(情緒) 爆發 <with, into>

▲ A bomb exploded on the bus and killed all the passengers. 炸彈在公車上爆炸，使所有的乘客喪生。

12. **invent** [ɪn`vɛnt] v. 發明

▲ Nikola Tesla invented the first alternating current motor. 尼古拉特斯拉發明了第一臺交流馬達。

13. **journey** [`dʒɝnɪ] n. [C] 旅行 [同] trip

▲ Before going on a journey, Helena packed everything she might need in a big suitcase. 出發去旅行前，Helena 將所有可能需要的東西打包在一個大皮箱裡。

journey [`dʒɝnɪ] v. 旅行

▲ After Ann retired from teaching, she has journeyed to six countries.
Ann 從教職退休後，已經去過六個國家旅行。

14. **learning** [ˈlɝnɪŋ] **n.** [U] 學習

▲ My part-time job is a great learning experience for me. 我的兼職工作對我來說是個很棒的學習經驗。

15. **leopard** [ˈlɛpɚd] **n.** [C] 豹

▲ Leopards are under the threat from illegal hunting.
豹正受非法狩獵的威脅。

💡 A leopard cannot change its spots. 【諺】本性難移。

16. **palm** [pɑm] **n.** [C] 手掌；棕櫚樹

▲ The fortune teller read her palm.
算命先生幫她看過手相。

💡 have sb in the palm of sb's hand ⋯把⋯攢在手掌心
(⋯完全掌控⋯)

17. **permission** [pɚˈmɪʃən] **n.** [U] 許可

▲ Students must get the teacher's permission to leave the classroom.
學生必須徵求老師的同意才能離開教室。

💡 give/grant sb permission 給⋯許可 | get/obtain sb's permission 得到⋯的許可

18. **pollute** [pəˈlut] **v.** 汙染

▲ The river was polluted by chemicals drained from the nearby factories.
這條河受到附近工廠排出的化學藥品汙染。

19. **presence** [ˈprɛzn̩s] **n.** [U] 出席 [反] absence；存在 [反] absence

▲ The singer was touched and surprised by the presence of so many fans.
這位歌手因為眾多粉絲出席感到又驚又喜。

💡 make your presence felt 突顯自己；對情勢發揮作用

20. **quit** [kwɪt] v. 停止；放棄 (quit | quit | quitting)

▲ Tina has decided to quit as CEO of the Taiwan branch. Tina 決定辭去臺灣區分公司執行長的職務。

21. **staff** [stæf] n. [sing.] 全體員工

▲ This kindergarten has a teaching staff of five.
這所幼兒園有五位教學人員。

💡 medical/nursing/coaching staff 醫務 / 護理 / 教練人員

staff [stæf] v. 任職

▲ This legal advice center is staffed mainly by volunteers and law students. 在這間法律諮詢中心工作的主要是志工和法律系學生。

22. **straw** [strɔ] n. [U] 稻草；[C] 吸管

▲ The little girl is putting on a straw hat with a ribbon bow. 這名小女孩正戴上一頂有蝴蝶結的草帽。

💡 clutch/grasp at straws 抓住救命稻草 (不放過任何微小的機會)｜ the final/last straw (壓垮駱駝的) 最後一根稻草

23. **tap** [tæp] v. 輕拍，輕敲 <on> (tapped | tapped | tapping)

▲ Stacey tapped me on the left shoulder.

Stacey 輕拍我的左肩。

💡 tap sth out 輕輕敲打…的節拍；敲擊鍵盤輸入…

tap [tæp] n. [C] 水龍頭 <on> [同] faucet

▲ Victor turned the tap on to wash his face.
Victor 打開水龍頭來洗臉。

💡 on tap 隨時可以使用的

---

24. **warn** [wɔrn] v. 警告，提醒 <about, against>

▲ People are warned against swimming in the polluted river. 大家受到警告不要在那受汙染的河川中游泳。

warning [`wɔrnɪŋ] n. [C][U] 警告，提醒

▲ The government recently issued a warning about cold temperatures. 政府近期發布低溫特報。

💡 advance/prior warning 事前預警｜without warning 毫無預警地，突然間

---

25. **zone** [zon] n. [C] 地區

▲ Both Taiwan and Japan are located in earthquake zones. 臺灣和日本都位在地震帶上。

💡 in the zone 處於最佳狀態

zone [zon] v. 指定…為某用途的區域

▲ This land was zoned for industrial use, not for housing. 這塊地過去指定為工業用地，而非住宅地。

💡 zone out 失神，恍神

Unit 4

1. **aboard** [ə`bord] prep. 搭乘 (火車、船和飛機等交通工具)

   ▲ Welcome aboard flight BR520 to Paris.
   歡迎搭乘 BR520 班機前往巴黎。

   aboard [ə`bord] adv. 上 (火車、船和飛機等交通工具)

   ▲ The bus is about to leave. All aboard!
   公車要離站了。乘客全部上車!

2. **adventure** [əd`vɛntʃə] n. [C][U] 冒險

   ▲ The speaker is telling the audience about his adventures in Africa.
   這位講者跟聽眾分享他在非洲的冒險故事。

   adventurous [əd`vɛntʃərəs] adj. 有冒險精神的,勇於嘗試新事物的

   ▲ Linda is adventurous in trying new food. You can find related videos on her YouTube channel.
   Linda 勇於嘗試新上市的食物。你可以在她的 YouTube 頻道找到相關的影片。

3. **afford** [ə`ford] v. 負擔得起

   ▲ The young couple can't afford a house now.
   這對年輕的夫妻現在在買不起一間房子。

   affordable [ə`fordəbḷ] adj. 買得起的,能夠負擔的 [反] unaffordable

   ▲ The clothes are both nice and affordable.

這些衣服物美價廉。

💡 affordable prices/housing 能夠負擔的價格 / 買得起的
房子

---

4. **background** [`bæk͵graʊnd] n. [C] 出身背景；(相片、畫
的) 背景

▲ The company has employees from different cultural
backgrounds. 這間公司有來自不同文化背景的員工。

---

5. **campus** [`kæmpəs] n. [C][U] 校園，校區

▲ My classmate hasn't decided whether to live on
campus or off campus.
我同學尚未決定要住校還是要外宿。

---

6. **carpenter** [`kɑrpəntɚ] n. [C] 木匠

▲ As a carpenter, my grandfather makes and repairs
wooden objects.
身為一個木匠，我的祖父製作和維修木製的東西。

---

7. **chill** [tʃɪl] n. [sing.] 寒意，涼意；[C] 著涼，風寒

▲ Esther could feel the chill in the air as soon as she
got up from bed.
Esther 一從床上起來就有感受到寒意。

💡 take the chill off sth 給⋯去除寒氣

chill [tʃɪl] v. 使冷卻，使變冷；冷靜，放輕鬆

▲ The pastry dough needs to be chilled for 30 to 45
minutes before baking.
酥皮麵團在烘烤前需要冷藏三十到四十五分鐘。

💡 chill sb to the bone 寒風刺骨；使…不寒而慄

chill [tʃɪl] adj. 寒冷的

▲ It's really frustrating to commute in the chill rain.
在寒冷的雨天通勤真的很叫人沮喪。

💡 the chill wind of sth …引起的問題

---

8. **coach** [kotʃ] n. [C] 教練；大型四輪馬車

▲ The team has a good winning record because they have a good coach.
這支隊伍擁有良好的獲勝紀錄，因為他們有個好教練。

coach [kotʃ] v. 訓練，指導

▲ Mrs. Ma coaches her students to interview for colleges. 馬老師訓練學生如何參與大學面試。

---

9. **creative** [krɪ`etɪv] adj. 有創造力的

▲ The company encourages employees to be creative.
這家公司鼓勵員工有創造力。

💡 creative thinking 創造性思考 | creative talents/abilities 創造天分 / 能力

---

10. **crispy** [`krɪspɪ] adj. 酥脆的 (crispier | crispiest)

▲ May loves crispy potato chips very much.
May 很愛酥脆的洋芋片。

---

11. **democratic** [ˌdɛmə`krætɪk] adj. 民主的

▲ In a democratic society, everyone has equal rights.
在民主社會裡，每個人都有平等的權利。

💡 democratic country/system/government/participation/decision 民主國家 / 制度 / 政府 / 參與 / 決策 | the Democratic Party 民主黨 (美國兩大政黨之一)

---

12. **dirt** [dɝt] **n.** [U] 塵土，泥土 [同] dust

▲ Ben washed the dirt off his rain boots before going into the house.
進入房子之前，Ben 把雨靴上的塵土洗掉。

💡 dirt poor/cheap 赤貧的 / 非常便宜的

---

13. **extreme** [ɪk`strim] **adj.** 極度的，極端的

▲ Climate change has caused extreme weather conditions to become more common these days.
近來氣候變遷已經使得極端天氣狀況變得更普遍。

extreme [ɪk`strim] **n.** [C] 極度，極端

▲ Gina used to be optimistic, but she has gone to the opposite extreme since her beloved passed away.
Gina 以前很樂觀，但自從她的摯愛過世後，她就走向相反的極端。

💡 in the extreme 非常，極其

extremely [ɪk`strimlɪ] **adv.** 非常，極其

▲ The lucky girl was extremely excited when she won a new car.
當這位幸運的女孩贏得一輛新車時，她非常地興奮。

---

14. **inventor** [ɪn`vɛntɚ] **n.** [C] 發明家

▲ Alexander Graham Bell is commonly regarded as the inventor of the first practical telephone.

亞歷山大格拉漢姆貝爾被多數人視作第一支實用電話的發明者。

---

15. **junk** [dʒʌŋk] n. [U] 廢棄物 [同] garbage

▲ The old man's home is full of junk, including broken chairs and old TV sets.

這個老人的家滿是廢棄物，包括壞掉的椅子和舊電視。

💡 junk mail/food 垃圾郵件 / 食物

junk [dʒʌŋk] v. 丟棄，扔掉

▲ According to the records, millions of tons of clothing are junked every year.

根據紀錄，每年有幾百萬噸的衣物被丟棄。

---

16. **litter** [ˋlɪtɚ] n. [U] 垃圾 [同] rubbish, trash, garbage

▲ There is litter everywhere in the park.

公園裡到處都是垃圾。

litter [ˋlɪtɚ] v. 到處亂丟 <with>

▲ It's heartbreaking to see the streets were littered with trash after the parade.

看到遊行後街上到處是亂丟的垃圾很讓人心痛。

---

17. **pineapple** [ˋpaɪn‚æpl̩] n. [C][U] 鳳梨

▲ We grow a lot of pineapples in Taiwan.

臺灣種很多鳳梨。

---

18. **precious** [ˋprɛʃəs] adj. 珍貴的，寶貴的

▲ Freedom is very precious, so we have to treasure it.

自由很寶貴，所以我們必須珍惜。

---

19. **previous** [ˈprivɪəs] adj. 先前的 [同] prior

▲ If you haven't read the previous chapter, you probably will have difficulty understanding the following story. 如果你不曾讀過前一章，你可能無法了解接下來故事的內容。

💡 previous to sth 在…之前

previously [ˈprivɪəslɪ] adv. 先前

▲ Restaurants that were previously bustling with customers are now closed or provide takeaway only. 以前擠滿顧客的餐廳現在不是關門就是只提供外賣。

20. **probable** [ˈprɑbəbl̩] adj. 有可能的 [反] improbable

▲ It is highly probable that Luke will quit his job owing to his illness. Luke 很可能因病辭職。

probability [ˌprɑbəˈbɪlətɪ] n. [C][U] 可能性 [同] likelihood (pl. probabilities)

▲ There is a strong probability that you suffer from depression if you feel like crying for more than two weeks.

如果你超過兩星期想哭，你非常可能是得了憂鬱症。

💡 in all probability 很有可能，十之八九

21. **representative** [ˌrɛprɪˈzɛntətɪv] adj. 典型的，有代表性的 <of> [反] unrepresentative

▲ That building is representative of Victorian architecture. 那幢建築物是典型的維多利亞式建築。

representative [ˌrɛprɪˈzɛntətɪv] n. [C] 代表 <of>

[同] delegate

▲ If you have any problems, feel free to contact one of our representatives for immediate support.

你如果有任何問題，歡迎隨時與我們的代表聯絡，以提供即時協助。

💡 representative of the UN 聯合國的代表 | Representative (美國) 眾議院議員

---

22. **strip** [strɪp] n. [C] 細長條

▲ Did you read that funny comic strip?

你有看過那篇有趣的連載漫畫嗎？

strip [strɪp] v. 剝掉 <off, from> [同] remove ；脫衣服 <off> [同] undress (stripped | stripped | stripping)

▲ To renovate his old house, Jerry needs to strip all the faded wallpaper off the walls first. 為了重新裝潢舊家，Jerry 需要先把牆上所有褪色的壁紙剝掉。

---

23. **stubborn** [ˋstʌbən] adj. 固執的 [同] obstinate

▲ Don't waste your breath. My brother won't listen because he is very stubborn.

不要白費口舌了。我弟弟不會聽的，因為他很固執。

💡 as stubborn as a mule 非常固執的 | stubborn pride 死要面子

---

24. **technique** [tɛkˋnik] n. [C][U] 技巧，技能 <for>

▲ The nanny has a wonderful technique for taking care of children. 這保姆照顧小孩很有一套。

---

25. **various** [ˋvɛrɪəs] adj. 各種的 [同] diverse

▲ Annie decided to quit her job and moved to another city for various reasons. Annie 基於種種因素決定要辭掉工作並搬去另一個城市。

Unit 5

1. **admire** [ədˋmaɪr] v. 欽佩，讚賞

▲ Tina admires Fiona for being able to express herself clearly in English. Tina 很佩服 Fiona 能夠以英語清楚地表達自己的想法。

2. **advertise** [ˋædvɚ͵taɪz] v. 登廣告

▲ The company is going to spend a lot of money advertising their new product on television.
這間公司將要花一大筆錢在電視上登新產品的廣告。

advertisement [͵ædvɚˋtaɪzmənt] n. [C] 廣告 (also ad)

▲ I put an advertisement for volunteers on Facebook.
我在臉書上登了徵志工的廣告。

💡 be an advertisement for sth 是⋯的活招牌

advertising [ˋædvɚ͵taɪzɪŋ] n. [U] 廣告業

▲ My cousin works in advertising.
我的表哥在廣告業工作。

3. **anxious** [ˋæŋkʃəs] adj. 擔心的 <about, for> [同] worried

▲ More and more people are anxious about the future of the country owing to the decreasing birth rate.

因出生率日益降低，越來越多人憂心國家的未來。

🔹 be anxious for sb 為…感到擔心

4. **benefit** [ˋbɛnəfɪt] n. [C][U] 益處；補助

▲ It will be to your benefit to read the book.
讀這本書將對你有益處。

🔹 give sb the benefit of the doubt 把…往好處想 |
unemployment/housing benefit 失業 / 房屋補助

benefit [ˋbɛnəfɪt] v. 得益於 <by, from>

▲ Only the poor will benefit from this law. It is not
applicable to the rich.
只有窮人得益於此法律。對富人不適用。

---

5. **casual** [ˋkæʒʊəl] adj. 休閒的，非正式的 [反] formal；輕
鬆的

▲ The employees are allowed to wear casual clothes.
員工可以穿休閒的服裝。

casually [ˋkæʒʊəlɪ] adv. 隨便地，輕便地

▲ Thomas was casually dressed in a T-shirt and jeans.
Thomas 隨便地穿著一件 T 恤和牛仔褲。

6. **chilly** [ˋtʃɪlɪ] adj. 寒冷的 (chillier | chilliest)

▲ I like to wrap myself up in a wool blanket to keep my
body warm on chilly winter nights. 在寒冷的冬夜，我
喜歡將自己包裹在羊毛毯裡，以保持身體溫暖。

7. **colorful** [ˋkʌləfəl] adj. 多采多姿的

▲ Emma led a colorful life after retirement.

Emma 退休後過著多采多姿的生活。

---

8. **decade** [ˈdɛked] n. [C] 十年
   ▲ I haven't seen my aunt for over a decade.
   我已經超過十年沒有見到我阿姨了。

---

9. **dishonest** [dɪsˈɑnɪst] adj. 不誠實的，欺騙的 [反] honest
   ▲ Joanna sued the dishonest traders for damages.
   Joanna 控告不老實的商人並要求賠償。
   dishonesty [dɪsˈɑnɪstɪ] n. [U] 不誠實
   ▲ The politician's dishonesty has landed him in trouble. 該名政治人物的不誠實讓他陷入麻煩之中。

---

10. **drunk** [drʌŋk] adj. 酒醉的
    ▲ Leo got completely drunk, so his friend called a taxi for him.
    Leo 喝得很醉，所以他朋友幫他叫了一輛計程車。
    drunk [drʌŋk] n. [C] 醉漢
    ▲ The drunk wanted another drink. 這醉漢想再喝一杯。

---

11. **fade** [fed] v. 褪色；衰退
    ▲ The dress faded after only a wash.
    那件洋裝洗一次就褪色了。

---

12. **fortune** [ˈfɔrtʃən] n. [U] 好運；[C] 財富
    ▲ Fortune smiled on me. I won the lottery.
    幸運女神對我笑。我中了樂透。

---

13. **jewel** [ˈdʒuəl] n. [C] 寶石 [同] gem

▲ The diver was thrilled at the possibility of finding some jewels in the sunken ship.
潛水夫想到有可能在沉船中發現一些寶石就很興奮。

14. **limb** [lɪm] n. [C] (人或動物的) 肢體
    ▲ The patient felt great pain when he tried to move his limbs. 這病人試著移動四肢時，覺得非常疼痛。
    ♥ out on a limb (意見) 無人支持或贊同

15. **luggage** [ˋlʌgɪdʒ] n. [U] 行李 [同] baggage
    ▲ Please help me put the heavy luggage in the car.
    請幫我把沉重的行李放進車子。

16. **normal** [ˋnɔrml̩] adj. 正常的 [反] abnormal
    ▲ An adult's normal body temperature is about 36°C to 37°C. 成人正常體溫大約是攝氏三十六到三十七度。
    normally [ˋnɔrml̩ɪ] adv. 正常地，通常
    ▲ Normally, Gloria is not so late.
    Gloria 通常不會那麼晚到。

17. **perform** [pɚˋfɔrm] v. 執行 [同] carry out；表演
    ▲ The doctor is performing a heart operation now.
    醫生現在正在執行心臟手術。

18. **profit** [ˋprɑfɪt] n. [C][U] 盈利，利潤
    ▲ George made a big profit from selling second-hand cars. George 靠賣二手車賺很多錢。
    profit [ˋprɑfɪt] v. 獲利 <by, from>
    ▲ A wise man profits by his mistakes.

智者從錯誤中獲益。

---

19. **proof** [pruf] n. [C][U] 證據，證物 [同] evidence
   ▲ The police have a lot of proof against the suspect.
   警方有很多不利於此嫌犯的證據。
   💡 living proof 活生生的證明 | the proof of the pudding
   布丁好不好，吃了才知道 (空談不如實證)

20. **release** [rɪ`lis] n. [C][U] 釋放；上映
   ▲ The release of the three hostages made the
   negotiators feel a thrill of excitement.
   三名人質的釋放使談判人員感到振奮。
   release [rɪ`lis] v. 釋放；發行
   ▲ The authorities released the political prisoners from
   the jails under international pressure.
   當局迫於國際壓力將政治犯從監獄釋放。

21. **responsibility** [rɪ,spɑnsə`bɪlətɪ] n. [C][U] 責任，職責
   <for> (pl. responsibilities)
   ▲ I will take full responsibility for the failure.
   我會對這次的失敗負全責。
   💡 have a responsibility to sb 對⋯負責

22. **salary** [`sælərɪ] n. [C][U] 薪水 (pl. salaries)
   ▲ Jack earns a salary of $500 per week.
   Jack 週薪五百美元。
   💡 annual/monthly salary 年 / 月薪 | boost/raise/cut/
   reduce salaries 提高 / 降低薪資

---

23. **structure** [ˋstrʌktʃɚ] **n.** [C][U] 結構，組織；[C] 建築物
   ▲ The first two chapters of the book discuss the changing political and social structure of the island.
   這本書的前兩章討論島上改變中的政治和社會結構。

24. **stuff** [stʌf] **n.** [U] 物品，東西
   ▲ What is the name of the stuff you used to mend the vase? 你用來修補花瓶的東西叫什麼？
   💡 do your stuff 做分內的事
   stuff [stʌf] **v.** 塞滿 <with> [同] fill
   ▲ When I returned from my vacation, my suitcase was stuffed with souvenirs.
   我渡假回來時，行李箱塞滿了紀念品。
   💡 stuff your face 大吃大喝

25. **tune** [tjun] **n.** [C] 曲子 [同] melody
   ▲ The pianist played several popular tunes.
   這位鋼琴師演奏了幾首熱門的曲子。
   💡 in/out of tune 音很準 / 走音
   tune [tjun] **v.** (為樂器) 調音
   ▲ The piano hasn't been tuned for years, so its pitch is not quite right.
   那架鋼琴已經很久沒調音了，所以音準不太對。
   💡 tune (sb/sth) out (對⋯) 置之不理

Unit 6

1. **afterward** [ˋæftə·wəd] adv. 之後，然後 (also afterwards)
   ▲ Maria and John went to the movies, and shortly afterward they had lunch in a Japanese restaurant.
   Maria 和 John 去看電影，隨後不久就去一家日式餐廳吃午餐。
   💡 shortly/soon afterward 隨後不久

2. **airline** [ˋɛrˌlaɪn] n. [C] 航空公司
   ▲ Low-cost airlines have become popular with the youth in recent years.
   廉價航空近年來很受年輕人歡迎。

3. **aware** [əˋwɛr] adj. 注意到
   ▲ I hope you are fully aware of the possible dangers.
   我希望你充分注意可能的危險。

4. **budget** [ˋbʌdʒɪt] n. [C] 預算 <on>
   ▲ Living on a tight budget, the student spent little money on recreation.
   由於預算拮据，所以這名學生在娛樂上花費甚少。
   💡 under/within/over budget 低於 / 符合 / 超出預算 |
   draw up a budget 編列預算
   budget [ˋbʌdʒɪt] v. 編預算 <for>
   ▲ Emily has budgeted for insurance this year.
   Emily 今年已經為保險編列預算。

5. **chat** [tʃæt] n. [C] 閒聊 <with>

▲ Ian had a chat with his neighbor about the new library in the neighborhood.
Ian 和他的鄰居閒聊關於社區新圖書館的事。

chat [tʃæt] v. 閒聊 <to, about> (chatted | chatted | chatting)

▲ The students got together and chatted about their idols. 學生們聚在一起閒聊著他們的偶像。

---

6. **clue** [klu] n. [C] 線索 <to, about>

▲ Police are still searching the house for clues to the identity of the murderer.
警方仍在屋內尋找凶手身分的線索。

💡 not have a clue/have no clue 一無所知，毫無頭緒

---

7. **comfort** [`kʌmfɚt] n. [U] 安慰 [同] consolation；[C] 舒適 (物品) (usu. pl.)

▲ No matter what difficulty Josh may encounter, he can always take comfort from his family's support. 無論遭遇什麼困難，Josh 都能從家人的支持中得到安慰。

comfort [`kʌmfɚt] v. 安慰

▲ The father tried to comfort his daughter.
這位父親試圖安慰他的女兒。

---

8. **dislike** [dɪs`laɪk] v. 不喜歡，討厭 [反] like

▲ Though I dislike exercising, I still persist in walking 10,000 steps a day.
雖然我不喜歡運動，但是我仍堅持每天走一萬步。

dislike [dɪsˋlaɪk] n. [C][U] 不喜歡，厭惡 (的事) <for, of> [反] liking

▲ Vanessa has a dislike for seafood.
Vanessa 討厭海鮮。

♥ take a dislike to... 開始討厭… | likes and dislikes 好惡

---

9. **dose** [dos] n. [C] (藥物) 一劑

▲ A low dose of the drug may still have side effects.
這種藥物低劑量仍可能有副作用。

dose [dos] v. 使服藥 <with>

▲ The doctor dosed me with sleeping pills.
醫生配安眠藥給我吃。

---

10. **efficient** [ɪˋfɪʃənt] adj. 有效率的 [反] inefficient

▲ We want to find an efficient method to speed up production. 我們想找一個有效率的方法來加速生產。

efficiently [ɪˋfɪʃəntlɪ] adv. 有效率地

▲ Ken uses his time efficiently.
Ken 有效率地使用他的時間。

---

11. **fancy** [ˋfænsɪ] adj. 花俏的；豪華的 [同] swanky (fancier | fanciest)

▲ I don't like this dress because it is too fancy.
我不喜歡這件洋裝，因為它太花俏了。

fancy [ˋfænsɪ] n. [sing.] 喜好，愛好 [同] whim

▲ Wanting to ride the roller coaster was a passing fancy. 想要搭乘雲霄飛車是一時的喜好。

fancy [ˋfænsɪ] v. 想要 [同] feel like；幻想 <as>

▲ Do you fancy a walk after dinner?
你想要在晚飯後散步嗎？

---

12. **global** [`globl] adj. 全球的
   ▲ Financial experts worried that the terrorist attack would affect the global economy.
   財經專家擔心這起恐怖攻擊將影響全球經濟。
   🕯 global warming (溫室效應引起的) 地球暖化效應

---

13. **jewelry** [`dʒuəlrɪ] n. [U] (總稱) 珠寶，首飾
   ▲ The actress couldn't have retrieved the three pieces of jewelry without the help of police. 這女演員若沒有警方的幫助是無法找回她失去的三件珠寶。

---

14. **magical** [`mædʒɪkl] adj. 有魔力的；令人愉快的，奇妙的 [同] enchanting
   ▲ The man's magical powers allow his followers to listen to him and do as he wishes. 這名男子的魔力令他的追隨者們聽從他，並依他的心願行事。

---

15. **mission** [`mɪʃən] n. [C] 使命，任務 <on>
   ▲ The general sent the soldier on a difficult mission.
   將軍派給這個士兵一項艱難的任務。

---

16. **plastic** [`plæstɪk] n. [U] 塑膠
   ▲ Many countries have already taken steps to reduce the use of plastic cups.
   許多國家已經採取措施減少塑膠杯的使用。
   plastic [`plæstɪk] adj. 塑膠的

▲ Do you believe paper bags are more environmentally friendly than plastic bags?
你認為紙袋比塑膠袋環保嗎？

17. **pure** [pjʊr] adj. 純的，不摻雜的 [反] impure；純粹的，完全的 (purer | purest)

▲ The necklace is made of pure gold, so it is very expensive. 這條項鍊是純金打造的，所以非常昂貴。

18. **purse** [pɝs] n. [C] 錢包

▲ I usually carry money in my purse.
我的錢通常都放在錢包裡。

19. **remain** [rɪ`men] v. 保持 [同] stay；剩下

▲ All the passengers on the plane should remain seated until the seat belt signs are switched off.
飛機上所有乘客應保持坐著，直到安全帶警示燈熄滅。

20. **sake** [sek] n. [U] 緣故，理由

▲ Scott quit his job for the sake of his health.
Scott 為了健康而辭去工作。

💡 for sb's sake/for the sake of sb 為了幫助…，為了…的利益

21. **scary** [`skɛrɪ] adj. 恐怖的，嚇人的 (scarier | scariest)

▲ Melody prefers scary movies. Melody 喜歡恐怖電影。

22. **significant** [sɪg`nɪfəkənt] adj. 重要的，顯著的 <for> [同] important

▲ The meeting is very significant for the cooperation between the two companies.

這次的會議對這兩個公司的合作很重要。

23. **suicide** [`suə,saɪd] n. [C][U] 自殺

▲ It is reported that the suicide rate has risen gradually in the past years.

據報導自殺率在過去幾年已經逐漸攀升。

24. **tight** [taɪt] adj. 緊的，小的 [反] loose；(時間、金錢) 緊的

▲ The dress seems to be too tight.

這件洋裝穿起來好像太緊了。

tight [taɪt] adv. 緊密地

▲ Since a typhoon is coming, please check all the windows are shut tight.

由於颱風要來了，請確認所有的窗戶都有緊閉。

25. **vivid** [`vɪvɪd] adj. (色彩) 鮮豔的；生動的，栩栩如生的

▲ Hebe's vivid yellow dress caught many people's attention. Hebe 鮮豔的黃色洋裝吸引了許多人的注意。

Unit 7

1. **ambition** [æm`bɪʃən] n. [C] 抱負，志向

▲ Ryan's ambition is to become a famous actor before forty. Ryan 的志向是要在四十歲之前成為名演員。

💡 realize/achieve/fulfill sb's ambition 實現…的抱負

2. **apart** [ə`pɑrt] adv. 分開地

▲ Harry stood with his feet wide apart.
Harry 兩腳分得很開地站著。

🔮 apart from... 不考慮…，除了…之外 | tell <u>sb/sth</u> apart 分辨…

3. **approve** [ə`pruv] v. 同意，贊成 <of>

▲ My father didn't approve of me studying abroad.
父親不贊成我出國念書。

4. **breath** [brɛθ] n. [C] 吸一下氣；[U] 呼吸

▲ Molly took a deep breath before she entered the interview room. Molly 在進入面試室前深吸一口氣。

🔮 hold <u>sb's</u> breath …屏住呼吸；屏息以待 | be/run out of breath 喘不過氣 | take <u>sb's</u> breath away 美得令…讚嘆

5. **capable** [`kepəbḷ] adj. 有能力的 <of>

▲ The old man is not capable of taking care of himself.
這名老人沒有照顧自己的能力。

6. **cherry** [`tʃɛrɪ] n. [C] 櫻桃 (pl. cherries)

▲ Bob picked some cherries from the tree in the backyard to make a cherry pie.
Bob 在後院的樹上摘了一些櫻桃要做櫻桃派。

🔮 the cherry on the cake 錦上添花之物

cherry [`tʃɛrɪ] adj. 櫻桃紅的，鮮紅色的

▲ The model has beautiful cherry lips.

這位模特兒有漂亮的櫻桃紅唇。

7. **column** [ˋkɑləm] n. [C] 石柱；(報紙、雜誌的) 專欄
   ▲ The town is famous for a row of Greek columns.
   這城鎮以擁有一排希臘風格的石柱而聞名。

8. **cradle** [ˋkredl̩] n. [C] 搖籃
   ▲ The mother rocked the cradle to stop her baby from
   crying. 這母親推動搖籃讓她的寶寶停止哭泣。
   cradle [ˋkredl̩] v. 托住，輕柔地抱著
   ▲ Most of the parents tend to cradle their babies in their
   left arms. 大部分的父母多用左臂抱嬰孩。

9. **dive** [daɪv] n. [C] 跳水
   ▲ The athlete is practicing her dives.
   這位運動員正在練習跳水。
   dive [daɪv] v. 潛水，跳水 <into> (dove, dived | dived |
   diving)
   ▲ The lifeguard dove into the pool to save a drowning
   boy. 這救生員跳入泳池中救一名溺水的男孩。

10. **downtown** [ˌdaʊnˋtaʊn] adj. 市中心的，商業區的
    ▲ Daniel has to go to the office in downtown Chicago
    for meeting.
    Daniel 需要去芝加哥城區的辦公室開會。
    downtown [ˌdaʊnˋtaʊn] adv. 在市中心地，在商業區地
    ▲ Let's go downtown to see the movies.
    我們去市區看電影吧。

downtown [ˌdaʊn`taʊn] n. [C] 市中心，商業區

▲ The rents in the heart of downtown are extremely high now. 市中心的房屋租金現在非常的高昂。

11. **emotional** [ɪ`moʃənl] adj. 情感的；情緒化的

▲ Parents should care about their children's emotional needs. 父母應當注意孩子的情感需求。

12. **flash** [flæʃ] n. [C] 閃光

▲ The child fears the flash of lightning.
這名小孩害怕閃電的閃光。

💡 a flash in the pan 曇花一現 | in a flash 轉瞬間

flash [flæʃ] v. 閃光；突然浮現

▲ Lightning flashes in the dark sky. 閃電劃過夜空。

13. **label** [`lebl] n. [C] 標籤 [同] tag, ticket

▲ The label on the product tells people what it contains.
這產品上的標籤告訴人們裡面含有什麼成分。

label [`lebl] v. 貼上標籤

▲ The doctor carefully labeled each of the bottles.
醫生小心地在每個瓶子上貼標籤。

💡 label sb/sth as sth 把…稱為 (貼標籤為)…

14. **medal** [`mɛdl] n. [C] 獎章

▲ The tennis player won the championship and received a gold medal.
這位網球選手贏得冠軍而獲頒金牌。

💡 gold/silver/bronze medal 金 / 銀 / 銅牌

15. **motor** [ˋmotɚ] n. [C] 馬達，引擎；汽車

   ▲ The electric fan needs a new motor.
   這臺電風扇需要新的馬達。

   motor [ˋmotɚ] adj. 汽車的

   ▲ In big cities, exhaust fumes from motor vehicles are the major source of air pollution. 在大城市裡，車輛所排放的廢氣是空氣汙染的主要來源。

---

16. **product** [ˋprɑdʌkt] n. [C] 產品 [同] goods；成果

   ▲ We are going to run a commercial on TV to promote our new product. 我們要在電視播廣告來促銷新產品。

   💡 dairy/meat/agricultural/commercial products 乳製品 / 肉製品 / 農產品 / 商品

---

17. **razor** [ˋrezɚ] n. [C] 刮鬍刀，剃刀

   ▲ Brian is shaving his beard with an electric razor.
   Brian 正在用電動刮鬍刀刮鬍子。

---

18. **remote** [rɪˋmot] adj. 遙遠的，偏僻的 [同] isolated (remoter | remotest)

   ▲ Nick lives in a remote village far from the city.
   Nick 住在離城市很遙遠的村莊裡。

---

19. **republic** [rɪˋpʌblɪk] n. [C] 共和國

   ▲ The Republic of China is a democratic country.
   中華民國是一個民主國家。

---

20. **security** [sɪˋkjʊrətɪ] n. [U] 安全 (保障)

▲The museum tightened security when the president visited. 博物館在總統參訪時加強安全措施。

21. **semester** [səˋmɛstɚ] n. [C] 學期

▲The first semester lasts from this September to next January. 第一學期是從今年九月到明年一月。

22. **shortly** [ˋʃɔrtlɪ] adv. 不久，很快

▲Usually lightning is shortly followed by thunder.
通常閃電過後不久會有雷聲。

💡 shortly after/before sth …不久之後 / 之前

23. **summit** [ˋsʌmɪt] n. [C] 山頂；高峰會議

▲After climbing the mountain for hours, we finally reached its summit.
爬了幾個鐘頭後，我們終於到達山頂。

24. **violence** [ˋvaɪələns] n. [U] 暴力

▲It is unwise to use violence to solve problems.
訴諸暴力手段來解決問題是不明智的。

25. **wheat** [wit] n. [U] 小麥

▲The farm workers are harvesting the wheat on the fields. 農場工人們正在收割田裡的小麥。

💡 wheat farm/field/crop/flour 麥田 / 小麥作物 / 麵粉

Unit 8

1. **advantage** [ədˈvæntɪdʒ] n. [C][U] 好處 [反] disadvantage
   ▲ Being tall is an advantage for a basketball player.
   個子高對籃球選手有利。
   ● take advantage of sb/sth 利用…；占…便宜 | to sb's advantage 對…有利的

2. **announce** [əˈnaʊns] v. 宣布 <to>
   ▲ The boss announced the new project to his employees. 老闆向他的員工宣布新的企劃案。
   announcement [əˈnaʊnsmənt] n. [C] 宣告，公告
   ▲ The government just made an announcement that there would be an increase in the fuel tax.
   政府剛做出了燃油稅增加的公告。

3. **apron** [ˈeprən] n. [C] 圍裙
   ▲ My father always wears an apron when cooking.
   我爸爸煮菜時總會穿圍裙。

4. **aside** [əˈsaɪd] adv. 在旁邊
   ▲ Ann stepped aside to make way for an old lady.
   Ann 退到旁邊讓路給老太太。
   ● aside from... 除…之外

5. **chest** [tʃɛst] n. [C] 胸部，胸腔
   ▲ Logan saw a doctor because he had chest pains.

Logan 因為胸部疼痛而去看醫生。

---

6. **citizen** [ˋsɪtəzn̩] n. [C] 公民

▲ Mr. Lin has applied to become a Polish citizen.
林先生已申請成為波蘭公民。

---

7. **compete** [kəmˋpit] v. 競爭 <with, against>

▲ Oliver has to compete with other candidates for the
job. Oliver 必須和其他求職者競爭這份工作。

---

8. **complaint** [kəmˋplent] n. [C] 抱怨 <to>

▲ John made a complaint to the manager about the
waiter's rude behavior.
John 跟經理抱怨服務生無禮的行為。

---

9. **credit** [ˋkrɛdɪt] n. [U] 賒帳 <on>；讚揚

▲ Mr. Wang bought the new house on credit.
王先生貸款買新屋。

credit [ˋkrɛdɪt] v. 歸於 <to>

▲ Samuel credits his success to his wife.
Samuel 把他的成就歸功於他太太。

---

10. **doubtful** [ˋdautfəl] adj. 感到懷疑的，不能確定的
<about>

▲ The manager was doubtful about Gail's ability to run
the big project.
經理對於 Gail 執行這個大企劃案的能力感到懷疑。

---

11. **drain** [dren] v. 瀝乾，排空；使筋疲力盡

▲ The cook drained the dumplings thoroughly.
這名廚師將餃子的水瀝乾。

drain [dren] n. [C] 下水道，排水管

▲ Vicky dropped her car key down the drain by accident.
Vicky 不小心將汽車鑰匙掉入下水道裡。

---

12. **flavor** [ˋflevɚ] n. [C][U] 味道 [同] taste

▲ Garlic and ginger are usually used to give flavor to dishes. 大蒜和薑通常用來為菜色增添味道。

flavor [ˋflevɚ] v. 為…加味道，增添風味 <with>

▲ Lisa flavored the drink with lemon.
Lisa 在飲料中加入檸檬調味。

---

13. **flood** [flʌd] n. [C][U] 洪水，水災

▲ Several houses were carried away by the great flood.
數間房屋被大洪水沖走了。

flood [flʌd] v. 淹水；湧進 [同] pour

▲ Many homes were flooded due to the heavy rain.
多戶人家因豪雨淹水。

---

14. **frequent** [ˋfrikwənt] adj. 頻繁的，經常的 [反] infrequent

▲ Fred makes frequent visits to Europe because he has business contacts with several European companies.
Fred 經常去歐洲，因為他與幾家歐洲公司有生意往來。

frequent [ˋfrikwənt] v. 常去，常到

▲ My friend and I met at a restaurant frequented by students. 我朋友和我約在一間學生常去的餐廳。

15. **information** [ˌɪnfəˋmeʃən] n. [U] 資訊，情報 <on, about>

▲ I want a good deal of information on this matter to make the decision.
我需要大量關於這件事的資訊以作出判斷。

16. **lawn** [lɔn] n. [C][U] 草地，草坪

▲ Iris is having a picnic on the lawn.
Iris 正在草地上野餐。

💡 mow/cut the lawn 修剪草坪

17. **medium** [ˋmidɪəm] adj. 中等的 [同] average；(肉) 中等熟度的

▲ Allen wears medium-sized pants.
Allen 穿中號的褲子。

medium [ˋmidɪəm] n. [C] 媒介 (pl. media, mediums)

▲ The Internet has become a medium of advertising.
網路已經變成廣告的媒介。

18. **neighborhood** [ˋnebəˌhʊd] n. [C] 鄰近地區，住宅區

▲ We live in a quiet neighborhood.
我們住的地區很安靜。

19. **regional** [ˋridʒənl] adj. 地區的，區域的

▲ The local people here speak with a regional accent.

這裡的本地人說話帶有地區性的口音。

---

20. **reveal** [rɪˋvil] v. 洩漏，透露 [同] disclose [反] conceal
   ▲ Oliver's facial expression revealed that he was lying.
   Oliver 的臉部表情透露他在說謊。

21. **shampoo** [ʃæmˋpu] n. [C][U] 洗髮精 (pl. shampoos)
   ▲ Nick often uses moisturizing shampoo for his dry hair. Nick 通常為他的乾燥髮質使用保溼型洗髮精。

   shampoo [ʃæmˋpu] v. 用洗髮精洗
   ▲ The hairdresser shampoos the customer's hair and then blows it dry. 理髮師洗客人的頭髮並將它吹乾。

22. **sink** [sɪŋk] n. [C] 水槽
   ▲ The dirty plates are piled up in the kitchen sink.
   廚房水槽堆滿了髒盤子。

   sink [sɪŋk] v. 下沉，下陷；降低 (sank, sunk | sunk | sinking)
   ▲ The *Titanic* sank in the North Atlantic Ocean in 1912. 鐵達尼號於 1912 年在北大西洋沉沒。

23. **suffer** [ˋsʌfɚ] v. 遭受，罹患 <from>
   ▲ More and more people are suffering from asthma owing to air pollution.
   有越來越多的人因為空氣汙染而罹患哮喘。

   suffering [ˋsʌfrɪŋ] n. [C][U] 痛苦
   ▲ The medicine relieved the patient's suffering, so he feels much better now.

藥物緩和了這個病人的痛苦，所以他現在覺得好多了。

24. **suspect** [sə`spɛkt] v. 懷疑 <of>

▲ The police suspected the woman of committing the crime. 警方懷疑這名女子犯下罪行。

suspect [`sʌspɛkt] n. [C] 嫌疑犯

▲ The man was the main suspect in the case. 這名男子是這個案子的主要嫌疑犯。

suspect [`sʌspɛkt] adj. 可疑的，不可靠的 [同] suspicious

▲ A suspect package was found in the railroad car. 火車車廂內發現了一個可疑的包裹。

25. **whistle** [`wɪsl̩] n. [C] 哨子

▲ The coach blew his whistle to ask the players to run toward him. 教練吹哨子要球員跑向他這邊。

whistle [`wɪsl̩] v. 吹口哨；吹哨子

▲ Kcn used to whistle his favorite tune on his way to school. Ken 過去經常在去上學的路上，用口哨吹他喜愛的曲子。

Unit 9

1. **advanced** [əd`vænst] adj. 先進的；高階的

▲ This is the most advanced jet plane in the world. 這是世界上最先進的噴射機。

2. **armed** [ɑrmd] adj. 武裝的 [反] unarmed

▲ The boundary disputes finally led to armed conflict between the two countries.

邊界爭端最終引發兩國的武裝衝突。

---

3. **assume** [ə`sum] v. 假定，假設；假裝，冒充；擔任

▲ The judge must assume (that) the suspect is innocent until he or she is proven guilty.

在被證明有罪之前，法官必須假定嫌疑犯無罪。

---

4. **attitude** [`ætə,tjud] n. [C] 態度 <to, toward>

▲ Kevin took an unfriendly attitude toward me.

Kevin 對我抱持著不友善的態度。

💡 positive/negative attitude 正面的 / 負面的態度

---

5. **cable** [`kebl] n. [C] 電纜

▲ The government laid cables between the two islands.

政府在兩座小島間埋設電纜。

cable [`kebl] v. 打越洋電報

▲ Emma's father cabled her some money yesterday.

Emma 的父親昨天利用越洋電報匯給她一些錢。

---

6. **client** [`klaɪənt] n. [C] 客戶，顧客 [同] customer

▲ The restaurant tried to handle the negative feedback from the clients.

這間餐廳試著處理來自顧客的負面評價。

---

7. **concert** [`kɑnsɝt] n. [C] 音樂會

▲ The queen attended the charity concert to raise funds for the orphans.

女王參加這場為孤兒募款的慈善音樂會。

💡 in concert with sb/sth 和…合作 | classical/rock/pop concert 古典 / 搖滾 / 流行音樂會

8. **constant** [ˋkɑnstənt] adj. 連續不斷的 [同] continual

▲ The children's constant fighting got on the mother's nerves. 孩子不斷爭吵使母親心煩。

constant [ˋkɑnstənt] n. [C] 常數

constantly [ˋkɑnstəntlɪ] adv. 不斷地 [同] continually

▲ Stir the curry constantly or you might burn it.
不斷攪拌咖哩，不然你可能會把它燒焦。

9. **creature** [ˋkritʃɚ] n. [C] 生物

▲ We should respect all living creatures on Earth.
我們應該尊重地球上所有的生物。

10. **crown** [kraʊn] n. [C] 王冠

▲ The princess wore a crown on her head.
公主頭上戴著王冠。

crown [kraʊn] v. 為…加冕

▲ Philip was crowned king at the age of 20.
Philip 在二十歲時被加冕為王。

11. **dump** [dʌmp] v. 扔下，丟下

▲ Bill dumped his shopping bags on the sofa as soon as he got home.
Bill 一回到家就把他的購物袋扔在沙發上。

dump [dʌmp] n. [C] 垃圾場

▲ All the garbage is taken to the dump in the suburbs.

所有的垃圾都會被運送到位於郊區的垃圾場。

💡 (down) in the dumps 情緒低落，不高興

12. **electricity** [ɪ,lɛk`trɪsətɪ] n. [U] 電力

▲ Wind power can be used to produce electricity.

風力可以用來發電。

💡 provide/supply electricity 供給電力

13. **fold** [fold] v. 摺疊，摺起 <up>

▲ Steven folded up his shirts neatly.

Steven 把他的襯衫摺得很整齊。

fold [fold] n. [C] 摺疊；摺痕

▲ The bug hid in the folds of the curtain.

小蟲藏在窗簾的摺縫裡。

14. **fur** [fɝ] n. [C][U] (動物的) 毛皮

▲ The cat's fur is very soft. 這隻貓的毛很軟。

15. **harbor** [`hɑrbɚ] n. [C] 港口

▲ Some ships came into the harbor to seek shelter during the storm.

暴風雨時，一些船隻駛入港口尋找遮蔽。

harbor [`hɑrbɚ] v. 藏匿 (罪犯或臟物)；懷有，心懷 (負面想法)

▲ Amy was sued for harboring a criminal.

Amy 被控告藏匿罪犯。

16. **liberty** [`lɪbɚtɪ] n. [C][U] 自由 (pl. liberties)

▲ People in democratic countries enjoy the liberty of free speech. 民主國家人民享受言論自由。

💡 be at liberty to V 被允許做…

17. **microwave** [ˋmaɪkrəˌwev] n. [C] 微波爐 (also microwave oven)

▲ It is very convenient to heat up leftovers in the microwave. 在微波爐加熱剩菜很方便。

microwave [ˋmaɪkrəˌwev] v. 微波 (食物)

▲ Customers in the convenience store microwave the food. 便利超商的顧客們微波食物。

18. **ongoing** [ˋɑnˌɡoɪŋ] adj. 不斷發展的，持續進行的

▲ The investigation of gunrunning is ongoing.
軍火走私的偵查還在持續進行中。

19. **relax** [rɪˋlæks] v. 放鬆

▲ Whenever I'm under stress, I'll play the guitar because it relaxes me.
每當我有壓力時，我會彈吉他，因為這會使我放鬆。

20. **roughly** [ˋrʌflɪ] adv. 粗魯地；大致上 [同] about, approximately

▲ Don't press the button roughly. You almost broke it.
不要粗魯地按按鍵。你差點把它弄壞。

💡 roughly speaking 大致上來說

21. **signal** [ˋsɪɡnl] n. [C] 信號 [同] sign

▲ The police officer gave the driver the signal to stop.

警察示意要司機停車。

signal [`sɪgl̩] v. 發出信號

▲ The police officer signaled the man to put his hands in the air. 警察示意要男子高舉雙手。

---

22. **talent** [`tælənt] n. [C][U] 天分，才能 <for>

▲ George has a talent for ballet.
George 有跳芭蕾的天分。

💡 talent competition/show 選秀比賽 / 演出

talented [`tæləntɪd] adj. 有天分的，有才能的

▲ Miranda is a talented archer.
Miranda 是個有天分的弓箭手。

---

23. **tasty** [`testɪ] adj. 美味的 (tastier | tastiest)

▲ It's the tastiest dish I have ever had!
這是我吃過最好吃的一道菜了！

---

24. **tourism** [`tʊrɪzm̩] n. [U] 旅遊業

▲ To boost tourism, the authorities have announced that visitors staying less than 90 days in the country do not need a visa. 為了促進觀光，官方宣布旅客至該國旅遊九十天內無需簽證。

---

25. **unique** [ju`nik] adj. 獨一無二的，專屬的 <to>；獨特的
[同] unusual

▲ The travel agency provides customized services that are unique to your needs.
這家旅遊業者提供客製化服務，滿足客戶專屬的需求。

unique [ju`nik] **n.** [C] 獨特的人或物

Unit 10

1. **advise** [əd`vaɪz] **v.** 建議，勸告
   ▲ I advised Zoe that she should take a rest.
   我建議 Zoe 要休息一下。
   💡 (strongly) advise sb against sth (強烈) 建議⋯不要⋯

---

2. **ash** [æʃ] **n.** [C][U] 灰，灰燼
   ▲ Don't drop cigarette ash in the trash can. It might cause a fire.
   別讓菸灰掉在垃圾桶裡。有可能引發火災。

---

3. **audience** [`ɔdɪəns] **n.** [C] 觀眾
   ▲ The talk show has an audience of several millions every week. 每週有數百萬觀眾收看此脫口秀。
   💡 an audience laughs/claps/cheers/boos 觀眾大笑 / 鼓掌 / 喝彩 / 喝倒彩

---

4. **automatic** [ˌɔtə`mætɪk] **adj.** 自動的 [反] manual
   ▲ Most convenience stores have automatic doors.
   大部分的便利商店都有自動門。

---

5. **clinic** [`klɪnɪk] **n.** [C] 診所
   ▲ I have an appointment at the clinic next Friday.
   我和診所預約下週五看診。

---

6. **comparison** [kəm`pærəsn̩] n. [C][U] 比較
   ▲ The teacher asked her students to make a comparison of the two writing styles.
   老師要學生比較這兩種寫作的風格。
   💡 in/by comparison with sb/sth 與…相比

7. **costly** [`kɔstlɪ] adj. 貴的 (costlier | costliest)
   ▲ It would be costly to buy a house in Taipei.
   在臺北買房子很貴。

8. **crew** [kru] n. [C] (船、飛機的) 全體工作人員；專業團隊
   ▲ The crew helped the passengers get off the plane after the pilot made an emergency landing.
   在機長緊急迫降後，機上工作人員協助乘客下機。

9. **crop** [krɑp] n. [C] 農作物
   ▲ The crops won't survive if there is a drought.
   若有乾旱，農作物將無法存活下來。
   crop [krɑp] v. 收成 (cropped | cropped | cropping)
   ▲ The strawberries haven't cropped as well as last year.
   草莓的收成沒有像去年一樣好。

10. **destroy** [dɪ`strɔɪ] v. 毀壞，破壞
    ▲ The historic church was totally destroyed in a fire.
    這間有歷史價值的教堂被大火徹底燒毀了。
    💡 destroy sb's confidence 破壞…的自信

11. **edit** [`ɛdɪt] v. 編輯；剪輯

▲ The school newspaper is written and edited by the students. 校刊由學生撰寫和編輯。

12. **exhibition** [,ɛksə`bɪʃən] n. [C][U] 展示 (會) <on> [同] exhibit

▲ A collection of Picasso's paintings will be on exhibition in the museum.

一系列畢卡索的畫作將在這個博物館展出。

13. **forever** [fə`ɛvə] adv. 永久地，永遠

▲ I will forever remember the day we met.

我會永遠記得我們相遇這一天。

💡 forever and ever 永久地

14. **hometown** [`hom,taʊn] n. [C] 家鄉，故鄉

▲ The young man left his hometown and went to a big city to look for a job.

那年輕人離開家鄉，到大城市去找尋工作。

15. **humor** [`hjumə] n. [U] 幽默；[C][U] 心情

▲ My friend has a great sense of humor.

我朋友富有幽默感。

💡 in a good/bad humor 心情好 / 壞的

16. **lover** [`lʌvə] n. [C] 戀人；愛好者

▲ There are pairs of lovers celebrating Valentine's Day in the restaurant.

有好幾對戀人在這家餐廳慶祝情人節。

17. **miracle** [ˋmɪrəkl̩] n. [C] 奇蹟

▲ It was a miracle that the driver wasn't hurt in the car crash. 駕駛在車禍中沒受傷是奇蹟。

💡 perform/work miracles/a miracle 創造奇蹟；有奇效

18. **outer** [ˋautɚ] adj. 外面的 [反] inner

▲ It is my dream to travel to outer space someday. 我的夢想是有一天能到外太空去旅行。

19. **pole** [pol] n. [C] 竿，柱；(地球的) 極

▲ Since Willy likes fishing, he has a variety of fishing poles. 由於 Willy 喜愛釣魚，他有各式各樣的釣魚竿。

20. **remind** [rɪˋmaɪnd] v. 使想起 <of>；提醒 <about, to>

▲ The old picture reminded me of my childhood. 這張舊照片使我想起童年。

💡 remind sb to V 提醒⋯做⋯

21. **silk** [sɪlk] n. [U] 絲，蠶絲

▲ A silkworm is a type of caterpillar which can produce silk. 蠶是一種會吐絲的毛毛蟲。

💡 artificial silk 人造絲

22. **sufficient** [səˋfɪʃənt] adj. 足夠的 [同] enough [反] insufficient

▲ Do we have sufficient time to complete the project? 我們有足夠的時間完成這項專案計畫嗎？

23. **threaten** [ˋθrɛtn̩] v. 威脅，恐嚇 <to>

▲ The terrorists threatened to set off the bombs.
恐怖分子威脅要引爆炸彈。

24. **traveler** [`trævlɚ] n. [C] 旅行者
▲ Lena is a frequent traveler to Paris.
Lena 是到巴黎旅行的常客。

25. **tropical** [`trɑpɪkl̩] adj. 熱帶的
▲ People should try hard to protect the tropical rainforests. 人們應該盡力保護熱帶雨林。

🍃 tropical island/region/climate 熱帶島嶼 / 地區 / 氣候

Unit 11

1. **agriculture** [`ægrɪ͵kʌltʃɚ] n. [U] 農業
▲ People in this area depend on agriculture for a living.
此地的人民以務農維生。

2. **attractive** [ə`træktɪv] adj. 有魅力的 <to>
▲ Everything about the singer is attractive to his loyal fans. 關於這位歌手的每件事對他的忠實粉絲來說都是很有魅力的。

🍃 find sb attractive 覺得⋯有魅力

3. **bacon** [`bekən] n. [U] 培根肉
▲ Please give me a slice of bacon. 請給我一片培根。

🍃 bring home the bacon 養家 | bacon and eggs 培根蛋 | save sb's bacon 幫助⋯脫離困境

4. **career** [kə`rɪr] n. [C] (終生的) 職業 <in>

▲ Pursuing a career in medicine, the young doctor committed himself to treating people in the poor village. 從事醫療職業，這位年輕醫師致力於治療在這貧困鄉村的人們。

💡 political/medical/academic career 政治 / 醫療 / 學術生涯

---

5. **clown** [klaʊn] n. [C] 小丑

▲ Nancy likes the clown best at the circus.
馬戲團中 Nancy 最喜歡小丑。

💡 class clown 班級小丑

clown [klaʊn] v. 搞笑 <around>

▲ My teacher was angry that all the students clowned around in class this morning. 我的老師對於今天早上所有學生在課堂上搞笑感到生氣。

---

6. **cricket** [`krɪkɪt] n. [C] 蟋蟀

▲ Male crickets chirp at night in order to attract female crickets. 雄性蟋蟀夜間發唧唧聲吸引雌性蟋蟀。

---

7. **criminal** [`krɪmənl] adj. 犯罪的

▲ People with a criminal record sometimes find it hard to get a job.
有犯罪紀錄的人們有時會發現很難找到工作。

criminal [`krɪmənl] n. [C] 罪犯

▲ Justice is done when criminals receive the punishment they deserve.

當罪犯受到應有的懲罰時，正義就伸張。

---

8. **dramatic** [drə`mætɪk] adj. 驟然的，戲劇性的

▲ Justin went abroad for only a few months, but you could notice a dramatic change in his behavior.

Justin 只有出國幾個月，但你可以注意到他的行為舉止驟然轉變。

---

9. **educate** [`ɛdʒə͵ket] v. (在學校) 教育 <about, in, on>

▲ Schools should educate children about the importance of recycling.

學校應該教育孩子資源回收的重要性。

---

10. **educational** [͵ɛdʒə`keʃən!] adj. 教育的

▲ A good children's book is not only fun but educational as well.

好的兒童讀物不僅有趣而且具有教育意義。

---

11. **expectation** [͵ɛkspɛk`teʃən] n. [C][U] 期望，預料

▲ Eric has to study hard to live up to his parents' expectations.

Eric 必須要用功念書以達到他父母的期望。

💡 against/contrary to all expectations 意想不到的是

---

12. **expressive** [ɪk`sprɛsɪv] adj. 富有表達力的

▲ The poem was expressive of the writer's ideas about life. 這首詩生動的表達作家對於生命的見解。

---

13. **frank** [fræŋk] adj. 直率的 <with, about>

▲ Annie is pretty frank about her opinions.
Annie 表達意見時相當直率。

💡 to be frank with you 直率地對你說

frankly [`fræŋklɪ] adv. 直率地

▲ John admitted his mistake frankly.
John 直率地承認自己的錯誤。

💡 frankly speaking 坦白地說｜quite frankly 相當坦率地說

---

14. **kingdom** [`kɪŋdəm] n. [C] 王國；領域 <of>

▲ The king ruled over a large kingdom.
國王統治領土廣大的王國。

---

15. **lung** [lʌŋ] n. [C] 肺

▲ Hogan breathed deeply to fill his lungs with fresh air.
Hogan 深呼吸使肺部充滿新鮮空氣。

---

16. **motel** [mo`tɛl] n. [C] 汽車旅館

▲ When traveling by car, you can choose a motel, where you can park your car outside the room.
開車旅行時，你可以選擇汽車旅館，那裡你的車子可以停在房外。

---

17. **paradise** [`pærə,daɪs] n. [C][U] 天堂 [同] heaven

▲ It is generally believed that good people will go to Paradise after they die.
一般人普遍相信好人死後會上天堂。

💡 shopper's paradise 購物者的天堂

---

18. **political** [pə`lɪtɪkl̩] adj. 政治的

▲ This country has several political parties.
這個國家有好幾個政黨。

politically [pə`lɪtɪklɪ] adv. 政治上

▲ Which political party will win the election is a politically sensitive issue.
哪個政黨會贏得選舉是一個政治上敏感的問題。

19. **prevent** [prɪ`vɛnt] v. 阻止，預防 <from>

▲ The heavy rain prevented my brother from going out.
大雨讓弟弟無法外出。

20. **reserve** [rɪ`zɝv] n. [C] 儲備物 (usu. pl.) <of>

▲ My parents keep a large reserve of water and food for typhoons. 我的父母為了颱風大量儲備水和食物。

reserve [rɪ`zɝv] v. 保留 <for>；預定

▲ Priority seats are reserved for the passengers in need.
這些博愛座是保留給有需要的乘客。

reserved [rɪ`zɝvd] adj. 矜持內向的 [同] shy

▲ Helen's new classmate is a very quiet and reserved person. Helen 的新同學是個很安靜又內向的人。

21. **sorrow** [`sɔro] n. [C][U] 悲傷

▲ A friend is someone that can share your joys and sorrows. 朋友是可以分享你的喜悅和悲傷的人。

22. **technical** [`tɛknɪkl̩] adj. 技術性的

▲ Josh played the piano with technical precision but little warmth.

Josh 彈奏鋼琴的技術精湛，但缺乏熱情。

---

23. **tower** [ˋtaʊɚ] n. [C] 塔

▲ I got to the top of Tokyo Tower to enjoy the panorama of the city.

我登上東京鐵塔的頂端欣賞城市全景。

💡 tower of strength (危難時) 可依靠的人

tower [ˋtaʊɚ] v. 聳立

▲ The new building towers in front of our house.

新的大樓聳立在我們的房子前。

💡 tower above/over sb/sth 比…優秀；比…高

---

24. **urban** [ˋɝbən] adj. 都市的 [反] rural

▲ Fiona cannot stand the hectic pace of urban life.

Fiona 無法忍受都市生活的繁忙步調。

---

25. **wealthy** [ˋwɛlθɪ] adj. 富裕的 [同] rich (wealthier | wealthiest)

▲ The wealthy old man decided to donate all his money to charities.

這位富裕的老先生決定把所有的錢都捐給慈善機構。

Unit 12

1. **additional** [əˋdɪʃən̩l] adj. 額外的，附加的 [同] extra

▲ There will be an additional charge for overweight baggage when you check in.
在登機報到時，過重的行李會收取額外的費用。

additionally [ə`dɪʃənˌlɪ] adv. 此外 [同] also

▲ Terry speaks good English. Additionally, he can also speak French and German well. Terry 的英語說得很好。此外他也可以講很好的法語和德語。

---

2. **arrest** [ə`rɛst] n. [C][U] 逮捕

▲ The thicf was quickly put under arrest.
小偷很快就被逮捕了。

arrest [ə`rɛst] v. 逮捕 <for>

▲ The police arrested the man for drunken driving.
警察逮捕了酒後駕車的男子。

---

3. **awful** [`ɔful] adj. 糟糕的，惡劣的

▲ Ben had to cancel the picnic because of the awful weather. 因為糟糕的天氣，Ben 必須取消野餐。

awfully [`ɔfulɪ] adv. 非常

▲ It's awfully kind of you. 你真的非常體貼。

---

4. **basement** [`besmənt] n. [C] 地下室

▲ Mrs. Lin stored the old furniture in the basement of her house. 林太太將舊家具放在她家的地下室。

💡 basement flat/apartment 地下室公寓

---

5. **cattle** [`kætl] n. [pl.] 牛隻 (cows, bulls, oxen 等總稱)

▲ A herd of cattle is grazing in the field.

一群牛正在田野上吃草。

💡 <u>beef/dairy</u> cattle 肉 / 乳牛

---

6. **complain** [kəm`plen] v. 抱怨 <about, of>

▲ Mr. Liu often complains about his monotonous job.
劉先生常抱怨他單調的工作。

---

7. **decorate** [`dɛkə,ret] v. 裝飾 <with>

▲ The church is decorated with flowers for the wedding. 教堂為了這場婚禮裝飾得滿是花朵。

---

8. **decrease** [dɪ`kris] v. 減少 <in, by> [反] increase

▲ People have to decrease the amount of water they use by 55% because of the worsening drought.
因為日益嚴重的乾旱，人們必須減少 55% 的用水量。

decrease [`dikris] n. [C][U] 減少 <in, of> [同] reduction [反] increase

▲ A gradual decrease in population will bring about an aging society. 人口的逐漸減少將使一個社會老化。

---

9. **designer** [dɪ`zaɪnɚ] n. [C] 設計師

▲ The show features the clothes made by the fashion designer, Jason.
這場秀是以時裝設計師 Jason 製作的服裝為特色。

---

10. **election** [ɪ`lɛkʃən] n. [C] 選舉

▲ The mayoral election will be held tomorrow.
明天會舉行市長選舉。

11. **engage** [ɪnˋgedʒ] v. 僱用

▲ The manager decided to engage Tom as an office assistant. 經理決定僱用 Tom 為行政助理。

💡 engage in 參加｜engage sb in conversation 與…攀談

engagement [ɪnˋgedʒmənt] n. [C] 約會；訂婚 <to>

▲ I'm going to have a dinner engagement with my old colleague tonight.
今晚我要和我以前的同事一起約吃晚飯。

engaged [ɪnˋgedʒd] adj. 已訂婚的 <to>；忙於…的，從事…的 <in>

▲ Nancy has got engaged to Mike, her classmate from senior high school.
Nancy 和她的高中同學 Mike 已訂婚。

12. **experiment** [ɪkˋspɛrəmənt] n. [C] 實驗 <on, with, in>

▲ It is in question whether scientists should do experiments on living animals.
科學家是否該做活體動物實驗仍在討論中。

💡 perform/conduct/do/carry out an experiment 做實驗

experiment [ɪkˋspɛrəmənt] v. 實驗 <with>

▲ The herbal doctor experiments with all kinds of plants. 這名草藥醫生拿各種植物來實驗。

13. **faith** [feθ] n. [U] 信仰；信任 <in>

▲ Rita has lost faith in Christianity since the church scandal erupted.
自從教堂醜聞爆發以來 Rita 對基督教喪失了信仰。

14. **gap** [gæp] n. [C] 縫隙，裂縫 <in, between>

▲ The little girl has a gap between her two front teeth.
這小女孩兩顆門牙之間有縫隙。

15. **majority** [mə`dʒɔrətɪ] n. [sing.] 大多數，大部分 <of>
[反] minority

▲ The majority of the elementary school students take part in after-school programs.
大多數的小學學生都參加了課後活動。

16. **march** [mɑrtʃ] n. [C] 遊行；進行曲

▲ People held a march for freedom.
人們為爭取自由而舉行遊行。

march [mɑrtʃ] v. 列隊行進

▲ The troops are marching along the street.
軍隊沿街列隊行進。

17. **mayor** [`meɚ] n. [C] 市長

▲ The mayor assured the public that he would do his best to fight crime.
市長向大眾保證他會盡力打擊犯罪。

18. **murder** [`mɜdɚ] n. [C] 凶殺案 [同] homicide

▲ A murder happened in the friendly neighborhood last night. 昨晚這個友善的地區發生一起凶殺案。

murder [`mɜdɚ] v. 殺害

▲ An old lady was murdered by the criminal, who broke into her apartment.

一個老婦人被闖進她公寓的罪犯殺害。

19. **politics** [ˋpɑləˏtɪks] n. [U] 政治 (學)

▲ Though both his father and grandfather are legislators, Albert is not interested in entering politics. 雖然他的父親及祖父都是立法委員，Albert 對於從事政治不感興趣。

20. **pollution** [pəˋluʃən] n. [U] 汙染

▲ The water pollution was due to the waste dumped by the factory. 水汙染是由工廠傾倒的廢棄物造成的。

♥ air/water pollution 空氣 / 水汙染

21. **routine** [ruˋtin] n. [C][U] 例行公事，慣例

▲ Checking emails has become my daily routine.
查看電子郵件已經成為我每天的例行公事。

routine [ruˋtin] adj. 例行的

▲ When you apply for a visa, you have to answer some routine questions.
當你申請簽證時，你必須回答一些例行的問題。

22. **squeeze** [skwiz] v. 擠出 <out>

▲ Joe squeezed toothpaste out from the tube onto his toothbrush. Joe 從牙膏管中擠出牙膏到牙刷上。

squeeze [skwiz] n. [C] 緊握

▲ Diana said goodbye to her boyfriend and gave his hand a gentle squeeze.
Diana 與她的男友說再見並緊握了一下他的手。

23. **territory** [ˈtɛrəˌtorɪ] n. [C][U] 領土 (pl. territories)

▲ The plane was shot down when it overflew enemy territory. 那架飛機在飛越敵人領土時被擊落。

---

24. **trunk** [trʌŋk] n. [C] 後車箱；樹幹

▲ Put your baggage in the trunk.
把你的行李放進後車箱。

---

25. **variety** [vəˈraɪətɪ] n. [sing.] 不同種類 <of>；[C] 品種 (pl. varieties)

▲ There is a wide variety of books available at the bookstore. 在這間書店裡有不同種類的書籍可買到。

💡 Variety is the spice of life. 【諺】多樣化是生活的調味。

Unit 13

1. **athlete** [ˈæθlit] n. [C] 運動員

▲ Only the top athletes in the world can win the gold medals in the Olympic Games.
只有世界頂尖的運動員才能在奧運會中獲得金牌。

---

2. **awkward** [ˈɔkwəd] adj. 笨拙的；令人尷尬的

▲ The child is still awkward using a knife and fork.
這個孩子使用刀叉仍舊笨拙。

awkwardly [ˈɔkwədlɪ] adv. 笨拙地

▲ The lady's uncomfortable shoes made her walk awkwardly.

女人的鞋子很不舒服，讓她走起來很笨拙。

---

3. **badly** [ˋbædlɪ] adv. 嚴重地 [反] well (worse | worst)

▲ Leo was badly hurt in the car accident.

　Leo 在車禍中受了重傷。

💡 badly hurt/injured 重傷

---

4. **beneath** [bɪˋniθ] prep. 在⋯下方 [同] underneath

▲ To get away from the sunshine, we sat beneath the tree. 為了避開陽光，我們坐在樹下。

💡 beneath sb 對⋯來說不夠好

---

5. **collection** [kəˋlɛkʃən] n. [C][U] 收藏品 <of>

▲ The baseball fan has a collection of baseball cards.

　這棒球迷有棒球卡的收藏品。

💡 art collection 藝術收藏

---

6. **cone** [kon] n. [C] 圓錐體

▲ The police officer put some traffic cones on the road to get drivers' attention.

　警察在這條路上放一些交通錐以取得駕駛的注意。

💡 ice cream cone 錐形冰淇淋甜筒

---

7. **democracy** [dɪˋmɑkrəsɪ] n. [C][U] 民主 (國家) (pl. democracies)

▲ Some of the democracies still have a royal family.

　一些民主國家仍有皇室存在。

---

8. **desire** [dɪˋzaɪr] n. [C][U] 慾望 <for>

▲ Seeking peace of mind, Rita has no desire for fame.
Rita 追求心裡安寧，對名聲沒什麼慾望。

💡 sb's heart's desire 渴望獲得之物 | overwhelming/
burning/strong/great desire 強烈的慾望

desire [dɪ`zaɪr] v. 希望

▲ A country that desires everlasting peace won't launch
a war against any other country in the world.
一個渴望持久和平的國家不會對世界上任何其他國家
發動戰爭。

9. **detect** [dɪ`tɛkt] v. 發現

▲ My father detected a gas leak and phoned the
emergency number immediately.
我父親發現瓦斯外洩並立刻打緊急救助電話。

10. **elevator** [`ɛlə,vetɚ] n. [C] 電梯

▲ Take the elevator to the 14th floor.
搭乘電梯到十四樓。

11. **enjoyable** [ɪn`dʒɔɪəbl] adj. 令人愉快的，有趣的

▲ Playing games or watching movies makes a long-
distance flight enjoyable.
玩遊戲或看電影使搭飛機的長途飛行變得愉快。

12. **fearful** [`fɪrfəl] adj. 害怕的；擔心的 <of, that>

▲ Gina is fearful of offending her teacher.
Gina 害怕會激怒她的老師。

13. **gesture** [`dʒɛstʃɚ] n. [C][U] 手勢 <of>

▲ After reaching the finish line, John raised his arms in the air in a gesture of victory. 抵達終點線後，John 在空中高舉雙手，做出勝利的手勢。

💡 make a...gesture 做出…的手勢

gesture [ˋdʒɛstʃɚ] v. 做手勢

▲ "Leave now," said the guard, gesturing at the gate. 「馬上離開」，守衛指著大門說道。

14. **impress** [ɪmˋprɛs] v. 給…留下深刻印象 <with, by>

▲ Joan impressed everyone at the party with her beauty. Joan 的美貌給派對的每個人留下深刻印象。

15. **meanwhile** [ˋmin,waɪl] n. [C][U] (與此) 同時

▲ Gary was cleaning the house. In the meanwhile, his wife went to school to pick up their children. Gary 打掃了房子。與此同時，他的妻子去學校接他們的小孩。

meanwhile [ˋmin,waɪl] adv. (與此) 同時

▲ Martha is cooking dinner. Meanwhile, her husband is setting the table. Martha 正在煮晚餐。與此同時，她的丈夫正在擺放餐具。

16. **missing** [ˋmɪsɪŋ] adj. 失蹤的 [同] lost

▲ The police have not found the missing boy so far. 警方到目前為止尚未找到失蹤的男孩。

17. **naked** [ˋnekɪd] adj. 赤裸的 [同] bare

▲ That is a painting of a naked woman and her children.

那幅畫作畫的是一個赤裸的女人與她的小孩。

💡 stark naked 一絲不掛 | half/partly naked 半裸 | stripped naked 脫光衣服 | naked eye 肉眼

---

18. **native** [`netɪv] adj. 原產的 <to>

▲ Corn is native to America. 玉米原產於美洲。

💡 go native 入境隨俗 | native language/tongue 母語

native [`netɪv] n. [C] 本地人 <of>

▲ The tourist dressed as if he were a native of the country he was visiting.
旅客打扮得就像他拜訪的國家的本地人一般。

---

19. **promote** [prə`mot] v. 促進，推動 [同] encourage；促銷；升職 <to>

▲ The YouTuber uploaded several videos to promote public awareness of school bullying.
這位 YouTube 創作者上傳了幾部影片來促進大眾對校園霸凌的認識。

---

20. **racial** [`reʃəl] adj. 種族的

▲ Laws on equality should be passed to stop racial discrimination. 平等法應該被通過來阻止種族歧視。

💡 racial prejudice/equality 種族偏見 / 平等

---

21. **rust** [rʌst] n. [U] 鏽

▲ Fred cleans and oils his bike regularly to prevent rust. Fred 定期將腳踏車清潔和上油以防生鏽。

rust [rʌst] v. 生鏽 [同] corrode

▲ If you leave the lawn mower outside in the rain, it will rust easily.

如果你把割草機放在外面淋雨，它很容易會生鏽。

22. **stadium** [ˋstedɪəm] n. [C] 體育場 (pl. stadiums, stadia)

▲ Some athletes are launching a crowdfunding campaign to build football stadiums in poor countries. 一些運動員正在網路籌募基金來在貧困的國家建足球場。

23. **theory** [ˋθiərɪ] n. [C][U] 理論 ， 學說 <in, of, that> (pl. theories)

▲ The scientist's plan, though excellent in theory, is impractical.

科學家的計畫雖然在理論上很好，但不實際。

💡 political/economic/literary theory 政治 / 經濟 / 文學理論

24. **twist** [twɪst] n. [C] 搓，扭轉

▲ You have to give the rope a few more twists.

你必須再搓幾下繩子。

💡 twists and turns 彎彎曲曲；曲折變化

twist [twɪst] v. 轉動；扭傷 (腳踝等)

▲ When Michelle feels nervous, she would keep twisting her ring.

當 Michelle 焦慮的時候，她會一直轉動戒指。

💡 twist sb's arm 向…施壓 | twist sb around your little finger

任意擺布 (常指非常喜歡自己的人)

25. **web** [wɛb] n. [C] 網

▲ A butterfly was caught in a spider's web.
一隻蝴蝶被蜘蛛網捉住。

💡 spin a web 織網

Unit 14

1. **awake** [ə`wek] adj. 醒著的

▲ Eric lay awake in bed for hours last night.
Eric 昨晚醒著躺在床上好幾個小時。

💡 stay/keep/remain awake 保持清醒

awake [ə`wek] v. 醒來 (awoke, awaked | awoken | awaking)

▲ Olivia was so nervous about the interview that she awoke very early this morning. Olivia 對於面試如此緊張以致於她今天早上很早就醒來了。

2. **bang** [bæŋ] n. [C] 砰、撞的聲音

▲ Ian heard a bang, which sounded like a gunshot.
Ian 聽見砰的一聲，聽起來像槍聲。

💡 with a bang 砰地一聲 | go out with a bang 圓滿結束

bang [bæŋ] v. 砰地擊打 <on, with>

▲ Jack was so mad that he banged the table with his fist. Jack 非常生氣而用拳頭砰地重擊桌面。

bang [bæŋ] adv. 正好

▲ The company's technology is bang up to date.
這家公司的技術是最新的。

3. **banker** [ˋbæŋkɚ] n. [C] 銀行家
▲ The child of the banker was kidnapped by two masked men in Paris. 這名銀行家的小孩在巴黎被兩個戴著口罩的男子綁架。

4. **beam** [bim] n. [C] 光線
▲ The beam of the car's headlights made me unable to open my eyes. 這車子車頭燈的光線讓我張不開眼。
💡 laser/electron beam 雷射光線 / 電波
beam [bim] v. 照射
▲ Light beamed through a hole in the curtain.
光線由窗簾上的小洞照射過來。

5. **bind** [baɪnd] v. 綁；束縛 (bound | bound | binding)
▲ The thief was bound hand and foot.
小偷的手腳被綁起來了。
💡 bind/tie sb hand and foot 綁住…的手腳

6. **confirm** [kənˋfɝm] v. 確認 <that>
▲ Leo called the airline to confirm his plane ticket.
Leo 打電話給航空公司確認機位。

7. **deposit** [dɪˋpɑzɪt] n. [C] 存款 <of>
▲ Roy makes a deposit of US$1,000 into his wife's account every month.
Roy 每個月都會在他妻子的戶頭存入一千美元。

💡 on deposit (錢) 存款的

deposit [dɪˋpɑzɪt] v. 儲存 (尤指金錢) <in>

▲ Betty deposited NT$10,000 dollars in her own account today.

Betty 今天在她自己的帳戶裡存了了新臺幣一萬元。

---

8. **determine** [dɪˋtɝmɪn] v. 確定 <how, what, who, that>

▲ Quizzes are used to determine how much students have learned. 測驗是被用來確定學生學到了多少。

determined [dɪˋtɝmɪnd] adj. 意志堅定的，堅決的 <to>

▲ Gina is determined to get the tough job done.

Gina 意志堅定的要把棘手的工作完成。

💡 bound and determined 一定要

---

9. **entry** [ˋɛntrɪ] n. [C][U] 進入 <to, into> [反] exit (pl. entries)

▲ Although the door was locked, the burglar gained entry to the house through a window in the backyard.

雖然門是鎖著，竊賊還是經由後院的一扇窗戶進入這房子。

---

10. **excellence** [ˋɛksl̩əns] n. [U] 優秀 <in, of>

▲ Constant practice can help you achieve excellence in your language skills.

不斷練習能幫助你的語言技巧變得傑出。

---

11. **familiar** [fəˋmɪljɚ] adj. 熟悉的 <with, to> [反] unfamiliar

▲ Since we just moved here, we are not familiar with the neighborhood.

因為我們剛搬來這裡，我們對這一區不太熟悉。

💡 on familiar terms 關係親密 | look/sound familiar 看 / 聽起來熟悉

---

12. **fond** [fɑnd] adj. 喜愛的 <of> (fonder | fondest)

▲ Patty is fond of juicy fruit like watermelons.

Patty 喜愛像是西瓜這類多汁的水果。

13. **graduate** [ˋgrædʒʊɪt] n. [C] 畢業生 <of, in>

▲ A college graduate cannot find a decent job easily because more and more people have a master's degree. 大學畢業生不容易找到好工作，因為越來越多人有碩士學位。

💡 graduate school/student 研究所 / 生

graduate [ˋgrædʒʊ͵et] v. 畢業 <from, with>

▲ My sister graduated from college this June.

我姊姊今年六月從大學畢業。

14. **leather** [ˋlɛðɚ] n. [U] 皮革

▲ The leather handbags are more expensive than those made of nylon. 皮革製的手提袋比尼龍製的貴。

---

15. **mighty** [ˋmaɪtɪ] adj. 巨大的 [同] great (mightier | mightiest)

▲ It's impossible for us to cross the mighty river.

我們不可能穿過這條巨大的河流。

💡 The pen is mightier than the sword. 【諺】筆比劍更有力量。 | high and mighty 趾高氣揚的

mightily [`maɪtḷɪ] adv. 非常

▲ All the students were mightily surprised by the result of their experiment. 所有同學都非常驚訝實驗結果。

---

16. **moisture** [`mɔɪstʃɚ] n. [U] 水分，溼氣

▲ Trees use their roots to absorb moisture from the soil. 樹木用根部來吸取土壤中的水分。

💡 absorb/retain moisture 吸取 / 保留水分

---

17. **necessity** [nə`sɛsətɪ] n. [C] 必需品 (usu. pl.)；[U] 需要

▲ Due to the earthquake, many victims lacked the basic necessities like food and water. 由於地震的緣故，許多的災民缺乏基本必需品，例如食物和水。

💡 basic/bare necessities 基本必需品

---

18. **operation** [ˌɑpə`reʃən] n. [C][U] 運作；操作；手術

▲ That machine is not in operation yet.
那部機器尚未使用。

💡 have/undergo an operation on/for... 接受…的手術 (身體部位)/ 因…動手術 (病因) | perform/carry out an operation 執行手術

---

19. **professor** [prə`fɛsɚ] n. [C] 教授 (abbr. Prof.)

▲ After years of hard work, Nina finally got promotion from associate professor to full professor of English literature.

經過多年努力，Nina 終於從英國文學的副教授升等為教授。

20. **rely** [rɪˋlaɪ] v. 依靠，依賴 <on, upon>

▲ You can rely on Nancy to help handle the difficult problem. 你可以依靠 Nancy 來幫忙處理這個難題。

21. **scarce** [skɛrs] adj. 缺乏的，稀有的 (scarcer | scarcest)

▲ When fresh vegetables are scarce in the winter, the country has to import them from other countries.
冬天新鮮蔬菜缺乏的時候，這個國家必須從其他國家進口。

💡 scarce resources 稀有資源 | make yourself scarce (為免麻煩) 避開

22. **stove** [stov] n. [C] 爐灶

▲ Gina put a pot on the stove and heated the milk.
Gina 將鍋子放在爐灶上來加熱牛奶。

23. **tend** [tɛnd] v. 易於…，傾向於… <to>；照料，照顧

▲ My brother tends to shout when he gets excited.
我弟弟一興奮就容易大叫。

24. **tide** [taɪd] n. [C] 潮汐的漲退；形勢

▲ Is the tide in or out this morning?
今天早上是漲潮還是退潮？

💡 high/low tide 高 / 低潮 | go/swim against the tide 逆潮流 | go/swim with the tide 趕潮流

25. **underwear** [ˋʌndɚ͵wɛr] n. [U] 內衣褲

▲ Wendy prepared some clothes and underwear for her graduation trip.

Wendy 為了畢業旅行準備了一些衣服和內衣褲。

Unit 15

1. **bacteria** [bækˋtɪrɪə] n. [pl.] 細菌 (sing. bacterium)

▲ The bacteria in drinking water spread the illness.

這疾病是由飲用水裡的細菌傳播。

2. **bare** [bɛr] adj. 赤裸的，裸露的 (barer | barest)

▲ You'd better not step onto the hot sandy beach in bare feet. 你最好不要赤腳踩在炎熱的沙灘上。

💡 with your bare hands 赤手空拳

bare [bɛr] v. 使裸露

▲ My mom told me not to bare my head in this cold weather, or I'll get a cold. 我母親叫我不要在寒冷的天氣中把頭裸露出來，否則會感冒。

💡 bare your heart/soul 吐露心聲

3. **bay** [be] n. [C] 海灣

▲ Our ship sailed into a beautiful bay with crystal water. 我們的船駛入一個有清澈水域的美麗海灣。

💡 at bay (動物) 被包圍 | hold/keep sth at bay 阻止 (令人不快的事)

4. **besides** [bɪ`saɪdz] adv. 此外
   ▲ Planes are more comfortable; besides, they are faster.
   飛機比較舒適，此外還比較快。

   besides [bɪ`saɪdz] prep. 除…之外
   ▲ That store sells many things besides furniture.
   那家店除了家具之外，還出售許多東西。

5. **bitter** [`bɪtɚ] adj. 苦的；痛苦的
   ▲ This medicine tastes bitter. 這藥有苦味。

6. **bloody** [`blʌdɪ] adj. 血腥的；流血的 (bloodier | bloodiest)
   ▲ That was a bloody battle with hundreds of soldiers slaughtered.
   那是場血腥的戰鬥，數以百計的士兵遭屠殺。

7. **conscious** [`kɑnʃəs] adj. 意識到的 <of> [同] aware
   ▲ The explorer was not conscious of what was awaiting him. 探險家沒意識到有什麼在等著他。

   consciousness [`kɑnʃəsnɪs] n. [U] 意識
   ▲ A responsible father has a clear consciousness of his duty. 一個負責的父親對於自身責任有清楚的意識。

8. **dime** [daɪm] n. [C] (美國、加拿大) 十分硬幣
   ▲ Ten dimes make one dollar.
   十個十分硬幣相當於一美元。
   💡 a dime a dozen 隨處可見

9. **elderly** [ˈɛldɚlɪ] adj. 年長的

▲ The elderly artist is invited to give a speech on art appreciation.

這位年長的藝術家應邀以藝術鑑賞為題發表演說。

---

10. **export** [ˈɛksport] n. [C] 出口商品 [反] import

▲ Tea is one of India's main exports.

茶葉是印度的主要出口商品之一。

export [ɪksˈport] v. 出口 <to> [反] import

▲ Our company's high-quality bicycles are exported to many countries.

我們公司的高品質腳踏車出口到許多的國家。

---

11. **fairly** [ˈfɛrlɪ] adv. 公平地

▲ Joe quit after he found out he had not been fairly treated by his boss.

發現受到老闆不公平地對待後，Joe 辭職。

---

12. **grab** [græb] v. 抓住 [同] seize (grabbed | grabbed | grabbing)

▲ Amy grabbed hold of the girl's arm before she fell.

Amy 在女孩跌倒前緊抓住她的手臂。

💡 grab sb's attention 吸引⋯的注意

grab [græb] n. [C] 抓住 <at, for>

▲ When the robber made a grab at the woman's bag, he fell. 當強盜抓住女人的包時，他跌倒了。

💡 up for grabs 人人皆可爭取

---

13. **handful** [ˈhænd͵fʊl] n. [C] 一把 (之量) <of>；[sing.] 少數 <of>

▲ The old lady gave a handful of candies to the kid.
老太太給這個孩子一把糖果。

14. **injury** [ˈɪndʒərɪ] n. [C][U] 損傷，傷害 (pl. injuries)

▲ Luca had to quit jogging because of his knee injury.
Luca 因為膝蓋損傷而必須停止慢跑。

💡 head/back/knee injury 頭部 / 背部 / 膝蓋損傷 | add insult to injury 雪上加霜 | sustain/receive an injury 受到傷害

15. **moral** [ˈmɔrəl] adj. 道德的

▲ A fable usually gives a moral lesson at the end of the story. 寓言故事的結尾常有一個道德教訓。

moral [ˈmɔrəl] n. [pl.] 道德 (～s)

▲ Some people have no business morals.
有些人沒有職業道德。

💡 public/private morals 公共 / 個人道德

16. **novelist** [ˈnɑvl͵ɪst] n. [C] 小說家

▲ My dream is to become a globally renowned novelist. 我的夢想是成為舉世聞名的小說家。

17. **occasion** [əˈkeʒən] n. [C] (某事發生的) 時刻；特殊場合

▲ I have helped Helen on several occasions.
我曾多次幫過 Helen 的忙。

💡 on occasion 偶爾，有時

18. **rate** [ret] n. [C] 比率

▲ The government has taken measures to boost the birth rate. 政府採取措施來提升出生率。

💡 at any rate 無論如何 | at this rate 照這樣下去 | the going rate for sth …的現行費用或酬金

rate [ret] v. 評價 <as>

▲ Jimmy doesn't rate Emily highly as a poet. Jimmy 對 Emily 身為詩人的評價不高。

---

19. **react** [rɪ`ækt] v. 反應，回應 <to>

▲ Some people like the new policy while others react differently. 有些人喜歡新政策，而有些人則不。

💡 react against sth 反抗；反對

---

20. **recognize** [`rɛkəg,naɪz] v. 認出 [同] identify

▲ My nephew has changed so much that I can't recognize him at all.
我姪子改變得太多以致於我根本認不出他來。

---

21. **scholarship** [`skɑlɚ,ʃɪp] n. [C] 獎學金 <to>

▲ Mike won a scholarship to the prestigious university due to his good grades. Mike 因為出色的成績而獲得這間有名望的大學的獎學金。

💡 on a scholarship 得到獎學金

---

22. **scientist** [`saɪəntɪst] n. [C] 科學家

▲ Some scientists agree that salmon locate home streams by smell.

部分科學家贊同鮭魚是靠嗅覺回到出生河川的說法。

---

23. **substance** [`sʌbstəns] n. [C] 物質
   ▲ Rita asked me if this powdery substance was harmful. Rita 詢問我這粉狀的物質是否有害。
   💡 illegal substance 毒品

---

24. **trend** [trɛnd] n. [C] 趨勢 <in>
   ▲ The upward trend in the price of gold still continues. 金價的上漲趨勢仍然持續中。

---

25. **union** [`junjən] n. [C] 工會 (also labor union) ; [U] 結合，合併
   ▲ Many employees joined a union to protect their rights. 很多僱員加入工會以保障他們的權益。

Unit 16

1. **barely** [`bɛrlɪ] adv. 勉強地，幾乎不能
   ▲ Wendy has barely enough money to pay her bills this month. Wendy 這個月勉強有足夠的錢來支付帳單。

---

2. **beetle** [`bitl] n. [C] 甲蟲
   ▲ The biologist did some research on different kinds of beetles. 生物學家對不同種的甲蟲做了一些研究。

---

3. **bore** [bor] v. 使厭煩，使討厭 <with>

▲ My neighbor always bores me with the same complaints. 鄰居總說同樣的抱怨使我感到厭煩。

💡 bore sb silly 使…覺得無聊透頂 | bore into sb 盯住…

bore [bor] n. [C] 令人討厭的人或事

▲ The boy is such a bore that nobody wants to be his friend. 這男孩是如此令人討厭的人以致於沒有人想當他的朋友。

---

4. **brake** [brek] n. [C] 剎車

▲ The scooter couldn't stop because the brakes failed. 這輛摩托車因為剎車失靈而無法停下來。

💡 slam/put on the brakes 踩剎車 | put the brakes on... 控制 | screech/squeal of brakes 尖銳的剎車聲

brake [brek] v. 剎車

▲ The driver braked hard when she saw a child running out into the road.
這駕駛一看見孩子奔向馬路就用力剎車。

---

5. **crash** [kræʃ] n. [C] 撞車事故，失事；碎裂聲

▲ The car crash killed five persons.
那起撞車事故中有五人喪生。

crash [kræʃ] v. 墜毀，猛撞 <into>

▲ The plane crashed shortly after take-off.
這架飛機在起飛不久後就墜毀。

---

6. **donkey** [`dɑŋkɪ] n. [C] 驢

▲ Can you tell the difference between a donkey and a mule? 你可以說出驢和騾的差異嗎？

💡 donkey's years 很長的時間

---

7. **exchange** [ɪks`tʃendʒ] n. [C][U] 交換
▲ The student exchange program allows students to study in one of the three colleges in Japan.
這個交換學生計畫允許學生到日本這三所大學的其中之一修課。
💡 in exchange for sth 作為…的交換
exchange [ɪks`tʃendʒ] v. 交換 <for>
▲ During the war, people would exchange all their valuables for any food due to food shortages.
在戰爭期間，人們因食物短缺而願意用他們所有的貴重物品交換任何食物。
💡 exchange sth with sb 和…交換…

---

8. **fairy** [`fɛrɪ] n. [C] 小仙子，小精靈 (pl. fairies)
▲ The little girl always imagines herself as a graceful fairy. 那小女孩總是想像自己是優雅的小仙子。
fairy [`fɛrɪ] adj. 幻想中的
▲ Vicky's father always reads her a fairy tale before she goes to sleep.
Vicky 的爸爸總在她睡前為她讀一則童話故事。

---

9. **fare** [fɛr] n. [C] 票價
▲ What is the train fare to Hualien?
往花蓮的火車票是多少錢？

---

10. **guidance** [`gaɪdn̩s] n. [U] 指導，引導 <on, about>

▲ Tim turned to his teacher for guidance on how to choose a major.

Tim 請老師給他一些選擇主修科目方面的指導。

---

11. **heal** [hil] v. 治癒 [同] cure

▲ Time heals all wounds. 時間會治療一切的創傷。

---

12. **honor** [ˋɑnɚ] n. [U] 榮譽

▲ The soldiers did not fight for their own lives but for the honor of their country. 這些軍人並非為個人生命而戰，而是為國家的榮譽而戰。

honor [ˋɑnɚ] v. 向…致敬，公開表彰 <for>

▲ The firefighter was honored for his bravery.
這名消防隊員因其英勇而受到表彰。

---

13. **mental** [ˋmɛntl] adj. 精神的，心理的

▲ Carol suffers from mental illness, whose symptoms include mood disorders and anxiety disorders. Carol 得了精神疾病，它的症狀包括情緒失調及焦慮症。

---

14. **nickname** [ˋnɪk͵nem] n. [C] 綽號

▲ The boy's friends give him the nickname "Rocky."
男孩被朋友取了綽號 Rocky。

nickname [ˋnɪk͵nem] v. 取綽號

▲ That pretty girl with fair skin was nicknamed "Snow White." 有著白皙皮膚的漂亮女孩被取了「白雪公主」的綽號。

---

15. **observe** [əbˋzɝv] v. 觀察 [同] monitor；遵守 [同] obey

▲ Farmers in ancient times would observe the stars to predict the weather.

古代的農夫會觀察星象以預測天氣。

16. **optimistic** [ˌɑptə`mɪstɪk] adj. 樂觀的 <about> [同] positive [反] pessimistic

▲ Willy is optimistic about his new job in the thriving city.

Willy 對於他在這個繁榮都市的新工作感到樂觀。

17. **reaction** [rɪ`ækʃən] n. [C][U] 反應，回應 <to>

▲ An emergency fund was set up in reaction to the devastating flood.

為了因應這個破壞極大的水災而設立緊急基金。

18. **represent** [ˌrɛprɪ`zɛnt] v. 代表；象徵 [同] symbolize

▲ The government spokesman represented the president at the conference.

政府發言人在這次會議中代表總統出席。

19. **scientific** [ˌsaɪən`tɪfɪk] adj. 科學的

▲ Scientific evidence has proved that doing exercise can make people look younger.

科學證據已經證實做運動可使人們看起來更年輕。

20. **scream** [skrim] v. 尖叫 <at, in, with> [同] shriek, yell

▲ Kelly screamed at Henry for breaking her favorite mug. Kelly 因為 Henry 打破她最喜歡的馬克杯而對他大吼大叫。

💡 scream in/with laughter/terror/pain 尖聲地笑 / 驚恐地尖叫 / 痛苦地尖叫 | scream your head off 大聲叫喊

scream [skrim] n. [C] 尖叫聲 <of> [同] shriek

▲ Jean let out a scream when she saw a cockroach in the kitchen.
當 Jean 在廚房看到一隻蟑螂時發出一聲尖叫。

---

21. **senior** [ˋsinjɚ] adj. 年長的 <to>；資深的 <to> [反] junior

▲ Most senior citizens live on social welfare while only a small percentage of them depend on their pensions.
大多數老年人靠社會福利過活，只有少部分人依靠自己的退休金生活。

senior [ˋsinjɚ] n. [C] 年長者

▲ Lily, my best friend, is ten years my senior.
我最要好的朋友 Lily 比我大十歲。

---

22. **superior** [sʊˋpɪrɪɚ] adj. 較好的，較優越的 <to> [反] inferior

▲ My new computer is superior to my old one.
我的新電腦比舊的好。

superior [sʊˋpɪrɪɚ] n. [C] 上司，上級

▲ Who is your immediate superior?
誰是你的頂頭上司？

---

23. **vacant** [ˋvekənt] adj. 空的 [同] unoccupied；(職位) 空缺的

▲ The hotel has no vacant rooms.

這間飯店沒有空的房間。

24. **vehicle** [ˋviɪkl] n. [C] 交通工具，車輛

▲ Vehicles are not permitted on this street, which is always filled with tourists.
所有的車輛都禁止進入這條總是擠滿遊客的街道。

25. **victim** [ˋvɪktɪm] n. [C] 受害者，犧牲者

▲ The government provided a temporary shelter for the earthquake victims.
政府為這些地震災民提供暫時的收容所。

💡 fall victim to sth 成為…的受害者；被…所傷害

Unit 17

1. **bold** [bold] adj. 勇敢的，無畏的 [同] brave

▲ The bold firefighters rescued dozens of people from the burning skyscraper. 勇敢的消防隊員從大火吞沒的摩天大樓救出裡面很多的人。

💡 (as) bold as brass 冒昧

2. **bowling** [ˋbolɪŋ] n. [U] 保齡球

▲ My friends and I like to go bowling on Saturday.
我朋友和我喜歡在星期六打保齡球。

3. **broadcast** [ˋbrɔdˏkæst] n. [C] 廣播節目

▲ Did you watch the news broadcast at noon, while eating lunch? 你吃午餐時看了中午的新聞廣播嗎？

💡 live broadcast 現場直播 | radio/television broadcast 電臺 / 電視節目

broadcast [`brɔd͵kæst] v. 廣 播 (broadcast, broadcasted | broadcast, broadcasted | broadcasting)

▲ Major TV stations used to broadcast news at 7 p.m. 主要的電視臺過去在晚間七點播報新聞。

---

4. **captain** [`kæptɪn] n. [C] 機長，船長

▲ The captain told us the location of the airplane. 機長告訴我們飛機的位置。

---

5. **civil** [`sɪvḷ] adj. 公民的；民事的

▲ The protesters marched to defend their civil rights. 抗議者遊行捍衛他們的公民權。

---

6. **cupboard** [`kʌbəˑd] n. [C] 櫥櫃

▲ The dishes are all stored in the kitchen cupboard. 碗盤全放置在廚房櫥櫃裡。

---

7. **eager** [`igəˑ] adj. 渴望的，熱切的 <to, for>

▲ Since Dora was eager to see what was inside the package, she tore it open immediately.
由於 Dora 想知道包裹裡面有什麼，她立即把它拆開。

---

8. **explore** [ɪk`splor] v. 探險；探究，探討 [同] analyze, look at

▲ Due to my passion for traveling, I have explored many parts of the world.

因為我熱愛旅遊，我已經探索世界多個地方。

---

9. **farther** [ˋfɑrðɚ] adv. 更遠地 [同] further
   ▲ Don't swim farther out into the ocean.
   不要再往海裡游去了。
   💡 farther afield 更遠離
   farther [ˋfɑrðɚ] adj. 更遠的 [同] further
   ▲ Olivia sat at the farther end of the table.
   Olivia 坐在桌子更遠的一端。

---

10. **fashionable** [ˋfæʃənəbl] adj. 時髦的 [反] unfashionable
    ▲ The singer is so fashionable that many people copy
    the way she dresses.
    這位歌手很時髦，以至於許多人模仿她的穿著。

---

11. **hesitate** [ˋhɛzə͵tet] v. 猶豫 <to>
    ▲ Don't hesitate to call me if you need anything.
    如果你需要任何東西，別猶豫打給我。

---

12. **indoors** [ˋɪn͵dorz] adv. 室內地 [反] outdoors
    ▲ The students in my class have to stay indoors today
    because it is raining heavily.
    因為下大雨，所以我班上學生今天必須待在室內。

---

13. **location** [loˋkeʃən] n. [C] 地點，位置
    ▲ That busy corner is a good location for a restaurant
    or a convenience store.
    那個繁忙的角落是開餐廳或超商的好地點。

14. **odd** [ɑd] adj. 奇怪的；奇數的 [反] even
    ▲ The man is an odd person who likes to wear shorts in winter. 這男人是個奇怪的人，喜歡在冬天穿短褲。

15. **onto** [ˋɑntu] prep. 到⋯上
    ▲ Suddenly, a man jumped onto the stage.
       突然有個男子跳到舞臺上。

16. **organize** [ˋɔrgənˏaɪz] v. 組織
    ▲ Who will organize the activity? 誰會組織這個活動？
    organized [ˋɔrgənˏaɪzd] adj. 安排有序的
    ▲ The office is well organized with everything neat and tidy. 辦公室井然有序。

17. **performance** [pɚˋfɔrməns] n. [C] 表演；[U] (工作、學業) 表現
    ▲ The world-famous rock band will give four performances in London.
       這個世界知名的搖滾樂團在倫敦將有四場表演。

18. **preparation** [ˏprɛpəˋreʃən] n. [C] 準備工作 (usu. pl.) <for>；[U] 準備 <for>
    ▲ Mary has been practicing swimming every day since last month, making preparations for the contest next week. Mary 自上個月以來每天都在練習游泳，為下星期的比賽作準備。

19. **reliable** [rɪˋlaɪəbl̩] adj. 可靠的，可信賴的 [同] dependable [反] unreliable

▲ The information came from a reliable source.
這個消息來自可靠的來源。

💡 reliable information/data 可靠的消息 / 資料

20. **request** [rɪˋkwɛst] n. [C] 要求，請求 <to>

▲ Tim made a request to his father for more pocket money. Tim 向父親要求更多的零用錢。

💡 on request 應要求 | at sb's request 依…的要求

request [rɪˋkwɛst] v. 要求，請求 <that>

▲ The boss requested that the work should be finished by the end of the month. 老闆要求月底前要完成工作。

21. **similarity** [͵sɪməˋlærətɪ] n. [C][U] 相 似 (處) <to, between> [同] resemblance [反] difference (pl. similarities)

▲ The murder case bears some similarities to the previous one.
這起謀殺案與前一起案子有一些相似之處。

22. **skinny** [ˋskɪnɪ] adj. 很瘦的，皮包骨的 (skinnier | skinniest)

▲ Tiffany is so skinny that her parents want her to put on some weight.
Tiffany 太瘦了以致於她父母希望她能增加一些重量。

23. **survey** [ˋsɝve] n. [C] 調查

▲ The survey shows that firstborn children are usually more responsible.

這份調查顯示老大通常比較負責任。

💡 conduct/carry out/do a survey 做調查｜survey shows/reveals 調查顯示

survey [sə`ve] v. 調查；勘查 [同] inspect

▲ Some of the voters who were surveyed said they were not satisfied with the outcome of the election.
一些接受調查的選民說他們不滿意這次選舉的結果。

---

24. **vary** [`vɛrɪ] v. 不同 [同] differ

▲ Prices of cellphones vary from store to store.
每一家店的手機價格都不同。

💡 vary in 在⋯有所不同

---

25. **violent** [`vaɪələnt] adj. 猛烈的；暴力的

▲ There was a violent volcanic eruption yesterday.
昨天有猛烈的火山爆發。

Unit 18

1. **bomb** [bɑm] n. [C] 炸彈

▲ A bomb exploded, injuring ten people.
炸彈爆炸，傷了十人。

💡 bomb explodes/goes off 炸彈爆炸｜plant a bomb 埋炸彈｜drop a bomb 投炸彈｜the bomb 原子彈｜be the bomb 極好

. **bomb** [bɑm] v. 轟炸，投下炸彈

▲ Planes bombed the city every night during World War II. 第二次世界大戰期間，飛機每晚轟炸這座城市。

💡 be bombed out 被炸毀

bombard [bɑm`bɑrd] v. 炮轟；(以問題、要求等) 困擾某人 <with>

▲ The enemy bombarded the fort. 敵人炮轟軍營。

---

2. **breast** [brɛst] n. [C] 乳房

▲ Women should have a check-up for breast cancer every year. 婦女應該每年做乳癌檢查。

---

3. **bush** [bʊʃ] n. [C] 灌木

▲ Mr. Chang trims the bushes around his house once a month. 張先生每個月修剪一次住家周圍的灌木叢。

💡 beat about/around the bush (說話) 拐彎抹角

---

4. **capture** [`kæptʃɚ] v. 俘虜；捕獲

▲ The soldiers were captured by the enemy.
這些士兵被敵軍俘虜。

capture [`kæptʃɚ] n. [U] 捕獲 <of>

▲ The capture of the robber took a lot of time and effort. 捕獲這強盜花了許多時間及力氣。

---

5. **dealer** [`dilɚ] n. [C] 商人

▲ Josh works as a second-hand car dealer.
Josh 是個二手車經銷商。

---

6. **editor** [`ɛdɪtɚ] n. [C] 編輯

▲ Debbie is a senior editor in the publishing house.

Debbie 是這間出版社的資深編輯。

---

7. **fence** [fɛns] `n.` [C] 柵欄

▲ My father spent a week building a fence around the garden. 我父親花一個星期的時間在花園周圍蓋柵欄。

🔔 sit on the fence 猶豫不決

fence [fɛns] `v.` (用柵欄) 圍住

▲ The horses were fenced in the farm. 馬兒被圍在農場。

---

8. **fuel** [ˋfjuəl] `n.` [C][U] 燃料

▲ Coal is used for fuel. 煤被用來做燃料。

🔔 add fuel to the fire 火上加油

fuel [ˋfjuəl] `v.` 為⋯添加燃料

▲ The amazing airplane can be fueled in the air without having to land.

這架令人驚奇的飛機可在空中加油，而無須降落。

🔔 fuel up 加油

---

9. **harmful** [ˋhɑrmfəl] `adj.` 有害的 <to>

▲ It is a known fact that smoking is harmful to health. 眾所周知吸菸對健康有害。

---

10. **humorous** [ˋhjumərəs] `adj.` 幽默的 [同] funny

▲ Living your life in a humorous way may make you healthier. 以幽默的方式過生活可能會讓你更健康。

---

11. **investigate** [ɪnˋvɛstəˏget] `v.` 調查

▲ The police are investigating the cause of the car accident.

警方正在調查這起車禍的原因。

12. **mosquito** [məˋskito] n. [C] 蚊子 (pl. mosquitoes, mosquitos)

▲ You had better put some ointment on that mosquito bite. 你最好在那個被蚊子叮的地方擦些藥膏。

13. **onion** [ˋʌnjən] n. [C][U] 洋蔥

▲ Let the onion cook for fifteen minutes before you add the chicken soup.
先將洋蔥煮十五分鐘後再加入雞高湯。

14. **oral** [ˋorəl] adj. 口頭的；口腔的

▲ To get a master's degree, a student has to pass not only a written exam but also an oral defense. 為了取得碩士學位，學生不僅必須通過筆試，還得通過口試。

♥ oral agreement/presentation/exam 口頭協議 / 報告 / 考試

oral [ˋorəl] n. [C] 口試

▲ To get a master's degree, a student has to pass not only a written exam but also an oral. 為了取得碩士學位，學生不僅必須通過筆試，還得通過口試。

15. **original** [əˋrɪdʒənl] adj. 原先的，最初的

▲ The original plan was quite different from the revised version. 原先的計畫和修改過的版本很不一樣。

original [əˋrɪdʒənl] n. [C] 原作

▲ This is not a copy; it's an original.

這不是複製品而是原作。

💡 in the original 以原文

---

16. **panic** [ˋpænɪk] n. [U] 恐慌，驚慌

▲ Panic spread through the audience when the fire alarm went off in the theater.
當火警警鈴在戲院響起時，觀眾們驚慌失措。

💡 get into a panic 慌張起來 | panic attack (突如其來的) 驚慌失措

panic [ˋpænɪk] v. 驚慌失措 (panicked | panicked | panicking)

▲ It is important not to panic during an earthquake.
地震時重要的是不要驚慌失措。

---

17. **property** [ˋprɑpɚtɪ] n. [U] 財產；[C] 性質，屬性 (usu. pl.) [同] quality, characteristic (pl. properties)

▲ The wealthy man divided his property among his sons. 富人將財產分給兒子們。

💡 personal property 個人財產

---

18. **protection** [prəˋtɛkʃən] n. [U] 保護 <from, against>

▲ Doctors warned that just one shot of the vaccine may not provide full protection against COVID-19. 醫生警告一劑疫苗可能無法針對新冠肺炎提供完整保護。

---

19. **resource** [rɪˋsors] n. [C] 資源 (usu. pl.)

▲ People must conserve natural resources for future generations because they are limited.

人們必須為未來的世代保存天然資源，因它們是有限的。

---

20. **solid** [ˋsɑlɪd] adj. 固體的；堅固的
   ▲ The solid form of water is ice. 水的固態是冰。

---

21. **somehow** [ˋsʌm͵haʊ] adv. 以⋯方式；不知為何
   ▲ Don't worry! We can find the way home somehow.
   別擔心！我們會有辦法找到回家的方式的。

---

22. **stable** [ˋstebḷ] adj. 穩定的 [同] steady [反] unstable
   ▲ The medical treatment kept the patient's condition
   stable. 醫療讓病人的病情保持穩定。

---

23. **toss** [tɔs] v. 拋，擲 <into>
   ▲ Allen screwed the paper into a ball and tossed it into
   the trash can. Allen 將紙揉成一團並丟進垃圾桶裡。
   ♥ toss up 丟硬幣決定 | toss sth out 丟棄⋯ | toss sth
   away 隨便地花掉或丟掉
   toss [tɔs] n. [C] 拋擲 (硬幣)
   ▲ Wendy won the coin toss and got a free drink.
   Wendy 在擲硬幣中猜對並得到一杯免費的飲料。
   ♥ toss of a coin 擲硬幣決定 | win/lose the toss 在擲硬
   幣中猜對 / 錯

---

24. **visible** [ˋvɪzəbḷ] adj. 看得見的 [反] invisible
   ▲ A lighthouse is visible in the distance.
   可以看見遠處有一燈塔。

💡 visible to the naked eye 肉眼可視 | clearly/barely visible 清晰可見 / 看不清楚

25. **yolk** [jok] n. [C][U] 蛋黃

▲ Don't eat raw egg yolk as it can be a source of food poisoning.

不要吃生蛋黃，因為它可能是食物中毒的來源。

Unit 19

1. **acceptable** [ək`sɛptəbl̩] adj. 可接受的 <to> [反] unacceptable

▲ After a long discussion, we finally came to a decision that was acceptable to all of us.

在長時間討論後，我們終於做出大家都能接受的決定。

2. **breathe** [brið] v. 呼吸

▲ Wendy was breathing hard because she ran all the way home. Wendy 因一路跑回家而大口喘氣。

💡 breathe your last 嚥氣 | breathe easier 鬆了口氣 | breathe life into sth 注入活力 | breathe deeply 深呼吸

3. **brick** [brɪk] n. [C][U] 磚

▲ There is a house of red brick at the foot of the hill.

山腳下有一棟紅磚房子。

💡 bricks and mortar 房產

4. **cafeteria** [ˌkæfə`tɪrɪə] n. [C] 自助餐廳
   ▲ Ken and I had dinner together in the cafeteria, which served cheap and delicious food. Ken 和我在自助餐廳享用晚餐，那裡提供便宜又好吃的食物。

5. **cleaner** [`klinə] n. [C] 清潔工
   ▲ As a cleaner, her daily duty is to mop the floor of this building.
   作為一位清潔工，她每日的職責是拖這棟大樓的地板。
   ♥ take sb to the cleaner's 騙光⋯的錢

6. **committee** [kə`mɪtɪ] n. [C] 委員會 <of, on>
   ▲ Mrs. Lin used to be on the parents' committee in her daughter's school.
   林太太曾是她女兒學校家長委員會的成員。

7. **deck** [dɛk] n. [C] 甲板
   ▲ Ella relaxed on the deck and enjoyed the beautiful sunset. Ella 在甲板上放鬆身心並享受美麗的夕陽。
   ♥ lower/upper deck 低 / 上層的甲板 | below deck 在主甲板下

8. **electronic** [ɪˌlɛk`trɑnɪk] adj. (尤指設備) 電子的
   ▲ The company uses electronic mail to send the latest information to the customers.
   這家公司用電子郵件寄送最新的資訊給顧客。
   ♥ electronic devices/components 電子設備 / 元件

9. **fighter** [`faɪtə] n. [C] 戰士，鬥士；戰鬥機

▲ Rita is highly regarded as a freedom fighter.
Rita 被譽為自由戰士。

---

10. **fund** [fʌnd] n. [C] 基金，專款

▲ The hospital has set up a fund to treat rare diseases.
這間醫院成立治療罕見疾病的基金。

💡 trust/pension fund 信託 / 退休基金 | fund of sth 充滿…的

fund [fʌnd] v. 資助

▲ The professor's research was funded by the government organization.
這教授的研究是由這個政府機構所資助。

---

11. **immediate** [ɪˈmidɪət] adj. 直接的 [同] instant；目前的

▲ The immediate response from the public to the entertainer's violence is to boycott his new album.
大眾對這個藝人暴力事件的直接反應是抵制他的新唱片。

💡 immediate problem/danger 即刻的 問題 / 危險 | immediate cause 直接原因 | with immediate effect 立即見效，生效 | the immediate future 近期

immediately [ɪˈmidɪətlɪ] adv. 立刻地 [同] at once

▲ The car burst into flames immediately after the accident. 事故發生後車子立刻燒了起來。

---

12. **industrial** [ɪnˈdʌstrɪəl] adj. 工業的

▲ The news has raised public awareness of the pollution in industrial areas.

這則新聞已經提高了大眾對工業區汙染的意識。

💡 industrial relations 勞資關係

13. **kidney** [ˋkɪdnɪ] n. [C] 腎臟

▲ The patient needs a kidney transplant, or she may die of kidney failure soon.

這病人需要腎臟移植，不然她很快可能會死於腎衰竭。

14. **muscle** [ˋmʌsl̩] n. [C][U] 肌肉

▲ Hank builds his muscles by lifting weights.

Hank 以舉重來鍛鍊肌肉。

💡 pull a muscle 拉傷肌肉 | not move a muscle 一動也不動

15. **opposite** [ˋɑpəzɪt] adj. 相反的 <to> |同| contrary ；對面的

▲ Rachel ended up marrying a man whose character was opposite to hers.

Rachel 最後跟與她個性相反的男人結婚。

opposite [ˋɑpəzɪt] n. [C] 相反的人或事物

▲ Darkness and daylight are complete opposites.

黑夜和白晝是完全相反的。

opposite [ˋɑpəzɪt] prep. 在…對面

▲ Andy and a girl sat opposite each other on the train.

火車上，Andy 坐在一位女生對面。

opposite [ˋɑpəzɪt] adv. 在…對面

▲ The man who lives opposite is an artist.

住在對面的男人是名藝術家。

16. **painter** [ˈpentɚ] n. [C] 畫家
▲ He is a portrait painter. 他是肖像畫家。
💡 portrait/landscape painter 肖像 / 風景畫家

17. **pause** [pɔz] n. [C] 暫停，停頓 <in>
▲ There was a pause before Mary answered the question. Mary 停頓了一下才回答這個問題。
pause [pɔz] v. 暫停，停頓 [同] stop
▲ Gary paused and looked around before going into the house. Gary 停下來環顧四周後才走進屋子裡。
💡 pause for breath/thought 停下來喘息 / 思索一下

18. **pilot** [ˈpaɪlət] n. [C] 飛行員
▲ Luke trained as a fighter pilot at the air force base. Luke 在空軍基地接受戰鬥機飛行員訓練。
💡 fighter/helicopter/bomber pilot 戰鬥機 / 直升機 / 轟炸機飛行員
pilot [ˈpaɪlət] v. 駕駛飛機
▲ Who is piloting that light aircraft? 誰在駕駛那架輕型飛機？

19. **reasonable** [ˈriznəbl̩] adj. 合理的，公道的 [反] unreasonable
▲ The workers struck for reasonable wages. 工人為了爭取合理的工資而罷工。

20. **rid** [rɪd] adj. 擺脫掉，免除

▲ We should get rid of our bad habits.
我們應該擺脫壞習慣。

rid [rɪd] **v.** 使擺脫 <of> [同] eliminate (rid │ rid │ ridding)

▲ The medicine rids me of the cough.
這個藥使我擺脫咳嗽。

---

21. **spite** [spaɪt] **n.** [U] 儘管;怨恨,惡意 [同] malice

▲ In spite of the heavy rain, the outdoor concert was held on time. 儘管下大雨,這戶外演唱會準時舉辦。

💡 in spite of oneself …不由自主地

---

22. **stare** [stɛr] **v.** 盯著看,凝視 <at>

▲ It is impolite to stare at others.
盯著別人看是不禮貌的。

💡 stare sth in the face 與 (令人不快的) 事情非常接近 │ be staring sb in the face …就在…眼前;…十分明顯

stare [stɛr] **n.** [C] 注視,凝視

▲ In the small town, foreigners often receive curious stares. 在這個小鎮,外國人常招來好奇的眼光。

---

23. **statue** [ˈstætʃʊ] **n.** [C] 雕像

▲ The Statue of Liberty is a landmark of New York City. 自由女神像是紐約市的一個地標。

💡 put up/erect a statue 豎立雕像 │ marble/stone/bronze statue 大理石 / 石頭 / 青銅雕像

---

24. **tough** [tʌf] adj. 艱難的；嚴格的 <on, with>；嚼不爛的
    [反] tender (tougher | toughest)
    ▲ Because of her tough childhood, Lisa always has a
    deep feeling of insecurity.
    因為艱困的童年，Lisa 總有很深的不安全感。
    💡 tough luck 活該 (表示不同情)

25. **vitamin** [ˋvaɪtəmɪn] n. [C] 維他命
    ▲ You don't need to take any vitamin pills if you have
    a balanced diet.
    如果你有均衡的飲食，你就不需要服用任何維他命錠。

Unit 20

1. **accurate** [ˋækjərɪt] adj. 精確的 [反] inaccurate
    ▲ My watch is very accurate, not a second fast or slow.
    我的錶非常準確，分秒不差。

2. **breeze** [briz] n. [C] 微風
    ▲ Fiona likes the feeling of a warm spring breeze.
    Fiona 喜歡春天溫暖微風吹拂的感覺。
    breeze [briz] v. 如風似地走
    ▲ Tim breezed in, although he was an hour late.
    Tim 如風似地走進來，儘管他已經遲到一小時了。

3. **bump** [bʌmp] n. [C] 碰撞聲
    ▲ The heavy box fell on the floor with a bump.

這個沉重的箱子掉在地上伴隨著碰撞聲。

bump [bʌmp] v. 撞上 <against, into> [同] hit, collide

▲ The truck bumped against the mountain wall when turning around a sharp curve.

那輛卡車急轉彎時撞上山壁。

💡 bump into sb 與⋯不期而遇 | bump sb off 謀殺⋯ | bump sth up 提高⋯(的數量)

---

4. **clip** [klɪp] n. [C] 夾子

▲ Gina fastened the notes with a paper clip.

Gina 用迴紋針把便條紙夾住。

💡 hair/tie clip 髮 / 領帶夾 | at a fast/good clip 迅速 | clip round/on the ear 一記耳光

clip [klɪp] v. (用夾子) 夾住 (clipped | clipped | clipping)

▲ Fred clipped several sheets of paper together.

Fred 把好幾張紙用夾子夾在一起。

---

5. **cotton** [ˈkɑtn̩] n. [U] 棉花

▲ Rita only buys the clothes made of pure cotton because it is comfortable.

Rita 只買純棉製作的衣服，因為很舒服。

---

6. **desirable** [dɪˈzaɪrəbl̩] adj. 令人嚮往的，值得擁有的 [反] undesirable

▲ It is desirable for my sister to be a flight attendant.

當空服員對我姊姊來說是令人嚮往的。

7. **emergency** [ɪˋmɝdʒənsɪ] n. [C][U] 緊急情況 (pl. emergencies)

▲ During a fire, you should follow the emergency exit signs to leave the building safely. 火災時你應該要沿著緊急出口標誌行進，安全地離開建築物。

💡 emergency landing/room 緊急迫降 / 急診室 | in case of emergency 有緊急狀況時

8. **fist** [fɪst] n. [C] 拳，拳頭

▲ Dylan punched the punching bag with his fists. Dylan 用拳頭捶打沙包。

💡 clench sb's fists …緊握雙拳

fist [fɪst] v. 把 (手) 握成拳頭

▲ Jimmy cannot fist his fingers into his palm because he sprained his index finger. Jimmy 無法將手指握進掌心成拳頭，因為他扭傷了食指。

9. **harm** [hɑrm] n. [U] 損害，傷害

▲ The heavy snow did great harm to the crops. 大雪對農作物造成很大的損害。

💡 do more harm than good 弊大於利 | there is no harm in 做…也沒壞處 | out of harm's way 安全地

harm [hɑrm] v. 傷害，損害

▲ Although the dog looks fierce, it won't harm anyone. 雖然這隻狗看起來很凶猛，但牠不會傷害任何人。

💡 harm a hair on sb's head 動…一根寒毛 | harm sb's image/reputation 傷害…的形象 / 聲望

10. **inferior** [ɪnˋfɪrɪɚ] adj. 次等的，較差的 <to> [反] superior

▲ To our disappointment, the latest model of the car is somewhat inferior to its previous version.
令人失望的是，這輛最新型的汽車不知為何比先前車種略為遜色。

💡 inferior/superior to... 比…低劣 / 出色的

inferior [ɪnˋfɪrɪɚ] n. [C] 部下，屬下 [反] superior

▲ The manager's inferiors all respect her because she is on the up and up.
這位經理的部下都很尊敬她，因為她值得信賴。

---

11. **kit** [kɪt] n. [C] 成套工具

▲ You should pack a first aid kit for the trip, just in case. 你應該為旅途帶個急救工具以防萬一。

---

12. **mobile** [ˋmobl̩] adj. 走動的

▲ Bob won't be mobile until the wound in his leg heals.
在腳傷痊癒之前，Bob 不能走動。

---

13. **organic** [ɔrˋgænɪk] adj. 有機的

▲ The restaurant only serves organic food, which is better for health.
這間餐廳只供應有機食物，那對健康較有益。

---

14. **outdoor** [ˋautˏdor] adj. 室外的 [反] indoor

▲ The rich man decided to build an outdoor swimming pool in his villa.

富豪決定要在他的別墅蓋一座室外游泳池。

---

15. **palace** [ˋpælɪs] n. [C] 宮殿，皇宮

▲ The luxurious five-star hotel looks like a palace.
這棟五星級的豪華旅館看起來像宮殿。

💡 royal/presidential palace 皇室 / 總統官邸 |
Buckingham Palace 白金漢宮

---

16. **plenty** [ˋplɛntɪ] pron. 大量，許多 <of>

▲ There are plenty of books in the library.
這座圖書館有豐富的藏書。

plenty [ˋplɛntɪ] n. [U] 大量，許多

▲ There is time in plenty for them to finish this work.
他們有大量的時間來完成這項工作。

plenty [ˋplɛntɪ] adv. 大量

▲ There is plenty more food in the VIP lounge at the
airport. 有更大量的食物在機場的貴賓休息室。

---

17. **reduce** [rɪˋdjus] v. 減少，降低 [同] cut

▲ Julia decided to go jogging every day to reduce her
weight. Julia 決定要每天慢跑來減重。

---

18. **religious** [rɪˋlɪdʒəs] adj. 宗教的；虔誠的 [同] devout

▲ The religious group is accused of charity fraud.
該宗教團體被控慈善詐騙。

---

19. **response** [rɪˋspɑns] n. [C] 回答 <to>；回應 <to>

▲ It was strange that Carol made no response to my
urgent request.

奇怪的是，Carol 沒有回覆我的緊急的請求。

---

20. **specific** [spɪ`sɪfɪk] adj. 明確的 <about> [同] precise；特定的 <to> [同] particular

▲ Your explanation is too general. Please give some specific examples.
你的解釋太籠統。請舉一些明確的例子。

---

21. **steady** [`stɛdɪ] adj. 持續的 [同] constant；穩定的，平穩的 [同] regular (steadier | steadiest)

▲ If the restaurant doesn't have a steady growth in sales, the owner may close it down. 如果這間餐廳的銷售沒有持續成長，這老闆可能會關閉它。

steady [`stɛdɪ] v. 使穩定；使鎮定

▲ Can you steady the ladder? 你能扶住梯子嗎？

steady [`stɛdɪ] adv. 穩定地

▲ Mindy has been going steady with her boyfriend for seven years; she sometimes wonders when he will propose. Mindy 和男友穩定地交往了七年；有時候她想知道何時他會求婚。

steady [`stɛdɪ] n. [C] 穩定交往對象 (pl. steadies)

▲ Eric has had a steady since last winter.
Eric 從去年冬天開始有一個穩定交往對象。

---

22. **stir** [stɜ] v. 攪拌 <with, in, into>；煽動，激發 (stirred | stirred | stirring)

▲ Sally stirred her milk tea with a spoon.
Sally 用湯匙攪拌她的奶茶。

💡 stir (up) hatred/anger/fears/trouble 激起仇恨 / 憤怒 /
恐懼 / 麻煩 | stir the blood 令人興奮

stir [stɝ] n. [C][U] 騷動 [同] commotion；攪拌

▲ The politician's scandal created quite a stir at the
time. 這名政客的醜聞在當時引起了很大的騷動。

💡 cause/create/make a stir 引起騷亂

---

23. **strength** [strɛŋθ] n. [C] 優點；[U] 力氣 [反] weakness

▲ William tried to analyze the strengths and
weaknesses of the new job.
William 試著分析這新工作的優缺點。

---

24. **trace** [tres] n. [C][U] 蹤跡，痕跡 <of>

▲ The hunters saw traces of a bear in the snow.
獵人們在雪地裡發現熊的蹤跡。

trace [tres] v. 追查到 [同] track；追溯

▲ The parents never give up tracing their missing
daughter.
這對父母從不放棄追查他們失蹤女兒的下落。

---

25. **vocabulary** [vəˈkæbjəˌlɛrɪ] n. [C] 字彙 (pl. vocabularies)

▲ Kevin's younger sister only knows a limited
vocabulary. Kevin 的妹妹只知道有限的字彙。

💡 develop/build/enlarge/enrich/expand sb's vocabulary
增加字彙 | command a vocabulary 掌握字彙

Unit 21

1. **angel** [ˈendʒəl] n. [C] 天使；仁慈的人

▲ There are two pictures of angels on the wall of the church. 在這教堂的牆壁上有兩幅天使群的畫作。

💡 be no angel 有時會表現得很壞

---

2. **boot** [but] n. [C] 靴子

▲ I bought a pair of riding boots in the clearance sale. 我在清倉大拍賣時買了一雙馬靴。

💡 leather/hiking/ski boots 皮 / 登山 / 滑雪靴

boot [but] v. 猛踢，猛踹

▲ The soccer player booted the ball straight out. 這名足球選手直直的將球踢了出去。

💡 boot sb out (of sth) 迫使…離開 (…)；迫使…辭去 (…)

---

3. **charm** [tʃɑrm] n. [C] 護身符；[U] 魅力

▲ The rabbit's foot is Lillian's lucky charm. 這個兔腳是 Lillian 的護身符。

charm [tʃɑrm] v. 吸引，迷住

▲ The audience was charmed by the violinist's performance. 觀眾被小提琴家的表演迷住了。

charming [ˈtʃɑrmɪŋ] adj. 迷人的 [同] attractive, appealing

▲ I can't forget Lydia's charming smile. 我無法忘記 Lydia 的迷人微笑。

💡 Prince Charming 白馬王子，夢中情人

4. **cooker** [ˋkʊkɚ] n. [C] 炊具 [同] stove

▲ You have to be careful when using a pressure cooker.
你使用壓力鍋時要小心一點。

---

5. **disk** [dɪsk] n. [C] 磁碟，光碟 (also disc)

▲ A hard disk can be used to store information from a
computer. 硬碟可用來儲存電腦的資料。

---

6. **envy** [ˋɛnvɪ] n. [U] 嫉妒，羨慕

▲ Cinderella's sisters stared with envy when Cinderella
was dancing with the prince.
灰姑娘和王子跳舞時，她的姊姊們嫉妒地瞪著看她。

♥ be green with envy 非常嫉妒 | be the envy of sb 令…
羨慕或嫉妒的對象

envy [ˋɛnvɪ] v. 嫉妒，羨慕

▲ George envied his younger sister because she seemed
to get all their parents' attention. George 嫉妒他的妹
妹，因為她似乎得到父母全部的關注。

---

7. **float** [flot] v. 漂浮，浮起 [同] drift；(聲音或氣味) 飄蕩

▲ There is a volleyball floating in the river.
那裡有一顆排球在河中漂浮。

float [flot] n. [C] 浮板

▲ To save energy, the swimmer held on to a float in the
swimming pool.
為了省力，這位泳客在游泳池中緊握著浮板。

---

8. **gasoline** [ˋgæslˏin] n. [U] 汽油 [同] petrol

▲ Cars mainly run on gasoline. 汽車主要靠汽油運轉。

gas [gæs] n. [C][U] 氣體；瓦斯 (pl. gases, gasses)

▲ We have to reduce the emission of greenhouse gases to prevent global warming.
我們必須減少溫室氣體的排放量來防止全球暖化。

---

9. **heater** [`hitɚ] n. [C] 暖氣設備

▲ A heater is used to heat the room.
暖爐是用來使房間暖和的。

---

10. **hopeful** [`hopfəl] adj. 抱有希望的 <of, about> [同] optimistic [反] hopeless

▲ The candidate is hopeful about the outcome of the election. 這位候選人對選舉結果抱有希望。

---

11. **jeep** [dʒip] n. [C] 吉普車

▲ A jeep can be used for driving on rough ground.
吉普車可以開在崎嶇的路面上。

---

12. **ladder** [`lædɚ] n. [C] 梯子

▲ Walking under a ladder is considered bad luck.
從梯子底下走過被認為是不吉利的。

---

13. **magnet** [`mægnɪt] n. [C] 磁鐵；磁石

▲ The magnet attracts bits of iron. 磁鐵會吸小鐵片。

---

14. **moist** [mɔɪst] adj. 溼潤的

▲ The flowers grew well in moist soil.
這些花在溼潤的土壤中長得很好。

---

15. **nest** [nɛst] n. [C] 鳥巢

▲ There is a bird's nest in the tree. 樹上有一個鳥巢。

nest [nɛst] v. 築巢

▲ Some swallows nested next to the window.
有幾隻燕子在窗戶旁築巢。

16. **penguin** [ˋpɛngwɪn] n. [C] 企鵝

▲ Penguins are native to the Antarctic.
企鵝是南極原產的動物。

17. **pump** [pʌmp] n. [C] 幫浦，抽水機

▲ The non-governmental organization installed pumps
in the village. 非政府組織在村莊安裝抽水機。

pump [pʌmp] v. 抽取

▲ The villagers pump clean water from the well.
村民把乾淨的水從井裡面抽上來。

18. **raw** [rɔ] adj. (肉) 生的；未經加工的

▲ You will probably get sick if you eat raw meat.
如果吃生肉你可能會生病。

19. **rush** [rʌʃ] n. [C][U] 衝，蜂擁而至

▲ The worshippers all came into the temple in a rush.
信眾全都湧入寺廟。

rush [rʌʃ] v. 使急速

▲ After the police got the call, they rushed to the scene
of the accident immediately.
警方接到電話後，立刻急速趕往事故現場。

20. **shrimp** [ʃrɪmp] n. [C] 蝦 (pl. shrimp, shrimps)

▲ My friend is allergic to shrimps. 我朋友對蝦子過敏。

21. **someday** [ˋsʌmˌde] adv. (將來) 有一天

▲ I hope I can visit Iceland someday.
我希望有一天能去冰島玩。

22. **stale** [stel] adj. (因久放而) 不新鮮的，走味的 [反] fresh
(staler | stalest)

▲ Don't eat that bread because it has gone stale.
不要吃那個麵包，因為它已經不新鮮了。

23. **teenage** [ˋtinˌedʒ] adj. 十幾歲的 (多指 13–19 歲的)

▲ This mobile app is very popular with teenage girls
and boys.
這個手機應用程式很受十幾歲的少女和少年歡迎。

24. **tub** [tʌb] n. [C] 盆子；浴缸 [同] bathtub

▲ Andrew used some tubs to grow plants and flowers.
Andrew 用一些盆子來種植植物和花卉。

25. **twin** [twɪn] n. [C] 雙胞胎之一

▲ The twins look so alike that I can hardly tell one
from the other. 這對雙胞胎看起來如此相像，以致於
我幾乎無法分辨他們。

Unit 22

1. **anyhow** [ˈɛnɪˌhaʊ] adv. 無論如何，不管怎樣 [同] anyway
   ▲ The doors were locked and we couldn't get in anyhow. 門鎖著，我們怎樣都進不去。

2. **brass** [bræs] n. [U] 黃銅
   ▲ Brass is a hard metal made of copper and zinc.
   黃銅是銅和鋅製成的硬質金屬。
   brass [bræs] adj. 銅管樂器的
   ▲ To be a good trumpet player, Joe practices the brass instrument eight hours every day. 為了要成為一名優秀的小喇叭手，Joe 每天演奏銅管樂器八個小時。

3. **chimney** [ˈtʃɪmnɪ] n. [C] 煙囪 (pl. chimneys)
   ▲ The smoke rising from a chimney always reminds me of my sweet home.
   煙囪冒出的煙總讓我想起我甜蜜的家。
   💡 smoke like a chimney 老菸槍

4. **cough** [kɔf] n. [C] 咳嗽
   ▲ The patient had a bad cough. 這位病人咳得很厲害。
   cough [kɔf] v. 咳嗽
   ▲ Ned was coughing a lot so I took him to the doctor's.
   Ned 咳得很厲害，所以我帶他去看醫生。

5. **ditch** [dɪtʃ] n. [C] 溝渠，壕溝

▲ The workers are digging ditches to prevent flooding during the typhoon seasons.
工人正在挖掘溝渠，以防止颱風季節的淹水狀況。

ditch [dɪtʃ] v. 丟棄，拋棄

▲ We decided to ditch the old bicycle and buy a new one. 我們決定要丟棄舊的腳踏車，再買一臺新的。

6. **faint** [fent] adj. 微弱的，不清晰的 [同] slight；感覺暈眩的

▲ The sound is too faint to be heard clearly.
這聲音太弱了聽不清楚。

💡 not have the faintest (idea) 一點也不知道

faint [fent] v. 暈倒 [同] pass out

▲ The runner fainted as soon as he crossed the finish line. 這跑者一越過終點線就暈倒了。

faint [fent] n. [sing.] 昏迷

▲ The old lady suddenly fell in a faint in the sun.
這位老太太突然在太陽下陷入昏迷。

7. **flock** [flɑk] n. [C] 一群 <of>

▲ Flocks of wild geese are flying south.
成群野雁正向南方飛去。

flock [flɑk] v. 聚集；蜂擁

▲ Birds of a feather flock together. 【諺】物以類聚。

8. **governor** [ˋgʌvɚnɚ] n. [C] 州長

▲ The amateur politician was elected as the governor.

這位政治素人被選為州長。

---

9. **hell** [hɛl] n. [U] 地獄
   ▲ The prison is like a hell on earth. 這監獄像人間地獄。

---

10. **horrible** [ˋhɔrəb!] adj. 可怕的 [同] terrible；糟糕的
    ▲ Waking up from a horrible nightmare, the little boy cried for his parents.
    這小男孩從可怕的惡夢中驚醒，哭喊著要他的父母。

---

11. **jet** [dʒɛt] n. [C] 噴出物；噴射機
    ▲ Jets of water spurted from the fountain.
    一股股水從噴泉噴出來。
    💡 jet lag 時差
    jet [dʒɛt] v. 搭飛機旅行 (jetted | jetted | jetting)
    ▲ Ann and Tom are jetting off for a honeymoon in Taiwan next week.
    Ann 和 Tom 下週要搭飛機去臺灣度蜜月。

---

12. **lately** [ˋletlɪ] adv. 最近
    ▲ The team went through a hard time last season, but lately things have been improving.
    這球隊上一季經歷一段困境，但最近情況已經改善。

---

13. **maid** [med] n. [C] 女傭
    ▲ The maid comes twice a week to clean our house.
    女傭一星期來打掃我們的房子兩次。
    💡 maid of honor/bridesmaid 伴娘

---

14. **multiply** [ˈmʌltəˌplaɪ] **v.** 乘;增加

▲ The math teacher asked the students to multiply 15 by 8. 數學老師請學生們用 8 乘 15。

15. **nun** [nʌn] **n.** [C] 修女

▲ The nun is saying her prayers in the church.
這位修女正在教堂裡禱告。

16. **penny** [ˈpɛnɪ] **n.** [C] 一分錢 (pl. pennies, pence)

▲ A penny saved is a penny earned.
【諺】省一分錢便賺一分錢。

🍀 worth every penny 值得每一分錢

penniless [ˈpɛnɪlɪs] **adj.** 身無分文的,一貧如洗的

▲ In the story, a rich girl fell in love with a penniless painter. 在這個故事中,一位富有的女孩愛上了身無分文的畫家。

17. **punch** [pʌntʃ] **n.** [C] 一拳 <in, on>

▲ The drunk man threw a punch at his friend.
喝醉的男子揮了他朋友一拳。

punch [pʌntʃ] **v.** 用拳猛擊 <in, on>

▲ The boxer punched his opponent in the chin.
拳擊手一拳打在對手的下巴。

18. **receipt** [rɪˈsit] **n.** [C] 收據 (also sales slip)

▲ The store should give you a receipt after you make a purchase. 買了東西之後,店家應該要給你收據。

19. **sack** [sæk] **n.** [C] (麻布、帆布等) 大袋子

▲ Sacks of flour and rice were donated to the earthquake victims by several charitable groups.

幾個慈善團體捐贈好幾大袋的麵粉和米給地震災民。

20. **sin** [sɪn] **n.** [C][U] 罪惡

▲ Many people think it is a sin to treat animals cruelly.

許多人認為虐待動物是一種罪惡。

sin [sɪn] **v.** 犯罪 (sinned | sinned | sinning)

▲ The soldier believes he has sinned against God.

這位士兵相信他已違背了上帝。

21. **spaghetti** [spə`gɛtɪ] **n.** [U] 義大利麵

▲ My parents like to have Italian food like spaghetti and pizza for lunch on weekends. 我父母週末喜歡吃義大利食物，像是義大利麵和披薩，當午餐。

22. **starve** [stɑrv] **v.** (使) 挨餓，餓死

▲ People starved to death during the long war.

人民在漫長的戰爭期間餓死。

23. **temper** [`tɛmpɚ] **n.** [sing.] 脾氣

▲ The boss has a short temper. 這個老闆很暴躁易怒。

💡 keep/lose sb's temper …不發 / 發脾氣 | fly/get into a temper 大發雷霆

24. **tunnel** [`tʌnl] **n.** [C] 地道，隧道

▲ The hostages escaped through a secret tunnel under the house.

人質們從房子底下的一條祕密通道逃了出去。

tunnel [ˋtʌnl] v. 挖掘地道，隧道

▲ The government decided to tunnel a route through the mountain. 政府決定穿山挖掘隧道。

25. **unite** [juˋnaɪt] v. 合併，結合

▲ The two companies were united to form a new one. 那兩家公司合併成為一家新公司。

Unit 23

1. **apologize** [əˋpɑləͺdʒaɪz] v. 道歉 <to>

▲ Ann apologized to her teacher for being late for school. Ann 因上學遲到而向老師道歉。

2. **bravery** [ˋbrevərɪ] n. [U] 勇敢 [同] courage [反] cowardice

▲ The soldier was awarded a medal for his bravery. 這士兵因其勇敢而獲頒勳章。

3. **chin** [tʃɪn] n. [C] 下巴

▲ The tutor rubbed his chin when he thought about that matter.
當這位家庭教師思考那件事時，他搓他的下巴。

💡 Chin up! 別氣餒！

4. **countable** [ˋkaʊntəbl] adj. 可數的 [反] uncountable

▲ The word "dream" is a countable noun, so it has a plural form.

dream 這個字是可數名詞，所以它有複數形。

---

5. **dizzy** [ˈdɪzɪ] adj. 頭暈的 (dizzier | dizziest)

   ▲ Tina felt dizzy after riding the roller coaster.
   Tina 坐完雲霄飛車後覺得頭暈。

   💡 the dizzy heights (of sth) (⋯的) 高位，要職

---

6. **fake** [fek] adj. 假的，偽造的 [同] counterfeit [反] genuine
   (faker | fakest)

   ▲ The man who sells fake medicine has been caught.
   販售假藥的男子已遭逮捕。

   fake [fek] v. 偽造 [同] forge

   ▲ Frank faked his wife's signature on the check.
   Frank 在支票上偽造妻子的簽名。

   fake [fek] n. [C] 贗品 [同] imitation [反] original

   ▲ The painting is a fake which is worthless.
   這幅畫是贗品，根本不值錢。

---

7. **fountain** [ˈfaʊntn̩] n. [C] 人工噴泉，噴水池

   ▲ There is a large fountain in the middle of the
   shopping mall. 該購物中心中間有大噴泉。

   💡 fountain pen 鋼筆

---

8. **grasp** [græsp] v. 緊抓，緊握 <by> [同] grip；理解

   ▲ The child grasped his mother by the arm.
   這小孩緊抓著他媽媽的手臂。

   💡 grasp the chance/opportunity 把握機會

   grasp [græsp] n. [C] 緊抓，緊握 (usu. sing.) [同] grip

▲ The rock climber kept a firm grasp of the rock.
這名攀岩者緊緊抓著岩石。

9. **helmet** [ˈhɛlmɪt] n. [C] 安全帽，頭盔

▲ Never forget to wear a helmet when you are riding a scooter. 騎機車時不要忘記戴安全帽。

10. **horror** [ˈhɔrɚ] n. [U] 恐懼 <in, of>

▲ The boy screamed in horror when he found himself in the dark house.
那男孩發現自己在這黑暗的房子裡時，他恐懼地大叫。

11. **juicy** [ˈdʒusɪ] adj. 多汁的 (juicier | juiciest)

▲ I like juicy and tender steak. 我喜歡多汁軟嫩的牛排。

12. **leap** [lip] n. [C] 跳躍

▲ Jim crossed the stream with a flying leap.
Jim 一個飛躍，跳過了小河。

leap [lip] v. 跳躍 <over> [同] jump (leaped, leapt | leaped, leapt | leaping)

▲ The horse leaped over the fence. 馬躍過了籬笆。

💡 leap out at sb 立即出現在…的視線內

13. **marble** [ˈmɑrbl̩] n. [C] 彈珠；[U] 大理石

▲ Many little boys like to play with marbles.
很多小男孩喜歡玩彈珠。

💡 lose sb's marbles …失去理智

14. **mushroom** [ˈmʌʃrum] n. [C] 蘑菇

▲ Mark became sick after eating some poisonous mushrooms. Mark 因為吃了些有毒的蘑菇而生病。

mushroom [ˋmʌʃrum] v. 如雨後春筍般增長

▲ The number of high-rise buildings has mushroomed in the past five years.
高樓大廈的數量在過去五年來如雨後春筍般地增長。

---

15. **oak** [ok] n. [C][U] 橡樹 (pl. oaks, oak)

▲ "Tie a Yellow Ribbon Round the Old Oak Tree" is a famous song. 〈繫條黃絲帶在老橡樹上〉是首名歌。

---

16. **pepper** [ˋpɛpɚ] n. [U] 胡椒粉；[C] 甜椒

▲ Can you pass the salt and pepper, please?
可以請你將鹽和胡椒遞過來嗎？

---

17. **queer** [kwɪr] adj. 古怪的，異常的 [同] odd

▲ Jeremy had a queer feeling that he was being followed. Jeremy 有個古怪的感覺，他覺得被跟蹤。

---

18. **receiver** [rɪˋsivɚ] n. [C] (電話) 聽筒；收件人

▲ Lauren picked up the receiver and dialed the number.
Lauren 拿起聽筒撥號。

---

19. **sauce** [sɔs] n. [C][U] 醬料

▲ The chef has cooked tomato sauce for pasta.
主廚已經煮好要搭配義大利麵的番茄醬了。

---

20. **sip** [sɪp] v. 啜飲 (sipped | sipped | sipping)

▲ Gary sipped coffee and read the newspapers this morning. Gary 今天早晨啜飲咖啡並閱讀報紙。

sip [sɪp] n. [C] 啜飲，一小口

▲ Sandy added some salt to the soup after taking a sip of it. 嘗了一小口湯後，Sandy 在湯裡加了一些鹽巴。

---

21. **spill** [spɪl] v. 溢出 ，灑出 <on> (spilled, spilt | spilled, spilt | spilling)

▲ One guest tripped and spilled coffee on the carpet of the restaurant.

一位客人絆倒並打翻咖啡在餐廳的地毯上。

💡 spill your guts (to sb) (向…) 傾訴心裡的話 | spill the beans 洩漏祕密

spill [spɪl] n. [C] 溢出 (物)

▲ Many marine animals were killed in the oil spill. 許多海洋動物死於這次的石油外洩。

---

22. **sting** [stɪŋ] n. [C] (動物或植物) 針，刺

▲ A bee dies when it loses its sting. 蜜蜂一旦失去螫針，便會死去。

sting [stɪŋ] v. 螫，叮 (stung | stung | stinging)

▲ The mountain climber's arm was stung by a bee. 這位登山者的手臂被蜜蜂螫到。

---

23. **tender** [ˈtɛndɚ] adj. 溫柔的 ；(蔬菜或肉等) 軟嫩的 [反] tough

▲ Rachel gave me a warm and tender smile. Rachel 給我一個溫暖又溫柔的微笑。

💡 at the tender age 年幼時期

24. **underlying** [ˌʌndəˈlaɪɪŋ] adj. 潛在的，根本的

▲ The government shouldn't ignore any underlying reason of the rising crime rate.
政府不應忽視任何犯罪率攀升的潛在原因。

25. **vase** [ves] n. [C] 花瓶

▲ The visitor knocked the vase over accidentally.
參觀者不小心打翻花瓶。

Unit 24

1. **assist** [əˈsɪst] v. 幫助，協助 <with, in>

▲ Doris assisted her brother with his homework.
Doris 協助弟弟做作業。

2. **brunch** [brʌntʃ] n. [U] 早午餐

▲ I am going to have brunch with my friend this Saturday. 這週六我要和朋友去吃早午餐。

3. **chip** [tʃɪp] n. [C] 碎片 (usu. pl.)；薯片 (usu. pl.)

▲ The camper threw some wood chips into the fire to keep it burning.
這露營者往火裡扔了一些木塊讓火繼續燒。

💡 have a chip on your shoulder 心理不平衡

chip [tʃɪp] v. 削 (chipped | chipped | chipping)

▲ The researchers chipped a lot of pieces off the rock.

研究人員們從岩石上削下許多碎片。

---

4. **crab** [kræb] n. [C] 螃蟹

▲ Crab season usually begins from September to December in Taiwan.
臺灣的螃蟹季通常從九月開始到十二月。

---

5. **dock** [dɑk] n. [C] 船塢；碼頭

▲ The ship is in dock for routine maintenance.
這艘船停在船塢，進行定時保養。

dock [dɑk] v. 進港，停泊

▲ The ship is scheduled to dock at Hualien tomorrow.
船隻計劃於明天在花蓮進港。

---

6. **faucet** [ˋfɔsɪt] n. [C] 水龍頭 [同] tap

▲ To conserve water, you should turn off the faucet immediately after use.
為了節約用水，你應該在使用水龍頭後立刻關上。

---

7. **freeze** [friz] v. 結冰；(因恐懼) 呆住 (froze | frozen | freezing)

▲ When water freezes, it becomes ice.
水冷凍後就變成冰。

💡 sb's blood freezes 嚇出一身冷汗

freeze [friz] n. [C] (暫時的) 凍結，停滯 (usu. sing.)

▲ Most of the workers faced a wage freeze in the past years. 大多數的員工過去幾年面臨薪資凍漲。

---

8. **grassy** [ˋgræsɪ] adj. 草茂密的 (grassier | grassiest)

▲ Some sheep are grazing in the grassy field.
一些羊在茂密的草原上吃草。

9. **hint** [hɪnt] n. [C] 提示

▲ Frank kept dropping a hint to me, but I couldn't take it. Frank 一直給我暗示，但我無法了解其意。

💡 broad hint 明顯的暗示

hint [hɪnt] v. 給提示，暗示 [同] imply

▲ The secretary hinted that she wanted a pay raise.
這祕書暗示她想要加薪。

10. **humid** [ˋhjumɪd] adj. 潮溼的

▲ The weather becomes very humid in the summer.
一到夏天天氣就變得很潮溼。

💡 humid air/climate 潮溼的空氣 / 氣候

11. **jungle** [ˋdʒʌŋgl̩] n. [C][U] 熱帶叢林

▲ Edward had some exciting adventures in the Amazon jungle.
Edward 在亞馬遜叢林裡經歷一些刺激的冒險。

12. **leisure** [ˋliʒɚ] n. [U] 閒暇

▲ Amber likes to do yoga in her leisure time.
Amber 空閒時喜歡做瑜伽。

💡 leisure activity/industry 休閒活動 / 產業 | at (sb's) leisure 當 (…) 有空時

13. **marker** [ˋmɑrkɚ] n. [C] 記號，標記；麥克筆

▲ The dancer had placed some markers on the floor.

這位舞者已經在地上放了一些記號。

---

14. **mystery** [ˋmɪstrɪ] **n.** [C][U] (事物) 神祕，奧祕 (pl. mysteries)

▲ The police never solved the mystery of the boy's disappearance. 警察從未解決這男孩失蹤的奧祕。

---

15. **omit** [oˋmɪt] **v.** 疏忽，遺漏，刪除 [同] leave out (omitted | omitted | omitting)

▲ You have omitted several important points in your report. 你的報告中漏掉了幾個要點。

---

16. **pigeon** [ˋpɪdʒən] **n.** [C] 鴿子

▲ The old man feeds pigeons in the park every morning. 這位老先生每天早上會到公園餵鴿子。

---

17. **quote** [kwot] **v.** 引述，引用 <from> [同] cite

▲ The student quoted a passage from Shakespeare. 這學生引用了一段莎士比亞的話。

quote [kwot] **n.** [C] 引文 <from>

▲ I included some quotes from the news report in my speech.
我在演講中涵蓋了一些來自此新聞報導的引文。

---

18. **relief** [rɪˋlif] **n.** [U] 寬慰，寬心；減輕

▲ It is a relief to know that the children have been rescued. 得知孩子們獲救，讓人鬆了一口氣。

💡 to sb's relief 令⋯放心的是

---

19. **saucer** [`sɔsɚ] n. [C] 茶托，茶碟

▲ The lady gave the stray dog a saucer of water.
這位女士給流浪狗一小碟水。

20. **skate** [sket] v. 溜冰

▲ Let's go skating in the park! 我們去公園溜冰吧！

💡 be skating on thin ice 如履薄冰，冒險

skate [sket] n. [C] 溜冰鞋

▲ Put on your ice skates. 穿上你的溜冰鞋。

💡 get/put your skates on 快點，把握時間

21. **spin** [spɪn] n. [C][U] 旋轉

▲ The car slid on the icy road and went into a spin.
車子在結冰的路上打滑，開始打轉。

💡 in a spin 忙得暈頭轉向

spin [spɪn] v. 旋轉 [同] turn, whirl (spun | spun | spinning)

▲ The ice skater began to spin faster and faster.
那位溜冰選手開始越轉越快。

💡 spin a coin 猜硬幣 | spin out of control (活動或事件)
迅速失控

22. **stitch** [stɪtʃ] n. [C] (縫紉的) 一針

▲ John cast some stitches to secure the two pieces of
cloth together.
John 多縫了幾針來將這兩塊布固定起來。

💡 a stitch in time (saves nine) 防微杜漸 (及時縫一針能
省九針)

stitch [stɪtʃ] v. 縫補，縫合 <up> [同] sew

▲ The doctor is stitching up the patient's wound.
醫生正在縫合這個病人的傷口。

23. **tent** [tɛnt] n. [C] 帳篷

▲ Do you know how to pitch a tent?
你知道如何搭帳篷嗎？

24. **unity** [`junətɪ] n. [C][U] 整體性；結合 [反] disunity (pl. unities)

▲ The film lacks unity. 這電影缺乏整體性。

25. **verse** [vɝs] n. [U] 韻文 <in> [同] poetry ； [C] (詩、歌的) 節

▲ This is a story written in verse.
這篇故事是用韻文寫成的。

Unit 25

1. **assistant** [ə`sɪstənt] n. [C] 助理，助手

▲ Clare had her assistant demonstrate the latest smartwatch to the clients.
Clare 請她的助理向客戶們示範最新款的智慧手錶。

assistant [ə`sɪstənt] adj. 輔助的，副的

▲ Fiona has been promoted to assistant manager.
Fiona 已經被升職為副理。

2. **bud** [bʌd] n. [C] 新芽 <in> ；花蕾

▲ The trees in the park were in bud in early spring.
公園裡的樹在初春時長出新芽。

bud [bʌd] **v.** 發芽 (budded | budded | budding)

▲ Many plants begin to bud in spring.
許多植物在春天開始發芽。

3. **chop** [tʃɑp] **n.** [C] (帶骨的豬或羊) 排

▲ The restaurant's signature dish is grilled lamb chop.
這間餐廳的招牌菜是烤羊排。

chop [tʃɑp] **v.** 砍，劈；切碎 (chopped | chopped | chopping)

▲ To keep warm, the hunter chopped wood to make a fire. 為了保暖，獵人砍木材來生火。

4. **crane** [kren] **n.** [C] 起重機；鶴

▲ The crane driver operated the crane to move the container. 起重機駕駛操作起重機來移動貨櫃。

crane [kren] **v.** 伸長脖子

▲ The kid craned his neck to see the parade.
這名小孩子伸長脖子看遊行。

5. **dolphin** [ˋdɑlfɪn] **n.** [C] 海豚

▲ A school of dolphins is leaping out of the water.
一群海豚正從水面跳出。

6. **feather** [ˋfɛðɚ] **n.** [C] 羽毛

▲ The little girl tickled her father's feet with a feather.
這小女孩用羽毛搔她父親的腳底。

💡 be as light as a feather (重量) 非常輕的 | a feather in
   your cap 可引以為傲的成就 | birds of a feather
   (flock together) 物以類聚

7. **geography** [dʒi`ɑgrəfɪ] n. [U] 地理學;(某地區的) 地理,
   地形
   ▲ Vincent is interested in human geography rather than
     physical geography.
     Vincent 喜歡人文地理而非自然地理。

8. **greenhouse** [`grin,haʊs] n. [C] 溫室
   ▲ The farmer grows some vegetables in the
     greenhouse. 這農夫在溫室裡種一些蔬菜。
   💡 the greenhouse effect 溫室效應 | greenhouse gas 溫
     室氣體 (尤指二氧化碳)

9. **historian** [hɪs`torɪən] n. [C] 歷史學家
   ▲ The historian will give a lecture on the civilization of
     ancient Rome.
     這位歷史學家將發表有關古羅馬文化的演說。

10. **hunger** [`hʌŋgɚ] n. [U] 飢餓 [同] starvation;[C] 渴望
    ▲ The student felt faint from hunger.
      這名學生因為飢餓感到暈眩。
    💡 die of hunger 死於飢餓
    hunger [`hʌŋgɚ] v. 渴望 <for, after>
    ▲ The nation hungers for an economic recovery.
      國民渴望經濟復甦。

11. **knight** [naɪt] n. [C] 騎士
   ▲ The knight finally killed the evil king at the end of the story.
   在故事的結尾，騎士終於殺了那個邪惡的國王。
   knight [naɪt] v. 授與爵位
   ▲ Jane was knighted for her services to the community.
   Jane 因為對社會的貢獻而被授與爵位。

---

12. **lemonade** [ˌlɛmənˈed] n. [U] 檸檬汁
   ▲ This homemade lemonade is really fresh.
   這個自製檸檬水很爽口。

---

13. **mathematical** [ˌmæθəˈmætɪkl̩] adj. 數學的
   ▲ Richard is considered a mathematical genius.
   Richard 被認為是數學天才。

---

14. **nap** [næp] n. [C] 小睡，打盹 [同] snooze
   ▲ Ella usually takes a nap after lunch.
   Ella 通常午餐後會小睡片刻。
   nap [næp] v. 小睡，打盹 (napped | napped | napping)
   ▲ Glen napped for an hour after he came home from school. Glen 放學回家後小睡了一個小時。

---

15. **outdoors** [ˌautˈdorz] adv. 在戶外 [反] indoors
   ▲ The rock concert was held outdoors last night.
   這場搖滾音樂會昨晚在戶外舉行。

---

16. **pill** [pɪl] n. [C] 藥丸，藥片

▲ Mr. Lee has to take pills to control his blood pressure every day.

李先生必須每天服用藥丸來控制他的血壓。

💡 sleeping/vitamin pill 安眠藥 / 維他命藥丸｜
sugar/sweeten the pill 緩和情況

17. **rag** [ræg] n. [C] 破布；[pl.] 破爛的衣服 (～s) <in>

▲ Mary used a rag to clean the floor.

Mary 用一塊破布擦地板。

18. **resist** [rɪˋzɪst] v. 抵制，反抗 [同] oppose；抗拒 (誘惑等)

▲ Many people strongly resisted raising income tax.

許多人強力抵制所得稅調漲。

19. **sausage** [ˋsɔsɪdʒ] n. [C][U] 香腸

▲ Jacob had some scrambled eggs, mushrooms, and sausages for breakfast.

Jacob 早餐吃一些炒蛋、蘑菇和香腸。

20. **ski** [ski] n. [C] 滑雪板 (pl. skis, ski)

▲ Tom brought his skis with him. Tom 帶著滑雪板。

ski [ski] v. 滑雪

▲ Tom wants to go skiing. Tom 想要去滑雪。

21. **steal** [stil] v. 偷竊 (stole｜stolen｜stealing)

▲ The best-selling author was accused of stealing ideas from the book.

這位暢銷書作家被控告偷竊該書的內容。

22. **stormy** [ˋstɔrmɪ] adj. 暴風雨的；激烈的 (stormier | stormiest)

▲ As the typhoon approaches, a stormy wind starts to blow. 隨著颱風接近，暴風雨般的風開始吹。

23. **terrific** [təˋrɪfɪk] adj. 很棒的

▲ Tommy looks terrific today.
Tommy 今天看起來棒極了。

24. **vest** [vɛst] n. [C] 背心

▲ The old man likes to wear a wool vest to keep warm.
這老人喜歡穿羊毛背心來保持溫暖。

25. **wage** [wedʒ] n. [C] (計時工資、日薪) 工資 (usu. pl.) [同] pay

▲ The laborers demanded higher wages because of long working hours.
工人們因為工時長而要求更高的工資。

Unit 26

1. **automobile** [ˋɔtəmoˏbil] n. [C] 汽車

▲ The automobile industry in this country is growing faster than any other country in the world. 這個國家汽車工業的增長速度勝過世界上任何其他國家。

2. **buffalo** [ˋbʌfəlo] n. [C] 水牛 (pl. buffaloes, buffalo)

▲ My grandparents raise some buffaloes on the farm.

我的祖父母在農場裡飼養一些水牛。

---

3. **cigarette** [`sɪgə,rɛt] n. [C] 香菸

▲ The woman lit a cigarette but soon put it out.
這女子點燃一支菸，但又很快把它弄熄。

---

4. **crawl** [krɔl] v. 爬行 <across>

▲ The baby crawled across the floor on his hands and knees. 嬰兒在地板上爬來爬去。

💡 be crawling with sb/sth 擠滿了⋯

crawl [krɔl] n. [sing.] 緩慢的速度

▲ The traffic usually slows to a crawl at the last day of vacation.
在假期最後一天，交通狀況通常會比較緩慢。

---

5. **doughnut** [`donət] n. [C] 甜甜圈 (also donut)

▲ We had doughnuts and latte for breakfast.
早餐我們吃甜甜圈和拿鐵咖啡。

---

6. **firework** [`faɪr,wɝk] n. [C] 煙火

▲ The government sets off fireworks to celebrate the country's birthday. 政府施放煙火以慶祝國慶日。

💡 firework display 煙火表演

---

7. **glance** [glæns] n. [C] 一瞥，掃視

▲ At first glance, the fallen leaf looks like a cockroach.
乍看之下，這片落葉很像蟑螂。

💡 take/give/have a glance (at sb) (對⋯) 匆匆一瞥

glance [glæns] v. 匆匆一瞥，掃視 <at, through>

▲ The shy girl glanced at the boy she liked and ran away. 這個害羞的小女孩匆匆瞥一下她喜歡的男孩後就跑走了。

8. **grin** [grɪn] n. [C] 露齒的笑，咧嘴的笑

▲ Luke gave me a wide grin.
Luke 給我一個大大的笑容。

grin [grɪn] v. 露齒笑，咧嘴笑 <at> (grinned | grinned | grinning)

▲ When I opened the door, my neighbor grinned at me.
當我打開門時，我的鄰居對我露齒笑。

💡 grin from ear to ear 笑得合不攏嘴 | grin and bear it 默默忍受

9. **holy** [`holɪ] adj. 神聖的 [同] divine, sacred (holier | holiest)

▲ A church is considered to be holy.
教堂被認為是神聖的。

💡 Holy cow! 天啊！(表示驚訝、恐懼等)

10. **icy** [`aɪsɪ] adj. 結冰的；極冷的 [同] freezing (icier | iciest)

▲ The roads became icy during the snowfall.
路面在下雪時結冰了。

11. **knot** [nɑt] n. [C] (繩等的) 結

▲ The clerk tied the ribbon in a beautiful knot and then attached it to the gift box.

店員把絲帶綁成一個美麗的結，然後再將它繫在禮盒上。

knot [nɑt] v. 打結 [反] untie (knotted | knotted | knotting)

▲ Karen wore a silk scarf loosely knotted around her neck. Karen 脖子上鬆鬆地繫著一條絲巾。

---

12. **lettuce** [ˋlɛtəs] n. [C][U] 萵苣，生菜

▲ Would you like some lettuce on your sandwich? 你的三明治要加些生菜嗎？

---

13. **melon** [ˋmɛlən] n. [C] 甜瓜，香瓜

▲ Debby ate a slice of melon for dessert. Debby 點心吃了一片香瓜。

---

14. **navy** [ˋnevɪ] n. [C] 海軍 (pl. navies)

▲ Ronald joined the navy when he was twenty. Ronald 在二十歲時加入海軍。

---

15. **oven** [ˋʌvən] n. [C] 烤箱

▲ Check the turkey in the oven to see if it is cooked thoroughly. 看看烤箱裡的火雞是不是烤好了。

---

16. **pint** [paɪnt] n. [C] 品脫 (液量單位，美國：0.473 公升 /1 品脫，英國：0.568 公升 /1 品脫)

▲ Please buy a pint of milk for me on your way home. 請你在回家路上幫我買一品脫的牛奶。

---

17. **ray** [re] n. [C] 光線；一線 (希望等) [同] glimmer

▲ A ray of sunlight came through the dark cloud.
一道陽光從烏雲中透出來。

---

18. **ripe** [raɪp] adj. 成熟的 [同] mature [反] unripe (riper | ripest)

▲ Peaches turn sweet when they are ripe.
桃子熟了以後會變甜。

---

19. **scale** [skel] n. [U] 規模；[C] 磅秤 (also scales)

▲ The full scale of the accident was reported in the morning news.
晨間新聞報導了這場意外的嚴重程度。

---

20. **skillful** [ˋskɪlfəl] adj. 熟練的

▲ Most of the teenagers are skillful at using social media. 多數的青少年很會用社交媒體。

---

21. **steam** [stim] n. [U] 蒸氣

▲ Steam is rising from the boiling soup.
蒸氣從煮沸的湯中冒出。

steam [stim] v. 冒著蒸氣，蒸

▲ The kettle is steaming on the stove.
水壺在爐上冒著蒸氣。

---

22. **subtract** [səbˋtrækt] v. 減去 [同] take away

▲ Subtract three from eight and you get five.
八減三得五。

---

23. **thankful** [ˋθæŋkfəl] adj. 感謝的 [同] grateful

▲ I'm thankful to you for giving me this chance.
我很感謝你給我這個機會。

24. **violet** [`vaɪəlɪt] adj. 藍紫色的
▲ The actor has beautiful violet eyes.
這名演員有一雙漂亮的藍紫色眼睛。

violet [`vaɪəlɪt] n. [C] 紫羅蘭
▲ Grandma planted some violets in her garden, and the small purple flowers made it look great.
奶奶在她的花園裡種一些紫羅蘭，這些紫色小花讓花園看起來很棒。

25. **warmth** [wɔrmθ] n. [U] 溫暖；親切，溫情
▲ The warmth of the fire made me feel sleepy.
溫暖的爐火使我覺得昏昏欲睡。

Unit 27

1. **avenue** [`ævə,nju] n. [C] 大道；方法，手段 [同] possibility
▲ Fifth Avenue in New York City is famous for the luxurious shops along its two sides.
紐約的第五大道因為兩旁的奢華商店而聞名。

2. **buffet** [bʌ`fe] n. [C] 歐式自助餐
▲ To keep in shape, you had better not have all-you-can-eat buffet too often.

為了保持健康，你最好不要常吃吃到飽自助餐。

---

3. **cinema** [ˋsɪnəmə] n. [C] 電影院 [同] movie theater
   ▲ What's on at the cinema now?
   電影院現在正在上映什麼電影？
   💡 go to the cinema 去看電影

---

4. **creator** [krɪˋetə] n. [C] 創作者
   ▲ Jerry Siegel and Joe Shuster are the creators of Superman. 傑瑞西格爾和喬舒斯特是超人的創作者。

---

5. **drag** [dræg] v. 拉，拖 (dragged | dragged | dragging)
   ▲ The boy dragged the heavy bag across the room.
   男孩拖著重重的袋子走過房間。
   drag [dræg] n. [sing.] 麻煩，瑣碎的事
   ▲ An hour's commute to work is really a drag.
   花一小時通勤上班真是件麻煩事。
   💡 be a drag on sb/sth 拖累…，成為…的累贅

---

6. **flame** [flem] n. [C][U] 火焰 <in>；強烈的情感
   ▲ The log cabin in the forest was in flames.
   森林裡的木屋熊熊燃燒起來。
   💡 burst into/put out the flames 燃起大火 / 熄滅火焰
   flame [flem] v. 燃燒
   ▲ The car hit the utility pole and flamed up.
   轎車撞到電線桿並起火燃燒。

---

7. **glory** [ˋglorɪ] n. [C] 榮耀或驕傲的事 ；[U] 榮耀 (pl. glories)

▲ The tall building was one of the glories of the city.
這棟高樓曾是這座城市的一大驕傲。

---

8. **grocery** [ˋgrosərɪ] n. [pl.] 食品雜貨 (-ries)；[C] 雜貨店 [同] grocery store (pl. groceries)

▲ Let's get some groceries. 去買些食品雜貨吧。

---

9. **horn** [hɔrn] n. [C] 角；喇叭

▲ The rhinos are illegally hunted for their horns.
為了獲取犀牛角，犀牛遭受非法狩獵。

💡 honk/beep/sound the horn 按喇叭

---

10. **import** [ˋɪmport] n. [C] 進口商品 [反] export

▲ Some imports like fruits and vegetables have quite an impact on the local farmers. 一些進口產品，像是水果和蔬菜，對本地農夫造成了不小的衝擊。

import [ɪmˋport] v. 進口 <from> [反] export

▲ Due to lack of natural resources, the country has to import oil, gas, and metals from other countries.
由於缺乏天然資源，這個國家必須從其他國家進口石油、天然氣和金屬。

---

11. **koala** [ˋkoɑlə] n. [C] 無尾熊

▲ Koalas are fed on eucalyptus leaves.
無尾熊以尤加利葉為主食。

---

12. **lick** [lɪk] v. 舔

▲ The cat licked the plate clean.
這隻貓把盤子舔乾淨。

lick [lɪk] n. [C] 舔一下
▲ May I have a lick of the honey?
我能不能嘗一口這個蜂蜜？

---

13. **melt** [mɛlt] v. 融化
▲ The snow melted in the sunlight. 雪在陽光下融化了。

---

14. **outline** [ˋaʊt͵laɪn] n. [C] 輪廓；大綱
▲ The teacher told the boy to draw an outline of the house and then give it colors.
老師叫男孩先畫出房子的輪廓，然後再上色。
outline [ˋaʊt͵laɪn] v. 勾畫…的輪廓；概述 [同] sketch
▲ Sue outlined the map of Taiwan on the blackboard.
Sue 在黑板上畫出臺灣地圖的輪廓。

---

15. **owl** [aʊl] n. [C] 貓頭鷹
▲ Lisa is a night owl. She always binge-watches the latest television season at night.
Lisa 是個夜貓子。她總在晚上追最新的電視劇。

---

16. **pit** [pɪt] n. [C] 深坑，深洞
▲ The cyclist fell into a pit by accident.
這個自行車騎士不小心掉到深洞裡。

---

17. **recorder** [rɪˋkɔrdɚ] n. [C] 錄音機；錄影機
▲ Tape recorders had been replaced by CD players.
錄音機已被 CD 播放器取代。

---

18. **rot** [rɑt] **v.** 腐爛 <away> [同] decompose (rotted | rotted | rotting)

▲ The fallen leaves rotted away and surrendered their nutrients to the soil.

落葉逐漸腐爛，將養分釋放至土壤中。

💡 rot in jail/prison 飽受牢獄之苦

rot [rɑt] **n.** [U] 腐壞，腐朽

▲ The damp has resulted in the rot of furniture.

潮溼導致家具腐壞。

💡 stop thc rot 阻止事態惡化

19. **scarf** [skɑrf] **n.** [C] 圍巾 (pl. scarves)

▲ Eric bought a silk scarf for his girlfriend as her birthday gift.

Eric 買了一條絲質圍巾給他女朋友當生日禮物。

20. **sleeve** [sliv] **n.** [C] 袖子

▲ The worker rolled up her sleeves and began to work.

工人捲起袖子開始工作。

21. **steep** [stip] **adj.** (斜坡) 陡峭的；(價格) 大起大落的

▲ The tower stands on the steep hill; it is not easy to reach there.

那座塔座落在險峻的山坡上；要到那裡不容易。

22. **suburb** [ˋsʌbɝb] **n.** [C] 郊區

▲ Yokohama is a suburb of Tokyo.

橫濱位於東京的郊區。

💡 the suburbs 郊區，城外

23. **thirst** [θɝst] n. [sing.] 口渴；渴望 <for> [同] craving
▲ After a workout, water is the best drink to quench your thirst. 水是運動後解渴的最佳飲品。

24. **volleyball** [ˋvɑlɪˏbɔl] n. [C][U] 排球 (運動)
▲ In recent years, there have been more and more people showing interest in volleyball.
近幾年來，有越來越多人對排球感興趣。

25. **waterfall** [ˋwɑtɚˏfɔl] n. [C] 瀑布
▲ The tourists came in sight of a great waterfall.
遊客們到可看見大瀑布的地方。

Unit 28

1. **awaken** [əˋwekən] v. 喚起 <to>
▲ People must be awakened to the danger of being overweight. 人們必須意識到體重過重的危險。

2. **bulb** [bʌlb] n. [C] 電燈泡
▲ The lamp takes a 20-watt bulb.
這盞燈用的是二十瓦的燈泡。

3. **circus** [ˋsɝkəs] n. [C] 馬戲團 (the ~)
▲ The children are excited about going to the circus.
小孩子們對要去馬戲團感到很興奮。

4. **cruel** [ˋkruəl] adj. 殘忍的 <to>

▲ That man is cruel to his dog.
  那個男人對他的狗很殘忍。

5. **dragonfly** [ˋdrægən͵flaɪ] n. [C] 蜻蜓 (pl. dragonflies)

▲ The professor specializes in the study of dragonflies.
  這位教授專門從事蜻蜓的研究。

6. **flashlight** [ˋflæʃ͵laɪt] n. [C] 手電筒

▲ I walked in the dark woods with a flashlight in my
  hand. 我拿著手電筒走在黑暗的樹林中。

7. **glow** [glo] n. [sing.] 光亮；喜悅，滿足 <of>

▲ The room was in complete darkness, except for a dim
  glow from my smartphone.
  房間一片漆黑，只有我智慧型手機發出的微弱光亮。

glow [glo] v. 發光

▲ The fireflies are glowing in the dark.
  螢火蟲在黑暗中發光。

8. **gum** [gʌm] n. [U] 口香糖 [同] chewing gum ； [C] 牙齦
  (usu. pl.)

▲ It is said that chewing gum is forbidden in Singapore.
  據說口香糖在新加坡是被禁止的。

9. **hourly** [ˋaʊrlɪ] adj. 每小時的

▲ Normally a lawyer charges an hourly fee for giving
  legal advice. 通常請律師給法律建議要按小時收費。

hourly [ˈaʊrlɪ] adv. 每小時地
▲ The trains run hourly. 火車一小時來一班。

---

10. **indoor** [ˈɪn‚dor] adj. 室內的 [反] outdoor
▲ Table tennis is an indoor sport.
乒乓球是室內運動。

---

11. **lace** [les] n. [U] 花邊，蕾絲；[C] 鞋帶 (usu. pl.) [同]
shoelace
▲ Some girls like to wear skirts with beautiful lace.
有一些女孩喜歡穿有漂亮花邊的裙子。
lace [les] v. 繫緊 <up>；摻少量的酒、毒藥等 <with>
▲ The man bent over to lace up his shoes.
這名男子彎腰繫緊鞋帶。

---

12. **loaf** [lof] n. [C] 一條 (麵包) (pl. loaves)
▲ My mother baked three loaves of bread.
媽媽烤了三條麵包。

---

13. **mend** [mɛnd] v. 修補 [同] fix
▲ The roof is leaking, so some workers are busy
mending it. 屋頂漏水，所以一些工人正在忙於修補。
💡 mend sb's ways …改過自新 | mend (sb's) fences
with sb 與…重修舊好

---

14. **overseas** [‚ovɚˈsiz] adv. 在海外 [同] abroad
▲ Many people travel overseas on their holidays.
很多人在假期期間去海外旅行。

overseas [͵ovɚˋsiz] adj. 海外的

▲ We have many overseas students at our university.
我們的大學裡有很多外國學生。

---

15. **ox** [ɑks] n. [C] (食用、勞役用的) 閹公牛 (pl. oxen)

▲ The farmers used to keep a lot of oxen for plow.
農夫們過去養很多牛來耕作。

---

16. **playful** [ˋplefəl] adj. 愛玩的

▲ Dodo is a playful little dog. He is very friendly toward human. Dodo 是隻愛玩的小狗。他非常親人。

---

17. **rectangle** [ˋrɛktæŋgl] n. [C] 長方形

▲ The math teacher drew a rectangle on the blackboard.
數學老師在黑板上畫了一個長方形。

---

18. **rumor** [ˋrumɚ] n. [C][U] 謠言

▲ Rumor has it that the mayor will resign.
謠傳市長將要辭職。

💡 start/spread a rumor 造謠 / 散布謠言

rumor [ˋrumɚ] v. 謠傳

▲ It's widely rumored that the CEO will be fired.
到處謠傳執行長要被資遣了。

---

19. **scissors** [ˋsɪzɚz] n. [pl.] 剪刀

▲ Be careful. This pair of scissors is very sharp.
小心一點。這把剪刀很銳利。

💡 nail scissors 指甲剪

20. **slender** [ˋslɛndɚ] adj. 苗條的，修長的 [同] slim

  ▲ This model has a slender figure and confidence.
  這位模特兒身材苗條並且有自信。

---

21. **stiff** [stɪf] adj. 僵硬的；嚴厲的

  ▲ Sitting at a computer all day gave me a stiff neck.
  整天坐在電腦前讓我的脖子僵硬。

  stiff [stɪf] adv. 非常，極其

  ▲ I am bored stiff. The movie is awful.
  我覺得非常無聊。這部電影很糟。

---

22. **suck** [sʌk] v. 吸吮

  ▲ Stop sucking your thumb. 不要吸吮你的拇指了。

  suck [sʌk] n. [C] 吸吮 (usu. sing.)

  ▲ The kitten is taking its suck of milk.
  這隻小貓正在吸奶。

---

23. **thread** [θrɛd] n. [C][U] 線

  ▲ My grandmother sewed the skirt with cotton thread.
  我奶奶用棉線縫製裙子。

  thread [θrɛd] v. 穿線

  ▲ My father put on his glasses and threaded a needle.
  我爸爸戴上眼鏡，把針穿了線。

---

24. **voter** [ˋvotɚ] n. [C] 選民

  ▲ Most of the voters are willing to poll and elect a new
  leader. 多數選民願意去投票並選出新的領導者。

---

25. **weapon** [ˋwɛpən] n. [C] 武器

▲ Silence is sometimes the most effective weapon.
沉默有時候是最有效的武器。

💡 nuclear/atomic weapons 核子武器

Unit 29

1. **baggage** [`bægɪdʒ] **n.** [U] 行李 [同] luggage, suitcase
   ▲ The passenger paid for his excess baggage.
   這位乘客為超重行李付費。

   💡 a piece of baggage 一件行李

2. **bull** [bʊl] **n.** [C] (未閹割的) 公牛
   ▲ Part of Peter's job is to milk the cows and feed the bulls on the farm.
   在農場裡擠牛奶和餵公牛是 Peter 的工作之一。

3. **clay** [kle] **n.** [U] 黏土，陶土
   ▲ The child broke a clay pot accidentally.
   這個小孩不小心打破一個陶罐。

4. **dam** [dæm] **n.** [C] 水壩
   ▲ Hoover Dam is one of the famous tourist attractions in the United States.
   胡佛水壩是美國其中一個知名景點。

   dam [dæm] **v.** 築壩 (dammed | dammed | damming)
   ▲ The government planned to dam Yangtze River.
   政府計劃在揚子江 (長江) 上建築水壩。

5. **drip** [drɪp] n. [sing.] 滴水聲

▲ I heard the drip of the rain from the roof which kept me awake all night.
我聽到雨從屋頂滴下來的聲音，這讓我徹夜未眠。

drip [drɪp] v. 滴下 (dripped | dripped | dripping)

▲ Because of the downpour, Theo's clothes are soaking wet and even his hair is dripping. 因為突然的傾盆大雨，Theo 的衣服溼透了，甚至連頭髮也在滴水。

6. **flesh** [flɛʃ] n. [U] (人或動物的) 肉；果肉

▲ Tigers and lions live on flesh.
老虎和獅子是肉食性動物。

7. **golf** [gɔlf] n. [U] 高爾夫球

▲ Henry spends most of his free time playing golf.
Henry 把大部分的休閒時間花在打高爾夫球上。

golf [gɔlf] v. 打高爾夫球

8. **hairdresser** [`hɛr͵drɛsɚ] n. [C] 美髮師

▲ Do you think I should go to the hairdresser to dye my hair brown?
你認為我應該去美髮師那裡把頭髮染成咖啡色嗎？

9. **housekeeper** [`haʊs͵kipɚ] n. [C] 女管家；(旅館、醫院等的) 清潔人員

▲ Mrs. Wang doesn't have to worry about housework because she has a housekeeper.
王太太不需要擔心家務，因為她有女管家。

10. **inner** [ˋɪnɚ] adj. 內部的；內心的

▲ It is safer to keep your wallet in the inner pocket of your jacket. 把皮夾放在你外套內裡的口袋比較安全。

---

11. **laughter** [ˋlæftɚ] n. [U] 笑，笑聲

▲ My classmates burst into laughter.
我的同學們突然大笑。

💡 roar/scream with laughter 大笑｜Laughter is the best medicine. 【諺】笑是佳良藥。

---

12. **locate** [ˋloket] v. 找到…的地點；設置 [同] site

▲ The police finally located the missing boy.
警察終於找到失蹤的男孩。

---

13. **merry** [ˋmɛrɪ] adj. 快樂的 [同] cheery (merrier｜merriest)

▲ Sandra is singing a merry tune.
Sandra 正唱著快樂的曲調。

---

14. **owe** [o] v. 欠 (錢)；將…歸功於 <to>

▲ Janet owed me NT$300 for the train ticket.
Janet 欠我火車票錢新臺幣三百元。

💡 owe sb an explanation/apology 虧欠…解釋 / 道歉

---

15. **pal** [pæl] n. [C] 朋友，夥伴

▲ Jamie has been my best pal since childhood.
Jamie 自童年起就是我最好的朋友。

💡 pen/cyber pal 筆 / 網友

---

16. **plug** [plʌg] n. [C] 插頭；塞子

   ▲ It is safer to take out the plug when you don't use the charger. 你不使用充電器時把插頭拔掉比較安全。

   plug [plʌg] v. 堵住，塞住 (plugged | plugged | plugging)

   ▲ Some leaves plugged up the drainpipe.
   一些葉子堵住排水管了。

17. **regret** [rɪ`grɛt] v. 感到遺憾，後悔 (regretted | regretted | regretting)

   ▲ Mandy doesn't regret giving up the chance of studying abroad.
   Mandy 不後悔放棄這個出國念書的機會。

   regret [rɪ`grɛt] n. [C][U] 遺憾，後悔 <at, for>

   ▲ The boss expressed deep regret for the factory closures. 老闆對於工廠的關閉深感遺憾。

   💡 with regret 遺憾地 | to sb's regret 令…遺憾的是

18. **satisfactory** [͵sætɪs`fæktrɪ] adj. 令人滿意的 [同] acceptable [反] unsatisfactory

   ▲ The teacher didn't think my report satisfactory and told me to write it again.
   老師不滿意我的報告，叫我再重寫一次。

19. **scout** [skaʊt] n. [C] 童子軍成員；星探

   ▲ As a scout, Anthony has learned some survival skills.
   身為童子軍，Anthony 學過一些求生技巧。

   scout [skaʊt] v. 偵查 <for>；尋找 <for>

▲ The camper is scouting for a place to pitch camp.
這位露營者在偵查搜尋地方紮營。

20. **slice** [slaɪs] n. [C] (切下食物的) 薄片 <of>

▲ Can I have a slice of beef? 我可以吃一片牛肉嗎？

♥ cut sth into slices 將…切成薄片

slice [slaɪs] v. 把…切成薄片

▲ Patty sliced some bread and tomatoes to make sandwich. Patty 把麵包和番茄切成薄片以做三明治。

21. **studio** [ˋstjudɪˏo] n. [C] 攝影棚；錄音室 (pl. studios)

▲ The director showed us around the studio.
導演帶我們參觀攝影棚。

22. **sum** [sʌm] n. [C] 金額

▲ Josh spent a large sum of money on clothes and shoes. Josh 花一大筆錢在衣服和鞋子上。

sum [sʌm] v. 總結，概述 <up> (summed | summed | summing)

▲ The writer summed up the main ideas in the last chapter. 作者在最後一個章節總結主要的觀念。

♥ to sum up 總而言之

23. **thumb** [θʌm] n. [C] 拇指

▲ The cook accidentally cut her thumb when she sliced the mushrooms.
這位廚師將蘑菇切片時不小心劃傷拇指。

💡 be all thumbs 笨手笨腳的 | under sb's thumb 受制
於…之下

thumb [θʌm] v. 用拇指作手勢

▲ The boy thumbed a ride to town.
那男孩搭便車到鎮上。

---

24. **wagon** [ˋwægən] n. [C] 四輪貨運馬車

▲ In some movies, we can see people traveling in
wagons. 在一些電影中，我們可以看見人們搭乘四輪
貨運馬車旅行。

---

25. **weave** [wiv] v. 編織 [同] knit ；(融合不同的事物) 編寫
(wove, weaved | woven, weaved | weaving)

▲ In ancient times, women should learn how to weave
clothes before they got married.
古時候，女人要在結婚前學會如何編織衣服。

weave [wiv] n. [C] 編法 (usu. sing.)

▲ The vest has a tight weave. 這背心有密實的織法。

Unit 30

1. **bait** [bet] n. [U] 餌；誘惑物

▲ Jerry likes fishing and often uses worms as bait.
Jerry 喜歡釣魚且通常用蟲當餌。

bait [bet] v. 裝誘餌

▲ The hunter baited the trap for rabbits.

這位獵人在捕兔器上裝誘餌。

---

2. **bullet** [ˋbʊlɪt] n. [C] 子彈

▲ The bullet hit the robber in the leg.
子彈射中搶匪的大腿。

💡 fire/shoot a bullet (開槍) 射了一發子彈

---

3. **closet** [ˋklɑzɪt] n. [C] 櫥櫃

▲ My closet is full of clothes.
我的衣櫃裡滿滿都是衣服。

---

4. **dare** [dɛr] aux. 敢於

▲ The students dare not break the class rules again for fear of being punished.
這群學生因為害怕被懲罰而不敢再違反班規。

dare [dɛr] v. 敢於

▲ The shy boy doesn't dare to ask the girl out.
這個害羞的男孩不敢約這女孩出去。

dare [dɛr] n. [C] 在激將法下做出的事

▲ Simon gets on a roller coaster on a dare.
Simon 受到激將登上雲霄飛車。

---

5. **drown** [draʊn] v. 淹死，溺死

▲ The kid fell into the river and was drowned in it.
那孩子掉進河裡被淹死了。

---

6. **flour** [flaʊr] n. [U] 麵粉

▲ Bread is made from flour. 麵包是麵粉做的。

---

7. **gossip** [ˋgɑsəp] n. [U] 閒話，流言蜚語
   ▲ The colleagues exchanged a few juicy pieces of office gossip during lunch break. 同事們在午休時交流一些辦公室內有趣的八卦新聞。
   💡 exchange/spread gossip 交流 / 傳播八卦 | a piece of gossip 一則流言 | hot/juicy/interesting gossip 特別有趣的八卦

   gossip [ˋgɑsəp] v. 散布流言 <about>
   ▲ The people in the town are gossiping about the new lover of the old man.
   鎮上的人民都在散布關於這位老翁新歡的流言。

8. **hallway** [ˋhɔl͵we] n. [C] 走廊，玄關
   ▲ The hallway leading to my bedroom is lined with framed photos of my family.
   通往我的臥室的走廊兩旁排列著裱框的家人照片。

9. **hug** [hʌg] n. [C] 擁抱 [同] embrace
   ▲ As soon as the grandmother saw her grandson, she gave him a big hug.
   祖母一看見她的孫子就給他一個大大的擁抱。

   hug [hʌg] v. 擁抱 [同] embrace (hugged | hugged | hugging)
   ▲ The little girl hugged her doll tightly.
   這個小女孩緊緊地抱住她的娃娃。

10. **innocent** [ˋɪnəsn̩t] adj. 無罪的 <of> [反] guilty；天真的 [同] naive

▲ The man was released when he was found innocent of any crime. 這名男子被判無罪的時候，他就獲釋了。

---

11. **laundry** [ˋlɔndrɪ] n. [C] 洗衣店 ；[U] 待洗的衣物 (pl. laundries)

▲ My husband always has his suits dry-cleaned in the laundry. 我丈夫總是把他的西裝送到洗衣店去乾洗。

---

12. **log** [lɔg] n. [C] 原木，木材

▲ Let's put another log on the fire.
我們再放一塊木頭進火裡吧。

log [lɔg] v. 伐 (木)，砍 (樹) (logged | logged | logging)

▲ The rainforests around the world are being logged for paper.
世界各地的熱帶雨林正被砍伐以供應紙張的需要。

---

13. **mess** [mɛs] n. [C][U] 髒亂 ；[sing.] 混亂局面，困境

▲ My friend always makes a mess in the kitchen when he tries to cook.
我朋友要煮飯時，總是把廚房弄得亂七八糟。

mess [mɛs] v. 弄髒 <up>

▲ I spent hours cleaning up the house, but it took my children only a few minutes to mess it up.
我花了好幾個小時打掃房子，但是我的小孩只花了幾分鐘就把它弄亂了。

💡 mess about/around 浪費時間

---

14. **pad** [pæd] n. [C] 護墊；便條本 [同] notebook

▲ The soccer player is wearing knee pads to protect his knees. 這位足球員穿著護膝以保護他的膝蓋。

pad [pæd] v. (用軟物) 填塞 (padded | padded | padding)

▲ The seats are padded with foam.
這些座椅被填塞了海綿乳膠。

---

15. **pancake** [ˋpænˌkek] n. [C] 薄煎餅

▲ Jenny likes to have pancakes for breakfast.
Jenny 喜歡早餐吃薄煎餅。

---

16. **politician** [ˌpɑləˋtɪʃən] n. [C] 政客，從政者

▲ The scandal of taking bribes ruined the career of the politician. 收賄醜聞毀了這政客的事業。

---

17. **restrict** [rɪˋstrɪkt] v. 限制 <to>

▲ The government announced policy to restrict freedom of movement into the country.
政府宣布限制自由入境的政策。

---

18. **saving** [ˋsevɪŋ] n. [pl.] 存款，儲蓄金 (～s)

▲ You should deposit your savings in a savings account. 你應該把存款存入銀行的儲蓄帳戶裡。

---

19. **screw** [skru] v. 用螺絲固定 <to>

▲ Tom screwed a picture to the wall.
Tom 用螺絲把畫作固定在牆上。

💡 screw sth up 把⋯搞砸 | screw up sb's courage ⋯鼓起勇氣

screw [skru] n. [C] 螺絲

▲ I tightened the screw with a screwdriver.
我用螺絲起子鎖緊螺絲。

---

20. **slope** [slop] n. [C] 斜坡 [同] incline；山坡

▲ The elementary school near my house is built on a slope. 我家附近的小學建造在一個斜坡上。

---

21. **summary** [`sʌmərɪ] n. [C] 概述，摘要 (pl. summaries)

▲ The teacher asked us to read the article and then write a summary of it.
老師要求我們看這篇文章，然後寫此文章的摘要。

---

22. **suspicion** [sə`spɪʃən] n. [C][U] 疑心，猜疑；嫌疑

▲ Her boyfriend's strange behavior aroused Melissa's suspicion.
她男友奇怪的行為舉止引起了 Melissa 的疑心。

💡 on/under/above/beyond suspicion 有 / 沒有嫌疑

---

23. **tighten** [`taɪtn̩] v. 拉緊 [反] loosen

▲ I tightened the strings on the guitar.
我把吉他的弦拉緊。

💡 tighten sth up 使⋯更嚴格 | tighten sb's belt ⋯勒緊腰帶，省吃儉用

---

24. **wander** [`wɑndɚ] v. 遊蕩 <around>；(思想) 游離，心不在焉

▲ The homeless man wanders around the street every day. 這個無家可歸的男人每天都在這條街上遊蕩。

wander [`wɑndɚ] n. [sing.] 遊蕩

▲ The tourists had a wander around this ancient city.
這群遊客在這個古老的城市遊蕩了一番。

25. **wipe** [waɪp] v. 擦拭，擦乾 <with, on>

▲ The girl wiped her dirty hands with a wet towel.
這女孩用溼毛巾擦她弄髒的手。

💡 wipe sth off/from... 從…擦去 (灰塵或液體等)

wipe [waɪp] n. [C] 擦，拭

▲ You need to give the dusty windows a quick wipe so
that we can see the views outside clearly. 你得擦一下
布滿灰塵的窗戶，我們才能清楚看得到窗外的風景。

Unit 31

1. **barn** [bɑrn] n. [C] 穀倉

▲ The farmer stored hay and some tools in the barn.
農夫將乾草和一些工具儲存在穀倉裡。

2. **bunch** [bʌntʃ] n. [C] 串，束

▲ Buck gave his girlfriend a bunch of roses.
Buck 送他的女友一束玫瑰。

3. **clothe** [kloð] v. 使穿衣服 [同] dress

▲ The models were clothed in the latest fashion.
模特兒們穿著最流行的時裝。

4. **darling** [`dɑrlɪŋ] n. [C] 親愛的人，寶貝

▲ My darling, I love you very much. 寶貝，我非常愛你。

darling [`dɑrlɪŋ] adj. 親愛的；可愛的

▲ Peter is my darling son. I won't let anyone hurt him.
   Peter 是我親愛的兒子。我不會讓任何人傷害他。

---

5. **drugstore** [`drʌg‚stor] n. [C] 藥妝店

▲ Many tourists buy medicine and cosmetics at drugstores in Japan.
   許多觀光客在日本的藥妝店購買藥品和化妝品。

---

6. **flute** [flut] n. [C] 長笛

▲ John plays the flute in the orchestra.
   John 在交響樂團中吹奏長笛。

---

7. **grasshopper** [`græs‚hɑpɚ] n. [C] 蚱蜢

▲ Most grasshoppers feed on crops.
   大部分的蚱蜢以農作物為食。

---

8. **hammer** [`hæmɚ] n. [C] 鎚子

▲ The paintings went under the hammer at an auction.
   這些畫被拍賣。

hammer [`hæmɚ] v. 用鎚子敲打；敲擊 [同] pound

▲ The carpenter is hammering the nail into the board.
   木工師傅正把釘子釘在木板上。

🔹 hammer sth into sb 向⋯灌輸⋯ | hammer out 充分討論出 (結果)

---

9. **hum** [hʌm] v. 嗡嗡作響；哼歌 (hummed | hummed | humming)

▲ I heard bees humming around flowers in the park yesterday. 我昨天聽到蜜蜂在公園的花叢嗡嗡叫。

10. **jail** [dʒel] n. [C] 監獄

▲ The man spent 10 years in jail for robbery.
這名男子因為搶劫而入獄十年。

💡 be put in/sent to jail 關入監獄 ｜ break jail 逃獄

jail [dʒel] v. 關入監獄 <for> [同] imprison

▲ The banker was jailed for 2 years for crime.
這名銀行家因罪入獄二年。

11. **lifetime** [ˋlaɪfˌtaɪm] n. [C] 終生，一輩子 (usu. sing.)

▲ Society has changed greatly during my lifetime.
在我的一生中，社會經歷了很大的變化。

12. **loose** [lus] adj. 寬鬆的 [同] slack [反] tight (looser ｜ loosest)

▲ It's more comfortable to wear loose clothes when you exercise. 你運動時穿寬鬆的衣服比較舒服。

💡 let/set sb/sth loose 使…自由；放開…

loosely [ˋluslɪ] adv. 鬆垮地

▲ The coat hung loosely on his body.
外套鬆垮地掛在他的身上。

13. **microphone** [ˋmaɪkrəˌfon] n. [C] 麥克風 <into> [同] mike, mic

▲ The chairman spoke into a microphone in the meeting. 主席在會議中透過麥克風說話。

14. **parade** [pə`red] n. [C] 遊行 [同] procession
  ▲ Many cities in the United States usually have parades on Independence Day.
    美國許多城市通常在獨立紀念日舉行遊行活動。
  parade [pə`red] v. 遊行 [同] procession
  ▲ The marchers will parade through the streets to fight for equal rights.
    示威者將在大街小巷遊行以爭取平權。

15. **pat** [pæt] v. 輕輕地拍 (patted | patted | patting)
  ▲ My friend patted me on the shoulder.
    我朋友拍拍我的肩膀。
  pat [pæt] n. [C] 輕拍
  ▲ Nina always gives her cat a pat on the head before she goes to work.
    Nina 上班前都會輕拍貓咪的頭。

16. **poll** [pol] n. [C] 民意調查 [同] survey；投票數 [同] ballot
  ▲ Most recent polls show that support for the government is declining.
    最近的民調顯示政府的支持率降低。
  poll [pol] v. (在選舉中) 得票
  ▲ The candidate polled over 75% of the votes.
    這候選人的得票超過 75%。

17. **ribbon** [`rɪbən] n. [C][U] 緞帶，帶子
  ▲ Nina wore a purple ribbon in her hair today.

Nina 今天在頭髮上紮了一條紫色的緞帶。

18. **scatter** [ˋskætɚ] v. 撒 <on, over, around>；驅散，散開
[同] disperse
▲ The workers are scattering gravel on the road.
工人把砂石撒在路上。

scatter [ˋskætɚ] n. [sing.] 零星，散落 [同] scattering
▲ Ann found a scatter of houses on the farm when she
looked out of the train window. 從火車車窗往外看，
Ann 發現有零星幾間房子在農場裡。

scattered [ˋskætɚd] adj. 散落的，分散的
▲ The weather forecast said there would be scattered
showers in the afternoon.
氣象預報說下午將有零星的陣雨。

19. **scrub** [skrʌb] n. [sing.] 刷洗，擦洗
▲ The street vender gives the food truck a good scrub
every day. 攤販老闆每天都會好好刷洗行動餐車。

scrub [skrʌb] v. (尤指用硬刷、肥皂和水) 擦洗，刷洗
(scrubbed | scrubbed | scrubbing)
▲ Mrs. Chen scrubbed the kitchen floor with a brush.
陳太太用刷子刷洗廚房的地板。

20. **snap** [snæp] v. 啪嗒一聲折斷 (snapped | snapped |
snapping)
▲ The rope snapped when we pulled it too tight.
當我們把繩子拉得太緊時，它就啪嗒一聲斷了。

snap [snæp] n. [C] 啪嗒聲

▲ My mother closed the jewelry box with a snap.
我母親啪嗒一聲闔上珠寶盒。

21. **surround** [sə`raʊnd] v. 圍繞，包圍
▲ Due to the scandal, the actor was surrounded by many reporters.
這名演員因為醜聞而被許多記者包圍。
surrounding [sə`raʊndɪŋ] adj. 周圍的 [同] nearby
▲ The plague spread to the surrounding villages.
瘟疫擴散到周圍的村落。

22. **swear** [swɛr] v. 發誓 [同] vow；咒罵 <at> (swore | sworn | swearing)
▲ Amy swore she knew nothing about the news.
Amy 發誓她對於這消息完全不知情。

23. **timber** [`tɪmbɚ] n. [U] 木材 [同] lumber
▲ Japan imports most of its timber from Thailand.
日本從泰國進口大多數的木材。

24. **wax** [wæks] n. [U] 蠟
▲ The special doll is made of wax.
這個特別的玩偶是由蠟製成的。
wax [wæks] v. 給⋯上蠟
▲ Henry waxes his car once a month.
Henry 一個月給他的車上一次蠟。

25. **wisdom** [`wɪzdəm] n. [U] 智慧

▲ The old man, with great wisdom and experience, gave me a piece of advice.

這位有著充分智慧和經驗的長者給了我一個建議。

Unit 32

1. **barrel** [ˋbærəl] **n.** [C] 桶；一桶之量

   ▲ The wine is put in oak barrels and left to mature in the cellar.

   這些葡萄酒被放在橡木桶中，並擺在地窖裡等它熟成。

2. **bundle** [ˋbʌndl̩] **n.** [C] 包，捆

   ▲ The singer receives a bundle of letters from her fans every day. 這歌手每天收到歌迷寄來的一大捆信。

3. **cock** [kɑk] **n.** [C] 公雞 [同] rooster

   ▲ At 5 a.m. the cock starts to crow.

   上午五點公雞開始啼叫。

4. **dash** [dæʃ] **n.** [sing.] 猛衝；少量

   ▲ When the door opened, the worshippers made a dash for the incense burner. 門一開，信徒朝著香爐猛衝。

   dash [dæʃ] **v.** 急奔 [同] rush；猛擊 <against>

   ▲ Dave dashed off without saying goodbye.

   Dave 沒說再見就匆忙離去。

5. **dumb** [dʌm] **adj.** 啞的；說不出話來的

   ▲ The girl has been deaf and dumb from birth.

那個女孩生來聾啞。

---

6. **foggy** [ˋfɑgɪ] adj. 有霧的，霧茫茫的 (foggier｜foggiest)
   ▲ It is usually damp and foggy in the season.
   這個季節通常又溼又起霧。
   💡 not have the foggiest (idea) 完全不知道

---

7. **greedy** [ˋgridɪ] adj. 貪心的 <for> (greedier｜greediest)
   ▲ Don't be so greedy for money. 別如此貪財。
   💡 greedy guts 貪吃鬼

---

8. **handkerchief** [ˋhæŋkɚtʃɪf] n. [C] 手帕 (pl. handkerchiefs, handkerchieves)
   ▲ Julia wiped away her tears with a handkerchief.
   Julia 用手帕擦掉眼淚。

---

9. **hut** [hʌt] n. [C] 小屋
   ▲ The mountain hut where the man lives hardly has any modern facilities.
   男子住的山中小屋裡幾乎沒有任何現代化設施。

---

10. **jazz** [dʒæz] n. [U] 爵士樂
    ▲ Brian is a huge fan of jazz. Brian 是個超級爵士樂迷。

---

11. **lighthouse** [ˋlaɪtˌhaʊs] n. [C] 燈塔
    ▲ A lighthouse shows ships the way into the port.
    燈塔指引船隻進港的路。

---

12. **loser** [ˋluzɚ] n. [C] 失敗者 [反] winner
    ▲ You have to learn to be a good loser.

你必須學習輸得起。

---

13. **missile** [`mɪsl̩] n. [C] 飛彈

    ▲ The army attacked a terrorist base with missiles.
      軍隊用飛彈攻擊一個恐怖分子的基地。

---

14. **parcel** [`pɑrsl̩] n. [C] 包裹 [同] package

    ▲ Parcels of food and clean water were delivered to the
      disaster area within 24 hours.
      食物及淨水包裹在二十四小時內被運送至災區。

    parcel [`pɑrsl̩] v. 打包 <up>

    ▲ The clerk parceled up the products to send.
      店員將要寄的產品打包起來。

---

15. **permit** [pə`mɪt] v. 許可，准許 (permitted | permitted |
    permitting)

    ▲ The teacher doesn't permit his students to chat in
      class. 老師不准學生上課時聊天。

    permit [`pɝmɪt] n. [C] 許可證

    ▲ You must get a permit so that you can fish here.
      你必須有許可證才能在這裡釣魚。

---

16. **porcelain** [`pɔrslɪn] n. [U] 瓷器

    ▲ Mr. Wang has a valuable porcelain collection in his
      house. 王先生家裡有珍貴的瓷器收藏品。

---

17. **roar** [ror] n. [C] 吼叫，咆哮

    ▲ The tiger in the zoo let out a roar when we walked
      past its cage.

當我們經過牠的籠子時，動物園裡的老虎發出一聲吼叫。

roar [ror] v. 吼叫，咆哮

▲ A lion was roaring in the cage. You could even hear it in the distance.

獅子在籠子裡吼叫。你甚至在遠處就可以聽到。

💡 roar with laughter 放聲大笑

---

18. **scholar** [ˋskɑlɚ] n. [C] (尤指大學的) 學者

▲ Mr. Wang is a distinguished scholar of ancient Greek civilization. 王先生是個傑出的古希臘文明學者。

---

19. **separation** [͵sɛpəˋreʃən] n. [C][U] 分開，分居

▲ The couple began to live together again after a separation of two years.

這對夫妻分居兩年後又開始住在一起。

---

20. **sometime** [ˋsʌm͵taɪm] adv. (過去或將來的) 某個時候

▲ My friend will call on me sometime next month.
我朋友將在下個月找個時間來拜訪我。

---

21. **survivor** [səˋvaɪvɚ] n. [C] 生還者

▲ The boy was the only survivor of the car crash.
這名男孩是這起車禍唯一的生還者。

---

22. **sword** [sord] n. [C] 劍，刀

▲ The brave king drew his sword to kill a poisonous snake. 英勇的國王拔劍殺了條毒蛇。

---

23. **tobacco** [tə`bæko] n. [U] 菸草

▲ The government is considering a ban on tobacco advertising in public places.

政府正在考慮公開場所禁止菸草廣告。

24. **weaken** [`wikən] v. 使虛弱 [反] strengthen

▲ The high fever weakened the patient.

發高燒使這位病人虛弱。

25. **wrap** [ræp] v. 包，裹 <in> (wrapped | wrapped | wrapping)

▲ Kelly felt cold and wrapped herself in a wool blanket. Kelly 覺得冷而把自己裹在羊毛毯裡。

wrap [ræp] n. [U] 包裝材料

▲ I bought a lot of cards and gift wrap for the Christmas party.

為了耶誕節派對，我買了許多賀卡和禮品包裝材料。

💡 keep sth under wraps 將…保密 | bubble wrap 氣泡布

Unit 33

1. **ache** [ek] n. [C] 疼痛 [同] pain

▲ Jerry felt a dull ache in his chest. He was afraid that he might have a heart disease.

Jerry 胸口隱隱作痛。他怕自己可能有心臟疾病。

ache [ek] v. 疼痛 [同] hurt

▲ Elsa's ankles ached from wearing the new pair of high heels.

Elsa 的腳踝因為穿這雙新的高跟鞋而疼痛。

---

2. **bead** [bid] n. [C] 珠子

▲ The actress walked the red carpet wearing a necklace of crystal bead.

這名女演員戴著一串水晶珠項鍊走紅毯。

bead [bid] v. 形成水珠

▲ After running for 30 minutes, the marathon runners' forehead was beaded with sweat.

跑了三十分鐘後，馬拉松跑者們的額頭汗水如珠。

---

3. **bury** [ˋbɛrɪ] v. 埋葬；掩蓋

▲ My grandparents were buried in the same cemetery.

我的祖父母被葬在同一個基地。

💡 bury oneself in sth 專心致志於… | bury sb's head in the sand …逃避現實

---

4. **cocktail** [ˋkɑk͵tel] n. [C] 雞尾酒

▲ My favorite cocktail is mojito.

我最喜歡的雞尾酒是莫希托。

---

5. **database** [ˋdetə͵bes] n. [C] 資料庫

▲ The company's reputation was damaged because its online database was hacked.

該公司商譽受損，因為它的線上資料庫遭駭客入侵。

---

6. **dumpling** [ˋdʌmplɪŋ] n. [C] 餃子

▲ Do you prefer beef or pork dumplings?
你喜歡牛肉還是豬肉水餃？

---

7. **follower** [`faloɚ] n. [C] 追隨者，信徒

▲ Although Sue lost the legislator's race, her followers want her to run for the president. 雖然 Sue 輸掉立法委員的選舉，她的追隨者想要她去參選總統。

---

8. **handy** [`hændɪ] adj. 便利的；有用的 [同] useful (handier | handiest)

▲ With the handy cash on delivery, more and more people shop online now.
有了方便的貨到付款服務，現今越來越多人上網購物。

---

9. **harvest** [`hɑrvɪst] n. [C][U] 收穫

▲ Due to climate change, the farmers have been having bad harvests for years.
由於氣候變遷，農民已經好幾年收成不好了。

harvest [`hɑrvɪst] v. 收割 (農作物)

▲ The heavy rain stopped the farmers from harvesting their crops. 大雨讓農夫們無法收割農作物。

---

10. **inn** [ɪn] n. [C] 小旅店；小酒館

▲ An inn is a small hotel. 小旅店指的是小型的旅館。

---

11. **jealous** [`dʒɛləs] adj. 嫉妒的 <of> [同] envious

▲ Ian is jealous of such a well-paid job that Mike has got. Ian 嫉妒 Mike 得到高薪的工作。

💡 make sb jealous 使⋯嫉妒

12. **lightning** [ˋlaɪtnɪŋ] n. [U] 閃電
   ▲ A flash of lightning lit up the sky.
   一道閃電照亮了天空。
   💡 Lightning never strikes (in the same place) twice.
   【諺】倒楣事不會總落在同一個人身上。

13. **mall** [mɔl] n. [C] 購物中心 (also shopping mall)
   ▲ The company planned to build a shopping mall in the
   downtown. 這間公司計劃在市中心蓋一座購物中心。

14. **mob** [mɑb] n. [C] 暴民
   ▲ The angry mob surrounded the mayor's official
   residence and was ready to rush in.
   一群憤怒的暴民包圍市長的官邸準備衝進去。
   mob [mɑb] v. 成群圍住
   ▲ The superstar was mobbed by his fans in the airport.
   這位巨星在機場被他的粉絲團團圍住。

15. **parrot** [ˋpærət] n. [C] 鸚鵡
   ▲ Can your parrot learn to talk like a human being?
   你的鸚鵡會學人說話嗎？
   parrot [ˋpærət] v. 鸚鵡學舌
   ▲ Don't parrot anything that others say. You need to
   practice critical thinking.
   不要鸚鵡學舌。你需要練習批判性思考。

16. **photographer** [fəˋtɑgrəfɚ] n. [C] 攝影師

▲ As a professional photographer, Tina always carries her camera.

身為一名職業攝影師，Tina 總是隨身攜帶相機。

17. **portion** [ˈpɔrʃən] n. [C] 一部分 ；(食物的) 一份 [同] serving

▲ The investor took away a large portion of the profit.

這位投資者拿走一大部分的利潤。

portion [ˈpɔrʃən] v. 分…份

▲ The central kitchen portions and packs thousands of in-flight meals a day.

這間中央廚房每天分裝數千份飛機餐。

18. **roast** [rost] adj. 烘烤的

▲ Would you like some roast beef for dinner?

你晚餐要吃一些烤牛肉嗎？

roast [rost] n. [C][U] 烤肉

▲ I prepared a roast for the potluck party.

我為百樂餐派對 (一人一菜派對) 準備了一大塊烤肉。

roast [rost] v. 烤 (肉)

▲ The cook roasted the chicken until it was golden brown. 廚師把雞肉烤至金黃色。

19. **seal** [sil] n. [C] 印章；海豹

▲ The file carried a seal of the President.

這份文件上有總統的印章。

💡 set/put the seal on sth 確保…萬無一失

seal [sil] v. 封住

▲ The worker sealed the boxes with tape in the factory.
工人在工廠裡用膠布把這些箱子封住。

---

20. **sexual** [ˋsɛkʃʊəl] adj. 性別的

▲ The woman thought her boss broke the sexual equality law.
這位女士認為她的老闆違反了性別平等法。

💡 sexual discrimination 性別歧視 | sexual assault/harassment 性侵害 / 騷擾 | sexual orientation/preference 性傾向

21. **spice** [spaɪs] n. [C][U] 香料；[U] 情趣

▲ Herbs and spices enrich the flavors of our food.
香草和香料豐富我們食物的味道。

spice [spaɪs] v. 加香料於…；使增添趣味 <up, with>

▲ Ben spiced his Coke with lemon.
Ben 用檸檬來幫可樂調味。

22. **swan** [swɑn] n. [C] 天鵝

▲ There are several swans gliding across the water.
那邊有幾隻天鵝在水面滑行。

23. **tag** [tæg] n. [C] 標籤 [同] label

▲ If you want to return the shirt purchased online, you can't remove its price tag. 如果你想退這件線上購買的襯衫，你就不能拿掉它的價格標籤。

tag [tæg] v. 貼標籤於… (tagged | tagged | tagging)

▲ The clerk tagged the items that would be sold.

店員在要賣的物品上面貼標籤。

24. **ton** [tʌn] n. [C] 噸 (pl. tons, ton)

▲ The total weight of the coal is roughly twenty tons.
煤礦總重約二十噸。

💡 tons of 大量的 | come down on sb like a ton of bricks 狠狠教訓…

25. **wed** [wɛd] v. 與…結婚 (wed, wedded | wed, wedded | wedding)

▲ After an 8-year relationship, the couple eventually decides to wed next spring.
交往八年後，這對情侶最後決定明年春天結婚。

Unit 34

1. **adviser** [əd`vaɪzɚ] n. [C] 顧問，忠告者 (also advisor)

▲ The investment adviser has a lot of fans.
這名投資顧問有很多粉絲。

2. **beast** [bist] n. [C] 野獸

▲ The lion is called the king of beasts.
獅子被稱為萬獸之王。

3. **buzz** [bʌz] n. [C] 嗡嗡聲

▲ The constant buzz of the old air-conditioner is really annoying.
這臺老舊冷氣持續發出的嗡嗡聲真的很惱人。

💡 give sb a buzz 打電話給…

buzz [bʌz] v. 嗡嗡作響

▲ There is something buzzing in the distance.
遠處有東西一直發出嗡嗡聲。

---

4. **coconut** [ˋkokənət] n. [C] 椰子

▲ People on some Pacific islands use coconuts as staples. 一些太平洋島嶼上的人們使用椰子作為主食。

---

5. **dawn** [dɔn] n. [U] 黎明 [同] daybreak, sunrise

▲ I must get up at the break of dawn.
我必須在黎明破曉時起床。

💡 from dawn to dusk 從早到晚 | at dawn 破曉時分

dawn [dɔn] v. 開始明朗，清楚

▲ After the police completed the investigation into the murder, the truth about this crime dawned. 警察完成對這樁謀殺案的調查後，這起案件的真相也明朗了。

💡 It dawns on sb that …開始理解

---

6. **dust** [dʌst] n. [U] 灰塵

▲ The house has been deserted for a long time, so there is dust everywhere.
這房子很久沒有人住了，所以到處都是灰塵。

💡 leave sb in the dust 使…望塵莫及

dust [dʌst] v. 拭去…的灰塵

▲ Mrs. Lin is busy dusting the table and bookshelf.
林太太正忙於擦去桌子和書架上的灰塵。

---

7. **freezer** [ˈfrizɚ] n. [C] 冷凍室，冷凍櫃

▲ I put the fresh steaks in the freezer to preserve them better. 我把新鮮牛排放在冷凍室以更好的保鮮它們。

8. **hanger** [ˈhæŋɚ] n. [C] 衣架

▲ My roommate needs more hangers to hang all his shirts and pants. 我的室友需要更多的衣架把他所有的襯衫和褲子掛起來。

9. **hay** [he] n. [U] 乾草

▲ When there is no grass in winter, they feed the cows on hay. 冬天沒有草的時候，他們就用乾草餵牛。

💡 Make hay while the sun shines. 【諺】打鐵趁熱，把握時機。

10. **inspect** [ɪnˈspɛkt] v. 檢查，審視 [同] examine

▲ The police inspected the scene of the crime, trying to figure out what had happened.
警察檢查犯罪現場，試著釐清到底發生什麼事。

11. **jelly** [ˈdʒɛlɪ] n. [C][U] 果凍 (pl. jellies)

▲ Children like to have jelly for dessert.
小孩子喜歡吃果凍當點心。

💡 turn to/feel like jelly (因恐懼或緊張而) 渾身癱軟

12. **lily** [ˈlɪlɪ] n. [C] 百合花 (pl. lilies)

▲ The meaning of lilies is purity. 百合花的花語是純淨。

13. **mankind** [mænˈkaɪnd] n. [U] 人類 [同] humankind

▲ Discovering fire is one of the most important events in the history of mankind.

發現火是人類歷史上最重要的事件之一。

14. **monk** [mʌŋk] n. [C] 修道士；僧侶

▲ The Catholic monks lead a simple life in the monastery.

這些天主教修道士在修道院中過著樸實的生活。

15. **passenger** [ˈpæsn̩dʒɚ] n. [C] 乘客

▲ All the passengers in a car must fasten their seat belts. 車上所有的乘客都要繫上安全帶。

16. **pine** [paɪn] n. [C][U] 松樹

▲ We like to take a walk in the pine forest.

我們喜歡在這松林裡散步。

17. **poster** [ˈpostɚ] n. [C] 海報 [同] placard

▲ Some students are putting up posters for the Christmas Eve party.

一些學生為了平安夜派對而張貼海報。

18. **rob** [rɑb] v. 搶劫 <of> (robbed | robbed | robbing)

▲ My cousin was robbed of his wallet in the park.

我的表哥在公園裡被搶了皮夾。

19. **sensible** [ˈsɛnsəbl̩] adj. 明智的；察覺到的

▲ It is sensible of Jimmy to follow his father's advice.

Jimmy 聽從他父親的勸告是明智的。

20. **sexy** [ˈsɛksɪ] adj. 性感的 (sexier | sexiest)

▲ I think the actor is very sexy.
我覺得那位演員非常性感。

21. **spinach** [ˈspɪnɪtʃ] n. [U] 菠菜

▲ Spinach is rich in iron. 菠菜含有豐富的鐵質。

22. **sweat** [swɛt] n. [U] 汗水 [同] perspiration

▲ The worker wiped the sweat off his face with a towel. 工人用毛巾擦去臉上的汗水。

💡 be/get in a sweat (about sth) (為…) 擔心

sweat [swɛt] v. 流汗 [同] perspire

▲ Karen sweated heavily after she finished the marathon. Karen 跑完馬拉松後汗流浹背。

💡 sweat like a pig 汗流浹背 | sweat over sth 埋頭做…

23. **talkative** [ˈtɔkətɪv] adj. 多話的

▲ I can't stand my colleague anymore! She is too talkative. 我受不了我的同事了！她太多話了。

24. **trader** [ˈtredɚ] n. [C] 商人，經商者

▲ Mr. Wu is a local trader who sells farm tools in the small town.
吳先生是個地方商人，在這個小鎮販售農具。

25. **weed** [wid] n. [C] 雜草

▲ Leo has removed the weeds from his garden.
Leo 已經清除完他花園裡的雜草。

weed [wid] v. 拔除雜草

▲ It is my turn to weed the yard today.
今天輪到我要拔除庭院裡的雜草。

Unit 35

1. **alley** [ˋælɪ] n. [C] 小巷，小弄
   ▲ It is dangerous to walk in a dark alley alone at night.
   晚上獨自走在暗巷裡很危險。

2. **berry** [ˋbɛrɪ] n. [C] 莓果，漿果 (pl. berries)
   ▲ Rich in antioxidants, berries are able to prevent heart disease and certain types of cancer. 莓果含有豐富的抗氧化劑，能預防心臟疾病和某些類型的癌症。

3. **canyon** [ˋkænjən] n. [C] 峽谷 [同] gorge
   ▲ The view of the Grand Canyon in the United States is splendid. 美國科羅拉多大峽谷的景色很壯觀。

4. **collar** [ˋkɑlɚ] n. [C] 衣領
   ▲ Ian was so mad that he grabbed the man by the collar and was about to hit him.
   Ian 氣到抓住這男子的領口想要打他。

5. **deed** [did] n. [C] 行為 [同] act
   ▲ By doing simple good deeds, you can bring happiness to people around you.
   藉由行小善，你可以將快樂帶給周遭的人。

💡 brave/charitable/evil deed 勇敢的 / 慈善的 / 邪惡的行為

---

6. **echo** [ˋɛko] n. [C] 回聲，回音 (pl. echoes)
   ▲ The reflection of sounds causes the echoes in the tunnel. 反射的聲音形成隧道裡的回音。

   echo [ˋɛko] v. 發出回音 <around> [同] reverberate
   ▲ The howls made by the wolves echoed around the canyon. 狼嚎在峽谷中迴盪著。

   💡 echo down/through the ages 流傳，影響後世

---

7. **fright** [fraɪt] n. [C] 驚嚇的經驗；[U] 驚嚇，恐怖
   ▲ People got such a fright when a fire broke out at the local factory during the night.
   夜晚當地的工廠突然起了大火，把大家嚇了一大跳。

---

8. **hasty** [ˋhestɪ] adj. 匆忙的，倉促的，草率的 [同] hurried (hastier | hastiest)
   ▲ You had better think twice, or you may regret your hasty decision.
   你最好三思，否則你可能會後悔你草率的決定。

   💡 hasty departure/meal/farewell 匆忙的離開 / 用餐 / 告別 | beat a hasty retreat 打退堂鼓

---

9. **heel** [hil] n. [C] 腳跟；鞋跟
   ▲ The new pair of shoes hurt my heels.
   這雙新鞋子磨破我的腳跟。

   heel [hil] v. 修理 (鞋跟)

▲ My leather shoes have worn down at the heel, so I get them heeled.
我皮鞋的鞋跟被磨平了，所以我拿它們去修理。

10. **inspector** [ɪn`spɛktɚ] n. [C] 檢查員，視察員
▲ While you are taking a train, a ticket inspector will check your ticket to ensure that you have paid the fare. 你搭火車時，查票員會檢查你的車票以確認你已經付車資。

11. **joyful** [`dʒɔɪfəl] adj. 快樂的，喜悅的 [同] happy [反] joyless
▲ The square is filled with joyful people celebrating the passing of the War.
廣場充滿了喜悅的民眾慶祝戰爭結束。

12. **lively** [`laɪvlɪ] adj. 熱烈的；精力充沛的 [同] animated, vivacious (livelier | liveliest)
▲ We had a lively discussion about the school fair in class today. 我們今天在課堂上熱烈討論學校園遊會。

13. **marvelous** [`mɑrvḷəs] adj. 令人驚嘆的，很棒的 [同] fantastic, splendid, wonderful
▲ We had a marvelous time at the Christmas party.
我們在耶誕派對中玩得很愉快。

14. **monster** [`mɑnstɚ] n. [C] 妖怪，怪物
▲ There are monsters in the stories of Greek mythology.

希臘神話的故事中有妖怪。

15. **passport** [`pæs,port] n. [C] 護照
▲ That man was arrested because he held a false passport. 那名男子因為持假護照而被逮捕。

16. **pitch** [pɪtʃ] n. [U] 音調；[sing.] 程度，強度
▲ The movie audiences kept crying out at the highest pitch during watching the horror movie.
電影觀眾在觀看這部恐怖片期間不斷高聲尖叫。
pitch [pɪtʃ] v. 投擲
▲ The gang of youths pitched stones to break the windows. 這幫小混混投擲石頭打碎窗戶。

17. **postpone** [post`pon] v. 延期，延後 <until> [同] put back [反] bring forward
▲ The baseball game has been postponed until next Tuesday. 這場棒球賽被延到下星期二。
postponement [post`ponmənt] n. [U] 延期
▲ The outbreak of the virus forced the postponement of all the planned large-scale events.
病毒爆發迫使所有安排好的大型活動延期。

18. **robbery** [`rɑbərɪ] n. [C][U] 搶劫 (pl. robberies)
▲ There were four robberies in the neighborhood last month, and the police were trying to trace the criminal.
該區上個月發生了四起搶案，警察正試圖追蹤罪犯。

19. **shadow** [ˋʃædo] n. [C] 影子；陰影

▲ The dog was barking at his own shadow.
這隻狗正對著牠自己的影子吠叫。

shadow [ˋʃædo] v. 跟蹤，尾隨；投下影子

▲ The police have shadowed the wanted man for several days. 警方已經跟蹤這名通緝犯好幾天了。

20. **shrink** [ʃrɪŋk] v. 縮水；減少 [反] grow (shrank, shrunk | shrunk, shrunken | shrinking)

▲ This sweater will shrink if you wash it in the washing machine. 如果你用洗衣機洗，這件毛衣就會縮水。

21. **spit** [spɪt] v. 吐出 (口水等) <out> (spit, spat | spit, spat | spitting)

▲ The boy drank the milk but spat it out immediately because he found it had gone sour. 那男孩喝了牛奶，但又立刻吐出來，因為他發現牛奶酸掉了。

🔮 spit blood 怒氣衝天地說，咬牙切齒地說

spit [spɪt] n. [U] 口水 [同] saliva

▲ Anna couldn't stop coughing because she was choked by her own spit.
Anna 止不住咳嗽因為她被自己的口水嗆到了。

🔮 spit and polish 仔細的清潔擦洗

22. **swell** [swɛl] v. 腫脹 <up>；增加 <to> (swelled | swelled, swollen | swelling)

▲ Put some ice on your injured ankle before it swells up. 在你受傷的腳踝腫起來前先冰敷。

swell [swɛl] n. [C] 海浪的起伏

▲ Watching the swell of the waves, I feel calm and peaceful. 看著海浪的起伏，我感到平靜祥和。

---

23. **tank** [tæŋk] n. [C] (儲存液體或氣體的) 箱，槽；坦克車

▲ The car flipped and crashed and the oil leaked from holes in the tank.

汽車翻覆撞毀，汽油從油箱的洞漏了出來。

---

24. **trail** [trel] n. [C] 小徑；蹤跡

▲ The hiker wandered from the mountain trail and got lost. 這名健行者在山間小徑俳徊而迷路了。

trail [trel] v. 拖曳

▲ The child trailed his coat behind him.

那孩子把他的外套拿在身後拖曳。

---

25. **weep** [wip] v. 哭泣，流淚 [同] cry, sob (wept | wept | weeping)

▲ The lady wept bitterly for the loss of her husband.

這位女士為她丈夫的死亡而痛哭。

Unit 36

1. **almond** [`ɑmənd] n. [C] 杏仁

▲ I think the smell of toasted almonds is wonderful, but my sister thinks it's awful.

我認為烤杏仁的味道很香，但我妹妹覺得糟透了。

2. **bet** [bɛt] <u>v.</u> 打賭 <on>；敢肯定 (bet, betted | bet, betted | betting)

▲ I wouldn't bet on that horse if I were you.
   如果我是你就不會去賭那匹馬。

🕯 I'll bet. 沒錯。 | You bet! 當然！

bet [bɛt] <u>n.</u> [C] 打賭 <on>

▲ My friend and I have got a bet on who will get higher score for the test.
   我朋友和我打賭，看誰的考試分數比較高。

🕯 <u>win/lose</u> a bet 贏了 / 輸掉打賭 | do sth on a bet 賭氣之下做… | <u>fair/good</u> bet 很可能發生的事 / 明智的決定

---

3. **carpet** [ˈkɑrpɪt] <u>n.</u> [C] 地毯

▲ We have fitted carpets in every room in the new house. 我們已在新家的每個房間鋪上地毯。

🕯 be on the carpet (因做錯事) 被上級長官訓斥

carpet [ˈkɑrpɪt] <u>v.</u> 鋪地毯

▲ The hotel lobby was carpeted in red.
   飯店大廳鋪上了紅色的地毯。

---

4. **colony** [ˈkɑlənɪ] <u>n.</u> [C] 殖民地 (pl. colonies)

▲ India was once a British colony.
   印度曾經是英國的殖民地。

colonize [ˈkɑləˌnaɪz] <u>v.</u> 使成為殖民地

▲ Hong Kong was colonized by the British Empire after the First Opium War.

香港在第一次鴉片戰爭過後，成為大英帝國的殖民地。

5. **deepen** [ˋdipən] v. 加深
   ▲ The teacher tried various ways to deepen the students' understanding of the economic theory. 這位老師嘗試各種方法來加深學生對此經濟理論的了解。

6. **elbow** [ˋɛl‚bo] n. [C] 手肘
   ▲ It is bad manners to rest your elbows on the table.
   把兩肘擱在桌上是很沒禮貌的。
   💡 at sb's elbow 緊跟著…
   elbow [ˋɛl‚bo] v. 用肘推擠
   ▲ The rude man elbowed his way to the front of the line. 這個粗魯的男子用肘推擠到隊伍的前面。
   💡 elbow sb out 強行使…離開 (職位、工作)

7. **frighten** [ˋfraɪtn̩] v. 使害怕，使受驚
   ▲ The sudden noise from the door frightened everyone in the house to death.
   門外突如其來的聲音把屋內的每個人嚇得要死。
   💡 frighten sb witless 把…嚇破膽 | frighten the life out of sb 把…嚇得魂不附體
   frightened [ˋfraɪtn̩d] adj. 害怕的，受驚的
   ▲ Some people are frightened of staying in small and closed spaces. 有些人害怕待在狹小封閉的空間。
   frightening [ˋfraɪtnɪŋ] adj. 可怕的，駭人的 [同] scary
   ▲ Going to the dentist's might be very frightening for both kids and adults.

看牙醫對小孩和成人來說可能都很可怕。

---

8. **hatch** [hætʃ] n. [C] 小窗口 [同] hatchway (pl. hatches)
   ▲ The cook passes the dishes through the serving hatch.
   廚師從送餐窗口將餐點送出。
   💡 escape hatch 逃生出口；解決困境的辦法 | Down the
   hatch! 乾杯！
   hatch [hætʃ] v. 孵化
   ▲ Chicken eggs usually take 21 days to hatch.
   雞蛋通常耗時二十一天孵化。

---

9. **hire** [haɪr] v. 租用 [同] rent；僱用
   ▲ The sales department hired a bus for the company
   trip. 銷售部門租了一輛巴士去員工旅遊。
   💡 hire purchase 分期付款
   hire [haɪr] n. [U] 租用；[C] 新僱員
   ▲ The sharing economy is booming. Bikes,
   motorcycles, cars, and even houses are for hire.
   共享經濟正蓬勃發展。自行車、機車、汽車甚至連房
   子都供租用。

---

10. **interrupt** [ˌɪntəˈrʌpt] v. 打斷
    ▲ Don't interrupt me while I'm speaking.
    我在說話時不要打斷我。

---

11. **junior** [ˈdʒunjɚ] adj. 年資較淺的 <to> [反] senior
    ▲ Mike is junior to me in the company.
    Mike 在公司比我資淺。

junior [ˋdʒunjɚ] n. [C] (大學) 三年級學生
▲ Donna is a junior in college. Donna 是大三的學生。

---

12. **lobby** [ˋlɑbɪ] n. [C] 大廳 [同] foyer (pl. lobbies)
▲ The lawyer will meet his client in the hotel lobby.
這位律師將在旅館大廳與客戶碰面。

---

13. **meadow** [ˋmɛdo] n. [C] 草地，牧場
▲ A flock of sheep is grazing in the meadow.
一群羊在草地上吃草。

---

14. **monthly** [ˋmʌnθlɪ] adj. 每月的，每月一次的
▲ *Fortune* is a monthly magazine. Each month a new
issue is published.
《財富》雜誌是月刊。每月出版新的一期內容。
monthly [ˋmʌnθlɪ] adv. 按月地
▲ White-collar workers are usually paid monthly.
白領階級通常領月薪。
monthly [ˋmʌnθlɪ] n. [C] 月刊 (pl. monthlies)
▲ Since reading habits are changing, the publisher
decided to discontinue the monthly.
由於閱讀習慣改變，這間出版社決定停刊這份月刊。

---

15. **pave** [pev] v. 鋪 (地面) <with>
▲ The road is paved with asphalt.
這條路是由柏油鋪成的。
💡 pave the way for sth 為…鋪路，使…容易進行 | the
streets are paved with gold (某城市) 很容易賺錢

pavement [ˋpevmənt] n. [C] 人行道 [同] sidewalk

▲ The students are walking on the pavement toward the school. 學生們走在往學校的人行道上。

16. **pity** [ˋpɪtɪ] n. [U] 同情，憐憫 <for> [同] sympathy；[sing.] 遺憾的事 [同] shame

▲ Rita feels pity for those who lost their homes during the earthquake.
Rita 很同情那些在地震中失去家園的人。

💡 have/take pity on 同情… | out of pity 出於同情

pity [ˋpɪtɪ] v. 同情，憐憫

▲ Emily pities her brother having to work under such pressure.
Emily 同情她的哥哥需要在高度壓力下工作。

pitiful [ˋpɪtɪfəl] adj. 令人同情的，可憐的 [同] pathetic

▲ The stray dog was a pitiful sight.
這隻流浪狗看起來可憐兮兮的。

17. **pottery** [ˋpɑtərɪ] n. [U] 陶器類

▲ After Mandy retired, she took up the hobby of making pottery.
Mandy 退休之後，她培養出製陶這個嗜好。

18. **robe** [rob] n. [C] 睡袍，浴衣 [同] bathrobe；長袍 (usu. pl.)

▲ After the shower, Henry put on a robe and went to the bedroom. 淋浴後，Henry 穿上浴衣走回房間。

19. **shallow** [ˈʃælo]　adj.　淺 的 [反] deep；膚淺的 [同]
superficial

▲ The river is shallow here, and you can walk across it.
這條河在這裡很淺，你可以步行穿越。

---

20. **sigh** [saɪ]　n.　[C] 嘆氣

▲ Hearing her sons fighting again, the mother let out a
sigh of disappointment.
這位母親聽到兒子們又在爭吵時失望地嘆了一口氣。

sigh [saɪ]　v.　嘆氣 <with>

▲ Daniel sighed with relief when he heard the good
news. Daniel 聽到好消息時鬆了一口氣。

---

21. **splash** [splæʃ]　n.　[C] 潑濺聲，噗通聲 (pl. splashes)

▲ Molly dived into the pool with a splash.
Molly 噗通一聲跳入池中。

💡 make/cause a splash 引起關注，引起轟動

splash [splæʃ]　v.　潑，濺

▲ Before jumping into the water, the swimmer splashed
cold water all over his body.
這游泳選手在跳入水中之前先用冷水潑灑全身。

---

22. **swift** [swɪft]　adj.　迅速的

▲ Swift action must be taken to stop the disease from
spreading. 必須採取迅速的行動以阻止此疾病蔓延。

💡 be swift to V 迅速的做…

---

23. **tow** [to]　n.　[sing.] 拖，牽引

▲ A wrecker gave me a tow when my car broken down on the way home.
我的車在回家路上拋錨後，一輛拖吊車將我的車拖走。

💡 in tow 緊跟著

tow [to] v. 拖，拉 <away>

▲ The wrecked car was towed away to a nearby garage.
這輛撞壞的車被拖到附近的修車場。

---

24. **tray** [tre] n. [C] 托盤

▲ The waiter carried some drinks on a tray.
服務生用托盤遞送一些飲料。

---

25. **whip** [wɪp] n. [C] 鞭子，皮鞭

▲ The man lashed his horse with a whip.
這男子用鞭子抽打他的馬。

whip [wɪp] v. 鞭打 (whipped | whipped | whipping)

▲ The cruel master whipped his servant who made a mistake. 這個殘忍的主人鞭打他犯錯的僕人。

Unit 37

1. **alphabet** [ˈælfə,bɛt] n. [C] 字母

▲ "The A.B.C." is a famous alphabet song.
〈英文字母歌〉是非常有名的字母歌。

alphabetic [ˌælfəˈbɛtɪk] adj. 依字母順序的 (also alphabetical)

▲ Arrange these words in alphabetic order.

把這些單字按字母順序排列。

2. **bleed** [blid] v. 流血 (bled | bled | bleeding)

▲ Sam's finger was bleeding because he cut it by accident. Sam 的手指在流血,因為他不小心切到它。

3. **carriage** [ˋkærɪdʒ] n. [C] (尤指舊時的) 四輪馬車

▲ The queen rode in a carriage at the parade.
女王在這個遊行中乘坐一輛四輪馬車。

4. **comma** [ˋkɑmə] n. [C] 逗號

▲ A comma is a sign used to separate different parts of a sentence.
逗號是用來分隔一個句子中不同部分的符號。

5. **dessert** [dɪˋzɝt] n. [C][U] 甜點

▲ I like to eat ice cream for dessert.
我喜歡吃冰淇淋當點心。

6. **elect** [ɪˋlɛkt] v. 選舉

▲ Who will the citizens elect for mayor?
市民們會選誰當市長?

elect [ɪˋlɛkt] adj. 當選而尚未就職的,候任的

▲ The president elect will take office in May.
候任的總統將於五月赴任執政。

7. **gallon** [ˋgælən] n. [C] 加侖 (液量單位,美國:3.785 公升/1 加侖,英國:4.546 公升/1 加侖)

▲ How much does a gallon of gasoline cost now?

現在一加侖的汽油要多少錢？

8. **hateful** [ˈhetfəl] adj. 十分討厭的，可惡的
▲ The smell and taste of coriander is very hateful to some people. 有些人十分討厭香菜的氣味和口味。

9. **historic** [hɪsˈtɔrɪk] adj. 歷史上著名的，有歷史意義的
▲ There are many historic sites on the island.
這座島嶼上有很多歷史遺跡。

10. **invitation** [ˌɪnvəˈteʃən] n. [C] 邀請
▲ Instead of accepting the invitation, the Internet celebrity turned it down.
這位網路名人沒有接受邀請，反而拒絕受邀。

11. **kangaroo** [ˌkæŋgəˈru] n. [C] 袋鼠 (pl. kangaroos)
▲ Kangaroos and koalas are native to Australia.
袋鼠和無尾熊是澳洲土生土長的動物。
🔖 kangaroo court 袋鼠法庭 (不公正的法庭)

12. **lock** [lɑk] n. [C] 鎖
▲ We had changed the lock after the house was broken in. 房子被小偷闖入後，我們就換了鎖。
lock [lɑk] v. 鎖上
▲ Be sure to lock up the classroom when you leave.
你離開的時候一定要鎖好教室的門窗。
🔖 lock sb out of sth 把⋯鎖在⋯外面 | lock horns over sth 為⋯爭論

13. **meaningful** [ˋminɪŋfəl] adj. 有意義的

▲ You can make your life more meaningful by helping others. 你可以藉著幫助別人讓生活更有意義。

💡 meaningful relationship/discussion/experience 重要的關係 / 討論 / 經歷

14. **moth** [mɔθ] n. [C] 蛾

▲ Moths which cause serious damage to fruit farms are one of the common pests.
蛾，對果園造成嚴重損害，是一種常見的害蟲。

15. **pea** [pi] n. [C] 豌豆

▲ Gina cooked roast chicken with peas and potatoes for dinner. Gina 煮烤雞配豌豆和馬鈴薯當晚餐。

16. **portrait** [ˋportrɪt] n. [C] 肖像

▲ There is a portrait of the president on the wall.
牆上有一幅總統的肖像。

17. **powder** [ˋpaʊdɚ] n. [C][U] 粉，粉末

▲ The nurse ground the medicine into powder for the kid to swallow.
護士將藥物磨成粉狀以讓這個孩童吞下。

💡 milk/curry/chili/soap powder 奶 / 咖哩 / 辣椒 / 洗衣粉 | take a powder 突然離開，溜走

powder [ˋpaʊdɚ] v. 上粉，撲粉

▲ The YouTuber teaches the viewers how to powder their faces in this video.

這名 YouTube 創作者在影片中教導觀眾如何上粉在臉上。

---

18. **rocket** [`rɑkɪt] n. [C] 火箭

▲ The government will increase the budget for the space program and launch more rockets into outer space. 政府將增加太空計畫的預算並發射更多火箭到外太空。

💡 It's not rocket science. 這並不難。

---

19. **shepherd** [`ʃɛpɚd] n. [C] 牧羊人

▲ There is always a close bond between a shepherd and his sheep. 牧羊人和他的羊之間總是有密切的關係。

---

20. **sincere** [sɪn`sɪr] adj. 真誠的，誠懇的 [同] genuine [反] insincere (sincerer | sincerest)

▲ Tim thinks Anna was not sincere in what she said. Tim 覺得 Anna 說的不是肺腑之言。

💡 sincere apology 真誠的道歉

---

21. **spoil** [spɔɪl] v. 毀掉 [同] ruin；寵壞，溺愛 (spoiled, spoilt | spoiled, spoilt | spoiling)

▲ Eating snacks before dinner can spoil your appetite. 晚餐前吃零食會破壞你的食慾。

💡 be spoilt for choice 選擇太多而難以決定

---

22. **tailor** [`telɚ] n. [C] (男裝) 裁縫師

▲ Kenton works as a tailor for the royal family. Kenton 為皇室擔任裁縫師。

💡 The tailor makes the man. 【諺】人要衣裝，佛要金裝。

23. **transport** [ˋtrænsport] n. [U] 運送，運輸 [同] delivery, transportation

▲ The employee is responsible for air transport of supplies. 這名員工是負責物資空運。

💡 public transport 大眾運輸 | means/form of transport 交通工具

transport [trænsˋport] v. 運送，運輸 [同] deliver

▲ The company often transports goods between the two places. 這間公司常在這兩地間運送貨物。

24. **tribe** [traɪb] n. [C] 部落，部族

▲ The whole tribe was wiped out by smallpox.
整個部落的人都死於天花。

25. **wicked** [ˋwɪkɪd] adj. 邪惡的 [同] evil

▲ There are usually brave young men, beautiful ladies, and wicked witches in fairy tales. 童話故事裡通常有英勇的少年、美麗的女子和邪惡的巫婆。

◆━━━━━━━━━━◆━━━━━━━━━━◆

Unit 38

1. **amaze** [əˋmez] v. 使吃驚 [同] astonish

▲ Doris amazed her friends by leaving her well-paid job to join the non-profit organization. Doris 辭掉高薪的工作加入非營利組織，讓她的朋友相當吃驚。

amazement [əˋmezmənt] n. [U] 驚訝 [同] astonishment

▲ I watched the animal show with amazement, in which all the animals could count.

我驚訝地看著動物秀，其中所有動物都會算數。

♥ to sb's amazement 令…驚訝的是

amazed [əˋmezd] adj. 驚訝的 [同] astonished

▲ I always remember the amazed expression on Joe's face when he heard the news.

我永遠記得當 Joe 聽到那消息時，他臉上訝異的表情。

amazing [əˋmezɪŋ] adj. 令人驚訝的 [同] astounding, incredible

▲ The boy ran at an amazing speed as if he had seen a ghost. 那男孩好像看到鬼似的，以驚人的速度奔跑。

---

2. **bless** [blɛs] v. 祝福；保佑 (blessed, blest | blessed, blest | blessing)

▲ The priest blessed the newlyweds.

牧師祝福這對新婚夫婦。

♥ bless you 保佑你 (對打噴嚏者所說的話) | be blessed with sth 有幸享有…

3. **cart** [kɑrt] n. [C] 手推車 [同] trolley

▲ We need a shopping cart because we will buy a lot of things today.

我們今天會買很多東西所以需要購物推車。

♥ put the cart before the horse 本末倒置

cart [kɑrt] v. 用車裝運

▲ Volunteers collected up the trash from the beach and then carted it away.

志工們把海灘上的垃圾收在一起後，用車裝運載走。

4. **confuse** [kən`fjuz] v. 將…混淆 <with>；使困惑

▲ I sometimes confuse Ray with his twin brother.

我有時會將 Ray 和他的雙胞胎弟弟混淆。

confused [kən`fjuzd] adj. 困惑的 <about>

▲ Tina is confused about Rita's decision of quitting the well-paid job. Tina 對於 Rita 辭掉這個薪水優渥工作的決定感到困惑。

confusing [kən`fjuzɪŋ] adj. 令人困惑的

▲ The complicated railroad system in the city is really confusing. 這個城市複雜的鐵路系統很令人困惑。

5. **devil** [`dɛvl̩] n. [C] 魔鬼 [同] demon

▲ The Devil is believed to be the most powerful evil spirit in some religions.

魔鬼在一些宗教中被認為是最強大的邪靈。

6. **element** [`ɛləmənt] n. [C] 元素；要素

▲ Hydrogen and Oxygen are the elements that make up water. 氫和氧是組成水的元素。

7. **gamble** [`gæmbl̩] n. [C] 冒險，賭博 (usu. sing.)

▲ It was a gamble for Lily to quit her current job and start her own business.

辭掉現職後創業對 Lily 來說是場冒險。

gamble [ˋgæmbḷ] v. 下賭注，賭博 <on> [同] bet；冒險 [同] risk

▲ Whether you gamble on horses or games, you have to take the risk of losing money.
無論你賭馬或賭球賽，你都得冒著輸錢的風險。

8. **headline** [ˋhɛd͵laɪn] n. [C] (報紙的) 標題

▲ Stacy barely had time to read the headlines before leaving for work.
Stacy 在上班出門前幾乎沒有時間看報紙的標題。

💡 hit/make the headlines 登上報紙頭條新聞

headline [ˋhɛd͵laɪn] v. 以⋯為標題

▲ The news was headlined "Unhealthy Happiness."
這篇新聞以「有害快樂」為標題。

9. **holder** [ˋholdɚ] n. [C] 持有者，擁有者

▲ Tom broke the record and became the holder of the world record.
Tom 打破紀錄，成為了世界紀錄的保持人。

10. **ivory** [ˋaɪvrɪ] n. [U] 象牙；[C] 象牙製品 (pl. ivories)

▲ The ban on the ivory trade aims to protect the wild elephants. 象牙交易禁令旨在保護野生大象。

💡 ivory tower 象牙塔 (比喻處於脫離現實、不知人間疾苦的狀態)

ivory [ˋaɪvrɪ] adj. 象牙色的

▲ The ivory dress looks good on you.

這件象牙色的洋裝穿在你身上很美。

---

11. **keyboard** [ˋki,bord] n. [C] 鍵盤；(電子) 鍵盤樂器
   ▲ The computer accepts input from the keyboard or the microphone.
   這臺電腦接受來自鍵盤或麥克風的聲控輸入。

---

12. **lollipop** [ˋlɑlɪ,pɑp] n. [C] 棒棒糖
   ▲ The babysitter gave the little boy a lollipop to stop him from crying.
   保姆給這小男孩一根棒棒糖，讓他停止哭泣。

---

13. **minus** [ˋmaɪnəs] prep. 減，減去
   ▲ Nine minus two is seven. 9 減 2 得 7。
   minus [ˋmaɪnəs] n. [C] 負號；缺點，不利條件 (pl. minuses)
   ▲ Don't forget to put a minus before a number less than zero. 在小於零的數字前別忘了加負號。
   minus [ˋmaɪnəs] adj. 負的；不利的；略低於的
   ▲ The temperature will fall to minus ten tomorrow.
   明天溫度將降至零下十度。

---

14. **napkin** [ˋnæpkɪn] n. [C] 餐巾，餐巾紙
   ▲ I wiped my mouth with a napkin. 我用餐巾擦嘴。

---

15. **peanut** [ˋpinət] n. [C] 花生
   ▲ The salted peanuts are too tasty to stop eating.
   這些鹽味花生真的好吃到讓人停不下來。

💡 peanut butter/oil 花生醬 / 油

---

16. **pour** [por] v. 倒 (液體)；湧入；(雨) 傾盆而下 <down>

▲ The waiter is pouring wine for guests at the table.
侍者為桌上的每位客人倒酒。

💡 pour sth out 毫無保留的表達…(感情或思想等)

---

17. **producer** [prə`djusɚ] n. [C] 生產者；製片人，製作人

▲ Brazil is one of the leading coffee producers in the world. 巴西是其中一個世界最大的咖啡出產國。

---

18. **romantic** [ro`mæntɪk] adj. 浪漫的，愛情的

▲ It is said that Paris is one of the most romantic cities in the world.
有人說巴黎是世界上最浪漫的城市之一。

romantic [ro`mæntɪk] n. [C] 浪漫主義者，耽於幻想的人

▲ Vivian is a hopeless romantic.
Vivian 是個無可救藥的浪漫主義者。

---

19. **shiny** [`ʃaɪnɪ] adj. 閃耀的，光亮的 [同] bright (shinier | shiniest)

▲ Tom has a shiny new car. Tom 有一部發亮的新車。

---

20. **skip** [skɪp] v. 蹦跳 [同] jump；略過 <over, to> (skipped | skipped | skipping)

▲ The kids skipped down the pavement happily after school.
孩子們放學後高興地沿著人行道蹦蹦跳跳往前走。

skip [skɪp] n. [C] 蹦蹦跳跳

▲ The little boy gave a skip of excitement.
小男孩興奮得蹦蹦跳跳。

21. **spray** [spre] n. [U] 水花
   ▲ We sat on the beach and enjoyed the spray from the sea. 我們坐在沙灘上，享受濺起的浪花。
   spray [spre] v. 噴灑 <with>
   ▲ Molly sprayed the plants with some water.
   Molly 用一些水噴灑植物。
   💡 spray sth on/onto/over sth 將…噴灑在…上

22. **tame** [tem] adj. 溫馴的 [反] wild (tamer | tamest)
   ▲ It is said that the power of love can transform a wild creature into a tame one. 據說愛的力量可以將野生動物轉化成一隻溫馴的動物。
   tame [tem] v. 馴化，馴服
   ▲ It is not easy to tame a lion. 要馴服獅子不容易。

23. **tricky** [ˋtrɪkɪ] adj. 狡猾的；難應付的 (trickier | trickiest)
   ▲ Foxes are considered to be tricky in many stories.
   狐狸在許多故事中被認為是狡猾的。

24. **troop** [trup] n. [C] 一群，一隊；[pl.] 軍隊 (~s)
   ▲ A troop of tourists was getting off the bus.
   一群遊客正從公車下車。

25. **widen** [ˋwaɪdn̩] v. 使寬廣 [同] broaden
   ▲ The river widens as it flows. 這條河越流越寬。

Unit 39

1. **ambassador** [æm`bæsədə] n. [C] 大使 <to>
   ▲ Paul is the British ambassador to Japan.
   Paul 是英國駐日大使。

2. **blouse** [blaʊs] n. [C] 女用襯衫 (pl. blouses)
   ▲ Mia wears a white silk blouse and a black skirt today.
   Mia 今天穿著一件白色絲質襯衫和一條黑色裙子。

3. **cast** [kæst] v. 投擲；(目光) 投向 (cast | cast | casting)
   ▲ Willy cast the line into the lake and waited for the fish to take the bait.
   Willy 把他的釣魚線拋進湖裡，等待魚兒上鉤。
   cast [kæst] n. [C] (戲劇或電影的) 全體演員陣容
   ▲ The film has a cast of more than twenty.
   這部電影有超過二十人的演員陣容。

4. **continent** [`kɑntənənt] n. [C] 大陸，大洲
   ▲ There are seven continents on Earth. 地球上有七大洲。

5. **dim** [dɪm] adj. 昏暗的 [反] bright (dimmer | dimmest)
   ▲ Don't read books in a dim light.
   不要在昏暗的光線下看書。
   dim [dɪm] v. 變暗 [反] brighten (dimmed | dimmed | dimming)
   ▲ The lights in the concert hall dimmed before the performance began.

在表演開始前，音樂廳的燈光暗下來。

6. **emperor** [ˋɛmpərɚ] **n.** [C] 皇帝

▲ The emperor ordered the soldiers to fight for his empire. 皇帝命令士兵為他的帝國而戰。

7. **gang** [gæŋ] **n.** [C] (朋友的) 一群；幫派組織

▲ Even though Ted made some new friends in college, he still missed the old gang. 即使 Ted 在大學中交了一些新朋友，他仍然想念他的老友們。

gang [gæŋ] **v.** 結黨 (反對他人) <up on, against>

▲ It's unreasonable to gang up on someone who behaves differently.
結黨反對行為舉止和他人不同的人是不合理的。

8. **headquarters** [ˋhɛd͵kwɔrtɚz] **n.** [pl.] 總部 (abbr. HQ)

▲ All the branch offices must report to the headquarters annually. 所有的分支機構每年都要向總部報告。

9. **homesick** [ˋhom͵sɪk] **adj.** 思鄉的，想家的

▲ Eddie felt homesick for Tainan when he first went to university. Eddie 剛上大學時，非常思念家鄉臺南。

10. **jar** [dʒɑr] **n.** [C] 廣口瓶，罐子

▲ You should keep your homemade jam in a jar and store it in the refrigerator.
你應該把自製的果醬放進罐子裡，並且儲存在冰箱。

jar [dʒɑr] **v.** 使煩躁，使不快 [同] grate (jarred | jarred | jarring)

▲ The traffic noise jarred on my nerves.
交通噪音使我很煩躁。

---

11. **kilometer** [kɪˋlɑmətɚ] n. [C] 公里 (abbr. km)
   ▲ The distance between the two towns is five kilometers. 這兩個城鎮的距離是五公里。

---

12. **lord** [lɔrd] n. [C] 貴族；上帝 (the Lord)
   ▲ It is said that Frank is the son of the lord.
   據說 Frank 是這名貴族的兒子。

---

13. **misery** [ˋmɪzrɪ] n. [C][U] 悲慘，痛苦 <in> [同] poverty, distress (pl. miseries)
   ▲ The old man lived in misery after his wife died.
   老先生自從喪妻之後就過著悲慘的生活。

---

14. **neat** [nit] adj. 整齊的
   ▲ Ann always keeps her room neat.
   Ann 總是保持房間整潔。

   neatly [ˋnitlɪ] adv. 整齊地
   ▲ The teacher tells us to write neatly in the test.
   老師叫我們考試時要字跡工整。

---

15. **pearl** [pɝl] n. [C] 珍珠
   ▲ The lady is wearing a pearl necklace.
   這位女士戴著一條珍珠項鍊。

---

16. **pretend** [prɪˋtɛnd] v. 假裝

▲ Nathan pretended to be sick, so he wouldn't have to go to school.

Nathan 假裝生病，這樣就可以不用去上學。

---

17. **pronounce** [prə`naʊns] v. 發音；發表意見，宣布

▲ The "b" in comb is not pronounced.

comb 的 b 不用發音。

💡 pronounce on/upon sth 發表對…的看法

---

18. **rotten** [`rɑtṇ] adj. 腐爛的，變質的；腐敗的，不誠實的

▲ Food goes rotten very quickly in hot and humid summer days. 食物在溼熱的夏天很快就腐敗。

---

19. **shorten** [`ʃɔrtṇ] v. 縮短，變短 [反] lengthen

▲ Days shorten when winter comes.

冬天來時，白晝會縮短。

---

20. **slave** [slev] n. [C] 奴隸 <to, of>

▲ Stop being a slave to ever-changing fashion.

不要做不停改變的時尚的奴隸。

slave [slev] v. 賣命工作，苦幹

▲ The whole team slaved away at the project this month. 整個團隊本月都在努力做此企劃案。

---

21. **spy** [spaɪ] n. [C] 間諜 (pl. spies)

▲ To everyone's surprise, the general has worked as an enemy spy.

出乎大家意料之外，這位將軍竟然是敵方間諜。

spy [spaɪ] v. 從事間諜活動 <for>

▲ The young man admitted spying for his country.
這年輕人承認為他的國家從事間諜活動。

💡 spy on sb/sth 監視，蒐集…

22. **tangerine** [ˌtændʒəˋrin] n. [C] 橘子
▲ The tangerine was peeled and divided into segments.
這顆橘子剝好皮也分成一瓣一瓣了。

23. **trumpet** [ˋtrʌmpɪt] n. [C] 小號，喇叭
▲ Lisa plays several instruments including trumpet, piano and violin.
Lisa 能演奏數種樂器，包括小號、鋼琴和小提琴。

💡 blow your own trumpet 自吹自擂，自我吹捧
trumpet [ˋtrʌmpɪt] v. 吹噓
▲ Daniel is trumpeting his daughter's accomplishments.
Daniel 到處吹噓他女兒的多才多藝。

24. **tug** [tʌg] n. [C] 拉，拽
▲ The naughty boy gave his classmate's hair a tug.
淘氣的男孩拉他同學的頭髮。

💡 tug-of-war 拔河比賽
tug [tʌg] v. 拉，拽 <at> (tugged | tugged | tugging)
▲ The little girl tugged at her mother's sleeve to get her attention. 小女孩拉她媽媽的袖子以取得她的注意。

25. **wrist** [rɪst] n. [C] 手腕
▲ Susan sprained her wrist while playing badminton.

Susan 打羽球時扭傷了她的手腕。

Unit 40

1. **ambulance** [`æmbjələns] n. [C] 救護車
   ▲ The man was in a bad car crash. Call an ambulance.
   這位男子發生嚴重的車禍。快叫救護車。

2. **bookcase** [`bʊk͵kes] n. [C] 書架
   ▲ I need to buy a new bookcase to put the novels.
   我需要買一座新書架來放小說。

3. **champion** [`tʃæmpɪən] n. [C] 冠軍，優勝者
   ▲ The man is the heavyweight champion of the world; no one can beat him.
   這名男子是世界重量級拳王，沒有人能贏他。

4. **controller** [kən`trolɚ] n. [C] 管理者，指揮者
   ▲ Christine became the controller after working for years in the company.
   Christine 在該公司工作多年後成為了管理者。
   💡 air-traffic controller 飛航管制員

5. **discount** [`dɪskaʊnt] n. [C] 折扣，打折 [同] reduction
   ▲ The store offers a discount of ten percent on cash purchases. 這間商店對於現金購買有打九折。
   discount [`dɪskaʊnt] v. 打折扣，不全置信，低估 [同] dismiss

▲ I always discount what he says.
對於他說的話，總是要打折扣。

💡 discount the possibility of sth 低估…的可能性

6. **energetic** [ˌɛnɚˈdʒɛtɪk] adj. 精力充沛的

▲ The puppy is very energetic and runs around in the yard. 這隻小狗精力充沛而在院子到處亂跑。

7. **garage** [ɡəˈrɑʒ] n. [C] 車庫；修車廠

▲ Please put the car away in the garage.
請把車停到車庫。

💡 garage sale 舊物拍賣 (多在自家的車庫進行)

8. **heap** [hip] n. [C] (凌亂的) 一堆 <of>

▲ Brook has a heap of clothes to fold before going to bed. Brook 在睡前還有一堆衣服要摺。

heap [hip] v. 堆積

▲ The big eater heaped a lot of food onto her plate.
這位食量大的人在她的盤子上堆了很多食物。

💡 heap praise/criticism on sb 大力讚揚 / 批評…

9. **honesty** [ˈɑnɪstɪ] n. [U] 誠實 [反] dishonesty

▲ The criminal finally answered the police's questions with his honesty. 罪犯終於誠實回答警察的問題。

💡 Honesty is the best policy. 【諺】 誠實為上策。 | in all honesty 說實話，其實

10. **jaw** [dʒɔ] n. [C] 下顎，下巴 [同] chin

▲ The boxer punched his opponent in the jaw.

這拳擊手一拳打在對手的下巴上。

💡 sb's jaw drops open … 大吃一驚

11. **kindergarten** [ˈkɪndɚˌɡɑrtn̩] n. [C] 幼兒園

▲ My son goes to kindergarten. 我兒子在上幼兒園。

12. **magician** [məˈdʒɪʃən] n. [C] 魔術師

▲ My uncle and aunt hired a magician for their son's birthday party.

我的叔叔和嬸嬸為兒子的生日會請了一個魔術師。

13. **mist** [mɪst] n. [C][U] 薄霧

▲ You had better drive with care with everything covered in mist.

一切都籠罩在霧裡，你最好小心駕駛。

mist [mɪst] v. 起霧

▲ My glasses misted up when I was enjoying hotpot.

我的眼鏡在吃火鍋時起霧。

misty [ˈmɪstɪ] adj. 有霧的 (mistier | mistiest)

▲ According to the weather forecast, it'll turn cold and misty tonight.

根據氣象報告，今晚會轉為寒冷、有霧的天氣。

14. **necktie** [ˈnɛkˌtaɪ] n. [C] 領帶 [同] tie

▲ Jason hates to wear a necktie. He says it makes him unable to breathe.

Jason 討厭戴領帶。他說那讓他無法呼吸。

15. **peel** [pil] v. 削 (水果或蔬菜的) 皮

▲Father is peeling some potatoes to make curry chicken. 父親正在削馬鈴薯的皮以做咖哩雞。

peel [pil] n. [C][U] (水果或蔬菜的) 外皮 [同] skin

▲Adding some grated orange peel to the cake can give it a pleasant fragrance.

加一些磨碎的橘子皮在蛋糕裡可以增添香味。

16. **pub** [pʌb] n. [C] (英國) 酒吧 [同] bar

▲The man had a beer in a pub during his last trip to the United Kingdom.

這名男子上次去英國時在一間酒吧裡喝了杯啤酒。

17. **rank** [ræŋk] n. [C][U] 級別，職位 [同] class；一列

▲Emily rose through the ranks to become production manager. Emily 級級攀升，當上生產部經理。

rank [ræŋk] v. 評定等級 <as>

▲Eva was ranked as one of the best tennis players in the league. Eva 被評為聯盟最傑出的網球選手之一。

18. **rug** [rʌg] n. [C] 小地毯，墊子

▲The children were asked to rub their shoes against the rug in the doorway before getting into the house.

孩子們被要求在進入房子前，要在門口的小地毯上磨擦他們的鞋子。

19. **shovel** [ˈʃʌvl] n. [C] 鏟子 [同] spade

▲Ronald cleared the snow from the driveway with a shovel. Ronald 用鏟子清除車道上的積雪。

shovel [ˈʃʌvḷ] v. 鏟起

▲ The family is busy shoveling snow away from their gate on a cold day.
這個家庭在冷天中忙著鏟除大門前的積雪。

20. **slippery** [ˈslɪprɪ] adj. 溼滑的 (slipperier | slipperiest)

▲ You have to be careful when walking on the slippery floor. 你走在這溼滑的地板上要小心。

21. **squirrel** [ˈskwɝəl] n. [C] 松鼠

▲ I saw some squirrels scurrying up the tree.
我看到一些松鼠快速跑到樹上去。

22. **tease** [tiz] v. 戲弄，取笑 <about>

▲ Some haters teased the actor about his looks.
一些網路酸民取笑這位演員的長相。

23. **truthful** [ˈtruθfəl] adj. 誠實的 <with> [同] honest [反] untruthful

▲ I think husband and wife should be truthful with each other. 我覺得夫妻彼此應誠實以對。

24. **tutor** [ˈtutɚ] n. [C] 家庭教師

▲ Tony's parents hired a tutor to help him with his math.
Tony 的父母幫他請了一位家庭教師來教他數學。

tutor [ˋtutɚ] v. 當家庭教師

▲ Beth tutored my older brother in math.
Beth 當過我哥哥的數學家教。

25. **yell** [jɛl] v. 吼叫 <at> [同] shout

▲ The man yelled at the waitress because she spilled some juice on his white shirt. 這名男子因為女服務生在他的白襯衫上灑了一些果汁而對她大吼。

yell [jɛl] n. [C] 喊叫聲 [同] shout

▲ Tom let out a yell of triumph when his favorite baseball player hit a home run. 看見最喜歡的棒球球員打出全壘打時，Tom 發出勝利的歡呼聲。

26. **youngster** [ˋjʌŋstɚ] n. [C] 年輕人 [反] elder

▲ Bending is an action that youngsters can do with ease, but it is quite hard for many elders. 彎腰是年輕人輕易做得到的動作，但對多數年長者卻相當困難。

27. **zipper** [ˋzɪpɚ] n. [C] 拉鍊 [同] zip

▲ The zipper is stuck, so I can't open my bag.
拉鍊卡住了，所以我沒辦法打開包包。

💡 do up/close/undo/open a zipper 拉上 / 拉開拉鍊

zipper [ˋzɪpɚ] v. 拉上拉鍊 [同] zip

▲ Zipper your coat up, or you will catch a cold.
拉上你外套的拉鍊否則你會感冒。

NOTE

Unit 1

1. **alert** [ə`lɜ·t] adj. 警覺的 <to>

   ▲ Parents should be alert to their children's strange behavior. 父母應該要對孩子的怪異行為有所警覺。

   alert [ə`lɜ·t] v. 向…發出警報 <to>

   ▲ The alarm rang, and it alerted me to the fire.
   警鈴大作,讓我意識到發生火災了。

   alert [ə`lɜ·t] n. [C][U] 警報

   ▲ A tsunami alert was issued immediately after the major earthquake occurred.
   發生大地震後立刻發布海嘯警報。

   ♥ on the alert 警戒

---

2. **anniversary** [,ænə`vɜ·sərı] n. [C] 週年紀念 (pl. anniversaries)

   ▲ Ben held a party to celebrate his parents' fiftieth wedding anniversary.
   Ben 舉辦一場派對慶祝他父母結婚五十週年紀念日。

---

3. **approval** [ə`pruvl̩] n. [U] 同意 [反] disapproval

   ▲ Sara took a week's leave with her supervisor's approval. Sara 取得主管同意後請了一星期的假。

---

4. **authentic** [ɔ`θɛntɪk] adj. 真實的 [同] genuine [反] inauthentic;正宗的 [同] genuine

   ▲ The businessman spent at least a million dollars acquiring this authentic Picasso painting.

這位商人花了至少一百萬元才購得這幅畢卡索的真跡。

---

5. **confidence** [ˋkɑnfədəns] n. [U] 信心 <in, that>；[C] 祕密
   ▲ Ian has confidence that he can win.
   Ian 有信心他能贏。
   💡 in confidence 私下地

---

6. **consist** [kənˋsɪst] v. 由…組成 <of>；存在於 <in>
   ▲ The tennis club consists of twelve boys and ten girls.
   網球社由十二個男孩和十個女孩組成。

---

7. **context** [ˋkɑntɛkst] n. [C] (事情發生的) 背景 <in>；上下文
   ▲ To fully understand what the drama tries to express, we should see it in historical context. 為了充分了解此戲劇想要表達什麼，我們必須審視它的歷史背景。

---

8. **creativity** [͵krie`tɪvətɪ] n. [U] 創造力
   ▲ Being a good artist requires a lot of creativity.
   身為一個好的藝術家需要有很多的創造力。

---

9. **endure** [ɪn`djʊr] v. 忍受 [同] bear
   ▲ People have to endure extreme heat when traveling in the desert.
   人們在沙漠旅行時必須忍受極度的燠熱。
   enduring [ɪn`djʊrɪŋ] adj. 持久的
   ▲ The war survivors hope for enduring peace and stability. 戰爭倖存者期待永久的和平和穩定。

---

10. **enthusiasm** [ɪn`θjuzɪˌæzəm] n. [U] 熱情 <for>

▲ Vince shows great enthusiasm for his work.
　Vince 對工作有極大的熱情。

🔮 arouse/lose enthusiasm 激起 / 失去熱情

11. **fragile** [`frædʒəl] adj. 易碎的 [同] breakable [反] strong；
脆弱的 [同] vulnerable [反] strong

▲ The parcel was labeled "Fragile."
　包裹上貼著「易碎」的標籤。

12. **habitual** [hə`bɪtʃʊəl] adj. 習慣性的

▲ Robert is a habitual drinker, and he almost gets drunk
　every day.
　Robert 是個嗜酒成性的人，他幾乎每天都喝醉。

13. **harmony** [`hɑrmənɪ] n. [U] 和諧 <in>

▲ In order to protect the earth, people should live in
　harmony with nature.
　為了保護地球，人們應該與大自然和平共存。

harmonious [hɑr`monɪəs] adj. 和諧的 [反]
inharmonious

▲ It's essential to establish a harmonious relationship
　with neighbors. 與鄰居建立和諧的關係很重要。

14. **initial** [ɪ`nɪʃəl] adj. 最初的 [同] first

▲ My initial impression of Susan changed after I had
　known her better. 我對 Susan 最初的印象在我進一步
　認識她後就改變了。

initial [ɪˈnɪʃəl] n. [C] (姓名的) 首字母 (usu. pl.)

▲ G.B.S. are the initials of George Bernard Shaw.
   G.B.S. 是 George Bernard Shaw 的名字首字母。

initial [ɪˈnɪʃəl] v. 在…上簽署姓名的首字母

▲ The CEO initialed the contract on the signature line.
   執行長在合約的簽名線上簽上姓名的首字母。

---

15. **intelligence** [ɪnˈtɛlədʒəns] n. [U] 智商，智慧

▲ The dolphin is an animal with high intelligence.
   海豚是智商很高的動物。

   💡 AI = artificial intelligence 人工智慧

---

16. **launch** [lɔntʃ] v. 發行；發射

▲ The new product is set to launch tomorrow.
   這個新產品已經準備好明天發行。

   💡 launch into 開始從事

launch [lɔntʃ] n. [C] 發表會；(火箭等的) 發射

▲ The new smartphone launch will take place in New
   York. 新款智慧型手機的發表會將會在紐約舉行。

---

17. **margin** [ˈmɑrdʒɪn] n. [C] (書頁的) 空白處 <in>；幅度，
    差額

▲ Please write your comments in the margin.
   請將你的意見寫在頁邊的空白處。

---

18. **overcome** [ˌovəˈkʌm] v. 克服 [同] defeat (overcame |
    overcome | overcoming)

▲ To achieve success, you should overcome all the difficulties. 為了成功，你應該克服所有的困難。

💡 overcome obstacles/problems 克服障礙 / 問題

19. **paragraph** [ˈpærəˌgræf] **n.** [C] 段落

▲ A paragraph usually contains five to ten sentences and focuses on one main idea. 段落通常包含五到十個句子，且專注於一個主要的想法。

20. **protein** [ˈprotin] **n.** [C][U] 蛋白質

▲ In addition to animal products, beans and nuts are also rich in protein.
除了動物製品外，豆類和堅果類也富含蛋白質。

21. **protest** [ˈprotɛst] **n.** [C][U] 抗議，反對 <against>

▲ The opposing party held a protest against the new policy. 反對黨舉行反新政策的抗議活動。

💡 under protest 不情願地

protest [prəˈtɛst] **v.** 抗議，反對 <against>

▲ Thousands of people gathered outside the AIT office, protesting against the U.S. pork imports.
數千人聚在美國在臺協會外面，抗議美豬進口。

22. **researcher** [rɪˈsɝtʃɚ] **n.** [C] 研究員

▲ According to some researchers, excessive vitamins are harmful to human health. 根據某些研究人員的說法，過量的維他命對人體健康有害。

23. **severe** [sə`vɪr] adj. 嚴厲的 [同] harsh；嚴重的 (severer | severest)

▲ Spanking is considered a severe punishment by some modern parents.
一些現代父母認為打屁股是嚴厲的懲罰。

severely [sə`vɪrlɪ] adv. 嚴重地

▲ The farm was severely damaged due to the typhoon.
農場因為颱風的關係嚴重受損。

---

24. **strengthen** [`strɛŋθən] v. 增強

▲ An ambassador's job is to strengthen the relationship between two countries.
大使的工作是要加強兩國的關係。

💡 strengthen sb's hand 加強⋯的權力

---

25. **sympathy** [`sɪmpəθɪ] n. [U] 同情

▲ The mayor expressed deep sympathy for the victims of that accident. 市長向那場意外的罹難者致哀。

Unit 2

1. **analysis** [ə`næləsɪs] n. [C][U] 分析 <of> (pl. analyses)

▲ We must make a careful analysis of the causes of the accident. 我們必須詳細分析事故發生的原因。

2. **arms** [ɑrmz] n. [pl.] 武器

▲ It is against the law for ordinary people to carry arms in Taiwan.

在臺灣，一般民眾攜帶武器是違法的。

---

3. **artificial** [ˌɑrtəˋfɪʃəl] adj. 人工的 [同] false [反] natural；不自然的 [同] fake

▲ An artificial flower may last forever.
人造花可永遠保存。

♥ artificial flavors 人工香料

---

4. **blend** [blɛnd] v. 使混和 <with> [同] mix；相稱 <with>

▲ Blend butter and flour before adding the other ingredients.
加入其他材料前，先把奶油和麵粉混和在一起。

blend [blɛnd] n. [C] 混和物

▲ Diego's dance is a blend of modern ballet and tango.
Diego 的舞蹈融合現代芭蕾與探戈舞。

---

5. **container** [kənˋtenɚ] n. [C] 容器；貨櫃

▲ Olivia kept her jewels in an unbreakable container.
Olivia 把她的首飾存放在一個打不破的容器裡。

---

6. **continuous** [kənˋtɪnjʊəs] adj. 不斷的，持續的

▲ There was something wrong with the air-conditioner because it made a continuous noise.
這臺冷氣出了問題，因為它持續發出噪音。

---

7. **contribution** [ˌkɑntrəˋbjuʃən] n. [C][U] 貢獻；捐款 <to> [同] donation

▲ Hawking's black hole theory is a major contribution to the modern science.

霍金的黑洞理論是現代科學的一大貢獻。

8. **depression** [dɪ`prɛʃən] n. [U] 憂鬱，憂鬱症；[C] 不景氣
   ▲ Lily traveled abroad in order to come out of her depression. 為了擺脫憂鬱，Lily 出國旅行。

9. **digital** [`dɪdʒɪtl] adj. 數位的，數字的
   ▲ A digital watch shows the time through digits rather than through hands.
   數位電子錶以數字而非以指針顯示時間。
   🔮 digital camera 數位相機

10. **equality** [ɪ`kwɑlətɪ] n. [U] 平等 [反] inequality
    ▲ Those laborers campaigned for social equality.
    那群勞工為爭取社會平等而發起運動。
    🔮 gender/racial equality 性別 / 種族平等

11. **experimental** [ɪk,spɛrə`mɛntl] adj. 實驗的
    ▲ The new treatment is still in the experimental stage.
    這種新療法還在實驗階段。
    🔮 experimental results/data 實驗結果 / 數據

12. **gallery** [`gælərɪ] n. [C] 畫廊 (pl. galleries)
    ▲ The modern art exhibition at the gallery is worth seeing. 這間畫廊的現代藝術展值得一看。
    🔮 art gallery 藝廊

13. **handwriting** [`hænd,raɪtɪŋ] n. [U] 字跡，筆跡

▲ Will's handwriting is very hard to read, so I have to call him to make sure of what he wants in the letter.
Will 的筆跡很難看得懂，所以我必須打給他以確認他在信上要求什麼。

14. **household** [`haʊs,hold] n. [C] (一戶) 家庭
▲ A growing number of households have pets nowadays. 現今有越來越多家庭養寵物。

household [`haʊs,hold] adj. 家用的
▲ Household chores are not just women's jobs.
家務事不是只屬於婦女的工作。

🌣 household products 家用產品

householder [`haʊs,holdɚ] n. [C] 住戶，居住者
▲ The householders have been informed to store water before the typhoon comes.
住戶已被通知在颱風來前做好儲水工作。

15. **intense** [ɪn`tɛns] adj. 強烈的，激烈的 [同] extreme
▲ The intense heat in the area killed many plants and trees. 這個地區的酷熱讓許多植物和樹木枯死。

🌣 intense pain 劇痛

16. **laboratory** [`læbrə,torɪ] n. [C] 實驗室 (abbr. lab) (pl. laboratories)
▲ Scientists from around the world work together in the cancer research laboratory. 來自世界各地的科學家在這癌症研究實驗室裡攜手合作。

17. **license** [ˈlaɪsn̩s] n. [C] 執照，許可證

▲ Peter passed the driving test and got a driver's license. Peter 通過駕駛考試取得駕照。

♥ under license 經過許可

license [ˈlaɪsn̩s] v. 批准，許可 <to>

▲ The restaurant is licensed to sell alcoholic drinks.
這家餐廳獲准販賣含酒精飲料。

18. **maturity** [məˈtjʊrətɪ] n. [U] 成熟

▲ Despite the young age, Owen showed great maturity when he faced difficulties.
儘管 Owen 年紀輕，他面對困難卻展現高度的成熟。

19. **oxygen** [ˈɑksədʒən] n. [U] 氧氣

▲ We cannot live without oxygen.
我們沒有氧氣不能生存。

20. **psychological** [ˌsaɪkəˈlɑdʒɪkl̩] adj. 心理的，精神的

▲ That child has psychological problems, which prevents him from interacting with other people.
那個孩子有心理上的問題，使他無法跟他人互動。

21. **quotation** [kwoˈteʃən] n. [C] 引文

▲ If you use a quotation in your paper, you must cite the source. 如果你在論文中使用引文，必須說明出處。

22. **research** [ˈrisɚtʃ] n. [U] 研究 <into, on>

▲ The experts are carrying out some research into the effects of music on children.

專家們正在進行一些關於音樂對小孩影響的研究。

💡 do/conduct research 做研究

research [rɪ`sɝtʃ] v. 研究 <into>

▲ Dr. Lin is researching into the causes of cancer and ways to prevent them.

林博士正在研究引發癌症的原因以及預防的方法。

---

23. **resistance** [rɪ`zɪstəns] n. [U] 抵抗 <to>；阻力

▲ When they came to arrest him, the man offered no resistance to the police.

警察來逮捕他的時候，那人沒有反抗。

💡 nonviolent resistance 非暴力抵抗

---

24. **surroundings** [sə`raundɪŋz] n. [pl.] 環境 [同] environment

▲ After Dylan moved to the new city, it took him a few weeks to get used to the new surroundings. 搬到新城市後，Dylan 花了幾個禮拜的時間適應新環境。

---

25. **tolerable** [`tɑlərəbl] adj. 可忍受的 [同] bearable [反] intolerable；尚可的 [同] reasonable

▲ The extreme cold in high mountain areas is barely tolerable to some tourists. 對一些觀光客而言，他們很難忍受高山極度低溫的天氣。

Unit 3

1. **appropriate** [ə`proprɪ͵et] adj. 適合的，合適的，恰當的
   <to, for> [同] suitable [反] inappropriate
   ▲ Jason made a speech highly appropriate to the occasion. Jason 發表了一個非常適合這場合的演講。
   💡 It is appropriate (for sb) to V (…) 做…是合適的

2. **association** [ə͵sosɪ`eʃən] n. [C] 協會 [同] organization；[C][U] 關聯 <between, with>
   ▲ Sally is interested in joining the student association.
   Sally 對於參與學生會很有興趣。
   💡 in association with 聯合…

3. **broke** [brok] adj. 破產的，身無分文的
   ▲ The businessman was flat broke after the investment failed. 投資失利後，這個商人徹底破產了。
   💡 go broke 破產 | go for broke 孤注一擲

4. **brutal** [`brutl] adj. 殘忍的，殘暴的
   ▲ The terrorists were arrested because they had been involved in the brutal attack.
   這些恐怖分子因參與這場暴力攻擊而遭到逮捕。

5. **community** [kə`mjunətɪ] n. [C] 社 區；社 群 (pl. communities)
   ▲ The crime rate is very low in this community.
   這個社區犯罪率很低。

6. **contribute** [kən`trɪbjʊt] v. 貢獻，捐贈 <to>；導致 <to>

▲ Penicillin, a type of antibiotic, has contributed greatly to mankind.
盤尼西林，一種抗生素，對人類有很大的貢獻。

7. **conventional** [kən`vɛnʃənl] adj. 常規的，傳統的 [反] unconventional

▲ Herbal medicine may provide a cure when conventional medicine cannot.
當傳統醫藥無效時，草藥也許能提供療效。

💡 conventional weapons 傳統武器

8. **cooperate** [ko`ɑpə͵ret] v. 合作，協力 <with> [同] collaborate

▲ The children cooperated with their parents in cleaning the rooms. 孩子們和父母親合力打掃房間。

9. **disability** [͵dɪsə`bɪlətɪ] n. [C][U] 身體缺陷，殘疾

▲ The disabled young man never lets his disability prevent him from doing whatever he wants to do. 這位殘障的年輕人從不讓他的身體缺陷阻礙他做想做的事。

💡 disability pension 殘障撫恤金 | learning/physical/mental disability 學習 / 身體 / 心理障礙

10. **essential** [ɪ`sɛnʃəl] adj. 必要的 <to, for> [同] vital [反] dispensable

▲ The sun is absolutely essential to the living things on earth. 太陽對於地球上的生命而言是不可或缺的。

essential [ɪˋsɛnʃəl] n. [C] 必需品 (usu. pl.) [同] necessity

▲ The old couple only brought the bare essentials with them when moving into the retirement home.
這對老夫婦只帶著必備的東西搬進退休之家。

---

11. **establish** [ɪˋstæblɪʃ] v. 建立，創立 [同] found, set up

▲ The oldest theater in this town was established in 1950. 這個小鎮最古老的劇院在 1950 年建立。

establishment [ɪˋstæblɪʃmənt] n. [C] 機構；[U] 建立 <of>

▲ There are many financial establishments set in the downtown business district.
有許多金融機構設立在市中心商業區。

---

12. **fasten** [ˋfæsn̩] v. 固定，繫緊 [同] do up [反] unfasten

▲ To ensure your safety, please fasten your seat belt during the flight.
為確保你的安全，請在飛航期間繫緊安全帶。

💡 fasten on/upon sth 集中注意力於…

---

13. **gene** [dʒin] n. [C] 基因

▲ Although the baby carried a defective gene, he looked normal.
雖然這個嬰兒帶有缺陷的基因，但他看起來很正常。

💡 dominant/recessive gene 顯性 / 隱性基因

---

14. **hardship** [ˋhɑrdʃɪp] n. [C][U] 苦難

▲ The soldier has gone through all kinds of hardships in the war. 這名軍人在戰爭中經歷了種種苦難。

💡 face/endure hardship 面臨 / 忍受苦難

15. **incident** [ˋɪnsədənt] n. [C] 事件

▲ The government refused to comment on the incident at the border. 政府拒絕就邊境的事件發表評論。

💡 without incident 平安無事

incidental [ˌɪnsəˋdɛntl] adj. 附帶的，伴隨的 <to>

▲ The bill includes several incidental charges.
這帳單包含了幾項雜支。

💡 incidental music 配樂

incidentally [ˌɪnsəˋdɛntlɪ] adv. 附帶地，順帶一提 [同] by the way

▲ Incidentally, our flight to Tokyo was canceled owing to the typhoon.
順帶一提，我們前往東京的班機因為颱風取消了。

16. **keen** [kin] adj. 激烈的；渴望的，喜愛的，感興趣的 <on> [同] eager

▲ Our team finally won the championship in the keen competition.
我們的隊伍最後在激烈的競爭中贏得冠軍。

💡 as keen as mustard 極感興趣

keenly [ˋkinlɪ] adv. 強烈地

▲ Bruce was keenly interested in wildlife photography.
Bruce 對野生動物攝影有強烈的興趣。

keenness [ˈkinnɪs] n. [U] 渴望，熱切

▲ Each contestant on the stage showed keenness for success. 每位臺上的參賽者顯得渴望成功。

---

17. **machinery** [məˈʃinərɪ] n. [U] 機器

▲ To reduce personnel expenses, the factory installed some machinery to replace workers. 為了減少人事開支，這間工廠安裝一些機器來取代工人。

---

18. **maximum** [ˈmæksəməm] adj. 最大極限的 (abbr. max)

▲ What is the maximum speed of that sports car? 那輛跑車最快可以開多快？

maximum [ˈmæksəməm] n. [C] 最大限度 (abbr. max) (usu. sing.) <of> (pl. maxima, maximums)

▲ Passengers are usually allowed to take a maximum of 20 kilograms on the flight. 乘客搭機時通常最多只能攜帶二十公斤。

---

19. **measure** [ˈmɛʒɚ] n. [C] 措施 (usu. pl.)；標準

▲ The police have taken strong measures against drunk driving. 警察已採取強烈手段防止酒後駕車。

💡 drastic/tough/extreme measures 嚴厲的 / 強硬的 / 極端的措施

---

20. **penalty** [ˈpɛnl̩tɪ] n. [C] 處罰 [同] punishment；(不利的) 代價 [同] disadvantage <for, of> (pl. penalties)

▲ Anyone who breaks the company rules will face penalties. 任何人違反公司規定將會面臨處罰。

💡 the death penalty 死刑

21. **psychologist** [saɪ`kɑlədʒɪst] n. [C] 心理學家

▲ The psychologist is an expert in child development.
那位心理學家是兒童發展的專家。

💡 clinical psychologist 臨床心理學家

22. **reference** [`rɛfrəns] n. [C][U] 提及 <to>；[C] 推薦函

▲ Greg made several references to his school life in London. Greg 提及一些他過去在倫敦的校園生活。

💡 with reference to 關於

23. **route** [rut] n. [C] 路線；方法 <to>

▲ We took the quickest route from the airport to the hotel. 我們走機場到飯店最快的路線。

💡 an alternative/escape route 替代 / 逃生路線

route [rut] v. 運送，傳送 <through, via>

▲ The new skincare products will be routed via Milan.
新的護膚產品將運送途經米蘭。

24. **tragedy** [`trædʒədɪ] n. [C][U] 悲慘的事；悲劇 (pl. tragedies)

▲ The wedding party ended in tragedy because the restaurant was on fire.
那場結婚派對以悲劇收場，因為餐廳失火了。

25. **universal** [ˌjunə`vɝsl̩] adj. 普遍的，通用的

▲ Extreme weather is a universal problem in the world.
極端天氣是全世界普遍的問題。

💡 a universal truth 普遍真理

universal [ˌjunəˋvɝsl] n. [C] 普遍現象

▲ It seems to be a universal in the world that parents want a better life for their children. 父母親希望子女有更好的生活似乎是全世界普遍的現象。

Unit 4

1. **athletic** [æθˋlɛtɪk] adj. 運動的；強壯的 [同] strong

▲ The athletic competition will be held next week. 運動比賽將於下週舉行。

2. **battery** [ˋbætərɪ] n. [C] 電池 (pl. batteries)

▲ The battery in the camera is dead and we have to replace it with a new one.

相機的電池沒電了，我們必須拿一個新的來替換。

💡 recharge sb's batteries 恢復…的體力 | battery life 電池壽命

3. **behavior** [bɪˋhevjɚ] n. [U] 行為，舉止

▲ Parents should teach their children to distinguish between socially appropriate and inappropriate behavior.

父母必須教導小孩區別社交中適當與不當的行為。

4. **canoe** [kəˋnu] n. [C] (用槳划的) 獨木舟

▲ Bella finally learned how to paddle a canoe by trial and error.

在不斷反覆嘗試後，Bella 最後學會如何划獨木舟。

canoe [kə`nu] v. 划獨木舟

▲ The man canoed along the river through the forest.
這男子划著獨木舟順流穿越森林。

---

5. **constructive** [kən`strʌktɪv] adj. 有建設性的，有用的

▲ The best way to put democracy into practice is to welcome constructive criticism from the opposition parties. 實踐民主的最佳方式就是歡迎反對黨有建設性的意見。

💡 constructive suggestions/advice 有建設性的建議 / 意見

6. **convince** [kən`vɪns] v. 使相信 <of, that>；說服 <to> [同] persuade

▲ The suspect tried hard to convince the judge of his innocence.
這個嫌疑犯努力試著使法官相信他的清白。

convinced [kən`vɪnst] adj. 確信的 <of, that> [反] unconvinced；虔誠的

▲ We are convinced that Ruth will win the race in the end. 我們確信 Ruth 最後將贏得比賽。

convincing [kən`vɪn͵sɪŋ] adj. 有說服力的

▲ No one believed what the politician said because it was not convincing.
沒人相信那位政治人物說的話，因為它沒有說服力。

💡 convincing victory/win 大比數獲勝

---

7. **cooperation** [ko͵ɑpə`reʃən] n. [U] 合作 <with, between>

▲ Since the witness is willing to be in full cooperation with the police, the case will be solved soon.

因為這名目擊證人願意全力配合警方調查，這起案件很快就能破案。

🕯 in close cooperation 緊密合作

8. **cooperative** [ko`ɑpərətɪv] adj. 合作的 [同] helpful [反] uncooperative

▲ The teacher asked the kids to be quiet, but they were not very cooperative.

老師要這些孩子們安靜點，但他們不太配合。

cooperative [ko`ɑpərətɪv] n. [C] 合作企業

▲ Last Sunday, we visited an agricultural cooperative and a rice factory.

上週日我們參觀了一家農業合作社與一間米工廠。

9. **economics** [͵ikə`nɑmɪks] n. [U] 經濟學

▲ Carol received a PhD in economics.

Carol 取得經濟學博士學位。

10. **estimate** [`ɛstəmɪt] n. [C] 估價 <of, for>

▲ The mechanic gave me a rough estimate of NT$8,000 for the repairs.

技工向我粗估修理費為新臺幣八千元。

🕯 a conservative/rough estimate 保守 / 粗略估計

estimate [`ɛstəmet] v. 估計 <at, that>

▲ After the fire, the store estimated the losses at two million NT dollars.
火災過後，該店家估計損失為新臺幣兩百萬元。

11. **ethnic** [`ɛθnɪk`] adj. 民族的，異國風味的
   ▲ Misunderstandings often occur among different ethnic groups. 不同種族間常會發生誤解。
   💡 ethnic clothes/dishes 民族服裝／料理 | ethnic minority 少數民族
   ethnic [`ɛθnɪk`] n. [C] 少數民族的一員
   ▲ We should treat all ethnics with respect.
   我們應該對於所有民族予以尊重。

12. **fetch** [fɛtʃ] v. 拿取，取回 [同] bring
   ▲ Please fetch me a plate from the cupboard.
   請幫我去櫥櫃拿一個盤子來。
   💡 fetch up 偶然來到
   fetch [fɛtʃ] n. [U] 拿取，取回
   ▲ Frank likes to play fetch with his new adopted dog in the yard.
   Frank 喜歡和他新領養的狗在庭院玩拋接遊戲。

13. **guilty** [`gɪltɪ`] adj. 內疚的 <about>；有罪的 <of> [反] innocent (guiltier | guiltiest)
   ▲ Karen felt guilty about forgetting her boyfriend's birthday again.
   Karen 為再次忘記她男友的生日而感到內疚。

💡 guilty conscience 問心有愧 | plead guilty 認罪

---

14. **humanity** [hju`mænətɪ] n. [U] 人類；仁慈

▲ Nuclear weapons are a threat to humanity.
核子武器是所有人類的一大威脅。

---

15. **install** [ɪn`stɔl] v. 安裝 [反] uninstall；正式任命 <as>

▲ Allen installed the new software to increase the processing speed of the computer.
Allen 安裝新的軟體以增加電腦執行的速度。

---

16. **landscape** [`lænskep] n. [C] 風景

▲ The painter depicted beautiful rural landscapes in her recent works.
這位畫家在她近期的作品中描繪美麗的鄉村風景。

landscape [`lænskep] v. 做景觀美化

▲ The city park was landscaped and it attracted many visitors. 城市公園經過美化後吸引了許多遊客。

---

17. **makeup** [`mek,ʌp] n. [U] 化妝品

▲ Many teenagers dress themselves up and wear some makeup for the Halloween parade.
許多年輕人為了萬聖節遊行裝扮自己。

---

18. **motivation** [,motə`veʃən] n. [U] 積極性；[C] 動機 <for>

▲ Emily lacks motivation and seldom involves herself in school activities.

Emily 缺乏積極性，很少參與學校活動。

---

19. **nowadays** [`nauə,dez] adv. 現在，現今 [同] today
▲ Nowadays, women have more opportunities than ever before. 現在女性比以前有更多機會。

---

20. **percentage** [pə`sɛntɪdʒ] n. [C] 百分比
▲ With the popularity of smartphones, a larger percentage of people can get easy access to the Internet.
隨著智慧型手機的普及，更多人能夠輕鬆上網。
💡 percentage points 百分點

---

21. **publisher** [`pʌblɪʃə] n. [C] 出版社
▲ At first, the author had difficulty finding a publisher for her new book.
最初這個作家很難找到出版社為她出新書。

---

22. **reflect** [rɪ`flɛkt] v. 反映 <in>；深思 <on, that>
▲ Wilson was fascinated by the still lake with the big round moon reflected in it.
Wilson 被這有著飽滿圓月倒影的寧靜湖面所吸引。

---

23. **satellite** [`sætḷ,aɪt] n. [C] 人造衛星 <by, via>
▲ People can watch the broadcast of the Olympic Games via satellite.
人們可以透過人造衛星收看奧運轉播。
💡 satellite town 衛星城市，大都市周圍的城鎮

---

24. **tragic** [ˈtrædʒɪk] adj. 悲慘的

▲ The director's death was a tragic loss to the entertainment industry.
這位導演的死對演藝界是個悲痛的損失。

💡 tragic heroes 悲劇英雄

---

25. **vessel** [ˈvɛsl] n. [C] 船 [同] ship；血管

▲ The fishing vessel was finally released ten months after it was hijacked by the pirates.
這艘漁船被海盜劫持十個月後才被釋放。

💡 a rescue/cargo vessel 救生 / 貨船

Unit 5

1. **absolute** [ˈæbsə͵lut] adj. 全然的；絕對的

▲ All of the hockey team members have absolute confidence in the coach's judgment.
所有曲棍球隊員都對於教練的判斷有全然的信心。

💡 in absolute terms 就其本身而言

absolutely [͵æbsəˈlutlɪ] adv. 全然地；當然

▲ Bill's poor health is absolutely related to his bad eating habits.
Bill 身體不好全然地與他不好的飲食習慣有關。

---

2. **annual** [ˈænjʊəl] adj. 一年一度的 [同] yearly；一年的 [同] yearly

▲ To most families in America, the annual celebration of Christmas is a very important event. 對於許多美國家庭而言，一年一度的耶誕節慶祝活動是一大盛事。

💡 annual meeting/report 年度會議 / 報告 | annual fee/budget 年費 / 年度預算

3. **atmosphere** [ˈætməsˌfɪr] n. [C][sing.] 大氣層 (the ~)；[sing.] 氣氛

▲ The toxic gases from these chemical factories caused damage to the atmosphere.
這些化學工廠排放的有毒氣體造成大氣層的汙染。

4. **breed** [brid] n. [C] 品種

▲ The Labrador retriever is my favorite breed of dog.
拉不拉多是我最喜歡的狗品種。

breed [brid] v. 繁殖 (bred | bred | breeding)

▲ The zoologist devotes himself to breeding endangered species.
那位動物學家致力於培育瀕臨絕種的物種。

breeding [ˈbridɪŋ] n. [U] 繁殖

▲ When is the breeding season for pandas?
熊貓的繁殖季節是什麼時候？

5. **cargo** [ˈkɑrgo] n. [C][U] (船或飛機載的) 貨物 (pl. cargoes, cargos)

▲ The cargo ship sank in the Indian Ocean.
這艘貨船在印度洋沉沒。

6. **communication** [kəˌmjunəˋkeʃən] n. [U] 溝通 <in, with, between>

▲ Sue and Eva will be in communication with each other by exchanging emails to practice their reading and writing skills. Sue 和 Eva 將以寫電子郵件的方式互相聯絡以練習讀寫技巧。

7. **consumer** [kənˋsumɚ] n. [C] 消費者

▲ Consumers need protection against dishonest dealers. 消費者須受到保護以對付不肖商人。

♥ consumer demand/rights 消費者需求 / 權益

8. **council** [ˋkaʊnsl] n. [C] (地方、鎮、市的) 政務委員會，議會

▲ The city council decided to build a library near the station. 市議會決議要在車站旁興建一座圖書館。

♥ student council 學生會

9. **critical** [ˋkrɪtɪkl] adj. 批評的 <of>；至關重要的 <to> [同] crucial

▲ Melody is always critical of the clothes her boyfriend wears. Melody 總是批評她男朋友穿的衣服。

♥ critical remark/decision 批判評論 / 重要決定

10. **cruelty** [ˋkruəltɪ] n. [C][U] 殘忍，殘酷 <of>；虐待 <to> [反] kindness (pl. cruelties)

▲ Those old soldiers suffered from the cruelty of the war. Some of them even lost their homes.

那些老兵經歷過戰爭的殘酷。有些人甚至失去他們的家。

▲ Julian was accused of cruelty to cats.
Julian 被指控虐待貓。

---

11. **eventual** [ɪ`vɛntʃuəl] adj. 最後的，最終的

▲ The outstanding runner was the eventual winner of the marathon.
這位傑出的跑者是這場馬拉松賽的最後贏家。

eventually [ɪ`vɛntʃulɪ] adv. 最後，終於

▲ Lydia has written her novel for years and it was published eventually yesterday.
Lydia 撰寫小說多年，昨日小說終於出版了。

---

12. **fiction** [`fɪkʃən] n. [U] 小說 [反] non-fiction；[C][U] 虛構的故事 [反] fact

▲ Nash is addicted to reading crime fiction.
Nash 沉迷於閱讀犯罪小說。

💡 a piece/work of fiction 一部小說

---

13. **genius** [`dʒinjəs] n. [C] 天才；[U] 才智，天賦 (pl. geniuses, genii)

▲ Mozart is a musical genius. 莫札特是個音樂天才。

💡 have a genius for sth 對⋯方面很有天分

---

14. **identical** [aɪ`dɛntɪkl̩] adj. 同樣的 <to, with>

▲ The reproduction looks almost identical to the original. 這件複製品看起來幾乎和原作一樣。

15. **influential** [ˌɪnfluˈɛnʃəl] adj. 有影響力的 <in>
▲ The legislators are influential in deciding on the government's policies.
立法委員對於決定政府的政策是有影響力的。

16. **interpret** [ɪnˈtɝprɪt] v. 解釋 <as>；口譯，翻譯
▲ Blaire's frequent absence from school is interpreted as a lack of interest in learning.
Blaire 經常上課缺席被解釋成缺乏學習興趣。

17. **manufacturer** [ˌmænjəˈfæktʃərə] n. [C] 製造商 [同] maker
▲ The car manufacturer urgently recalled all the defective vehicles.
這個汽車製造商緊急召回所有有瑕疵的車子。

18. **memorial** [məˈmorɪəl] adj. 紀念的，追悼的
▲ Many friends and relatives attended Jackson's memorial service.
很多朋友及親人參加了 Jackson 的追悼會。
memorial [məˈmorɪəl] n. [C] 紀念碑 <to>
▲ The statue was built as a memorial to the soldiers killed in the war. 這個紀念碑是為了戰死的軍人而建。

19. **numerous** [ˈnjumərəs] adj. 許多的，大量的 [同] many
▲ Our office gets numerous phone calls every day.
我們辦公室每天接到無數的電話。
💡 too numerous to mention/list 不勝枚舉

20. **observation** [ˌɑbzɚˈveʃən] n. [C][U] 觀察 <of>；[C] 評論 <on, about>

▲ The patient was kept under close observation in the hospital. 這名病人留院接受密切觀察。

---

21. **predict** [prɪˈdɪkt] v. 預測，預料 <that> [同] forecast

▲ The report predicted that domestic and international travel would increase by the end of the year.
報導預測國內外旅遊到年底前可能會增加。

predictable [prɪˈdɪktəbl̩] adj. 可預測的，可預料的

▲ Andrew felt bored with the drama because the plot was so predictable.
Andrew 對這齣劇感到無聊，因為劇情太好預測了。

---

22. **quarrel** [ˈkwɔrəl] n. [C] 爭吵 <about, over, with>

▲ Ella had a quarrel with her sister about some trivial things last week.
Ella 上星期因一些瑣事和她妹妹吵架。

quarrel [ˈkwɔrəl] v. 吵架 <about, over, with>

▲ Before the couple divorced, they often quarreled over money matters.
這對夫妻離婚前經常因為金錢的問題吵架。

quarrelsome [ˈkwɔrəlsəm] adj. 愛爭吵的 [同] argumentative

▲ Craig is a quarrelsome person, so it's not surprising that he got into an argument with his neighbors. Craig 是一個愛爭吵的人，因此他與鄰居們爭論是不意外的。

23. **reform** [rɪˋfɔrm] n. [C][U] 改革，改進 <of, to>

▲ The government carried out a series of reforms to the educational system.
政府對於教育系統實行了一系列的改革。

💡 push through reforms 使改革通過

reform [rɪˋfɔrm] v. 改革

▲ The citizens hope that the welfare system can be reformed. 市民希望福利制度能進行改革。

reformation [͵rɛfəˋmeʃən] n. [C][U] 改革；[sing.] 宗教改革 (the ～)

▲ Our performance for the last two seasons shows signs of declining and all we need is a radical reformation. 我們上兩季的表現呈現下滑趨勢，現在我們能做的就是徹底的改革。

---

24. **significance** [sɪgˋnɪfəkəns] n. [U] 重要 <of, for, to> [反] insignificance

▲ The winning of this award has great significance to the director. It means that his work has been recognized. 獲獎對這名導演特別重要。這表示他的作品已經受到肯定。

---

25. **transform** [trænsˋfɔrm] v. 徹底改變 <into>

▲ The sleepy town has been transformed into a bustling city. 這座寂靜的小鎮轉變為繁忙的都市。

Unit 6

1. **absorb** [əb`zɔrb] v. 吸收 (液體、氣體等)

   ▲ You can use the sponge to absorb the water on the kitchen floor.

   你可以用海綿把廚房地板上的水吸起來。

   🔍 be absorbed in... 沉迷，沉浸於…

2. **application** [ˌæplə`keʃən] n. [C] 申請 <for>；[U] 應用

   ▲ We regret that your application for a loan has not been accepted. 我們很抱歉你的貸款申請未獲准。

   🔍 fill in/out an application form 填申請表

3. **attraction** [ə`trækʃən] n. [U] 吸引力

   ▲ Horror movies hold no attraction for me.

   恐怖電影對我沒有吸引力。

   🔍 hold/have an attraction for/towards... 對…有吸引力

4. **cabinet** [`kæbənɪt] n. [C] 櫥櫃 [同] cupboard

   ▲ The antique collector had an ancient china cabinet in the living room.

   這位古董收藏家在客廳有個古老的瓷器陳列櫃。

5. **carrier** [`kærɪɚ] n. [C] 運輸工具 (車或船)；搬運工

   ▲ They transported helicopters and troops by a freight carrier. 他們用運輸艦來運送直升機跟軍隊。

   🔍 aircraft carrier 航空母艦

6. **construction** [kən`strʌkʃən] n. [C] 建築物；[U] 建造
   ▲ This temple is a construction made of wood and metal. 這棟廟宇是由木頭和金屬組成的建築物。

7. **contest** [`kɑntɛst] n. [C] 競爭，比賽
   ▲ Ten students entered the contest for a NT$100,000 scholarship, and the most hard-working one won it.
   十名學生競爭新臺幣十萬元的獎學金，而最用功的人得到這筆獎學金。
   contest [kən`tɛst] v. 角逐
   ▲ Robert stands a good chance since only three people are contesting the prize.
   Robert 很有機會，因為只有三個人在角逐此獎項。

8. **criticism** [`krɪtə,sɪzəm] n. [C][U] 批評，挑剔 <of, about> [反] praise
   ▲ There was a lot of criticism of the president's speech.
   總統的演說引起了很多批評。

9. **curiosity** [,kjʊrɪ`ɑsətɪ] n. [U] 好奇心
   ▲ To satisfy my curiosity, I decided to find out the stranger's identity.
   為了滿足我的好奇心，我決定查出這陌生人的身分。
   ♥ out of curiosity 出於好奇 | Curiosity killed the cat.
   【諺】好奇心會害死貓。(過於好奇會惹禍上身)

10. **definite** [`dɛfənɪt] adj. 明確的 [同] clear [反] indefinite
    ▲ What I want is a definite answer.

我要的是一個明確的答覆。

definitely [ˋdɛfənɪtlɪ] adv. 毫無疑問地 [同] certainly

▲ Florida is definitely the best city I've ever been to.
佛羅里達毫無疑問地是我去過最棒的城市。

---

11. **evidence** [ˋɛvədəns] n. [U] 證據 <of, on, for>

▲ Scientists are looking for the evidence of the existence of life on other planets.
科學家們正尋找其他星球有生命存在的證據。

evidence [ˋɛvədəns] v. 透過…證明

▲ This movie was a blockbuster, as evidenced by a box office success.
這部電影是賣座鉅片，透過它成功的票房就能證明。

---

12. **evident** [ˋɛvədənt] adj. 明顯的 [同] obvious, clear

▲ It is evident that hard work will pay off in the end.
顯而易見的，努力工作最後會得到回報。

evidently [ˋɛvədəntlɪ] adv. 顯然地 [同] obviously, clearly；據說 [同] apparently

▲ According to the statistics, evidently, the drug has serious side effects.
根據數據顯示，顯然地，這個藥有嚴重的副作用。

---

13. **flexible** [ˋflɛksəbl] adj. 可彎曲的 [反] rigid；可變通的，靈活的 [同] pliable [反] inflexible

▲ Rubber is a flexible material. 橡膠是可彎曲的材質。

14. **grace** [gres] n. [U] 優雅 <with> [同] gracefulness

▲ The Princess of Wales walked on to the stage with grace. 威爾斯王妃優雅地走上舞臺。

grace [gres] v. 使增添光彩

▲ This character actor graces the whole movie.
這名性格的演員使這部電影增添光彩。

15. **ignorance** [ˋɪgnərəns] n. [U] 無知 <of, about>

▲ I was shocked by the young man's ignorance of his own country's history.
這年輕人對自己國家歷史的無知令我吃驚。

💡 in ignorance of sth 不知道⋯

16. **intention** [ɪnˋtɛnʃən] n. [C][U] 意圖 <of>

▲ Maggie had no intention of attending Sophie's birthday party. Maggie 無意參加 Sophie 的生日派對。

17. **knob** [nɑb] n. [C] 圓形的門把

▲ Terry turned the knob to open the door to the backyard. Terry 轉動圓形門把以打開通往後院的門。

18. **merit** [ˋmɛrɪt] n. [C] 優點 (usu. pl.) <of> [同] strength

▲ PowerPoint presentations have the merit of being clear. PowerPoint 簡報的優點是清晰。

merit [ˋmɛrɪt] v. 值得 [同] deserve

▲ The issue of discrimination certainly merits attention.
歧視議題無疑值得大家關注。

19. **moderate** [ˋmɑdərɪt] adj. 中等的，適度的；普通的
   ▲ Moderate exercise such as walking for half an hour every day is fundamental to good health.
   中等強度的運動如每天步行半小時對健康很重要。

20. **occasional** [əˋkeʒən̩] adj. 偶爾的
   ▲ The weather forecast says it will be cloudy with occasional showers tomorrow.
   氣象預報說，明天是多雲偶爾有陣雨的天氣。
   occasionally [əˋkeʒən̩lɪ] adv. 偶爾
   ▲ We live in different cities, but we meet occasionally for a chat.
   我們住在不同的城市，但是偶爾會碰面聊天。

21. **prime** [praɪm] adj. 首要的 [同] main
   ▲ Asian tourists are the prime target for pickpockets in the area. 亞洲遊客是這個地區扒手們的首要的目標。
   💡 prime minister 首相 | prime number 質數
   prime [praɪm] n. [sing.] 全盛時期
   ▲ John is a successful dancer in the prime of his life.
   John 在他人生中的全盛時期是一個成功的舞者。

22. **rebel** [ˋrɛb̩l] n. [C] 反叛者
   ▲ The rebel forces tried to overthrow the government.
   反叛軍試圖推翻政府。
   rebel [rɪˋbɛl] v. 反抗；反叛 <against, at>
   ▲ In some countries, people will face the death penalty for rebelling against the government.

在某些國家，人民會因反抗政府而面臨死刑。

---

23. **refugee** [ˌrɛfjʊˋdʒi] n. [C] 難民

▲ The volunteers from the charity helped deliver food and clothes to the refugees in Syria. 慈善機構的志工們幫忙分送食物和衣服給敘利亞的難民。

---

24. **spark** [spɑrk] n. [C] 火花

▲ I struck sparks from that flint. 我在打火石上打出火花。

spark [spɑrk] v. 發出火花；引起 [同] cause

▲ The flame of the candle sparked in the wind.
蠟燭的火焰在風中發出火花。

---

25. **tremble** [ˋtrɛmbl̩] v. (通常因寒冷、害怕或情緒激動) 顫抖 <with> [同] quiver

▲ Pamela's hands trembled as she opened the envelope.
Pamela 拆開信封時手在顫抖。

tremble [ˋtrɛmbl̩] n. [U] 顫抖 (a ～)

▲ There was a tremble in his voice. 他的聲音顫抖著。

Unit 7

1. **adequate** [ˋædəkwɪt] adj. 足夠的 <for> [反] inadequate

▲ The food is adequate for five people.
這些食物足夠五個人吃。

adequately [ˋædəkwɪtlɪ] adv. 充足地 [同] sufficiently [反] inadequately

▲ My classmates are not adequately prepared for the final exam. 我同學並沒有充足地準備期末考。

adequacy [ˋædəkwəsɪ] n. [U] 適當性 [反] inadequacy

▲ The adequacy of health care has been brought into question. 醫療保健是否足夠受到質疑。

2. **category** [ˋkætəˏgorɪ] n. [C] 種類，類別 [同] class (pl. categories)

▲ This song falls into the category of K-pop music.
這首歌屬於韓國流行音樂。

categorize [ˋkætəgəˏraɪz] v. 分類 [同] classify

▲ How do biologists categorize animals?
生物學家如何對動物進行分類？

categorization [ˏkætəgəraɪˋzeʃən] n. [U] 分類 [同] classification

▲ The categorization of students according to grades still exists in many schools.
許多學校仍存在著按照成績對學生進行分類。

3. **celebration** [ˏsɛləˋbreʃən] n. [C] 慶祝會；[U] 慶祝

▲ My parents held a celebration on their 25th wedding anniversary. 我父母舉行結婚二十五週年慶祝會。

4. **charity** [ˋtʃærətɪ] n. [C] 慈善事業；[U] 慈悲 (pl. charities)

▲ The charity originates in Sydney, but it has become an international one now. 這個慈善機構源自雪梨，但它現在已經變成國際型的組織。

💡 Charity begins at home. 【諺】慈善從家中做起。

---

5. **competition** [ˌkɑmpə`tɪʃən] n. [C] 比賽；[U] 競爭 <for>

▲ Ella entered the swimming competition and took first place. Ella 參加了游泳比賽並得到了第一名。

---

6. **declare** [dɪ`klɛr] v. 宣布

▲ The new police chief declared war on drugs.
新的警察局長宣布掃毒。

---

7. **delight** [dɪ`laɪt] n. [C] 使人高興的人或物；[U] 高興 <with> [同] joy

▲ Gary takes delight in watching horror movies, so he never misses one.
Gary 喜歡看恐怖片，所以他從來不錯過任何一部。

💡 the delights of sth …的樂趣

delight [dɪ`laɪt] v. 使高興

▲ Jill's good manners delighted her parents.
Jill 良好的行為舉止讓她的父母很開心。

💡 delight in sth 從…中取樂

---

8. **dependent** [dɪ`pɛndənt] adj. 需要照顧的 [反] independent

▲ The man has to be on welfare because he is unemployed and has three dependent children.
這個男子必須靠社會救濟過日子，因為他失業又有三個需要照顧的孩子。

💡 dependent on/upon sth 由…來決定

dependent [dɪˋpɛndənt] **n.** [C] 要照顧的人

▲ You should write down the name of your dependent to complete the application form.
你需要將你要照顧的人的姓名寫下以完成申請表。

dependence [dɪˋpɛndəns] **n.** [U] 依賴 <on, upon> [反] independence

▲ People need to reduce their dependence on oil as a source of energy.
人們需要減少將石油作為能源燃料的依賴。

---

9. **desperate** [ˋdɛspərɪt] **adj.** 拼命的；嚴重的

▲ Trapped in the net, the fish made desperate efforts to escape. 這條魚被網住而拼命的要逃脫。

desperately [ˋdɛspərɪtlɪ] **adv.** 非常地

▲ Mr. Lee seems desperately busy today, so I won't bother him.
李先生今天似乎非常地忙碌，所以我不會打擾他。

desperation [ˌdɛspəˋreʃən] **n.** [U] 奮力一搏

▲ In desperation, the woman jumped out of the window to escape from the fire.
情急之下，女子跳出窗外以逃離大火。

---

10. **exception** [ɪkˋsɛpʃən] **n.** [C][U] 例外

▲ Bruce is a workaholic and works every day, but today is an exception because it is his wedding day.
Bruce 是工作狂，每天都工作，但是今天例外，因為今天是他的結婚日。

💡 make no exception(s) 沒有例外 | take exception to sth/sb 因為…而不悅

11. **fossil** [ˈfɑsl] **n.** [C] 化石
▲ It is surprising that fossils of fish have been found in the rocks gathered from the mountains. 在山上採集到的岩石中竟然發現魚的化石，真是令人驚訝。
fossil [ˈfɑsl] **adj.** 化石的
▲ It's not good for the environment to burn fossil fuels like oil and coal.
燃燒像是石油或煤炭這樣的化石燃料對環境不太好。

12. **guarantee** [ˌgærənˈti] **v.** 保證
▲ I cannot guarantee you will be satisfied with our plan. 我不能保證你會滿意我們的計畫。
guarantee [ˌgærənˈti] **n.** [C] 保證 [同] assurance
▲ No matter how hard you try, there is no guarantee that you will succeed.
無論你多努力也無法保證你會成功。

13. **illustrate** [ˈɪləstret] **v.** 用例子說明 [同] demonstrate
▲ The following examples illustrate how advertisements influence consumer buying behavior.
下列例子說明廣告如何影響消費者的購買行為。

14. **interact** [ˌɪntɚˈækt] **v.** 互動 <with>
▲ Our teacher doesn't allow us to interact with each other during class.

我們的老師不允許我們在課堂上與彼此互動。

---

15. **legend** [ˈlɛdʒənd] n. [C] 傳說
▲ Legend has it that the hero killed a fierce tiger with his bare hands and saved the boy in time. 傳說這英雄徒手殺了一隻凶猛的老虎且及時解救男孩。

---

16. **messenger** [ˈmɛsṇdʒɚ] n. [C] 信差
▲ The messenger delivered this document to the king secretly. 信差祕密地遞送了這份文件給國王。
💡 shoot the messenger 責備帶來壞消息的人

---

17. **multiple** [ˈmʌltəpl̩] adj. 多數的 [同] many
▲ My boss asked me to make multiple copies of the reports before the meeting.
我老闆請我在會議前把報告影印數份。

multiple [ˈmʌltəpl̩] n. [C] 倍數
▲ Thirty five is the lowest common multiple of 5 and 7.
三十五是五和七的最小公倍數。

---

18. **offense** [əˈfɛns] n. [C] 犯罪行為 [同] crime ；[U] 冒犯 <to>
▲ Drug dealing is an offense that can carry the death penalty.
毒品交易是一種可以被判處死刑的犯罪行為。

---

19. **phenomenon** [fəˈnɑməˌnɑn] n. [C] 現象 (pl. phenomena)
▲ A rainbow is a natural phenomenon after the rain.

彩虹是雨後的自然現象。

20. **physical** [`fɪzɪkl̩] adj. 身體的

▲ Physical exercise is good for the body, especially for the heart and circulatory system.
體能運動對身體很好，尤其是心臟與循環系統。

physically [`fɪzɪkl̩ɪ] adv. 身體上地

▲ The tennis player was physically and mentally exhausted after the game.
這名網球球員在比賽過後身心俱疲。

21. **productive** [prə`dʌktɪv] adj. 多產的 [反] unproductive

▲ Alexander is a productive writer and has written three books in the past six months.
Alexander 是多產的作家，過去六個月他寫了三本書。

22. **recall** [rɪ`kɔl] v. 想起 [同] recollect；召回

▲ I can't recall seeing any stranger outside the house then. 我不記得那時有看到任何陌生人在房子外面。

recall [`ri,kɔl] n. [U] 記性；[C] 召回 (usu. sing.) <of>

▲ It is amazing that the little girl has total recall of the long speech. 令人感到驚奇的是這名小女孩清楚記得這段長篇演說。

23. **reluctant** [rɪ`lʌktənt] adj. 不情願的 <to> [反] willing

▲ Although the party was over, the girl was reluctant to leave. 雖然派對結束了，但這女孩不情願離開。

reluctantly [rɪ`lʌktəntlɪ] adv. 不情願地

▲ Kevin reluctantly agreed to go with us.
Kevin 不情願地同意和我們一起去。

---

24. **surgery** [ˋsɝdʒərɪ] n. [U] 外科手術

▲ Walking slowly or stretching muscles can help speed up recovery from heart surgery.
慢走或伸展肌肉有助於加快從心臟外科手術中恢復。

💡 have/undergo/do/perform/carry out surgery 接受 / 執行手術 | surgery on/for sth 在…(部位)/ 為…(疾病) 的手術

---

25. **triumph** [ˋtraɪəmf] n. [C] 大成功，大勝利 <over, of>

▲ The new play was a triumph.
這齣新戲是一次大成功。

triumph [ˋtraɪəmf] v. 戰勝，打敗 <over>

▲ Modern medicine has triumphed over smallpox.
現代醫學戰勝了天花。

triumphant [traɪˋʌmfənt] adj. 勝利的

▲ When they learned that their team had won the game, triumphant shouts were heard everywhere among the students. 一得知他們的球隊贏了比賽，到處都可以聽見學生勝利的歡呼。

Unit 8

1. **admission** [ədˋmɪʃən] n. [C][U] 承認 [同] confession ；
入場許可 <to>

▲ It is generally believed that silence is an admission of guilt. 一般認為緘默即是承認有罪。

2. **circular** [ˋsɝkjələ] adj. 圓形的
   ▲ A large vase full of flowers is sitting in the center of the circular table.
   在圓桌正中央有個插滿花的大花瓶。

3. **collapse** [kəˋlæps] n. [U] 倒塌，瓦解
   ▲ The collapse of the building left 20 people dead.
   這棟建築的倒塌造成二十人死亡。

   collapse [kəˋlæps] v. 倒塌；崩潰
   ▲ The wooden bridge collapsed under the weight of the truck. 木橋在卡車的重壓下倒塌了。

4. **contrast** [ˋkɑntræst] n. [C][U] 對比，對照 <with, to>
   ▲ Tom, by contrast with Bob, is well behaved.
   跟 Bob 對比起來，Tom 很守規矩。

   contrast [kənˋtræst] v. 形成對比，對照 <with>
   ▲ Toby's radical political ideas contrast with the objective views held by his friends. Toby 激進的政治觀點和朋友們的客觀想法形成強烈的對比。

5. **convention** [kənˋvɛnʃən] n. [C][U] 傳統，常規
   ▲ In my country, it is a convention to wear black clothes at funerals.
   在我的國家，喪禮上穿黑色衣服是項傳統。

6. **defeat** [dɪˋfit] n. [C][U] 失敗

▲ Much to our disappointment, we suffered an unexpected defeat in the championship game. 令我們失望的是，我們在冠軍賽中遭受沒有預期到的挫敗。

defeat [dɪˋfit] v. 擊敗 [同] beat

▲ Eventually, Dana defeated the other opponents in the election after months of fierce competition. 經過數個月的激烈競爭，Dana 最終在選舉中打敗其他對手。

7. **deserve** [dɪˋzɝv] v. 值得，應得 <to>

▲ Jeremy deserves the promotion for his good work. 以 Jeremy 良好的工作表現來看，他應該得到晉升。

8. **disorder** [dɪsˋɔrdɚ] n. [U] 凌亂，雜亂 <in> [反] order

▲ The files on Fred's desk were all in disorder.
Fred 桌上的文件亂七八糟。

disorder [dɪsˋɔrdɚ] v. 使失調

▲ Taking too much medicine may disorder your immune system. 吃太多藥可能會使你的免疫系統失調。

disorderly [dɪsˋɔrdɚlɪ] adj. 雜亂的

▲ My cousin's belongings were in a disorderly mess. 我表妹的東西雜亂無章。

9. **distinguish** [dɪˋstɪŋgwɪʃ] v. 區分，區別 <from, between> [同] differentiate

▲ The baby was born color-blind, so he has difficulty distinguishing between red and green.
這名嬰兒生來就是色盲，所以他很難區分紅色和綠色。

10. **exhibit** [ɪg`zɪbɪt] n. [C] 展覽品

▲ All the exhibits at the museum are valuable works of art. 這間博物館的所有展覽品都是珍貴的藝術作品。

exhibit [ɪg`zɪbɪt] v. 展出 [同] display, show

▲ The company exhibited its new products at the trade fair. 這間公司在貿易展中展出新產品。

11. **explosive** [ɪk`splosɪv] adj. 易爆炸的

▲ Firecrackers contain explosive materials and must be handled with care.

鞭炮含有易爆炸的物質，必須小心處理。

explosive [ɪk`splosɪv] n. [C][U] 炸藥

▲ Explosives are sometimes used to blow up a building before a new one can be erected.

炸藥有時候會被用來拆除建築，然後再蓋新的。

12. **frame** [frem] n. [C] 畫框

▲ The portrait of Mr. Lin was put in a wooden frame. 林先生的肖像被鑲在木製畫框中。

frame [frem] v. 鑲了框

▲ A number of their wedding pictures were framed and put on the walls.

他們許多的結婚照鑲了框並掛在牆上。

13. **gulf** [gʌlf] n. [C] 海灣

▲ The Gulf of Mexico is a large ocean basin near the southeastern United States.

墨西哥灣是靠近美國東南方的一大片海洋盆地。

---

14. **immigrant** [ˋɪməgrənt] n. [C] (外來的) 移民
    ▲ New York City with immigrants from all over the world is a melting pot.
    紐約，有來自世界各地的移民，是個大熔爐。

---

15. **invest** [ɪnˋvɛst] v. 投資 <in>
    ▲ Emma invested some of her savings in stocks.
    Emma 投資部分存款在股票上。
    investment [ɪnˋvɛstmənt] n. [C][U] 投資
    ▲ Education is an investment in the future.
    教育是對未來的投資。

---

16. **magnificent** [mægˋnɪfəsn̩t] adj. 壯觀的 [同] splendid
    ▲ They sat on the beach, enjoying the magnificent sunset. 他們坐在沙灘上，欣賞壯麗的日落。
    magnificently [mægˋnɪfəsn̩tlɪ] adv. 極好地
    ▲ Angie is doing magnificently at her new job.
    Angie 把新工作做得極好。
    magnificence [mægˋnɪfəsn̩s] n. [U] 極好；壯麗
    ▲ The audience marveled at the magnificence of the performance. 觀眾對極佳的表演嘆為觀止。

---

17. **miserable** [ˋmɪzrəbl̩] adj. 悲慘的
    ▲ After his parents passed away, the little boy led a miserable life.
    父母過世後，這小男孩過著悲慘的生活。

miserably [ˋmɪzrəblɪ] adv. 悲慘地
▲ The old lady was crying miserably.
老太太痛苦地哭泣。

18. **nevertheless** [ˌnɛvəðəˋlɛs] adv. 不過，儘管如此 [同]
nonetheless
▲ It is raining. Nevertheless, Joe still wants to go jogging. 現在正在下雨。不過 Joe 還是想去慢跑。

19. **oppose** [əˋpoz] v. 反對
▲ The locals strongly opposed the government tearing down the old theater.
當地居民強烈反對政府拆除舊戲院。

20. **profession** [prəˋfɛʃən] n. [C] (需要專業技能的) 職業
▲ Eva was encouraged to go into the legal profession.
Eva 被鼓勵從事法律相關工作。

21. **recovery** [rɪˋkʌvrɪ] n. [sing.][U] 康復 <from>
▲ I hope you make a full recovery from the illness.
祝你從疾病中完全康復。

22. **refer** [rɪˋfɝ] v. 提到，談及 <to, as> (referred | referred | referring)
▲ Michelle often refers to her older sister as her guardian angel.
Michelle 常把姊姊稱作她的守護天使。

23. **representation** [ˌrɛprɪzɛnˋteʃən] n. [U] 代表；代表權

▲ The underprivileged need effective representation in parliament. 弱勢群體在國會中需要有力的代表。

24. **tendency** [ˋtɛndənsɪ] n. [C] (思想或行為等) 傾向 <to> (pl. tendencies)

▲ Susan's tendency to speak ill of her neighbors got herself into trouble.
Susan 喜歡說鄰居壞話的傾向使她陷入麻煩中。

25. **urgent** [ˋɝdʒənt] adj. 緊急的 [同] pressing

▲ The captain of the fishing boat received an urgent message informing him of an approaching typhoon.
漁船船長收到緊急訊息，通知他颱風的逼近。

Unit 9

1. **abandon** [əˋbændən] v. 拋棄

▲ The sailors decided to abandon ship as it began sinking fast.
當船開始快速下沉時，船員們決定要棄船。

abandoned [əˋbændənd] adj. 被拋棄的

▲ An abandoned baby was found in front of my house.
我家門前發現了一個棄嬰。

2. **adopt** [əˋdɑpt] v. 採用；領養

▲ The school adopted a new method of teaching English. 這所學校採用新的英語教學法。

adoption [əˋdɑpʃən] **n.** [U] 採用；[C][U] 收養

▲ The government encourages the adoption of renewable energy in this area.
政府鼓勵這個地區採用再生能源。

3. **civilization** [ˌsɪvl̩əˋzeʃən] **n.** [U] 文明

▲ The nuclear war would end modern civilization.
核子戰爭將終結現代文明。

4. **colleague** [ˋkɑlig] **n.** [C] 同事 [同] co-worker

▲ My husband introduced his colleagues to me at the party. 在宴會中，我丈夫向我介紹他的同事。

5. **creation** [krɪˋeʃən] **n.** [U] 創造 <of>

▲ The only thing that Tom is interested in is the creation of wealth. Tom 唯一有興趣的事是創造財富。

6. **defend** [dɪˋfɛnd] **v.** 防禦，防衛 <against, from>

▲ The soldiers vowed to defend their country against the enemy. 士兵宣誓對抗敵人以保衛國家。

7. **detective** [dɪˋtɛktɪv] **n.** [C] 偵探 (abbr. Det.)

▲ Kobe hired a private detective to find out if his wife had an affair.

Kobe 僱用私家偵探來調查他太太是否有外遇。

detective [dɪˋtɛktɪv] **adj.** 偵探的

▲ Mike is going to adapt the classic detective story for movie.

Mike 將要把這個經典的偵探故事改編成電影。

---

8. **distinguished** [dɪˋstɪŋgwɪʃt] adj. 傑出的
▲ In addition to being a statesman, Churchill was also a distinguished writer.
除了政治家外，邱吉爾也是傑出的作家。

---

9. **economic** [ˌɛkəˋnɑmɪk] adj. 經濟的
▲ The economic situation is getting worse in the shadow of the trade war.
經濟情勢在貿易戰的陰影下越來越糟。

---

10. **exposure** [ɪkˋspoʒɚ] n. [U] 暴露，接觸 <to>
▲ Prolonged exposure to radiation may cause cancer.
長期暴露在輻射中可能會致癌。

---

11. **fulfill** [fʊlˋfɪl] v. 實現，達到 (目標)
▲ Eventually Amy fulfilled her dream of studying abroad. Amy 終於實現了出國讀書的夢想。
fulfillment [fʊlˋfɪlmənt] n. [U] 實現
▲ Maggie was happy about the fulfillment of her dream of being a dancer.
Maggie 對於能夠實現當舞者的夢想相當開心。

---

12. **gender** [ˋdʒɛndɚ] n. [C][U] 性別 [同] sex
▲ The gender of a baby can be known about 4 months after pregnancy.
大約在懷孕後四個月就可以看出嬰兒的性別。

---

13. **harsh** [hɑrʃ] adj. 嚴厲的 [同] severe

▲ The scientist's new scientific theory was met with harsh criticism.

這位科學家的新科學理論受到嚴厲的批評。

14. **including** [ɪnˋkludɪŋ] prep. 包括 (abbr. incl.) [反] excluding

▲ The Thanksgiving feast will cost nearly NT$8,000, including a turkey and several bottles of white wine.

感恩節大餐會花費將近新臺幣八千元，其中包括一隻火雞與數瓶白酒。

15. **infant** [ˋɪnfənt] n. [C] 嬰孩

▲ The infant is sleeping in the cradle.

這嬰孩在搖籃裡睡覺。

16. **investigation** [ɪn͵vɛstəˋgeʃən] n. [C][U] 調查 <of, into>

▲ The police have conducted an investigation into the mysterious murder case.

警方已經開始調查這起離奇的謀殺案件。

💡 be under investigation 正在展開調查中

17. **literature** [ˋlɪtərətʃɚ] n. [U] 文學

▲ With a passion for reading and writing, John chose to major in literature in college. 出於對閱讀和寫作的熱情，John 選擇在大學主修文學。

18. **minister** [ˋmɪnɪstɚ] n. [C] 部長 <of, for>

▲ The Minister of Education is going to give a speech.

教育部長將要發表演說。

---

19. **monitor** [ˈmɑnətɚ] n. [C] 監視器

▲ The security guard is watching the monitors and has to report to his supervisor if there is any unusual activity. 警衛看著監視器，有任何不尋常的活動都要向長官報告。

monitor [ˈmɑnətɚ] v. 監看

▲ The doctor monitored the patient's heartbeat and blood pressure. 醫生監看病人的心跳和血壓。

20. **occupation** [ˌɑkjəˈpeʃən] n. [C] 職業；[U] 占領

▲ Gina's previous occupation was bus driver, but now she works as a server in a restaurant. Gina 先前的職業是公車司機，但是現在在餐廳當服務生。

21. **overlook** [ˌovɚˈluk] v. 忽略；俯瞰

▲ You should not overlook any detail of the contract. 你不該忽略合約的任何細節。

22. **promising** [ˈprɑmɪsɪŋ] adj. 有前途的，有希望的

▲ The boss has decided to hire Tom because he thinks he is a promising young man. 老闆決定僱用 Tom，因為他認為他是個有前途的年輕人。

23. **refusal** [rɪˈfjuzl] n. [C][U] 拒絕

▲ When David asked Linda out, she gave him a flat refusal. 當 David 約 Linda 出去時，她斷然拒絕他。

---

24. **reservation** [ˌrɛzɚˈveʃən] n. [C] 預定

▲ I'll make a reservation for dinner at the famous restaurant. 我要在那家有名的餐廳預定晚餐的位子。

25. **transfer** [ˈtrænsfɚ] n. [C][U] 轉調 (地點、工作、環境) <to>

▲ The police officer asked for a transfer to her hometown. 這警察請求轉調去她的家鄉。

transfer [trænsˈfɚ] v. 搬移 (transferred | transferred | transferring)

▲ The cargo was transferred from the ship to the dock. 貨物從船上搬移到碼頭。

Unit 10

1. **abstract** [ˈæbstrækt] adj. 抽象的 [反] concrete

▲ It is said that children have developed their capability of abstract thinking by the age of twelve.
據說小孩在十二歲時已經發展出抽象思考的能力。

2. **agency** [ˈedʒənsɪ] n. [C] 代理機構 (pl. agencies)

▲ My brother works for a travel agency.
我哥哥在旅行社上班。

💡 through the agency of 由於⋯的推動下

3. **classification** [ˌklæsəfəˈkeʃən] n. [C][U] 分類，類別

▲ There are millions of different classifications of insects.

昆蟲的分類有上百萬種。

---

4. **competitive** [kəm`pɛtətɪv] adj. 競爭的
   ▲ Only those who are creative and innovative can survive in this highly competitive world. 只有具備創造力和創新的人才能在這個競爭激烈的世界中存活。

---

5. **defense** [dɪ`fɛns] n. [C][U] 防禦 <of, against>
   ▲ The high walls were built as a defense against the enemy. 這些高牆是為了防禦敵人而建的。

---

6. **differ** [`dɪfɚ] v. 有區別 <from, in>
   ▲ The United States greatly differs from China in political systems.
   美國與中國在政治體制方面有很大的區別。

---

7. **distribution** [ˌdɪstrə`bjuʃən] n. [C][U] 分配，分發
   ▲ The government officials discussed the unequal distribution of wealth. 政府官員討論財富分配不均。

---

8. **durable** [`djurəbl̩] adj. 耐用的，持久的 [同] hard-wearing
   ▲ Jeans were first made to be durable because they were designed for miners.
   牛仔褲最初做得很耐穿，因為是設計給礦工穿的。

---

9. **extent** [ɪk`stɛnt] n. [U] 程度 <of>
   ▲ The extent of the damage caused by the big fire is still unknown now.

大火造成的損害程度目前仍不清楚。

💡 to the extent of 到達相當程度 | to some extent 到達某種程度 | to such extent 到⋯的程度

---

10. **furthermore** [ˋfɝðɚ͵mor] adv. 而且，此外 [同] moreover

▲ The book is worth reading. It gives useful information, and furthermore, it is interesting.
這本書值得一讀，既提供實用的知識又有趣味。

---

11. **generation** [͵dʒɛnəˋreʃən] n. [C] 一代 (人)，同代人

▲ It takes time and effort to bridge the generation gap between parents and children.
彌補父母與子女間的代溝需要時間和努力。

---

12. **hesitation** [͵hɛzəˋteʃən] n. [C][U] 猶豫

▲ Lance told the truth without the slightest hesitation.
Lance 毫不猶豫地說出真相。

---

13. **impact** [ˋɪmpækt] n. [C][U] 影響，衝擊 <on>

▲ Every important decision we make will have a lasting impact on our future. 每個我們所做的重要決定將對我們的未來有長遠的影響。

impact [ɪmˋpækt] v. 衝擊，對⋯產生影響 <on> [同] affect

▲ The war among the petroleum exporting countries will definitely impact on the prices of gasoline. 這場石油輸出國間的戰爭將絕對會對汽油價格造成衝擊。

---

14. **ingredient** [ɪnˋgridɪənt] n. [C] 材料；成分

▲ I bought all the ingredients needed for making cookies. 我買了做餅乾所需的全部材料。

15. **involve** [ɪnˋvɑlv] v. 包含 [同] entail

▲ My new job involves traveling around the world.
我的新工作包含環遊世界。

involvement [ɪnˋvɑlvmənt] n. [U] 參與，投入 <in, with> [同] participation

▲ The environmentalists' continued involvement in the campaign against the dumping of chemicals in the ocean gradually raised public awareness.
環保人士持續參與反對傾倒化學物在海中的活動漸漸引起公眾的意識。

involved [ɪnˋvɑlvd] adj. 參與

▲ Our teacher encouraged us to get involved in some extracurricular activities.
我們的老師鼓勵我們參與一些課外活動。

16. **modest** [ˋmɑdɪst] adj. 適中的，不大的

▲ All I need is not a mansion but a modest house with a small garden.
我所需要的不是豪宅而是有小花園的小房子。

modestly [ˋmɑdɪstlɪ] adv. 謙虛地

▲ "I would never have succeeded without your help," he said modestly.
他謙虛地說：「如果沒有你的幫忙我不可能會成功。」

17. **needy** [ˋnidɪ] adj. 貧窮的 [同] poor, penniless
(needier | neediest)

▲The woman often donates money to the needy families. 這位女士常常捐錢給貧苦人家。

18. **objective** [əbˋdʒɛktɪv] n. [C] 目標 [同] goal

▲The manager urged her team to achieve the objective of increasing sales by 20%.

經理督促她的團隊要達成增加 20% 銷售量的目標。

objective [əbˋdʒɛktɪv] adj. 客觀的 [同] unbiased [反] subjective

▲As a reporter, Katie tried to give a more objective report of the event.

身為記者，Katie 試著對此事件做更客觀的報導。

19. **overnight** [͵ovɚˋnaɪt] adv. 在晚上，過夜

▲Since we needed to take an early flight, we could only stay overnight at the airport.

因為必須搭早班機，我們只能在機場住一晚。

overnight [͵ovɚˋnaɪt] adj. 一整夜的

▲After an overnight talk, the committee finally reached a conclusion.

經過一整夜的商討，委員會終於達成結論。

20. **peer** [pɪr] n. [C] 同儕 (usu. pl.)

▲The best way to deal with peer pressure is to have confidence in yourself.

應付同儕壓力最好的方法就是對自己有信心。

peer [pɪr] v. 仔細看，費力看 <at, into>

▲ Isabella peered at the approaching figure through the fog. Isabella 盯著霧中接近的身影。

---

21. **prompt** [prɑmpt] v. 促使，導致 [同] provoke

▲ What prompted Jeff to quit the well-paid job?
什麼原因促使 Jeff 辭去這份高薪的工作？

prompt [prɑmpt] adj. 迅速的 [同] immediate

▲ We need a prompt solution to the problem.
我們需要一個迅速的解決之道。

prompt [prɑmpt] n. [C] 給…提詞

▲ Henry gave me a prompt when I forgot my lines on stage. 當我在舞臺上忘了臺詞時，Henry 給我提詞。

promptly [`prɑmptlɪ] adv. 迅速地

▲ Jason replied to the letter promptly.
Jason 迅速地回覆來信。

---

22. **relieve** [rɪ`liv] v. 緩解 (令人不快的局勢)

▲ The new economic policy aims to relieve the inflation. 新經濟政策目的是在減輕通貨膨脹。

relieved [rɪ`livd] adj. 放心的，寬慰的

▲ Lisa felt relieved when her son returned home safely.
當兒子平安歸來時，Lisa 就放心了。

---

23. **restriction** [rɪ`strɪkʃən] n. [C] 限制 <on> [同] limitation

▲ To ensure safety, there is a speed restriction in the residential areas; one can never drive faster than 30 kilometers per hour.

為了保障安全，住宅區有速限；開車時速不得超過三十公里。

---

24. **species** [ˋspiʃɪz] **n.** [C] (生物分類) 種 [同] type (pl. species)

▲ The lion and tiger are two different species of cats.
獅子與老虎是貓科中兩個不同的物種。

---

25. **vast** [væst] **adj.** (數量) 龐大的 [同] huge

▲ Vast amounts of money and effort have been put into the research on causes of cancer.
大量的金錢和努力被投入癌症原因的研究。

Unit 11

1. **accent** [ˋæksɛnt] **n.** [C] 重音；口音

▲ The accent is on the first syllable. 重音在第一音節。

accent [ˋæksɛnt] **v.** 在⋯標上重音

▲ Accent the following words on the proper syllables.
在下列單字的正確音節位置標上重音。

---

2. **adjust** [əˋdʒʌst] **v.** 調整 [同] adapt

▲ Grace adjusted her schedule so that she could make time to visit her friends.
Grace 調整她的行程，以便安排時間去拜訪朋友。

adjustment [əˋdʒʌstmənt] **n.** [C][U] 調整 <to, for>

▲ The mechanic made some adjustments to the brakes.

技工調整過剎車系統。

---

3. **appreciation** [ə͵priʃɪˋeʃən] n. [U] 感謝 <of, for>；鑑賞
   力 <of, for>

   ▲ I want to show them my appreciation by sending
   them a thank-you card.
   我想以寄感謝卡的方式向他們表示謝意。

   💡 in appreciation of... 感謝⋯

---

4. **coarse** [kors] adj. 粗糙的 [同] rough [反] smooth
   (coarser | coarsest)

   ▲ Her hands are red and coarse due to heavy
   housework. 由於繁重的家務，她的手又紅又粗糙。

---

5. **consult** [kənˋsʌlt] v. 商量 <with>

   ▲ I must consult with my advisers before giving you a
   definite answer.
   在給你明確的答案之前，我必須和顧問們商量。

---

6. **defensive** [dɪˋfɛnsɪv] adj. 防禦性的 [反] offensive

   ▲ The troops deployed defensive weapons around the
   town. 軍隊在城鎮周圍部署防禦性武器。

---

7. **despite** [dɪˋspaɪt] prep. 儘管 [同] in spite of

   ▲ Peter went mountain climbing despite the bad
   weather. 儘管天氣不好，Peter 還是去爬山。

---

8. **diligent** [ˋdɪlədʒənt] adj. 勤勉的 <in, about>
   [同] hard-working

▲ The students were diligent in their studies.
學生們勤勉的學習。

---

9. **diverse** [daɪˋvɝs] adj. 各式各樣的；不同的
   ▲ The U.S. is a culturally diverse country.
   美國是一個多元文化的國家。

---

10. **dynasty** [ˋdaɪnəstɪ] n. [C] 王朝 (pl. dynasties)
    ▲ The dynasty ruled for more than three hundred years.
    這個王朝統治超過了三百年。

---

11. **facility** [fəˋsɪlətɪ] n. [sing.] 才能 <for> [同] talent；[C] 設
    施 (usu. pl.) (pl. facilities)
    ▲ Helen has a facility for writing. Helen 擁有寫作的才能。
    💡 public facilities 公共設施

---

12. **goods** [gʊdz] n. [pl.] 商品
    ▲ Household goods are cheaper in this department
    store. 這間百貨公司的家用品價格較便宜。
    💡 deliver/come up with the goods 不負所望

---

13. **incredible** [ɪnˋkrɛdəbl] adj. 不可思議的 [同]
    unbelievable
    ▲ It was incredible that Irene won the first prize.
    真令人無法相信 Irene 竟然得到第一名。

---

14. **inspire** [ɪnˋspaɪr] v. 鼓舞
    ▲ The story of this man inspired many people not to
    give up their dreams.

男子的故事鼓舞許多人不要放棄他們的夢想。

inspiring [ɪnˋspaɪrɪŋ] adj. 鼓舞人心的 [反] uninspiring

▲ I met an inspiring teacher when I was in high school.
我在高中時遇到一位鼓舞人心的老師。

---

15. **insurance** [ɪnˋʃʊrəns] n. [U] 保險

▲ Jenny took out travel insurance before she went abroad. Jenny 出國前投保旅遊險。

insure [ɪnˋʃʊr] v. 投保，給⋯保險 <for, against>

▲ The sculpture is insured for three million dollars.
這個雕塑投保了三百萬元。

---

16. **isolation** [ˌaɪslˋeʃən] n. [U] 孤獨 <from>；隔離 <from>

▲ Living alone may cause a feeling of isolation.
獨居可能會導致孤獨感。

---

17. **monument** [ˋmɑnjəmənt] n. [C] 紀念碑 <to>

▲ People often put up a monument to a famous person in order to remember him or her.
人們常為名人設立紀念碑以紀念他或她。

---

18. **neglect** [nɪˋglɛkt] n. [U] 忽視 <of>；疏於照顧

▲ Jimmy was blamed for neglect of his duty.
Jimmy 因怠忽職守而受責備。

neglect [nɪˋglɛkt] v. 忽視；疏於照顧

▲ Jimmy has neglected his health for years, so he is ill now. Jimmy 多年來忽視了自己的健康，所以他現在生病了。

19. **pace** [pes] n. [C] 一步 [同] step；[U] 步調

▲ When Karen saw Victor, she took a few paces toward him. 當 Karen 看到 Victor 時，她向他邁了幾步。

pace [pes] v. 踱步

▲ Louis was so nervous that he paced up and down in the hall. Louis 緊張到在大廳裡走來走去。

20. **persuasive** [pəˋswesɪv] adj. 有說服力的

▲ Your excuse is not very persuasive. I don't think your teacher will buy it.

你的藉口沒什麼說服力。我想你的老師不會相信的。

persuasively [pəˋswesɪvlɪ] adv. 有說服力地

▲ The lawyer is talking persuasively to the jury.

這位律師正有說服力地對陪審團說話。

21. **philosophy** [fəˋlɑsəfɪ] n. [U] 哲學；[C] 人生哲學 (pl. philosophies)

▲ Luke majors in philosophy in college.

Luke 在大學主修哲學。

22. **pursue** [pəˋsu] v. 從事；追求

▲ Matt left his hometown to pursue a career in journalism in the big city.

Matt 離開家鄉去大城市從事新聞工作。

23. **renew** [rɪˋnju] v. 更新；(中斷後) 再繼續 [同] resume

▲ The toothbrush should be renewed every three months. 牙刷每三個月就需要更換一次。

24. **retreat** [rɪ`trit] n. [C][U] 撤退 [反] advance

▲ The general ordered a retreat of all his soldiers.
將軍下令他所有的士兵撤退。

retreat [rɪ`trit] v. 撤退 <from> [反] advance

▲ The defeated soldiers gave up their weapons and retreated from the battlefield.
敗戰的士兵拋棄武器而且從戰場撤退。

25. **revolution** [ˌrɛvə`luʃən] n. [C][U] 革命 [同] rebellion；旋轉 [同] spin

▲ A bloodless revolution broke out in that country.
那個國家爆發了一場不流血的革命。

Unit 12

1. **acceptance** [ək`sɛptəns] n. [U] 接受

▲ His acceptance into a good college pleased his father.
一所好大學接受他的入學申請令他父親很高興。

2. **access** [`æksɛs] n. [U] 通道 <to>

▲ The main access to the gym is on the right side.
進入體育館的主要通道是在右手邊。

access [`æksɛs] v. (從電腦) 讀取 (資料)

▲ Customers can access their bank accounts by smartphone.
顧客可以經由智慧型手機讀取他們的銀行帳戶。

3. **ashamed** [əˋʃemd] adj. 羞愧的，慚愧的 <of> [反] unashamed
▲ You should be ashamed of your behavior.
你應為自己的行為感到羞愧。

4. **aspect** [ˋæspɛkt] n. [C] 層面 <of> [同] point
▲ We should consider all aspects of the problem.
我們應通盤考量這個問題。

5. **comedy** [ˋkɑmədɪ] n. [C] 喜劇 (pl. comedies)
▲ Unlike tragedies, comedies are meant to make people laugh. 與悲劇不同，喜劇的目的是讓人發笑。

6. **contrary** [ˋkɑntrɛrɪ] n. [C] 相反 (the ~) [同] reverse (pl. contraries)
▲ I thought that he was older than me. However, the contrary was true.
我以為他年紀比我大。然而，事實跟我預期的相反。
contrary [ˋkɑntrɛrɪ] adj. 相反的 <to> [同] opposing
▲ Contrary to all expectations, all went well.
與預料的相反，一切順利。

7. **demonstrate** [ˋdɛmən͵stret] v. 顯示 [同] show
▲ Research has demonstrated that eating fast food frequently is harmful to health.
研究顯示常常吃速食對健康有害。

8. **discipline** [ˋdɪsəplɪn] n. [U] 紀律，訓練

▲ The school enforces strict discipline to ensure that the students obey school rules.
這間學校執行嚴格紀律以確保學生遵守校規。

💡 self-discipline 自我要求

discipline [ˋdɪsəplɪn] v. 處罰；教養

▲ The naughty student is often disciplined by the teacher. 這調皮的學生常被老師處罰。

9. **dominant** [ˋdɑmənənt] adj. 主導的，主要的

▲ Christianity has achieved a dominant position in western thought.
基督教在西方思想中占有主導的地位。

10. **efficiency** [ɪˋfɪʃənsɪ] n. [U] 效率 [反] inefficiency

▲ A good employee is someone who works with efficiency. 一名好員工是工作有效率的人。

11. **fantastic** [fænˋtæstɪk] adj. 極好的 [同] great

▲ Joan had a fantastic time at the costume party last night. Joan 在昨晚的化妝舞會玩得很開心。

12. **infection** [ɪnˋfɛkʃən] n. [U] 感染

▲ Washing hands before eating can efficiently reduce the risk of infection.
飯前洗手能有效降低感染的風險。

13. **instinct** [ˋɪnstɪŋkt] n. [C][U] 直覺，本能 [同] intuition

▲ My instinct tells me that something bad has happened to Maria.

我的直覺告訴我 Maria 遭遇了不好的事。

---

14. **labor** [`leba-`] n. [U] 勞動

▲ The workers who were exploited decided to withdraw their labor. 受剝削的工人決定罷工。

labor [`leba-`] v. 辛勞工作，苦幹 <over>

▲ Ann has labored over the report for three days.
Ann 為這份報告奮鬥三天了。

---

15. **learned** [`lɝnɪd`] adj. 學識淵博的

▲ We like to turn to the learned professor for advice.
我們喜歡向這位學識淵博的教授尋求建議。

---

16. **mild** [maɪld] adj. (天氣) 溫和的

▲ This city is chosen as one of the most livable cities in the world because of its mild climate. 這城市因其溫和的氣候而被選為世界上最適合居住的城市之一。

mildly [`maɪldlɪ`] adv. 溫和地

▲ The man mildly answered the reporter's questions.
這男子溫和地回答記者的問題。

---

17. **mysterious** [mɪ`stɪrɪəs`] adj. 神祕的

▲ The big sunglasses that the woman was wearing covered almost half of her face and made her look mysterious. 那名女子正戴著大墨鏡，幾乎遮住了她的半張臉，讓她看起來很神祕。

mysteriously [mɪ`stɪrɪəslɪ`] adv. 神祕地

▲ The money mysteriously disappeared that night.

那天晚上錢神祕地不見了。

---

18. **occupy** [ˋɑkjəˏpaɪ] **v.** 占領

▲ The army finally occupied the city after a long battle.
歷經長久戰役後，軍隊終於占領了城市。

occupied [ˋɑkjəˏpaɪd] **adj.** 有人使用的

▲ The restroom is occupied. 洗手間有人。

---

19. **passive** [ˋpæsɪv] **adj.** 被動的，消極的

▲ The students are passive in class. They just quietly listen when the teacher lectures. 這些學生在課堂上是被動的。當老師講課時他們僅是安靜聆聽。

---

20. **percent** [pəˋsɛnt] **n.** [C] 百分之⋯

▲ Only thirty percent of the students passed the exam.
只有 30% 的學生通過考試。

---

21. **philosophical** [ˏfɪləˋsɑfɪkl̩] **adj.** 豁達的 <about>

▲ Don't be discouraged and try to be philosophical about this problem.
不要氣餒，試著豁達一點看待這個問題。

philosophically [ˏfɪləˋsɑfɪklɪ] **adv.** 豁達地

▲ Mary and Tommy talked philosophically about death. Mary 和 Tommy 豁達地談論死亡。

---

22. **pursuit** [pəˋsut] **n.** [U] 追趕；追求

▲ The speeding car went through a red light with two police cars in pursuit.

這輛車超速闖紅燈，兩輛警車緊追在後。

23. **rainfall** [`ren,fɔl] n. [C][U] 降雨量
▲ The desert area is characterized by low annual rainfall. 這個沙漠地區以年降雨量低為特色。

24. **reputation** [,rɛpjə`teʃən] n. [C] 名聲，名譽
▲ This college has a good academic reputation.
這所大學具有極高的學術聲望。

25. **revise** [rɪ`vaɪz] v. 修訂，修改
▲ The online dictionary is revised every three months to keep up with the rapidly evolving language.
這網路字典每三個月進行一次修訂，以適應快速發展的語言。

Unit 13

1. **accidental** [,æksə`dɛntl] adj. 意外的 [反] deliberate
▲ The police suspected that the death of the rich businessman was not accidental, so they decided to conduct a closer investigation. 警察懷疑那位富商的死不是意外，所以他們決定進行更詳密的調查。
accidentally [,æksə`dɛntlɪ] adv. 意外地 [反] deliberately
▲ I met my college classmate on the street accidentally.
我在街上巧遇我大學同學。

2. **assistance** [ə`sɪstəns] n. [U] 幫助，援助

▲ Charlie always comes to my assistance whenever I am in trouble. 每當我有困難時，Charlie 總會來幫我。

3. **bankrupt** [`bæŋkrʌpt] adj. 破產的
   ▲ Tom has been declared bankrupt. Tom 被宣告破產。
   bankrupt [`bæŋkrʌpt] v. 使破產 [同] ruin
   ▲ The huge loss would bankrupt the car company.
   此項重大損失將使這家汽車公司破產。
   bankrupt [`bæŋkrʌpt] n. [C] 破產者
   ▲ Stella was declared a bankrupt last year.
   去年 Stella 被宣告破產。
   bankruptcy [`bæŋkrʌpsɪ] n. [C][U] 破 產 (pl. bankruptcies)
   ▲ This large company was forced into bankruptcy.
   這家大公司被迫宣告破產。

4. **code** [kod] n. [C][U] 密碼 (pl. codes)
   ▲ I received a letter written in code, but I didn't know how to break it.
   我收到一封密碼信，但我不知如何破解。
   code [kod] v. 用密碼寫
   ▲ Henry coded his letter to Nicole so that nobody could read it except her and himself. Henry 用密碼寫信給 Nicole，如此一來除了她和他本人之外無人能懂。

5. **commerce** [`kɑmɚs] n. [U] 商業，貿易 [同] trade
   ▲ The government is trying to promote local commerce and industry.

政府正嘗試推廣當地商業及工業。

---

6. **convey** [kən`ve] v. 傳達（思想、感情等）[同] communicate；運送

▲ We can make use of pictures to convey messages to people who cannot read.
我們可以利用圖畫把訊息傳達給不識字的人。

---

7. **dense** [dɛns] adj. 密集的 (denser | densest)

▲ Due to a dense population and limited farmland, fifty percent of the food in the country is imported from abroad. 因為密集的人口及有限的農地，這個國家 50% 的糧食是從國外進口。

---

8. **disguise** [dɪs`gaɪz] v. 假扮，喬裝 <as>

▲ The actress disguised herself as a nun so that no one would recognize her.
這名女演員把自己喬裝成修女好讓別人認不出她來。

disguise [dɪs`gaɪz] n. [C][U] 喬裝，偽裝 <in>

▲ The homeless man sitting on the bench turned out to be a policeman in disguise.
坐在長凳上的流浪漢實際上是警察喬裝的。

---

9. **elementary** [ˌɛlə`mɛntərɪ] adj. 基礎的

▲ Louisa is taking an elementary German course.
Louisa 正在上基礎德文課程。

---

10. **emphasis** [`ɛmfəsɪs] n. [C][U] 強調，重視 <on> [同] stress (pl. emphases)

▲ This senior high school puts great emphasis on academic achievements. 這所高中很重視學業成就。

---

11. **forecast** [`for͵kæst] n. [C] 預報

▲ The weather forecast says that it will be sunny and hot tomorrow. 天氣預報說明天天氣是晴朗炎熱的。

forecast [`for͵kæst] v. 預報 [同] predict (forecast, forecasted | forecast, forecasted | forecasting)

▲ The weatherman is forecasting the weather for tomorrow. 氣象播報員正在預報明天的天氣。

---

12. **informative** [ɪnˋfɔrmətɪv] adj. 給予知識的，提供資訊的 [同] instructive

▲ Linda gave an informative lecture.
Linda 發表了一場具知識性的演說。

---

13. **instruct** [ɪnˋstrʌkt] v. 教導 <in>

▲ The professor instructed us in American literature.
這位教授教導我們美國文學。

---

14. **issue** [ˋɪʃʊ] n. [C] 議題

▲ More and more people focus on environmental issues. 越來越多人關注環境議題。

💡 at issue 討論的焦點

issue [ˋɪʃʊ] v. 公布

▲ The actor issued a denial of the fake news that he was married.
這位演員發表聲明否認不實新聞報導他已婚的事。

15. **largely** [ˋlɑrdʒlɪ] adv. 主要地

▲ His failure is largely due to his laziness.
他的失敗大部分是因為懶惰。

---

16. **objection** [əbˋdʒɛkʃən] n. [C][U] 反對 <to>

▲ They had no objection to giving a party this weekend. 他們不反對這週末舉行派對。

♀ raise an objection to sth 對…提出異議

---

17. **otherwise** [ˋʌðɚˏwaɪz] adv. 否則

▲ Study hard; otherwise, you'll regret it.
用功讀書，否則你會後悔。

---

18. **outcome** [ˋaʊtˏkʌm] n. [C] 結果 <of> [同] result

▲ The outcome of the election surprised everyone.
選舉的結果令大家驚訝。

---

19. **permanent** [ˋpɝmənənt] adj. 永久的 [反] impermanent, temporary

▲ In my opinion, there is little chance of permanent peace in the world. Wars always happen. 依我看，世界上不太可能有永久的和平。戰爭總會發生。

♀ permanent job 固定工作

---

20. **pessimistic** [ˏpɛsəˋmɪstɪk] adj. 悲觀的 <about> [同] gloomy [反] optimistic

▲ My father is pessimistic about the current economic situation. 我的父親對目前的經濟情勢感到悲觀。

21. **portable** [ˋportəbl̩] adj. 手提式的，可攜帶的
   ▲ A portable computer is a computer that can be easily moved from one place to another.
   手提電腦是容易隨身攜帶的電腦。

22. **recognition** [ˌrɛkəgˋnɪʃən] n. [U] 認出；[sing.] 承認 [同] acceptance
   ▲ After reconstruction, the town has changed beyond recognition. 重建後，這城鎮已變得讓人認不出來。

23. **reduction** [rɪˋdʌkʃən] n. [C][U] 減少，縮小 <in, of> [反] increase
   ▲ With the introduction of new energy, there will be a reduction in the prices of oil.
   隨著新能源引進，油價勢必會下降。

24. **resemble** [rɪˋzɛmbl̩] v. 與…相似
   ▲ The twins closely resemble each other. It's almost impossible for others to tell one from the other.
   這對雙胞胎非常相像。旁人幾乎無法分辨他們。

25. **ruin** [ˋruɪn] v. 毀壞 [同] wreck
   ▲ Historians predict that the third world war will ruin all civilization.
   歷史學家預測第三次世界大戰將毀壞所有文明。
   ruin [ˋruɪn] n. [C] 廢墟；[U] 毀壞 [同] destruction
   ▲ These ruins were once the royal palace.
   這些廢墟曾是王宮。

Unit 14

1. **accomplish** [əˋkɑmplɪʃ] v. 完成，實現 [同] achieve
   ▲ The government attempted to accomplish its objective of reducing the unemployment rate.
   政府嘗試達成減少失業率的目標。

   accomplishment [əˋkɑmplɪʃmənt] n. [C] 成果 [同] achievement；[U] 完成
   ▲ The accomplishments of these scientists are amazing.
   這些科學家的研究成果驚人。

2. **authority** [əˋθɔrətɪ] n. [C] 當局；[U] 權力 <to, over> (pl. authorities)
   ▲ The school authorities haven't announced the result of the contest. 學校當局尚未公布競賽結果。

3. **capitalism** [ˋkæpətḷˏɪzəm] n. [U] 資本主義
   ▲ Capitalism is based on free markets of the world.
   資本主義以全球自由市場為基礎。

4. **concentrate** [ˋkɑnsṇˏtret] v. 專心 <on>
   ▲ Simon concentrated on memorizing English words.
   Simon 專心背英文字彙。

5. **cope** [kop] v. (成功地) 應付，處理 <with> [同] manage
   ▲ I have more work than I can cope with.
   我工作多得無法應付。

6. **delicate** [ˋdɛləkət] adj. 易碎的，脆弱的 [同] fragile；精細的

▲ Please handle the delicate china plates with care.
請小心處理這些易碎的瓷碟。

delicately [ˋdɛlɪkətlɪ] adv. 小心翼翼地

▲ The housekeeper placed all the glass containers delicately into a box.
管家小心翼翼地把所有玻璃容器放進盒子。

delicacy [ˋdɛləkəsɪ] n. [C] 佳肴；[U] 易碎 (pl. delicacies)

▲ This stewed soup is considered a delicacy in many Asian countries.
這燉湯在許多亞洲國家被認為是佳肴。

7. **destruction** [dɪˋstrʌkʃən] n. [U] 破壞

▲ The strong earthquake caused widespread destruction. 這場強震造成大範圍的破壞。

8. **dismiss** [dɪsˋmɪs] v. 解散

▲ The teacher dismissed the class as the bell rang.
老師在鈴聲響時下課。

dismissal [dɪsˋmɪsl] n. [C][U] 解僱

▲ The government has introduced a new law on unfair dismissal. 政府對無理解僱定出一項新法規。

9. **eliminate** [ɪˋlɪməˏnet] v. 排除 <from>

▲ To lose weight, Jimmy eliminates fried foods from his diet. 為了減重，Jimmy 將炸物排除在他的飲食外。

elimination [ɪ,lɪmə`neʃən] n. [U] 消除

▲ You may find the answer by a process of elimination. 你可以用消去法得到答案。

---

10. **engineering** [,ɛndʒə`nɪrɪŋ] n. [U] 工程學

▲ My brother majored in electronic engineering in college. 我哥哥在大學主修電子工程。

---

11. **formula** [`fɔrmjələ] n. [C] 方法 <for>；公式 (pl. formulas, formulae)

▲ There is no formula for success. 成功沒有一定的方法。

---

12. **inspiration** [,ɪnspə`reʃən] n. [U] 靈感 <from>

▲ Artists often draw inspiration from natural beauty. 藝術家常從自然美中獲取靈感。

---

13. **instructor** [ɪn`strʌktɚ] n. [C] 教練

▲ The swimming instructor is teaching the beginners how to hold their breath underwater. 游泳教練正在教初學者如何在水底下憋氣。

---

14. **literary** [`lɪtə,rɛrɪ] adj. 文學的

▲ Great literary works stand the test of time with universal themes and profound thoughts. 偉大的文學作品，有普世的主題和深刻的想法，經得起時間的考驗。

---

15. **outstanding** [aʊt`stændɪŋ] adj. 傑出的，優秀的 [同] excellent

▲ With years of hard work, Michael has proven himself to be an outstanding basketball player. 經過多年努力，Michael 證明自己是個傑出的籃球球員。

16. **overthrow** [ˌovɚˈθro] v. 推翻 (overthrew | overthrown | overthrowing)

▲ The civilians overthrew their military government and established a democratic republic.
這群平民推翻軍政府，建立了民主共和國。

17. **photography** [fəˈtɑgrəfɪ] n. [U] 攝影

▲ Fred loves photography, and he even wants to major in it in college.
Fred 熱愛攝影，而且他甚至想在大學主修攝影。

18. **plot** [plɑt] n. [C] (故事的) 情節

▲ The plot of the play is so complicated that I get confused.
這齣戲劇的情節如此複雜，以致於我都搞糊塗了。

plot [plɑt] v. 密謀 <to, against> [同] conspire (plotted | plotted | plotting)

▲ The people plotting to overthrow the government were arrested and executed.
這些密謀推翻政府的人們被逮捕處死。

19. **potential** [pəˈtɛnʃəl] adj. 潛在的 [同] possible

▲ The experts warn of the potential danger of genetically modified foods.

專家警告基因改造食物的潛在危險。

potential [pə`tɛnʃəl] n. [U] 潛力 <for>

▲ The island has great potential for oil drilling.
該小島很具有探勘石油的潛力。

potentially [pə`tɛnʃəlɪ] adv. 潛在地

▲ Some buildings are potentially dangerous after the earthquake. 地震過後有些建築有潛在的危險。

---

20. **preserve** [prɪ`zɝv] v. 維持

▲ The leader hoped to preserve the peace in the area.
領導者希望能維持這個地區的和平。

preserve [prɪ`zɝv] n. [C] 保護區

▲ No camping and hunting are allowed in the forest preserve. 此森林保護區禁止露營及狩獵。

preservative [prɪ`zɝvətɪv] n. [C][U] 防腐劑

▲ No artificial preservatives have been added to this homemade bread.
這自製的麵包裡沒有添加人工的防腐劑。

---

21. **resign** [rɪ`zaɪn] v. 辭職 <from>

▲ The sales manager resigned from the company due to his poor health.
這業務經理因健康問題向公司辭去職務。

22. **resolution** [ˌrɛzə`luʃən] n. [C] 決心 [同] determination

▲ Every year, Karen makes a New Year's resolution, but she never keeps it.
每年 Karen 都會許一個新年新希望，但她從未實現它。

resolute [ˈrɛzəˌlut] adj. 堅決的 [同] determined, headstrong [反] irresolute

▲ The explorer was resolute in carrying out his plan.
探險家堅決執行他的計畫。

resolutely [ˈrɛzəˌlutlɪ] adv. 堅決地

▲ Emma resolutely refused to give up.
Emma 堅決不放棄。

---

23. **retain** [rɪˈten] v. 保留

▲ The company retains the right to change the prices at any time. 本公司保留隨時改變價格的權利。

24. **scenery** [ˈsinərɪ] n. [U] 風景

▲ The breathtaking scenery of Grand Canyon National Park attracts many tourists annually. 大峽谷國家公園令人驚嘆的景色每年都吸引很多觀光客。

25. **theme** [θim] n. [C] 主題

▲ Teenage rebellion is the main theme of the new film.
青少年叛逆是這部新電影的主題。

Unit 15

1. **accuracy** [ˈækjərəsɪ] n. [U] 準確性 [反] inaccuracy

▲ The accuracy of the reports in newspapers is always questionable. 報紙上報導的準確性總是令人質疑。

2. **alcohol** [ˈælkəˌhɔl] n. [U] 酒 (精)

▲ The doctor told the patient not to drink alcohol.
醫生吩咐病人不能喝酒。

---

3. **biology** [baɪ`ɑlədʒɪ] n. [U] 生物學

▲ Biology is mainly the study of plants and animals.
生物學主要是對植物和動物的研究。

biologist [baɪ`ɑlədʒɪst] n. [C] 生物學家

▲ Being a professional biologist, William dedicates himself to biomedical research.
身為專業的生物學家，William 獻身於生物醫學研究。

---

4. **carve** [kɑrv] v. 雕刻 <out of, from>

▲ The sculptor carved the statue out of marble.
這雕刻家將大理石雕刻成雕像。

---

5. **concerning** [kən`sɜnɪŋ] prep. 關於

▲ Mike can't think of any solution concerning the problem. 關於此問題，Mike 想不出任何解決之道。

---

6. **digest** [`daɪdʒɛst] n. [C] 摘要，文摘 [同] summary

▲ My favorite magazine is *Reader's Digest*.
我最喜歡的雜誌是《讀者文摘》。

digest [daɪ`dʒɛst] v. 消化；理解

▲ You should chew your food thoroughly so that it can be digested easily. 你應該細嚼食物以利消化。

---

7. **disaster** [dɪz`æstɚ] n. [C][U] 災禍 [同] catastrophe

▲ It is almost impossible for humans to predict natural disasters.

人類幾乎無法預測天災。

---

8. **district** [ˈdɪstrɪkt] n. [C] 地區，區域
   ▲ Alan lived close to the shopping district of the town.
   Alan 住在城裡的購物區附近。

9. **enormous** [ɪˈnɔrməs] adj. 巨大的 [同] huge, immense
   ▲ Bruce lost an enormous sum of money because of
   bad investments.
   Bruce 因為投資不當而輸掉一大筆錢。

10. **era** [ˈɪrə] n. [C] 時代，年代
    ▲ The new president is taking the country into a new
    era with reforms. 新總統用改革帶領國家進入新時代。

11. **financial** [faɪˈnænʃəl] adj. 財務的
    ▲ More and more companies are faced with financial
    difficulties with the economy going down.
    隨著經濟蕭條，越來越多的公司面臨財務困境。
    financially [faɪˈnænʃəlɪ] adv. 財務地
    ▲ Sam is struggling financially because he doesn't have
    a permanent job.
    Sam 為財務苦苦掙扎，因為他沒有一份固定的工作。
    💡 financially embarrassed 拮据的

12. **fort** [fort] n. [C] 要塞 [同] fortress
    ▲ The general asked his soldiers to hold down the fort.
    將軍要求他的士兵守住要塞。

---

13. **intellectual** [ˌɪntl̩`ɛktʃʊəl] adj. 有智能的

   ▲ To have more intellectual powers, you must read more. 要有知識，就一定要多讀書。

   intellectual [ˌɪntl̩`ɛktʃʊəl] n. [C] 知識分子

   ▲ Many scholars and intellectuals attended the conference on educational reform.
   許多學者和知識分子參加了這個教育改革的會議。

14. **interaction** [ˌɪntɚ`ækʃən] n. [C][U] 互動，交流 <between, with>

   ▲ The interaction between the workers and the management is quite important.
   勞資雙方的互動溝通很重要。

15. **magnetic** [mæg`nɛtɪk] adj. 有磁性的；富有魅力的

   ▲ It is believed that migratory birds can sense the magnetic field of the Earth and thus are able to find their way on their seasonal movements.
   據信候鳥能察覺地球的磁場，因此能夠在季節性的遷徙時找到路徑。

16. **participation** [pɑrˌtɪsə`peʃən] n. [U] 參加，參與 <in>

   ▲ Through active participation in class discussions, students can learn to express their own opinions.
   透過積極參與課堂討論，學生們可以學習表達自己的觀點。

17. **portray** [por`tre] v. 描寫，描繪

▲ The award-winning writer portrays life in the country vividly. 這位得獎的作家生動地描寫鄉村生活。

---

18. **primitive** [`prɪmətɪv] adj. 原始的 [反] advanced, modern

▲ Some primitive tools have been found underground. 有些原始的工具在地底下被發現。

---

19. **privilege** [`prɪvlɪdʒ] n. [C][U] 特權

▲ In ancient times, only the nobles could enjoy the privilege of education.

在古代，只有貴族有受教育的特權。

💡 enjoy/exercise a privilege 享受 / 行使特權

privilege [`prɪvlɪdʒ] v. 給予特權 [同] favor

▲ The policy privileges the wealthy but neglects the poor. 政策給予富人特權但是忽視貧窮的人們。

privileged [`prɪvlɪdʒd] adj. 擁有特權的

▲ As a member of the privileged class, Jack enjoys more benefits than ordinary citizens. 身為特權階級的一員，Jack 比普通的老百姓享有更多的利益。

---

20. **prominent** [`prɑmənənt] adj. 重要的，著名的

▲ Smartphones play a prominent role in our daily lives. 智慧型手機在我們每天的生活中扮演著重要的角色。

prominently [`prɑmənəntlɪ] adv. 突出地

▲ Susan's red hair makes her stand out prominently among the crowd.

Susan 的紅頭髮使她在人群中很突出。

---

21. **reward** [rɪ`wɔrd] n. [C][U] 獎賞，報酬 <for>

▲ My teacher gave me a book as a reward for getting good grades.

我的老師給我一本書作為得到好成績的獎賞。

reward [rɪ`wɔrd] v. 獎賞 <with, for>

▲ The company rewarded its employees with bonuses for their hard work.

公司用獎金獎賞員工的努力工作。

---

22. **rhythm** [`rɪðəm] n. [C][U] 韻律，節奏

▲ We were dancing to the rhythm of the music.

我們隨著音樂的韻律起舞。

rhythmic [`rɪðmɪk] adj. 有節奏的

▲ The rhythmic sound of the rain hitting the tin roof is like a song.

雨有節奏的打在錫屋頂上的聲音就像一首歌。

rhythmically [`rɪðmɪk̩lɪ] adv. 有節奏地

▲ Thomas rhythmically played his drums.

Thomas 有節奏地打鼓。

---

23. **scoop** [skup] n. [C] (挖冰淇淋或粉狀物的) 勺子

▲ Two scoops of ice cream, please. 請給我兩球冰淇淋。

scoop [skup] v. 舀出

▲ The crew were desperately busy scooping out the water from the sinking ship.

船員們拼命地忙著把水舀出在下沉的船外。

24. **shelter** [ˈʃɛltɚ] n. [C] 收容所

▲ Those homeless children stayed temporarily in the shelter. 那些無家可歸的孩童暫時待在這個收容所。

shelter [ˈʃɛltɚ] v. 庇護，保護

▲ Andy was arrested for sheltering the wanted man. Andy 因庇護通緝犯被逮捕。

25. **visual** [ˈvɪʒʊəl] adj. 視覺的，視力的

▲ Using visual aids is a good way to make your speech clearer and more memorable. 使用視覺輔具是讓你的演講更清楚且更難忘的好方法。

visualize [ˈvɪʒʊəlˌaɪz] v. 想像 [同] imagine

▲ Can you visualize what you will be like in ten years? 你能想像自己十年後的樣子嗎？

Unit 16

1. **acid** [ˈæsɪd] n. [C][U] 酸

▲ High concentration of vinegar is a strongly corrosive acid. 高濃度的醋是強腐蝕性的酸。

acid [ˈæsɪd] adj. 酸的

▲ Sugar-free lemonade is quite acid. 無糖檸檬汁相當酸。

💡 acid rain 酸雨

2. **bond** [bɑnd] n. [C] 羈絆，束縛 <between, with>

▲ There is a close bond between the dog and its master. ·

這隻狗和牠的主人之間有著緊密的關係。

bond [bɑnd] v. 黏合 <to>；建立關係 <with>

▲ Sharon used the glue to bond the photo to the wall.

Sharon 用膠水將照片黏在牆上。

3. **campaign** [kæm`pen] n. [C] 活動 <against, for>

▲ The internet celebrity attempted to launch a nationwide campaign against tobacco.

這位網路名人試圖舉辦全國禁菸活動。

💡 advertising campaign 廣告宣傳活動

campaign [kæm`pen] v. 參加活動 <against, for>

▲ The non-governmental organization has been campaigning for human rights.

這個非政府組織一直參與支持人權的運動。

4. **clumsy** [`klʌmzɪ] adj. 笨拙的 (clumsier | clumsiest)

▲ The waiter was so clumsy that he spilled wine on the guest's suit.

這個服務生笨手笨腳的，把酒潑灑到客人的西裝上。

5. **conscience** [`kɑnʃəns] n. [C][U] 良心

▲ Nancy's conscience prevents her from doing anything against the law.

Nancy 的良心不讓她做任何違法的事。

💡 in good conscience 憑良心說

6. **dispute** [dɪ`spjut] n. [C][U] 爭論 <over, with>

▲ The dispute over the construction of the new chemical factory seems never-ending.
有關於設立新的化學工廠的爭論似乎不會結束。

💡 in dispute 在爭論中

dispute [dɪ`spjut] v. 爭論

▲ Whether the educational system should be reformed is a topic that has been hotly disputed recently.
教育制度是否應該被改革至今仍引起激烈的爭論。

---

7. **drill** [drɪl] n. [C] 鑽子；[C][U] 練習，演習

▲ Many children are afraid of the sound of a dentist's drill. 很多小孩害怕牙鑽的聲音。

drill [drɪl] v. 鑽；反覆練習 <in>

▲ The woodpecker drilled some holes in the wood in search of food. 啄木鳥在木頭上鑽一些洞尋找食物。

---

8. **economy** [ɪ`kɑnəmɪ] n. [C] 經濟；[C][U] 節儉 (pl. economies)

▲ The economy was weak, so consumer confidence was low. 經濟疲弱，所以消費者信心不足。

---

9. **evaluate** [ɪ`vælju͵et] v. 評估，評價 [同] assess；鑑定⋯ 的價值

▲ Daniel had to evaluate the situation before making a decision. Daniel 下決定之前必須先評估狀況。

---

10. **expand** [ɪk`spænd] v. 擴大 <into> [反] contract；膨脹

▲ The night market is rapidly expanding into a tourist attraction with booming tourism. 隨著旅遊業的蓬勃發展，這個夜市快速擴大成為觀光景點。

💡 expand on 對⋯詳細說明

---

11. **functional** [ˋfʌŋkʃənl̩] adj. 實用的 [同] utilitarian；功能性的；運作中的

▲ This piece of furniture is both functional and decorative. 這件家具既實用又美觀。

---

12. **intensity** [ɪnˋtɛnsətɪ] n. [U] 強烈，強度 <of>

▲ We are amazed at the intensity of the artist's emotions.
我們對於此藝術家的情感強烈程度感到驚訝。

---

13. **interfere** [ˌɪntəˋfɪr] v. 干涉，介入 <in, with> [同] meddle

▲ Jacob accused me of interfering in his private affairs.
Jacob 指責我干涉他的私事。

---

14. **manual** [ˋmænjʊəl] n. [C] 使用手冊

▲ Vera read the instruction manual carefully before she operated the machine.
Vera 在操作機器前仔細閱讀使用手冊。

manual [ˋmænjʊəl] adj. 用手操作的 [反] automatic；體力的

▲ Bruce will replace the manual machine with an automatic one.

Bruce 將使用自動化機器汰換這臺手動機器。

💡 manual mode 手動模式

---

15. **moreover** [mor`ovɚ] adv. 而且 [同] in addition

▲ Albee decided to buy the house because it is in a good location and, moreover, the price is reasonable. Albee 決定買這間房子，因為地點很好，而且價錢也合理。

---

16. **peculiar** [pɪ`kjuljɚ] adj. 奇怪的 [同] odd；獨特的 <to>

▲ It is peculiar that the car key is nowhere to be found. 奇怪的是汽車鑰匙哪裡都找不到。

peculiarly [pɪ`kjuljɚlɪ] adv. 奇 怪 地；特 別 [同] especially

▲ Dr. Wu has found that some animals behave peculiarly before an earthquake. 吳博士發現有些動物在地震前行為怪異。

---

17. **popularity** [ˌpɑpjə`lærətɪ] n. [U] 受歡迎，流行

▲ With many years of hard work, the actress has finally won worldwide popularity and fame. 經過多年的努力，這位女演員終於贏得世界各地的歡迎和聲譽。

---

18. **possession** [pə`zɛʃən] n. [U] 擁有；[C] 所有物 (usu. pl.) [同] belongings

▲ After her husband passed away, Lily took possession of his house. 在 Lily 丈夫過世後，她繼承他的房子。

💡 in possession of 擁有… | colonial possession 殖民地

---

19. **privacy** [ˋpraɪvəsɪ] n. [U] 隱私

▲ No matter who you are, you have no right to violate others' privacy. 無論你是誰，都無權侵犯他人的隱私。

💡 invade/protect sb's privacy 侵犯 / 保護…的隱私

20. **publication** [͵pʌbləˋkeʃən] n. [U] (書) 出版；公布 <of>；[C] 出版物

▲ The dictionary is ready for publication now.
這本字典目前已經準備出版了。

21. **regarding** [rɪˋgɑrdɪŋ] prep. 關於 [同] concerning, with regard to

▲ The politician refused to give any comments regarding the results of the election.
這個政客拒絕對選舉結果做任何評論。

22. **rural** [ˋrʊrəl] adj. 鄉村的 [反] urban

▲ There are more job opportunities in urban areas than in rural areas. 都市地區的工作機會較鄉村地區多。

23. **scratch** [skrætʃ] n. [C] 刮傷，抓痕

▲ Fortunately, Nick only had some scratches after falling off his bicycle.
幸運地，Nick 從腳踏車上跌下來後只有一些擦傷。

💡 without a scratch 毫髮無傷地

scratch [skrætʃ] v. 搔，抓

▲ Yvonne kept scratching the mosquito bites on her legs. Yvonne 一直抓她腿上的蚊子叮咬處。

24. **sculpture** [ˋskʌlptʃɚ] n. [C][U] 雕塑品

▲ The Museum of Modern Art displays some interesting sculptures.

現代藝術博物館展出一些有趣的雕塑品。

25. **tribal** [ˋtraɪbl̩] adj. 部落的

▲ The tribal chiefs were invited to discuss the issue of wildlife conservation.

部落的首領們被邀請來協商此野生動植物保護議題。

💡 tribal art 部落藝術

Unit 17

1. **academic** [͵ækəˋdɛmɪk] adj. 學術的 [反] non-academic；學業的

▲ Many college students prefer to buy academic books from secondhand bookstores.

許多大學生偏好在二手書店購買學術書籍。

💡 academic subject/qualification 學科 / 學歷

2. **agent** [ˋedʒənt] n. [C] 代理商，代理人；特務

▲ Our agent in Tokyo deals with all our business in Japan.

我們在東京的代理商經辦我們在日本的所有業務。

💡 travel agent 旅行社代辦人

3. **capacity** [kəˋpæsətɪ] n. [C][U] 容量 <of>；能力 <for>

(pl. capacities)

▲ The new movie theater has a seating capacity of 400.
這家新戲院有四百個座位。

💡 storage capacity 儲存容量 | at full capacity (工廠) 全
力生產

4. **circulation** [ˌsɝkjə`leʃən] n. [U] 循環；流傳 <in>；[C]
發行量 (usu. sing.)

▲ Sam gets cold hands and feet because of poor
circulation. Sam 因血液循環差而手腳冰冷。

5. **combination** [ˌkɑmbə`neʃən] n. [C][U] 結合；混和

▲ For Sally, honey and lemon are a perfect
combination. 對 Sally 而言，檸檬和蜂蜜是完美的結合。

💡 combination lock 密碼鎖

6. **conservative** [kən`sɝvətɪv] adj. 保守的；傳統的 [同]
traditional

▲ The conservative views of Eva's parents caused the
family conflict.
Eva 父母的保守觀念導致這場家庭衝突。

conservative [kən`sɝvətɪv] n. [C] 保守者

▲ Some conservatives are strongly opposed to the new
school rule. 一些保守者強力反對學校的新規定。

7. **distinct** [dɪ`stɪŋkt] adj. 有區別的 <from>；明顯的 [反]
indistinct

▲ Visiting a place in person is quite distinct from just
seeing the photo of it.

親自參訪某地和光看照片是相當不同的。

💡 as distinct from 而不是

---

8. **dynamic** [daɪˋnæmɪk] adj. 有活力的 [同] energetic

▲ Mike is a dynamic person, who enthusiastically participates in various activities. Mike 是個充滿活力的人，他熱中參與各式各樣的活動。

---

9. **ensure** [ɪnˋʃʊr] v. 確保 <that>

▲ Please ensure that all the students have got on the tour bus before you set off for the next destination. 出發前往下一個目的地前，請你確保所有學生都已經上遊覽車了。

---

10. **explosion** [ɪkˋsploʒən] n. [C][U] 爆炸；[C] (情感) 爆發；激增

▲ The huge explosion of the bombs could be heard in the distance. 從遠方就可以聽到炸彈的爆炸巨響。

💡 gas/nuclear explosion 氣體 / 核爆炸

---

11. **facial** [ˋfeʃəl] adj. 臉部的

▲ From her father's facial expressions, Dana could tell that he was very disappointed.
從父親臉上的表情看來，Dana 看得出他很失望。

💡 facial recognition 臉部辨識

---

12. **furious** [ˋfjʊrɪəs] adj. 狂怒的 <with, about, at, that>；猛烈的

▲ The boss got furious with me about the serious mistake I had made.

老闆對我所犯下的嚴重錯誤感到震怒。

---

13. **intensive** [ɪnˋtɛnsɪv] adj. 密集的

▲ Erin took an intensive course in German for her trip to Germany.

Erin 為了去德國的旅行修了德文的密集課程。

💡 intensive training 密集訓練

---

14. **lousy** [ˋlaʊzɪ] adj. 糟糕的，差勁的 (lousier | lousiest)

▲ What a lousy day! The heavy rain ruined our plan.

多麼糟的一天！大雨毀了我們的計畫。

---

15. **minimum** [ˋmɪnəməm] adj. 最小的，最少的 (abbr. min)

▲ The cost of living is high, so the government is considering raising the minimum wage.

生活費用很高，所以政府考慮調高最低工資。

minimum [ˋmɪnəməm] n. [C] 最小限度；最小值 (abbr. min) (pl. minima, minimums)

▲ The project will take a minimum of ten days.

這件工作至少要花十天。

---

16. **polish** [ˋpɑlɪʃ] n. [sing.] 擦亮；[C][U] 上光劑

▲ Andy gave his shoes a polish before going to work this morning.

Andy 今天早上上班前先把他的鞋子擦亮。

polish [ˋpɑlɪʃ] v. 擦亮

▲ Zoe spent the entire afternoon polishing the floor carefully. Zoe 花了一整個下午仔細將地板擦亮。

💡 polish up 改進，加強技能

17. **precise** [prɪ`saɪs] adj. 精確的，準確的 [同] exact

▲ Sonar is often used to pinpoint the precise location of schools of fish.
聲納通常被用來確定魚群的精確位置。

💡 to be precise 確切的說

precisely [prɪ`saɪslɪ] adv. 精確地，準確地

▲ The police have not figured out precisely what caused the car accident.
警方還未查出造成這場車禍的確切原因為何。

18. **realistic** [ˌrɪə`lɪstɪk] adj. 實際的，務實的 <about>；逼真的

▲ When you make a promise, you have to be realistic about your capabilities.
當你在做出承諾時，要實際考量自己的能力。

19. **satisfaction** [ˌsætɪs`fækʃən] n. [U] 滿意 <with, from> [反] dissatisfaction

▲ The doctor gained satisfaction from seeing his patients getting well.
醫生從看見病人痊癒中得到滿足感。

💡 to sb's satisfaction 讓…滿意的是

20. **signature** [`sɪgnətʃɚ] n. [C] 簽名

▲ It's illegal to forge others' signatures.
偽造他人簽名是違法的。

💡 put sb's signature to sth 在…上簽…的名字

signature [ˋsɪgnətʃɚ] adj. 專屬於某人的，招牌的

▲ Fish stew is one of Jessie's signature dishes.
燉魚是 Jessie 的招牌菜之一。

---

21. **site** [saɪt] n. [C] (建物的) 位置 <of, for>；遺跡

▲ This fire truck rushed to the site of the burning factory after getting the report.
接到通報後，消防車趕往失火工廠的位置。

site [saɪt] v. 座落於

▲ The new children's hospital will be sited next to the city hall. 新的兒童醫院將會座落於市政府旁。

---

22. **slight** [slaɪt] adj. 輕微的，少量的 [反] big；苗條的，瘦小的 [反] stocky

▲ There is only a slight difference between the male and female birds. 這些公鳥與母鳥只有些微的不同。

💡 not in the slightest 一點也不

slight [slaɪt] n. [C] 輕視，冷落 [同] insult

▲ Kate suffered slights from her sons because they had a big fight last night.
Kate 受到兒子的冷落，因為他們昨晚大吵一架。

slight [slaɪt] v. 冷落，輕視 [同] insult

▲ Greg felt slighted because his colleagues didn't invite him to the barbecue party. Greg 覺得受到冷落，因為

他的同事沒邀請他去烤肉派對。

23. **status** [`stetəs] n. [C][U] 地位，身分；[C] 狀況 (usu. sing.) (pl. statuses)

▲ Women's social status has been raised over the years.
女性的社會地位在這幾年已被提升。

🍃 marital status 婚姻狀況

24. **transportation** [ˌtrænspɚ`teʃən] n. [U] 交通工具；運輸

▲ No means of transportation is accessible to the remote mountain hut.
沒有任何交通工具可以到達那偏僻的山間小屋。

25. **volunteer** [ˌvɑlən`tɪr] n. [C] 志工

▲ The retired diplomat works in the school as a volunteer to help those with reading difficulties.
這位退休的外交官在學校擔任義工，幫助閱讀有困難的學生。

volunteer [ˌvɑlən`tɪr] v. 自願 <for, to>

▲ The kind man volunteered to help those in need in return for the help he had received in the past.
這位善心人士自願幫助貧困的人，以回報他過去曾受過的恩惠。

Unit 18

1. **acquire** [ə`kwaɪr] v. 獲得 [同] obtain；學會

▲ Kyle managed to acquire the out-of-print book after a long search.

經過長久搜尋後，Kyle 設法取得了這本已絕版的書。

2. **ancestor** [ˈænsɛstə] n. [C] 祖先 [同] forebear；原型，先驅 <of> [同] forerunner

▲ In search of his roots, Henry wants to find out where his ancestors came from.

為了尋根，Henry 想要找出祖先來自何處。

3. **artistic** [ɑrˈtɪstɪk] adj. 藝術的；有藝術造詣的

▲ The chef is famous for the artistic presentation of his dishes. 這位主廚以其藝術般的擺設菜餚而著名。

4. **circumstance** [ˈsɝkəmˌstæns] n. [C] 狀況 (usu. pl.)；情勢

▲ The poor family's financial circumstances don't allow them to buy a house or even rent one. 這個貧苦家庭的財務狀況不允許他們買房子甚或是租房子。

5. **comment** [ˈkɑmɛnt] n. [C][U] 評論 <about, on>

▲ Do you want to make any comments about the service at the restaurant?

你對這家餐廳的服務有任何意見嗎？

💡 No comment. 不予置評。

comment [ˈkɑmɛnt] v. 發表意見 <on, that>

▲ The piano teacher commented favorably on Leo's performance. 鋼琴老師讚賞 Leo 的演出。

6. **concrete** [kɑnˋkrit] adj. 具體的
   ▲ Ivy won't understand unless you give her a concrete example. 除非給 Ivy 具體的例子，否則她不會明白。
   💡 concrete evidence 具體的證據
   concrete [ˋkɑnkrit] n. [U] 混凝土
   ▲ The sidewalk is made of concrete.
   這條人行道是混凝土做的。
   concrete [kɑnˋkrit] v. 用混凝土修築
   ▲ The construction workers are concreting the road outside the store.
   建築工人正在用混凝土修築商店外的道路。

7. **consistent** [kənˋsɪstənt] adj. 一致的，符合的 <with>；始終如一的
   ▲ The professor's lectures are not always consistent with what the textbook says.
   這名教授的授課內容並不總是與課本上說的一致。

8. **device** [dɪˋvaɪs] n. [C] 裝置
   ▲ With the advances in technology, many clever electronic and medical devices are introduced to the market.
   隨著科技進步，許多精巧的電子和醫療裝置問世了。
   💡 Bluetooth device 藍牙裝置

9. **distribute** [dɪˋstrɪbjut] v. 分送，分發 <to> [同] give out
   ▲ The church distributed food and clothing to the poor.

教堂分送食物和衣物給窮人。

---

10. **electronics** [ɪˌlɛk`trɑnɪks] **n.** [U] 電子學

▲ Ronan decided to major in electronics in college.
Ronan 決定在大學主修電子學。

---

11. **expose** [ɪk`spoz] **v.** 暴露 <to>；揭露，揭發 [同] reveal

▲ Firefighters are often exposed to danger.
消防隊員常處於危險中。

---

12. **fame** [fem] **n.** [U] 名譽

▲ The pop singer rose to fame as soon as his first album was released.
這位流行歌手一發行第一張專輯就迅速成名。

💡 fame and fortune 名利

---

13. **formation** [fɔr`meʃən] **n.** [U] 組成 <of>；形成 <of>

▲ After years of war, the formation of the new government seems to bring people some hope. 歷經多年戰爭後，新政府的組成似乎帶給人民一些希望。

💡 in formation 以⋯隊形

---

14. **generosity** [ˌdʒɛnə`rɑsətɪ] **n.** [U] 慷慨，大方 <to>

▲ The superstar's profound generosity to the poor has won her the title "the kindest woman on Earth."
這位巨星對窮人的極度慷慨使她贏得「地球上最仁慈女性」的封號。

---

15. **intimate** [ˋɪntəmɪt] adj. 親密的

▲ Only intimate friends were invited to Terry's party.
只有親密好友獲邀參加 Terry 的派對。

intimate [ˋɪntəmɪt] n. [C] 密友

▲ Colin is an intimate of mine. I always share my life with her.
Colin 是我的密友。我總是和她分享我的生活。

---

16. **luxurious** [lʌgˋʒʊrɪəs] adj. 豪華的

▲ This five-star hotel is regarded as one of the most luxurious hotels in Japan.
這間五星級的飯店被認為是日本最奢華的飯店之一。

---

17. **mutual** [ˋmjutʃʊəl] adj. 互相的

▲ Friendship should be based on mutual understanding and trust. 友誼應以彼此的了解和信任為基礎。

♥ mutual friend 共同朋友

mutually [ˋmjutʃʊəlɪ] adv. 互相地

▲ Sam and Vicky will find a mutually convenient location for their next meeting. Sam 和 Vicky 將會找到一個對於下次會議互相方便的地點。

♥ mutually exclusive 互斥的

---

18. **possess** [pəˋzɛs] v. 擁有

▲ Heroes in comic books, such as Superman and Spider-Man, possess super power.
漫畫裡的英雄如超人和蜘蛛人擁有超能力。

19. **prevention** [prɪˋvɛnʃən] n. [U] 預防 <of>

▲Jimmy has been working on the prevention of lung cancer for years.

Jimmy 多年努力在找出預防肺癌的方法。

💡 Prevention is better than cure. 【諺】預防勝於治療。

20. **recipe** [ˋrɛsəpɪ] n. [C] 食譜 <for>

▲Lena has a special recipe for lemon cake, which is popular among her friends.

Lena 有個特別的檸檬蛋糕的食譜，很受她朋友歡迎。

21. **scarcely** [ˋskɛrslɪ] adv. 幾乎不 [同] hardly ；一…就… [同] hardly, barely

▲We could scarcely see anything through the thick fog. 我們在濃霧中幾乎什麼都看不見。

22. **software** [ˋsɔft͵wɛr] n. [U] 軟體

▲Don't forget to install anti-virus software on your new computer. 不要忘了在你的新電腦安裝防毒軟體。

23. **solar** [ˋsolɚ] adj. 太陽的，太陽能的

▲A solar panel is used to convert energy from the sun into electricity. 太陽能板被用來把太陽能轉換成電力。

💡 solar system 太陽系

24. **submarine** [ˋsʌbmə͵rin] n. [C] 潛水艇

▲The submarine was attacked by a destroyer and soon sank to the bottom of the sea.

這艘潛水艇受到驅逐艦攻擊並且很快沉入海底。

submarine [`sʌbməˌrin] adj. 海底的，海面下的

▲ Students are watching a video about how submarine cables are laid under the sea.

學生們正在觀看海底電纜如何被安置於海底的影片。

---

25. **virus** [`vaɪrəs] n. [C] 病毒；電腦病毒 (pl. viruses)

▲ Monkeypox virus was first discovered in monkeys at a Danish lab. 猴痘病毒最初是在丹麥一間實驗室的猴子體內發現的。

♥ virus infection 病毒感染

Unit 19

1. **adapt** [ə`dæpt] v. 使適應 <to>；改編 <for>

▲ It usually takes me one month to adapt to a new environment. 我通常需要一個月適應一個新的環境。

adaptable [ə`dæptəbl] adj. 能適應的 <to>；適應力強的

▲ Cockroaches are adaptable to a wide range of environments. 蟑螂能適應廣泛的環境。

---

2. **apparent** [ə`pɛrənt] adj. 顯而易見的 [同] obvious

▲ With the evidence at the scene of the crime, it is apparent that the man is guilty.

有了在犯罪現場的證據，這名男子顯然有罪。

apparently [ə`pɛrəntlɪ] adv. 明顯地

▲ Bob looked sad when he got the report card. Apparently, he didn't do well on the final exams.

Bob 拿到成績單時看上去很傷心。顯然，他的期末考試成績不好。

---

3. **composition** [ˌkɑmpə`zɪʃən] n. [U] 構成；(音樂) 創作
▲ The scientist is studying the composition of the fossil to find clues about how the species evolved.
尋找有關這物種如何進化的線索，這名科學家正在研究此化石構成內容。

---

4. **concentration** [ˌkɑnsn̩`treʃən] n. [U] 專注，專心 <on>
▲ When playing tennis, you should have all your concentration on the ball.
打網球時，你應該要將注意力集中在球上。
💡 lose concentration 失去專注

---

5. **construct** [kən`strʌkt] v. 建造 <from, out of, of>
▲ The high-rise building is constructed of steel and concrete. 這棟大樓是用鋼筋混凝土建造而成。

---

6. **content** [`kɑntɛnt] n. [U] 內容；[pl.] 內容物；目錄 (~s)
▲ Although the novel is selling well, I think it lacks content. 雖然這本小說賣得很好，我覺得它內容空洞。
content [kən`tɛnt] adj. 滿足的，滿意的 <with, to>
▲ Ed, who has high expectations of himself, isn't content with his first live performance.
Ed 自我期望很高，對他第一次現場表現不滿意。
content [kən`tɛnt] v. 使滿足，使滿意

▲ Rachel contented herself with a glass of red wine after working overtime.

加班後的一杯紅酒就讓 Rachel 很滿足。

contentment [kən`tɛntmənt] n. [U] 滿足

▲ The exhausted man gave a sigh of contentment when taking a hot bath.

這個筋疲力盡的男人在泡熱水澡時發出滿足的嘆息。

---

7. **demand** [dɪ`mænd] n. [C] 要求 <for, on> ; [U] 需要 <for>

▲ Since Ivy's current job makes great demands on her time, she has no time for her hobby. 因為 Ivy 目前工作要投入很多時間，所以她沒空從事她的嗜好。

💡 on demand 在有需求時

demand [dɪ`mænd] v. 要求 <that>

▲ The police demanded that the criminal should drop his weapon. 警方要求罪犯放下武器。

💡 demand sth from sb 向⋯要求⋯

demanding [dɪ`mændɪŋ] adj. 要求高的

▲ The physics class is very demanding; Sean has to spend three hours every day doing the required assignments. 這門物理課要求很高，Sean 每天必須花三個小時寫規定的作業。

---

8. **earnest** [`ɝnɪst] adj. 認真的，誠摯的

▲ The passionate young man has an earnest desire to do something beneficial to society.

這個熱情的年輕人熱切希望能對社會做些有益的事。

earnest [ˋɝnɪst] n. [U] 認真 <in>

▲ The research team works in earnest, hoping to find a cure for the rare disease. 這個研究團隊認真地工作，希望能找出治療罕見疾病的方法。

9. **elsewhere** [ˋɛls͵wɛr] adv. 別處

▲ This piece of jewelry is one of a kind; you won't be able to find anything like this elsewhere.
這件珠寶獨一無二，你在別的地方絕對找不到一樣的。

10. **feedback** [ˋfid͵bæk] n. [U] 回饋 <on, from>

▲ The feedback from the audience on the new movie was quite negative.
觀眾對於新電影的回饋是相當負面的。

11. **founder** [ˋfaʊndɚ] n. [C] 創立者

▲ A monument was put up in front of the hospital in memory of its founder.
一個紀念碑被立在醫院的前面以紀念它的創立者。

12. **genuine** [ˋdʒɛnjʊɪn] adj. 真正的 [同] real, authentic [反] false；真誠的 [同] sincere

▲ The shoes are more expensive because they are made of genuine leather. 這鞋比較貴因為是真皮做的。

genuinely [ˋdʒɛnjʊɪnlɪ] adv. 確實

▲ Howard was genuinely interested in classical music.
Howard 確實對古典音樂有興趣。

13. **graduation** [ˌgrædʒʊˋeʃən] n. [C][U] 畢業 (典禮)
    ▲ After graduation from college, Sean went to Singapore to work for the sake of a higher salary.
    為了較高薪，Sean 大學一畢業就去新加坡工作。

14. **invade** [ɪnˋved] v. 侵略；侵犯
    ▲ The troops planned to invade tonight.
    軍隊計劃今晚要侵略。

15. **invention** [ɪnˋvɛnʃən] n. [C][U] 發明；捏造的故事
    ▲ With the invention of the Internet, we can easily connect with people around the world. 隨著網路的發明，我們可以容易地與世界各地的人聯繫。

16. **manufacture** [ˌmænjəˋfæktʃɚ] n. [U] 大量生產
    ▲ Recycled materials are used in the manufacture of various products such as shoes, clothes, and even stadium seats. 回收材料被用於生產各種產品，例如鞋子、衣服甚至還有運動場椅子。
    manufacture [ˌmænjəˋfæktʃɚ] v. (大量) 生產；捏造
    [同] fabricate
    ▲ The factory manufactures good-quality parts, and thus its market share is high.
    這間工廠生產優質的零件，因此市占率很高。

17. **namely** [ˋnemlɪ] adv. 即，也就是說
    ▲ That restaurant is popular for two reasons, namely good food and low prices.

那家餐廳受歡迎有兩項原因，即美食與低價。

---

18. **procedure** [prəˋsidʒɚ] n. [C] 程序，步驟 <for>

▲ George followed standard procedures for setting up the printer. George 遵循標準程序裝設印表機。

---

19. **promotion** [prəˋmoʃən] n. [C][U] 促銷 <of>；升遷；[U] 促進 <of>

▲ The supermarket is doing a special promotion of Japanese cookies. 這家超市正在做日本餅乾的促銷。

---

20. **remarkable** [rɪˋmɑrkəbl̩] adj. 非凡的；引人注目的 <for>

▲ With great effort, David made remarkable progress in English. David 的英文因為努力有非凡的進步。

remarkably [rɪˋmɑrkəblɪ] adv. 非凡 [同] surprisingly

▲ Helen performed remarkably well in the speech contest. Helen 在演講比賽中表現非常地好。

---

21. **secure** [sɪˋkjʊr] v. 獲得；保衛 <against, from>；拴牢 <to sth>

▲ Naomi worked so hard to secure the top in the team. Naomi 為了在團隊裡取得最高地位很努力工作。

secure [sɪˋkjʊr] adj. 安心的 [反] insecure；安全的 <against, from>；堅固的 (securer | securest)

▲ Saving money makes Maya feel secure about the future. 存錢讓 Maya 對未來感到安心。

💡 secure job/income 可靠的工作 / 收入

22. **spare** [spɛr] adj. 備用的 (sparer │ sparest)

▲ Stanley put the spare key in the mailbox just in case.
  Stanley 把備用鑰匙放在信箱中，以防萬一。

💡 spare time 空閒時間

spare [spɛr] v. 抽出 (時間)；避免

▲ Though Hank is busy, he still spares some time to play basketball with his son every week.
  雖然 Hank 忙碌，他仍每週抽出時間和他兒子打籃球。

spare [spɛr] n. [C] 備用品

▲ Jasmine's skirt got stained with oil, but fortunately she has a spare in her bag. Jasmine 的裙子沾上油汙，但幸好她包包裡有備用的裙子。

---

23. **suspicious** [sə`spɪʃəs] adj. 懷疑的，可疑的 <of, about>

▲ It is a small town, so the local people are suspicious of strangers.
  這是個小城鎮，所以當地人對陌生人存有戒心。

---

24. **tortoise** [`tɔrtəs] n. [C] 陸龜

▲ Unlike many turtles, most tortoises live in dry regions.
  不像許多海龜，大部分的陸龜住在乾燥的地區。

---

25. **website** [`wɛb͵saɪt] n. [C] 網站

▲ Please visit our website to get more information about the products we sell.
  請上我們的網站了解我們銷售產品的更多資訊。

Unit 20

1. **aggressive** [əˋgrɛsɪv] adj. 有攻擊性的；積極的
   ▲ Some dogs are aggressive by nature.
   有些狗天生具有攻擊性。

---

2. **alternative** [ɔlˋtɜnətɪv] adj. 可替代的；非傳統的，另類的
   ▲ There is no alternative means of transportation to the town except the bus.
   到鎮上除了公車外沒有其他可替代的交通工具。
   💡 alternative energy 可替代能源
   alternative [ɔlˋtɜnətɪv] n. [C] 可替代的方案或選項 <to>
   ▲ We wonder if there is an alternative to the business plan. 我們想知道是否有這個商業計畫的可替代方案。
   💡 have no alternative but to V 除了…別無選擇
   alternatively [ɔlˋtɜnətɪvlɪ] adv. 要不，或者
   ▲ You can take a flight to Green Island or alternatively get there by boat.
   你可以搭飛機去綠島或者是搭船也可以到那裡。

---

3. **anxiety** [æŋˋzaɪətɪ] n. [U] 焦慮 <about, over> [同] concern；渴望 <to, for>
   ▲ There is growing public anxiety over the soaring house prices. 大眾對高漲的房價越來越焦慮。

---

4. **associate** [əˋsoʃɪˏet] adj. 副的

▲ The associate director remarked on the new science fiction movie in the press conference.

這名副導演在記者會上談論到新的科幻電影。

associate [əˋsoʃɪˏet] n. [C] (生意) 夥伴，同事 [同] colleague

▲ Nydia is one of my business associates.

Nydia 是我其中一位生意夥伴。

associate [əˋsoʃɪˏet] v. 聯想 <with>

▲ People usually associate Paris with the latest fashions. 人們經常將巴黎與最新流行聯想在一起。

---

5. **concept** [ˋkɑnsɛpt] n. [C] 概念，觀念 <of, that>

▲ Ben has no concept of money management. No wonder he often borrows money from his friends.

Ben 沒有金錢管理概念。難怪他總是和他的朋友借錢。

---

6. **consequence** [ˋkɑnsəˏkwɛns] n. [C] (常指不好的) 結果 <of, for>

▲ If you are going to do something risky, you should be prepared to take the consequences.

如果你要做有風險的事情，你就該準備好承擔後果。

💡 of little consequence 不重要的

---

7. **consume** [kənˋsum] v. 消耗；攝取

▲ The new model of smartphone consumes less electricity than the old one.

新款的智慧型手機較舊款的更不耗電。

8. **curse** [kɝs] n. [C] 詛咒 <on, upon>

▲ In the fairy tale, the witch put a curse on the arrogant prince. 在這則童話中，<u>巫婆對傲慢的王子下詛咒</u>。

curse [kɝs] v. 詛咒，咒罵 <for>

▲ Tony cursed the man for hitting his car.
Tony 咒罵那個撞到他車子的男子。

9. **diversity** [daɪˋvɝsətɪ] n. [U] 多樣性 ; 差異 (usu. sing.) <of> [同] variety

▲ Singapore is known for its cultural and linguistic diversity. 新加坡以文化和語言多樣性聞名。

💡 biological diversity 生物多樣性 | a diversity of opinions 不同的看法

10. **elastic** [ɪˋlæstɪk] adj. 有彈性的

▲ Wearing pants made of elastic materials offers more comfort when you do exercise.
運動時穿彈性布料做成的褲子會比較舒服。

elastic [ɪˋlæstɪk] n. [U] 鬆緊帶

▲ Claire used a piece of elastic to make a belt loop.
Claire 使用一條鬆緊帶做成一條腰帶。

11. **encounter** [ɪnˋkaʊntɚ] n. [C] 邂逅 , 不期而遇 <with, between>

▲ Wilson had an encounter with his uncle during his flight to Sydney.
Wilson 在飛往雪梨途中巧遇他的叔叔。

encounter [ɪnˋkaʊntɚ] v. 不期而遇；遭遇

▲ Fanny encountered her ex-boyfriend in the restaurant. Fanny 在餐廳巧遇她的前男友。

💡 encounter difficulties/resistance 遭遇困難 / 抵抗

---

12. **foundation** [faʊn`deʃən] n. [C] 地基 (usu. pl.)；基金會；基礎；[U] 建立

▲ The builders have been digging the foundations for two weeks. 建築工人已經挖地基挖了兩週。

---

13. **fundamental** [ˌfʌndə`mɛntl] adj. 基礎的，基本的 [同] basic；重要的 <to> [同] essential

▲ As a senior employee, you shouldn't have made such a fundamental mistake.
身為資深員工，你不應犯如此基本的錯誤。

fundamental [ˌfʌndə`mɛntl] n. [C] 基本原則 (usu. pl.)

▲ Rebecca taught the new staff the fundamentals of the customer service.
Rebecca 教導新員工關於客戶服務的基本原則。

---

14. **grateful** [`gretfəl] adj. 感激的，感謝的 <for, to> [反] ungrateful

▲ Sandy is grateful for all her parents have done for her. Sandy 對於她父母親為她所做的一切心懷感激。

---

15. **identify** [aɪ`dɛntəˌfaɪ] v. 辨別 <as>；有同感 <with>

▲ The experienced police officer successfully identified the beggar as the murderer.
這位經驗豐富的警官成功辨別出這乞丐就是謀殺犯。

16. **invasion** [ɪn`veʒən] n. [C][U] 侵略，入侵 <of>；侵犯 <of>

▲ The Nazi invasion of Poland led to the outbreak of World War II.
德國納粹入侵波蘭造成第二次世界大戰爆發。

17. **marathon** [`mærə͵θɑn] n. [C] 馬拉松賽跑

▲ Albert broke his own record in the marathon last month.
Albert 在上個月的馬拉松賽跑打破他自己的紀錄。

♥ run the marathon 參加馬拉松

18. **opera** [`ɑpərə] n. [C][U] 歌劇

▲ Elaine and her family are going to watch an opera tonight. Elaine 和她的家人今晚要去看歌劇。

♥ Taiwanese opera 歌仔戲

19. **professional** [prə`fɛʃənl] adj. 職業的；專業的

▲ Richard is a professional photographer, who has taken many great photos.
Richard 是位職業攝影師，他拍出了許多好作品。

♥ professional training 專業訓練

professional [prə`fɛʃənl] n. [C] 專家，專業人士

▲ You should consult with a health professional before taking these supplements.
在服用這些營養補充物前，你該先諮詢保健專家。

20. **profitable** [`prɑfɪtəbl̩] adj. 賺錢的，獲利的 [反] unprofitable

▲ The publishing business is not highly profitable because few people want to buy paper books now.
出版業不怎麼賺錢，因為現在很少人願意買紙本書。

21. **proposal** [prə`pozl̩] n. [C] 提議；求婚

▲ Eddie's proposal was turned down because few people agreed on it.
Eddie 的提議因很少人贊同而被否決。

🍏 put forward/submit a proposal 提出提議

22. **remedy** [`rɛmədɪ] n. [C] 療法 <for> [同] cure；補救辦法 <for> [同] solution (pl. remedies)

▲ An effective remedy for the rare disease has not been discovered so far.
目前還沒有找到有效治療此罕見疾病的療法。

🍏 beyond remedy 無藥可救

remedy [`rɛmədɪ] v. 補救 [同] put right

▲ Sammy tried to find a way to remedy the problem.
Sammy 嘗試找尋方法去補救問題。

23. **spiritual** [`spɪrɪtʃʊəl] adj. 精神的，心靈的 [反] material

▲ The Bible brings many people spiritual comfort in times of sorrow.
《聖經》為許多人在悲傷時刻帶來精神慰藉。

24. **split** [splɪt] v. 劈開 <in>；分成 <into> (split｜split｜splitting)

▲ Lightning split the trunk in two.
閃電把樹幹劈成兩半。

split [splɪt] n. [C] 分歧 <between, in, within> [同] rift；裂縫

▲ The new policy has caused a split between the opposition and the government.
新政策導致反對黨與政府之間產生了分歧。

25. **sympathetic** [ˌsɪmpə`θɛtɪk] adj. 有同情心的 <to> [反] unsympathetic

▲ We are sympathetic to those who lost their families in the natural disasters.
我們同情那些在天災中失去家人的人。

💡 lend a sympathetic ear to sb 以能同理的態度傾聽⋯的問題

Unit 21

1. **analyze** [`ænḷˌaɪz] v. 分析

▲ The assignment is to analyze the main theme of the novel. 作業是要分析小說的主題。

2. **assemble** [ə`sɛmbḷ] v. 集合 [反] disassemble

▲ Angry workers assembled in front of the factory, asking for higher pay and better working conditions.

憤怒的工人聚集在工廠前面，要求加薪和改善工作環境。

---

3. **bridegroom** [`braɪd,grum] n. [C] 新郎 (also groom)

▲ The bride and the bridegroom exchanged vows at the altar. 新郎與新娘在聖壇交換誓言。

---

4. **chorus** [`korəs] n. [C] 合唱團 [同] choir

▲ Boris sings with the Taipei City Chorus.
Boris 是臺北市立合唱團的一員。

---

5. **confusion** [kən`fjuʒən] n. [C][U] 混亂；困惑

▲ Rumors of war threw the stock exchange into confusion. 戰爭的謠言使股票市場陷於混亂。

---

6. **criticize** [`krɪtə,saɪz] v. 批評 <for> [反] praise

▲ The policy was criticized for its unreasonable demand. 此政策因其不合理要求而飽受批評。

---

7. **cushion** [`kuʃən] n. [C] 坐墊，靠墊 (also pillow)

▲ There are no chairs in this room, and we have to sit on the floor cushions.
這房間裡沒有椅子，我們必須坐在地板坐墊上。

cushion [`kuʃən] v. 對⋯起緩衝作用

▲ Lisa's fall was cushioned by the deep snow.
深的積雪對 Lisa 的跌落起緩衝作用。

💡 cushion the blow 緩解打擊

---

8. **embassy** [`ɛmbəsɪ] n. [C] 大使館 (pl. embassies)

▲ If you lose your passport abroad, report to the police
and contact the embassy.
如果你在國外遺失護照，向警方報案並與大使館連絡。

9. **emerge** [ɪ`mɝdʒ] v. 出現 <from, into>

▲ Dr. Lee emerged as a strong rival to the president.
李醫生以總統勁敵之姿出現。

10. **frequency** [`frikwənsɪ] n. [U] 頻率，次數 <of>

▲ The high frequency of his phone calls annoyed me.
他高頻率的來電打擾了我。

11. **globe** [glob] n. [C] 地球儀；世界 (the ~)

▲ The father used a globe to teach his children about
geography. 父親用地球儀教授孩子地理學。

12. **hatred** [`hetrɪd] n. [U] 憎恨，敵意

▲ The leader of the political party was accused of
stirring up racial hatred.
這個政黨的領袖被指控激起種族仇恨。

13. **imaginative** [ɪ`mædʒə,netɪv] adj. 富有想像力的 [同]
inventive [反] unimaginative

▲ The imaginative writer has created many good
stories. 這位想像力豐富的作家創作出許多精采的故事。

14. **insert** [ɪn`sɝt] v. 插入 <in, into, between>

▲ The old man's hands are too shaky to insert the key
into the lock.

這位老人的手顫抖得太厲害以致於無法將鑰匙插入鎖中。

insert [ˋɪn,sɝt] n. [C] 插頁

▲ The newspaper has an insert on the new products.
報紙上有新產品的插頁。

15. **leisurely** [ˋliʒɚlɪ] adj. 悠閒的

▲ Penny and I enjoyed a leisurely brunch at home on Sunday. 我和 Penny 週日在家吃悠閒的早午餐。

16. **mislead** [mɪsˋlid] v. 誤導 (misled | misled | misleading)

▲ The sly criminal tried to mislead the police into believing the story he made up.
這名狡猾的犯人試著用他編造的故事來誤導警方。

misleading [mɪsˋlidɪŋ] adj. 易誤導的

▲ Many advertisements give misleading information to consumers. 很多廣告給消費者容易誤導的資訊。

17. **muddy** [ˋmʌdɪ] adj. 泥濘的 (muddier | muddiest)

▲ The road became muddy and slippery after the rain.
雨後道路變得泥濘和溼滑。

18. **partial** [ˋpɑrʃəl] adj. 部分的；偏心的 [同] biased [反] impartial

▲ The patient may only make a partial recovery.
這位病人僅部分的康復。

💡 be partial to sth 偏好，喜好…

19. **prosperous** [ˋprɑspərəs] adj. 繁榮的，成功的 [同] affluent
   ▲ The small town has changed into a prosperous city
   because of rapid industrial development.
   因為工業快速的發展，這個小鎮已經變成繁榮的城市。

20. **psychology** [saɪˋkɑlədʒɪ] n. [U] 心理學
   ▲ Alex is interested in the human mind and behavior,
   so he wants to major in psychology. Alex 對於人類
   的心智與行為很感興趣，所以想要主修心理學。

21. **robber** [ˋrɑbɚ] n. [C] 搶劫犯
   ▲ The bank robber was arrested this morning.
   銀行搶劫犯今天早上被捕。

22. **singular** [ˋsɪŋgjələ] adj. 單數的；特別的
   ▲ The singular form of "thieves" is "thief."
   thieves 的單數形是 thief。
   singular [ˋsɪŋgjələ] n. [sing.] 單數 (the ∼)
   ▲ "Child" is the singular of "children."
   child 是 children 的單數。

23. **stab** [stæb] n. [C] 刺傷；突然的一陣感覺 <of>
   ▲ The robber died from a stab to the stomach.
   搶劫犯因為腹部刺傷而死亡。
   💡 have/make a stab at sth 嘗試
   stab [stæb] v. 刺 <in> (stabbed | stabbed | stabbing)
   ▲ The robber stabbed the woman in the chest.
   搶劫犯刺傷那女子的胸部。

💡 stab sb in the back 陷害…

24. **syllable** [ˋsɪləbl] n. [C] 音節
  ▲ There are three syllables in the word "restaurant."
  restaurant 這個字有三個音節。

25. **vacancy** [ˋvekənsɪ] n. [C] (職位) 空缺 <for> (pl. vacancies)
  ▲ There is a vacancy for manager in the marketing department. 行銷部門有開經理職缺。

Unit 22

1. **appoint** [əˋpɔɪnt] v. 委任，任命 <as>
  ▲ Hank was appointed as manager of the sales department. Hank 被任命為業務部門的經理。
  appointment [əˋpɔɪntmənt] n. [C] (相) 約 <with>；
  [C][U] 任命 <as>
  ▲ Mike has an appointment with me at noon.
  Mike 中午與我有約。
  💡 by appointment 按約定

2. **assembly** [əˋsɛmblɪ] n. [C] 集會 (pl. assemblies)
  ▲ The assembly consisted of people who concerned about human rights. 那集會由關心人權的人士組成。

3. **broom** [brum] n. [C] 掃把
  ▲ My mother bought a new broom to clean the floor.

我母親買了一支新掃把來掃地。

💡 a new broom sweeps clean 新官上任三把火

---

4. **civilian** [sə`vɪljən] adj. 一般平民的

▲ You cannot tell he is a general because he is in civilian clothes.

因他身穿便服，你無從得知他是一名將軍。

civilian [sə`vɪljən] n. [C] 平民

▲ The missile hit the village and killed hundreds of innocent civilians.

飛彈擊中村莊，使數百位無辜的平民喪命。

---

5. **congratulate** [kən`grætʃə͵let] v. 恭喜 <on>

▲ Let me congratulate you on your marriage.

祝你們締結良緣。

congratulation [kən͵grætʃə`leʃən] n. [U] 祝賀；[pl.] 恭喜 (你) <on> (～s)

▲ The president received a lot of calls of congratulation on her election victory.

總統接到許多通祝賀她勝選的電話。

---

6. **curve** [kɜv] n. [C] 轉彎

▲ Drive carefully because there is a sharp curve in the road. 要小心開車，因為這條路有個急轉彎。

💡 ahead of/behind the curve 跟上潮流 / 落伍 | throw sb a curve 給…出難題

curve [kɜv] v. 彎曲

▲ The road curves sharply to the right.

這條路向右急轉彎。

---

7. **defensible** [dɪˋfɛnsəbl] adj. 易於防守 (also defendable)
   [反] indefensible
   ▲ A castle built on a cliff is defensible.
   蓋在峭壁上的城堡易於防守。

8. **empire** [ˋɛmpaɪr] n. [C] 帝國
   ▲ In the 6th century, the Byzantine emperor ruled a
   vast empire stretching from Europe to Asia and to
   North Africa. 六世紀時，拜占庭帝王統治橫跨歐、亞
   及北非的大帝國。

9. **enclose** [ɪnˋkloz] v. 隨信附上；圍繞
   ▲ The man enclosed a check with this letter.
   男子隨信附上支票一張。

   enclosure [ɪnˋkloʒɚ] n. [C] 附件
   ▲ Details of the proposal can be found in the
   accompanying enclosure.
   你可以在附件裡看到企劃案的細節。

10. **freshman** [ˋfrɛʃmən] n. [C] 大一新生 (pl. freshmen)
    ▲ One of the traditions in this college is to give a party
    to welcome the freshmen.
    這所大學的傳統之一就是舉辦派對歡迎大一新生。

11. **grammar** [ˋgræmɚ] n. [U] 文法
    ▲ There are too many errors of grammar in your
    composition.

你的作文有太多文法上的錯誤。

---

12. **hawk** [hɔk] n. [C] 鷹

▲ Kevin can see really well; he has eyes of a hawk.
Kevin 可以看得很清楚,他的眼睛如鷹一般銳利。

hawk [hɔk] v. 叫賣 [同] peddle

▲ Rita hawks fruit in the street. Rita 在街上叫賣水果。

---

13. **imitation** [ˌɪmə`teʃən] n. [C][U] 模仿 <of>

▲ The comedian did an imitation of that politician and had his audience roaring with laughter.
這名喜劇演員模仿那位政客,使觀眾大笑不已。

---

14. **intuition** [ˌɪntu`ɪʃən] n. [U] 直覺 <that>

▲ The monk has an intuition that something terrible is going to happen. 這位僧侶直覺有壞事要發生。

---

15. **liar** [`laɪɚ] n. [C] 說謊的人,騙子

▲ The boy is the biggest liar that I have ever met.
男孩是我見過最會說謊的人。

---

16. **misunderstand** [ˌmɪsʌndɚ`stænd] v. 誤解
(misunderstood | misunderstood | misunderstanding)

▲ Don't misunderstand me. I've no intention of offending anybody.
不要誤會我。我沒有要冒犯任何人的意思。

misunderstanding [ˌmɪsʌndɚ`stændɪŋ] n. [C][U] 誤會

▲ They must have had a misunderstanding.

他們之間一定曾經有誤會。

---

17. **nationality** [ˌnæʃənˈælətɪ] n. [C][U] 國籍 (pl. nationalities)

▲ Nicky was born in New York City, so he has American nationality.
Nicky 在紐約市出生，所以他有美國國籍。

💡 dual nationality 雙重國籍

---

18. **partnership** [ˈpɑrtnɚˌʃɪp] n. [U] 合夥關係，夥伴關係

▲ My aunt has gone into partnership with a friend to start a restaurant. 我阿姨和朋友合夥開了一家餐廳。

---

19. **publicity** [pʌbˈlɪsətɪ] n. [U] 宣傳

▲ Emma thinks the actor's love affair is just a publicity stunt.
Emma 認為這位男演員的戀情只是個宣傳噱頭。

---

20. **publish** [ˈpʌblɪʃ] v. 出版，發表

▲ The fans are all very excited that the new volume of the comic book is finally published.
粉絲們都很興奮這部漫畫終於出版最新一集了。

---

21. **rusty** [ˈrʌstɪ] adj. 生鏽的 (rustier | rustiest)

▲ Will stainless steel go rusty? 不鏽鋼會生鏽嗎？

---

22. **sketch** [skɛtʃ] n. [C] 素描 <of>

▲ Suzanne drew a rough sketch of the mountain before it rained. Suzanne 在下雨前粗略地畫下了山的素描。

💡 sketch from nature 寫生

sketch [skɛtʃ] **v.** 畫素描

▲ The little boy is sketching the panda in the zoo.
那個小男孩正在動物園裡畫熊貓。

💡 sketch sth in 提供關於…的細節 | sketch sth out 概述

---

23. **stem** [stɛm] **n.** [C] (花草的) 莖

▲ The sunflower has a tall flower stem.
向日葵有高聳的花莖。

💡 from stem to stern 從頭到尾

stem [stɛm] **v.** 起源於 ，由…造成 <from> (stemmed |
stemmed | stemming)

▲ Tim's failure obviously stemmed from a lack of
planning. Tim 的失敗很明顯地是由於缺乏計劃。

---

24. **technician** [tɛk`nɪʃən] **n.** [C] 技師

▲ As a car technician, Anne is so good that she can fix
any car within 12 hours. 身為汽車技師，Anne 非常優
秀所以能在十二小時內修好任何車。

---

25. **violate** [`vaɪə,let] **v.** 違反，違背 [同] flout

▲ Anyone who violates the law will be punished
cruelly in the country.
任何人在這個國家犯法都會受到嚴厲處罰。

Unit 23 📖

1. **aquarium** [əˋkwɛrɪəm] **n.** [C] 水族箱 (pl. aquariums, aquaria)

   ▲ There is an aquarium in our living room.
   我們的客廳裡有一個水族箱。

2. **assign** [əˋsaɪn] **v.** 定出 <for>；指派

   ▲ We assigned a date for the next meeting.
   我們決定出了下次開會的日期。

   💡 assign sb to sth 指派…做

   assignment [əˋsaɪnmənt] **n.** [C] 工作

   ▲ My assignment was to obtain the necessary money.
   我的工作是籌措需要的款項。

   💡 on assignment 執行任務

3. **bulletin** [ˋbʊlətn̩] **n.** [C] 公告；新聞快報

   ▲ Sam put an ad on the bulletin board.
   Sam 在公告欄上貼了一則廣告。

4. **clarify** [ˋklærə͵faɪ] **v.** 闡明，澄清

   ▲ Could you clarify your first statement, please?
   請闡明你的第一個論述好嗎？

5. **conquer** [ˋkɑŋkɚ] **v.** 克服

   ▲ If you want to be a teacher, you must conquer your fear of speaking in front of people.
   如果你要當老師，就必須克服在人群前說話的恐懼。

6. **damp** [dæmp] adj. 溼的 ，潮溼的 [同] moist (damper, more damp | dampest, most damp)

▲ Wipe off the dirt with a damp cloth. 用溼布拭去灰塵。

damp [dæmp] n. [U] 潮溼

▲ After heavy rain, I felt the damp on my clothes.
大雨過後，我感覺到衣服上的潮溼。

damp [dæmp] v. 使潮溼

▲ If the shirts are too dry to iron, damp them a little.
假如襯衫太乾不好燙，可以把它們弄溼一點。

7. **delightful** [dɪ`laɪtfəl] adj. 令人愉快的

▲ Everyone had a delightful time at the year-end party.
大家在年終派對開心極了。

8. **endanger** [ɪn`dendʒɚ] v. 危害

▲ David endangered his life by driving recklessly.
David 的魯莽駕駛危及自己的生命。

9. **entertain** [ˌɛntɚ`ten] v. 娛樂 <with>

▲ Let me entertain you with a song.
讓我唱一首歌來娛樂你們。

entertainment [ˌɛntɚ`tenmənt] n. [C][U] 娛樂

▲ Nancy and I watch TV for entertainment.
Nancy 和我看電視當作娛樂。

10. **frost** [frɔst] n. [C][U] 霜

▲ Everything outside is covered by frost in early November. 十一月初，戶外所有的景物都被霜所覆蓋。

♥ heavy/hard frost 嚴重的霜

frost [frɔst] v. 結霜 <up, over>

▲ All the windows of the house frosted up overnight.
這個房子的所有窗戶在一夜之間都結霜了。

---

11. **grammatical** [grə`mætɪkl] adj. 文法上的

▲ Each language has a unique grammatical structure.
每一種語言都有其獨特的文法結構。

---

12. **helicopter** [`hɛlɪ,kɑptə] n. [C] 直升機

▲ One helicopter was sent to rescue the crew from the sinking ship. 一架直升機被派往搜救沉船上的船員。

---

13. **immigrate** [`ɪmə,gret] v. (外來的) 移民

▲ Bill's father immigrated to New Zealand from Germany. Bill 的父親從德國移民到紐西蘭。

---

14. **lecture** [`lɛktʃə] n. [C] 講座，課 <to, on, about>

▲ The scholar is going to give a lecture to the students on biology.
那位學者將向學生講授關於生物學的講座。

lecture [`lɛktʃə] v. 講課，講授 <on>

▲ The professor lectures on literature at the university.
教授在大學講授文學。

---

15. **lifeguard** [`laɪf,gɑrd] n. [C] 救生員

▲ Upon hearing someone calling for help in the swimming pool, the lifeguard jumped into the water immediately.

一聽到有人在游泳池裡呼救，救生員立刻跳入水中。

16. **modesty** [ˋmɑdəstɪ] **n.** [U] 謙虛

▲ Nick's natural modesty prevented him from being spoilt by fame.

Nick 天性謙虛使他不會因為出名而得意忘形。

💡 in all modesty 毫不誇張地說

17. **negotiate** [nɪˋgoʃɪ,et] **v.** 談判，協商 <with>

▲ The two companies negotiated with each other for months before they finally signed a contract.

在最後簽署合約前，這兩間公司協商數個月。

18. **pasta** [ˋpɑstə] **n.** [U] 義大利麵食

▲ You can taste all kinds of pasta and pizza when traveling in Italy. 當你在義大利旅行時，你能嘗到各式各樣的義大利麵食和披薩。

19. **quilt** [kwɪlt] **n.** [C] 棉被

▲ Several volunteers worked together in the church to make quilts for the homeless.

幾位志工一起在教堂縫製棉被給無家可歸的人。

quilt [kwɪlt] **v.** 縫棉被

▲ My uncle watched a teaching video to learn to quilt.

我叔叔看一段教學影片學習縫棉被。

20. **radar** [ˋredɑr] **n.** [C][U] 雷達 (裝置)

▲ The research team is going to set up a radar system on top of the mountain.

研究團隊將在山頂架設一個雷達裝置。

💡 on/off sb's radar …知道 / 不知道 | beneath the/sb's radar 被…忘記，被…忽視

---

21. **scold** [skold] v. 責罵 <for>

▲ The mother scolded her son for making a scene.
母親因為兒子大吵大鬧而責罵他。

scold [skold] n. [C] 責罵

▲ Jimmy's teacher gave him a bad scold.
Jimmy 的老師給他嚴厲的責罵。

---

22. **skyscraper** [`skaɪ,skrepɚ] n. [C] 摩天大樓，超高層建築

▲ Taipei 101 used to be the tallest skyscraper in the world. 臺北 101 過去曾是世界最高的摩天大樓。

---

23. **strive** [straɪv] v. 努力，奮鬥 <to>

▲ Though the runner fell, he still strove to reach the finish line. 雖然那名跑者摔倒，他仍努力跑到終點。

---

24. **tense** [tɛns] adj. 緊張的 (tenser | tensest)

▲ You are too tense. Try to relax!
你太緊張了。試著放輕鬆點吧！

tense [tɛns] v. (使) 緊繃

▲ The athlete's muscles tensed as he got ready to run at a full speed. 運動員在準備要全力衝刺時，肌肉緊繃。

💡 tensed up 緊張的

tense [tɛns] n. [C][U] 時態

▲We use past tense when describing things that have happened.

我們使用過去時態來描述已經發生的事情。

---

25. **violation** [ˌvaɪəˈleʃən] n. [C][U] 違反，違背 <of> [同] flout

▲Oliver was in violation of the company's regulations by copying the files.

Oliver 複製檔案違反了公司的規則。

Unit 24

1. **assurance** [əˈʃʊrəns] n. [C] 保證 [同] guarantee, promise

▲You have my assurance that I'll return the money to you by Friday. 我向你保證我會在星期五之前還錢。

---

2. **assure** [əˈʃʊr] v. 向…保證 <of>

▲The manager can assure us of Ted's loyalty to the company.

經理可以向我們保證 Ted 對公司是忠誠的。

---

3. **burglar** [ˈbɝglɚ] n. [C] (入室) 竊賊

▲The police believed the burglar broke into the house through the kitchen window.

警察認為竊賊從廚房窗戶潛入屋內。

---

4. **cliff** [klɪf] n. [C] 峭壁

▲ Waves crashing against the base of a cliff over time can form a sea cave.

波浪持續拍打在懸崖底部一段時間會形成海蝕洞。

---

5. **consequent** [`kɑnsə,kwɛnt] adj. 隨之而來的，因…而起的 [同] resultant

▲ The closure of the factory and the consequent loss of jobs have caused many problems.

工廠的關閉和隨之而來的失業造成了很多的問題。

consequently [`kɑnsə,kwɛntlɪ] adv. 因此

▲ The house is on the hill and consequently it commands a view of the whole town.

那間房子在山丘上，因此能眺望全鎮。

---

6. **deadline** [`dɛdlaɪn] n. [C] 截止日期 <for>

▲ Reporters always work under pressure to meet the deadline. 記者總是在趕稿件截止日期的壓力下工作。

🔘 meet/extend the deadline 趕上 / 延長截止日期

---

7. **demonstration** [,dɛmən`streʃən] n. [C][U] 演示，示範 <of>；[C] 示威活動 <against>

▲ The teacher gave a clear demonstration of what should be achieved.

老師清楚說明要達成的目標是什麼。

---

8. **enforce** [ɪn`fors] v. (強制) 執行

▲ The government intends to enforce tougher laws to decrease the crime rate.

政府想要執行更嚴格的法律來降低犯罪率。

enforcement [ɪn`fɔrsmənt] n. [C][U] 執行

▲ Singapore's strict law enforcement has made it one of the safest tourist destinations in the world. 新加坡嚴格的執法使它成為世界上最安全的旅遊勝地之一。

💡 law enforcement officer 執法官員

---

9. **equip** [ɪ`kwɪp] v. 配備 <with> (equipped | equipped | equipping)

▲ The building is fully equipped with fire safety equipment. 這棟大樓完整備有消防設備。

equipment [ɪ`kwɪpmənt] n. [U] 設備

▲ Mary rents the camping equipment instead of buying. Mary 租用露營設備而非購買。

---

10. **frown** [fraʊn] n. [C] 皺眉

▲ The teacher looked at the naughty student with a frown. 老師皺眉地看著那個調皮的學生。

frown [fraʊn] v. 皺眉 <at>

▲ Alan frowned at his son, who came home at midnight. Alan 對他半夜才回家的兒子皺起眉頭。

💡 frown on/upon sth 不贊成…

---

11. **graph** [græf] n. [C] 圖表

▲ This graph shows how sharply the city's crime rate has declined. 此圖表顯示了該市的犯罪率急遽下降。

graph [græf] v. 用圖表表示

▲ Our professor asked us to graph data.
我們的教授要求我們將數據用圖表表示。

---

12. **hive** [haɪv] n. [C] 蜂窩 [同] beehive；人群嘈雜之處

▲ The naughty boy lit a fire that disturbed the hive, and this caused the bees to attack him.
這個頑皮的男孩點火騷擾蜂窩，這讓蜜蜂攻擊他。

💡 hive of activity/industry 繁忙的場所

---

13. **immigration** [ˌɪməˈgreʃən] n. [U] 移民 (入境) <into>

▲ Canada has a strict policy on immigration into the country. 加拿大對於入境移民有嚴格的政策。

---

14. **lecturer** [ˈlɛktʃərə] n. [C] (大學) 講師 <in>

▲ Max is a lecturer in computer engineering at the university. Max 是大學資訊工程學的講師。

---

15. **lipstick** [ˈlɪpˌstɪk] n. [C][U] 脣膏，口紅

▲ Sophie applied some lipstick as a final touch of her makeup. Sophie 擦了些口紅作為化妝最後的修飾。

---

16. **mule** [mjul] n. [C] 騾子

▲ Mr. Chen is as stubborn as a mule. 陳先生十分固執。

---

17. **nightmare** [ˈnaɪtˌmɛr] n. [C] 惡夢，夢魘

▲ Our trip to Rome turned into a nightmare after our passports were stolen.
羅馬之旅在護照被偷後成了一場惡夢。

18. **paw** [pɔ] n. [C] 爪子

   ▲ My pet dogs destroyed my new sofa with their dirty paws. 我的寵物狗用牠們的髒爪子毀了我的新沙發。

   paw [pɔ] v. 用爪子抓 <at>

   ▲ The cat pawed at the stuffed animal.
   那隻貓用爪子撥弄絨布玩偶。

---

19. **rage** [redʒ] n. [C][U] 盛怒，暴怒

   ▲ Mr. Chang flew into a rage when he learned that his son had skipped class.
   當張先生知道他兒子蹺課後，他勃然大怒。

   🕯 be all the rage 風靡一時

   rage [redʒ] v. 肆虐

   ▲ The typhoon raged across the southern part of the island. 颱風肆虐島嶼的南部。

---

20. **raisin** [ˈrezn̩] n. [C] 葡萄乾

   ▲ My favorite ice cream flavor is rum raisin.
   我最喜歡的冰淇淋口味是蘭姆葡萄乾。

---

21. **settler** [ˈsɛtlɚ] n. [C] 移居者

   ▲ The early settlers had a hard time adapting themselves to the new environment.
   早期的移民者難以適應新環境。

---

22. **spear** [spɪr] n. [C] 矛；魚叉

   ▲ In ancient times, people fought their enemies with spears and swords.

古時候，人們用矛和劍與敵人戰鬥。

spear [spɪr] v. (用尖物) 戳，刺

▲ Tyson speared a piece of meat with his fork and put it into his mouth. Tyson 用叉子戳起一塊肉放進嘴裡。

23. **stroke** [strok] n. [C] 中風

▲ The stroke paralyzed the right side of the old man's body. 老人因中風而身體右半邊癱瘓。

stroke [strok] v. 撫摸

▲ Dora stroked her daughter's hair and then started to braid it. Dora 撫摸她女兒的頭髮，然後開始編辮子。

24. **tickle** [`tɪkl̩] v. 搔癢

▲ The woman tickled the baby's feet, and this made him laugh loudly.
女子搔了搔這嬰兒的腳，這讓他大笑。

💡 tickle sb's fancy 勾起…的興趣

tickle [`tɪkl̩] n. [sing.] 搔…的癢

▲ My mom gave me a tickle to wake me up.
我母親搔我的癢來叫醒我。

25. **voluntary** [`vɑlən.tɛrɪ] adj. 自願的 [反] involuntary, compulsory

▲ After several hours of internal struggle, the suspect made a voluntary confession.
經過幾個小時的內心掙扎，嫌犯自動認罪了。

Unit 25

1. **atom** [ˋætəm] n. [C] 原子
   ▲ A molecule of carbon dioxide has one carbon atom and two oxygen atoms.
   二氧化碳分子有一個碳原子和兩個氧原子。

2. **autograph** [ˋɔtə͵græf] n. [C] 親筆簽名
   ▲ After the death of the celebrity, his autographs become extremely valuable.
   在這個名人去世後，他的親筆簽名變得非常值錢。
   autograph [ˋɔtə͵græf] v. 在⋯上親筆簽名
   ▲ The athlete autographed the poster as a gift to her fans.
   運動員在海報上親筆簽名，作為送給她粉絲的禮物。

3. **cane** [ken] n. [C] 拐杖；藤條
   ▲ The old man has to walk with a cane as he has balance problems.
   因為有平衡問題，這老人必須拄著拐杖走路。

4. **commit** [kəˋmɪt] v. 犯 (罪、錯) (committed | committed | committing)
   ▲ A murder was committed on this street last night.
   昨晚這條街上發生了一件謀殺案。
   💡 commit oneself ⋯表態 | commit suicide 自殺

5. **constitution** [͵kɑnstəˋtjuʃən] n. [C] 憲法

▲ The Supreme Court has the authority to interpret the Constitution. 最高法院有權解釋憲法。

---

6. **decoration** [ˌdɛkəˈreʃən] n. [U] 裝潢，裝飾

▲ My sister majors in interior decoration.
我姊姊主修室內裝潢。

---

7. **determination** [dɪˌtɝməˈneʃən] n. [U] 決心 <to>

▲ Tim's determination to pass the entrance exam made him keep on studying hard. Tim 一定要通過入學考試的決心敦促他不斷努力用功。

---

8. **enlarge** [ɪnˈlɑrdʒ] v. 放大

▲ My parents enlarged the photo they liked best and hung it on the wall.
我父母把他們最喜歡的照片放大並掛在牆上。

💡 enlarge on/upon sth 詳細說明

enlargement [ɪnˈlɑrdʒmənt] n. [U] 擴充 <of>

▲ We are going to hire more people and hope the enlargement of the team will increase the production.
我們將僱用更多人，希望藉由擴充團隊可以增加生產。

---

9. **evaluation** [ɪˌvæljuˈeʃən] n. [C] 評估

▲ The manager will carry out an evaluation of the new project. 經理將會評估新的企劃案。

---

10. **furnish** [ˈfɝnɪʃ] v. 為…配備家具 <with>

▲ The rented room is well furnished with a bed, a desk, and a wardrobe.

這間租來的房間有著完善的設備，包括床、桌子和衣櫥。

---

11. **gratitude** [ˋgrætə,tjud] n. [U] 感謝，感激 [反] ingratitude

▲ Let me express my deep gratitude for your great contribution to this company.

讓我向你對這公司的莫大貢獻表示深深的感謝。

---

12. **homeland** [ˋhom,lænd] n. [C] 祖國

▲ When the old man returned to his homeland fifty years later, no one recognized him.

當這老人五十年後回到祖國時，沒有人能認出他來。

---

13. **impose** [ɪmˋpoz] v. 強制實行 <on, upon>

▲ The government imposed a ban on smoking in public places. 政府禁止在公共場所抽菸。

---

14. **lengthen** [ˋlɛŋθən] v. 加長，使變長 [反] shorten

▲ As summer approaches, the days will lengthen, and the nights will shorten.

隨著夏天接近，白天會加長而夜晚會縮短。

---

15. **liquor** [ˋlɪkɚ] n. [U] 烈酒

▲ Whiskey and brandy are liquor.

威士忌和白蘭地是烈酒。

---

16. **murderer** [ˋmɝdərɚ] n. [C] 凶手，殺人犯 [同] killer

▲ The police are trying to find out who the murderer is.

警方正設法找出凶手是誰。

💡 mass murderer 殺人狂

---

17. **nuclear** [`njukliɚ] adj. 核能的
   ▲ The construction of the new nuclear power plant caused considerable controversy.
   興建新的核能發電廠引起極大的爭議。

18. **peep** [pip] n. [C] 偷看
   ▲ The teacher took a peep into the library and found Henry was dozing.
   老師往圖書館內看了一眼，發現 Henry 在打瞌睡。

   peep [pip] v. 偷看，窺視 <at, into, through>
   ▲ Since there was no response to my knocking, I tried to peep into the room through the keyhole. 因為我敲門沒有回應，我試著透過鑰匙孔向房間裡窺視。

19. **reception** [rɪ`sɛpʃən] n. [C] 招待會，歡迎會
   ▲ After the wedding, there will be a reception.
   婚禮之後會有招待會。

   receptionist [rɪ`sɛpʃənɪst] n. [C] 接待員
   ▲ Emma told the receptionist that she had come for the 10:00 appointment.
   Emma 告訴接待員她來赴十點的會面。

20. **reflection** [rɪ`flɛkʃən] n. [C] 倒影，映像
   ▲ The queen is looking at her reflection in the mirror.
   皇后看著鏡中自己的倒影。

---

21. sew [so] **v.** 縫紉，做針線活 <on> (sewed | sewn, sewed | sewing)

▲ Rod sewed a button on his shirt.

Rod 在他的襯衫縫上鈕扣。

💡 sew up 縫合

sewing [`soɪŋ] **n.** [U] 縫紉

▲ Lena is very good at sewing. Lena 很善於裁縫。

22. splendid [`splɛndɪd] **adj.** 壯麗的

▲ The girl exclaimed in amazement when she was looking at the splendid sunset.

那女孩看著壯麗的日落景象時發出驚嘆聲。

23. sue [su] **v.** 控告 <for>

▲ Ita sued her ex-husband for entering her house without permission.

Ita 控告她前夫未經允許就進入她家。

24. timetable [`taɪm,tebl] **n.** [C] 時刻表

▲ You can find out the times of your bus in that timetable. 你可以在那個時刻表中找到你的公車時間。

25. welfare [`wɛl,fɛr] **n.** [U] 福祉 <of>

▲ In a divorce case, the welfare of the children would be the top priority.

在離婚的案件中，孩子的福祉會是優先考量的事。

💡 on welfare 接受社會救濟

Unit 26

1. **atomic** [ə`tɑmɪk] adj. 原子的
   ▲ The United States dropped atomic bombs in Japan during World War II.
   美國於第二次世界大戰時在日本投下了原子彈。

---

2. **bargain** [`bɑrgɪn] n. [C] 便宜貨
   ▲ I bought this dress at a clearance sale, and it was a real bargain.
   我在清倉大拍賣時買這件洋裝，真的很便宜。
   🍃 make a bargain 達成協議
   bargain [`bɑrgɪn] v. 討價還價
   ▲ My father bargained with the real estate agent for a lower price. 父親跟房屋仲介殺價。
   🍃 bargain sth away 便宜拋售⋯

---

3. **capitalist** [`kæpətl̩ɪst] n. [C] 資本家
   ▲ Several capitalists invested in the business, hoping to make a profit within the next few months. 一些資本家投資該企業，希望可以在接下來幾個月內獲利。

---

4. **companion** [kəm`pænjən] n. [C] 夥伴，同伴
   ▲ The dog is the old man's closest companion.
   這隻狗是這老人最親密的夥伴。

---

5. **consultant** [kən`sʌltn̩t] n. [C] 顧問

▲ Philip works as a management consultant for the newly established company.

Philip 在這間新創立的公司擔任管理顧問。

6. **depart** [dɪ`pɑrt] v. 出發，離開 <for, from> [同] leave

▲ The train will depart for Rome from Milan in one hour. 這班火車將在一小時內從米蘭出發至羅馬。

7. **dew** [dju] n. [U] 露水

▲ The morning dew gathered on the grass.

清晨的露水聚集在草地上。

8. **exaggerate** [ɪg`zædʒə,ret] v. 誇大，誇張

▲ Don't exaggerate, and just tell me the truth.

不要誇大其詞，只要告訴我實情。

9. **explanation** [,ɛksplə`neʃən] n. [C][U] 解釋，說明 <of, for>

▲ The student gave an explanation for being late for school this morning.

這學生解釋今天早上上學遲到的原因。

10. **gaze** [gez] n. [C] 凝視 (usu. sing.)

▲ My grandmother looked at me with a steady gaze as if seeing me for the first time.

我奶奶目不轉睛地看著我，好像是第一次見到我一樣。

gaze [gez] v. 凝視 <at> [同] stare

▲ Richard gazed at the stars in the sky, trying to locate Polaris.

Richard 抬頭凝望著星星，試著找到北極星。

---

11. **grave** [grev] n. [C] 墳墓，墓穴

▲ Sue's grandmother has been buried in the grave.
Sue 的祖母已經下葬。

grave [grev] adj. 嚴重的 (graver | gravest)

▲ If you try to cross the broken bridge, you will put your life in grave danger.
如果你要過這條毀壞的橋，你將處於極大的危險之中。

---

12. **honeymoon** [ˋhʌnɪˌmun] n. [C] 蜜月

▲ The married couple went to Venice on their honeymoon. 這對夫妻前往威尼斯度蜜月。

honeymoon [ˋhʌnɪˌmun] v. 度蜜月

▲ We are planning to honeymoon in France.
我們正計劃去法國度蜜月。

---

13. **impression** [ɪmˋprɛʃən] n. [C] 印象 <of>

▲ Everyone's first impression of Troy is his friendly smile. Troy 給大家的第一印象是親切的笑容。

---

14. **librarian** [laɪˋbrɛrɪən] n. [C] 圖書館管理員

▲ The librarian can help you find the book you are looking for.
圖書館管理員可以幫忙找到你要尋找的書。

---

15. **loan** [lon] n. [C] 貸款

▲ Mr. Wu took out a loan in order to buy a new house.
吳先生申請貸款去買新房子。

💡 loan shark 放高利貸者

loan [lon] v. 借出 <to>

▲ The paintings were loaned by the Louvre Museum to the National Palace Museum.

這些畫作由羅浮宮出借給國立故宮博物院。

---

16. **murmur** [`mɝmɚ] n. [C] 低語

▲ The teacher heard a low murmur from the students.

這個老師聽見學生們竊竊私語。

murmur [`mɝmɚ] v. 低聲說 <to>

▲ It was strange that Victor kept murmuring to himself.

Victor 不斷喃喃自語，真是奇怪。

---

17. **obtain** [əb`ten] v. 獲得 [同] get

▲ Bonnie managed to obtain a ticket to the concert.

Bonnie 設法拿到了音樂會的票。

---

18. **perfume** [`pɝfjum] n. [C][U] 香水 [同] fragrance

▲ Sally wore perfume to the party.

Sally 擦了點香水去舞會。

perfume [`pɝfjum] v. 使香氣瀰漫

▲ Annie's room is perfumed with the smell of flowers.

Annie 的房間瀰漫著花的芳香。

---

19. **recreation** [ˌrɛkrɪ`eʃən] n. [C][U] 娛樂，消遣

▲ What do you like to do for recreation?

你喜歡做什麼休閒活動？

---

20. **register** [`rɛdʒɪstɚ] v. 註冊 <for> [同] enroll

▲ You must register for the course you want to take.
你必須註冊你要選修的課。

register [ˋrɛdʒɪstɚ] n. [C] 登記簿 <in>

▲ The clerk can't find my name in the hotel register.
職員在旅館登記簿裡找不到我的名字。

---

21. **shade** [ʃed] n. [U] 陰涼處，陰暗處

▲ Andy is reading in the shade of a big tree.
Andy 在一棵大樹下的陰涼處讀書。

🔘 put sb/sth in the shade 讓⋯黯然失色

shade [ʃed] v. 遮擋 (光線)

▲ Flora used a book to shade her face from the sun.
Flora 用書遮住臉不被太陽曬到。

---

22. **stingy** [ˋstɪndʒɪ] adj. 吝嗇的，小氣的 <with> (stingier |
stingiest)

▲ The rich man is very stingy and never donates money
to the charity.
這個有錢人很吝嗇，從不捐錢給慈善機構。

---

23. **telegraph** [ˋtɛlə͵græf] n. [U] 電報

▲ People in the past used to send urgent messages by
telegraph. 人們在過去會用電報傳送緊急的訊息。

telegraph [ˋtɛlə͵græf] v. 打電報

▲ Sam telegraphed an urgent message to William.
Sam 打電報傳送緊急的訊息給 William。

---

24. **timid** [ˋtɪmɪd] adj. 膽怯的 [同] shy [反] confident

▲ Clara has been unfairly treated, but she is too timid to protest.

Clara 一直受到不公平對待，但她太膽怯不敢抗議。

25. **withdraw** [wɪθ`drɔ] v. 領款 <from> (withdrew | withdrawn | withdrawing)

▲ To repay the debts, I must withdraw all my money from the bank account.

為了償還債務，我必須從銀行戶頭把全部的錢領出來。

withdrawal [wɪθ`drɔl] n. [C][U] 提款

▲ The teller is explaining to the old man that there is no charge for withdrawals. 銀行出納員正在向那位老人解釋提款並不會被收取費用。

Unit 27

1. **accountant** [ə`kauntənt] n. [C] 會計師

▲ The rich businessman hires an accountant to take care of his taxes.

這位富有的商人僱用會計師來處理他的稅務。

2. **attach** [ə`tætʃ] v. 連接 <to> [同] stick

▲ My brother helped me attach the printer to my desktop computer.

我哥哥幫我將印表機連接上我的桌上型電腦。

attachment [ə`tætʃmənt] n. [C] (機器的) 附件

▲ The attachments of the vacuum cleaner are all in the box. 這吸塵器所有的附件都在這箱子裡。

3. **barrier** [ˋbærɪɚ] n. [C] 隔閡，障礙
   ▲ To bring people of all ages together, we must work hard to remove social barriers. 為了使各年齡層的人更緊密結合，我們必須努力消除社會隔閡。

4. **catalogue** [ˋkætḷͺɔg] n. [C] 目錄 (also catalog)
   ▲ The goods in the mail-order catalogue look fancy. 這郵購目錄上的商品看起來很不錯。
   catalogue [ˋkætḷͺɔg] v. 記錄
   ▲ The experimental data was catalogued by the researchers. 實驗資料由研究人員記錄。

5. **compose** [kəmˋpoz] v. 構成 <of> [同] consist of
   ▲ A molecule of water is composed of one oxygen atom and two hydrogen atoms.
   一個水分子是由一個氧原子和兩個氫原子組合而成。

6. **continual** [kənˋtɪnjʊəl] adj. 不停的 [同] constant [反] sporadic
   ▲ Your continual interruptions have ruined my work schedule. 你不停地打擾毀了我的工作進度。

7. **departure** [dɪˋpɑrtʃɚ] n. [C][U] 啟程，離開 <for, from> [反] arrival
   ▲ Frank changed his US dollars for euros before his departure for Paris.

Frank 在前往巴黎前把他的美元換成歐元。

---

8. **dignity** [ˈdɪgnətɪ] n. [U] 尊嚴，自尊 <with>
   ▲ The tennis player admitted defeat with dignity.
   那位網球選手很有尊嚴地接受失敗。

---

9. **exhaust** [ɪgˈzɔst] n. [U] (引擎排出的) 廢氣
   ▲ Car exhaust fumes are one of the main reasons for air
   pollution. 汽車廢氣是空氣汙染的主因之一。

   exhaust [ɪgˈzɔst] v. 耗盡 [同] use up
   ▲ These earthquake victims exhausted their supply of
   food within a week.
   這些地震災民在一週內把所有糧食吃完了。

   exhausted [ɪgˈzɔstɪd] adj. 筋疲力竭的 [同] worn out
   ▲ The family was completely exhausted after their long
   journey. 這一家人從長途旅行回來後非常疲累。

   exhaustion [ɪgˈzɔstʃən] n. [U] 筋疲力竭
   ▲ Sunny suffers from nervous exhaustion because of the
   overwork. Sunny 因過度工作而飽受神經疲勞之苦。

---

10. **extend** [ɪkˈstɛnd] v. 擴展，擴大
    ▲ In order to strengthen national defense, the government
    planned to extend its mandatory military service to one
    year. 為了加強國防，政府計畫將義務兵役延長至一年。

---

11. **gear** [gɪr] n. [C][U] 排檔 <in>
    ▲ Whenever you put the car in gear, it is supposed to
    start rolling forward or backward.

每當車子上檔，它應該會開始往前或往後行駛。

gear [gɪr] v. 使適合於 <to, toward>

▲ The playground is geared toward children under the age of 12. 遊戲場適合十二歲以下的小孩。

---

12. **greasy** [ˋgrisɪ] adj. 油膩的 [同] oily (greasier | greasiest)

▲ The greasy French fries are bad for health.
這些油膩的薯條對健康不好。

---

13. **horizon** [həˋraɪzn̩] n. [sing.] 地平線 <on>

▲ At dawn, the sun appeared on the horizon.
黎明時，太陽出現在地平線上。

💡 broaden/expand/widen sb's horizons 開闊眼界

---

14. **injure** [ˋɪndʒɚ] v. 傷害，損害 [同] hurt, harm

▲ Jeremy injured his foot while playing basketball.
Jeremy 打籃球時腳受傷了。

injured [ˋɪndʒɚd] adj. 受傷的

▲ The surgeon operated on Nina's injured leg last week. 外科醫生上週在 Nina 受傷的腿上動手術。

injured [ˋɪndʒɚd] n. [pl.] 傷者 (the ~)

▲ The injured in the car crash were taken to the nearby hospital right away.
這場車禍的傷者馬上被送到附近的醫院。

---

15. **limitation** [ˌlɪməˋteʃən] n. [C][U] 限 制 <on> [同] restriction

▲ There are severe limitations on the use of nuclear power in that country.

那個國家對核能的使用有嚴格的限制。

16. **lobster** [`lɑbstɚ] n. [C] 龍蝦；[U] 龍蝦肉

▲ The feature of a lobster is its two large claws.
龍蝦的特色就是牠的兩隻大鉗。

17. **noble** [`nobl] adj. 高尚的 (nobler | noblest)

▲ The mayor praised the man for his noble deed.
市長讚揚這男子高尚的行為。

noble [`nobl] n. [C] 貴族

▲ The billionaire lives a luxurious life like a noble.
這個億萬富翁過著如貴族般的奢侈生活。

18. **option** [`ɑpʃən] n. [C] 選擇

▲ Because of bad business, the owner had no option but to close the grocery store.
由於生意很慘澹，店主別無選擇只好將雜貨店收起來。

19. **philosopher** [fə`lɑsəfɚ] n. [C] 哲學家

▲ The philosopher always talks wisely.
這位哲學家說話總是很有智慧。

20. **recycle** [ri`saɪkl] v. 回收利用

▲ We have to recycle plastic, cans, and even old clothes to make the most of the resources we have.
我們必須回收塑膠、罐子甚至於舊衣物以善用我們所擁有的資源。

21. **registration** [ˌrɛdʒɪ`streʃən] n. [U] 註冊

▲ The student registration form is used to enroll a student who is new to this school.
學生註冊表格適用於加入本校的新生。

💡 registration fee 掛號費

---

22. **shady** [`ʃedɪ] adj. 陰涼的，陰暗的 [同] dim (shadier | shadiest)

▲ We had a long walk under the shady trees.
我們在陰涼的樹下散步了很久。

---

23. **stocking** [`stɑkɪŋ] n. [C] 長筒襪

▲ Fiona is a little girl who is wearing a pair of stockings. Fiona 是正穿著一雙長筒襪的小女孩。

---

24. **tension** [`tɛnʃən] n. [U] (精神上的) 緊張，焦慮

▲ Taking a walk can relieve tension and stress.
散步可以消除緊張和壓力。

---

25. **tolerant** [`tɑlərənt] adj. 寬容的，寬大的 <of, toward> [反] intolerant

▲ I am not tolerant of racism. 我不能容忍種族歧視。

Unit 28

1. **accuse** [ə`kjuz] v. 指控，譴責 <of>

▲ Gina accused me of being a liar. Gina 指責我說謊。

2. **audio** [`ɔdɪo] adj. 聲音的，錄音的

▲ Audio cassettes and videotapes have been replaced by compact discs.
錄音帶與錄影帶已被影音光碟所取代。

audiovisual [ˌɔdɪoˈvɪʒʊəl] adj. 視聽的

▲ Audiovisual aids are widely applied in language learning. 視聽教具被廣泛使用在語言學習上。

---

3. **blade** [bled] n. [C] 刀片，刀身

▲ Watch out for the sharp blade of the knife. You may hurt yourself. 小心這銳利的刀鋒。你可能會傷到自己。

---

4. **chemistry** [ˈkɛmɪstrɪ] n. [U] 化學

▲ Elsa majors in chemistry at college.
Elsa 在大學主修化學。

---

5. **composer** [kəmˈpozɚ] n. [C] 作曲家

▲ Mozart is one of the greatest composers in classical music. 莫札特在古典音樂界是最偉大的作曲家之一。

---

6. **copper** [ˈkɑpɚ] n. [U] 銅

▲ The old woman wears a bracelet made of copper.
這位老太太戴著銅製的手鐲。

copper [ˈkɑpɚ] adj. 銅的

▲ His grandfather gave him an old copper coin.
他祖父給他一枚老銅幣。

---

7. **devise** [dɪˈvaɪz] v. 設計，想出

▲ To save money, we should devise a method to cut electricity bills.

為了省錢，我們應該要想出一個降低電費的方法。

8. **diligence** [ˋdɪlədʒəns] n. [U] 勤勉
  ▲ Helen showed great diligence in studying French.
  Helen 非常勤勉地學習法文。

9. **expansion** [ɪkˋspænʃən] n. [C][U] 擴張，擴大
  ▲ The rapid expansion of the industrial area causes many traffic problems.
  工業區的快速擴張導致很多的交通問題。

10. **faithful** [ˋfeθfəl] adj. 忠誠的，忠貞的 [同] loyal
  ▲ Terry was overcome with grief because his faithful dog died. Terry 悲痛欲絕，因為他忠誠的狗死了。

11. **germ** [dʒɝm] n. [C] 細菌
  ▲ Wash your hands to kill the germs before you eat.
  吃飯前先洗手來殺死細菌。

12. **grind** [graɪnd] v. 研磨，磨碎 (ground | ground | grinding)
  ▲ Tom used a coffee grinder to grind the coffee.
  Tom 用咖啡研磨機來研磨咖啡豆。
  💡 grind sb down 折磨，欺壓…
  grind [graɪnd] n. [sing.] 苦差事
  ▲ Working under the burning sun is a real grind.
  在大太陽底下工作真的是一件苦差事。

13. **horrify** [ˋhɔrə͵faɪ] v. 使震驚 [同] appall

▲ The news of her best friend's death horrified Tina.
好友死亡的消息讓 Tina 震驚。

horrified [ˋhɔrəˌfaɪd] adj. 驚懼的

▲ Students were horrified to see this scary movie.
學生們看到這部恐怖電影都感到害怕。

horrifying [ˋhɔrəˌfaɪɪŋ] adj. 令人驚懼的 [同] horrific

▲ All the children were terrified of this horrifying scene. 所有孩子對這令人恐懼的景象都感到害怕。

---

14. **inspection** [ɪnˋspɛkʃən] n. [C][U] 檢查，檢驗

▲ Movie theaters and restaurants that fail the annual safety inspection will not be allowed to do business.
沒有通過每年安全檢查的電影院和餐廳將不准營業。

---

15. **linen** [ˋlɪnɪn] n. [U] 亞麻，亞麻布

▲ Shirts made of linen are cool and comfortable to wear in summer.
亞麻布製的襯衫在夏天穿既涼爽又舒服。

---

16. **loyal** [ˋlɔɪəl] adj. 忠實的，忠誠的 <to>

▲ Duke is very loyal to his friends.
Duke 對他的朋友很忠誠。

loyally [ˋlɔɪəlɪ] adv. 忠實地

▲ Tony always loyally supports his favorite baseball team. Tony 總是忠實地支持他最喜歡的棒球隊。

---

17. **nonsense** [ˋnɑnsɛns] n. [U] 胡說，胡扯 [同] rubbish

▲ Don't listen to John. He is talking nonsense.

別聽 John 說的話。他在胡扯。

18. **orbit** [`ɔrbɪt] n. [C] 軌道 <in>

▲ The satellite is in orbit around the Earth.
這顆衛星正沿著地球的軌道運行。

• **orbit** [`ɔrbɪt] v. 沿軌道運行

▲ The Earth orbits the sun. 地球繞著太陽運行。

19. **physicist** [`fɪzəsɪst] n. [C] 物理學家

▲ Mike hopes to become a distinguished physicist.
Mike 希望成為傑出的物理學家。

20. **refund** [`rifʌnd] n. [C] 退款

▲ We guarantee refunds if you are not satisfied with
our products.
如果你不滿意我們的產品，我們保證退費。

💡 tax refund 退稅 | demand/claim a full refund 要求完
全退款

refund [rɪ`fʌnd] v. 退費 [同] reimburse

▲ When the performance was canceled, the admission
fee was refunded. 表演取消，退還入場費。

refundable [rɪ`fʌndəbl̩] adj. 可退費的

▲ Tickets to the ball game are not refundable.
球賽的票不得退票。

21. **regulate** [`rɛgjə,let] v. 管理，管控

▲ The laws that regulate the use of food additives have
been under discussion recently.

管控食品添加物使用的法律最近正受到討論。

---

22. **shave** [ʃev] v. 剃去 (毛髮) <off>

▲ Willy shaved his beard off with an electric razor.
Willy 用電動刮鬍刀剃掉鬍子。

shave [ʃev] n. [C] 刮臉

▲ William needs a shave before having an interview.
William 在面試前需要刮臉。

---

23. **suggestion** [səg`dʒɛstʃən] n. [C] 建議

▲ My older sister made a valuable suggestion about
how to keep in shape.
關於如何保持健康，我姊姊給了我寶貴的建議。

---

24. **terror** [`tɛrɚ] n. [U] 恐懼 <in> [同] fear

▲ Kitty screamed in terror as if she had seen a ghost.
Kitty 像見鬼一樣害怕地尖叫。

---

25. **tomb** [tum] n. [C] 墳墓 [同] grave

▲ Not until the tomb of Tutankhamun was discovered
did people know more about his life. 直到圖坦卡門的
墓被發現，人們才知道更多關於他的生活。

Unit 29

1. **acquaintance** [ə`kwentəns] n. [C] 泛泛之交

▲ Chris is more of an acquaintance than a friend.

與其說 Chris 是朋友，不如說只是泛泛之交。

2. **autobiography** [ˌɔtəbaɪˋɑɡrəfɪ] n. [C] 自傳 (pl. autobiographies)

▲ The retired general is composing his autobiography to let his descendants know more about his life.
這位退役的將軍正在撰寫他的自傳，以讓後代子孫更了解他的生平。

3. **blessing** [ˋblɛsɪŋ] n. [C] 祝福

▲ My father gave us his blessing for our marriage.
我父親祝福我們的婚姻。

💡 a blessing in disguise 因禍得福

4. **cherish** [ˋtʃɛrɪʃ] v. 珍惜，珍愛 [同] treasure

▲ I cherish the memories of my working holiday in Australia. 我珍惜在澳洲打工渡假的回憶。

5. **conference** [ˋkɑnfərəns] n. [C] 會議 <on>

▲ Last week, I attended a conference on physics in Paris. 上週我出席在巴黎舉行的物理學會議。

6. **cord** [kɔrd] n. [C][U] 繩

▲ The war criminal broke the cords that were used to bind his hands and feet and managed to escape.
那個戰犯弄斷了用來綁住手腳的繩子，設法逃脫了。

💡 the umbilical cord 臍帶

7. **devote** [dɪˋvot] v. 奉獻 <to>

▲ Mother Teresa devoted her life to the poor and the sick in India.

德蕾莎修女將一生奉獻給印度的窮人及病人。

devoted [dɪˋvotɪd] adj. 全心奉獻的，全心全意的

▲ It is not easy to be a devoted father at home and a dedicated supervisor at work simultaneously.

在家是個全心奉獻的父親，同時在工作上又是個盡忠職守的上司實在很不容易。

---

8. **diplomat** [ˋdɪpləˏmæt] n. [C] 外交官

▲ Leo is interested in relations between countries, so he works hard to be a diplomat.

Leo 對國際關係有興趣，所以他努力要成為外交官。

---

9. **fantasy** [ˋfæntəsɪ] n. [C][U] 妄想 (pl. fantasies)

▲ The poor man has a fantasy of getting rich overnight.

這位貧窮的人妄想一夜致富。

---

10. **farewell** [ˏfɛrˋwɛl] n. [C] 再見，告辭

▲ At the end of the party, the host exchanged farewells with the guests. 派對結束時，主人和客人互相道別。

💡 a farewell party 告別會

---

11. **gigantic** [dʒaɪˋgæntɪk] adj. 巨大的 [同] enormous, huge

▲ A gigantic shopping mall is about to be built in downtown Los Angeles.

一座巨大的購物中心即將在洛杉磯的市中心興建。

---

12. **halt** [hɔlt] n. [sing.] 停止 [同] stop

▲ The bus suddenly came to a halt in the middle of the road. 公車突然在路中間停下來。

💡 come to a halt 使停止

halt [hɔlt] v. 停下 [同] stop

▲ Traffic halted because of the heavy snow.
交通因為大雪中斷。

13. **hose** [hoz] n. [C] 橡皮水管 (pl. hose, hoses)

▲ I used a hose to water the flowers and plants in the yard. 我用橡皮水管為庭院裡的花和植物澆水。

hose [hoz] v. 用水管澆水、沖洗 <down>

▲ Mr. Chen hosed down the garden last Saturday.
陳先生上週六用水管澆花園的花。

14. **insult** [ˋɪnsʌlt] n. [C] 侮辱

▲ It was an insult that Jimmy didn't come to my grandfather's funeral.
Jimmy 沒來參加我祖父的葬禮對我來說是一種侮辱。

💡 add insult to injury 雪上加霜

insult [ɪnˋsʌlt] v. 侮辱

▲ Lucas insulted me by calling me a fool.
Lucas 叫我傻瓜來侮辱我。

15. **logic** [ˋlɑdʒɪk] n. [U] 邏輯

▲ Many people don't see the logic behind the reporter's statement. 許多人不明白這位記者說法背後的邏輯。

16. **measurable** [ˋmeʒrəbl̩] adj. 顯著的

▲ There has been a measurable improvement in your work. 你的工作有明顯的進步。

17. **nursery** [`nɝsərɪ] n. [C] 幼兒園，托兒所 (pl. nurseries)

▲ A nursery provides childcare when both the parents have to work during the day. 父母白天都要上班的話，幼兒園可以提供照顧小孩的服務。

18. **orchestra** [`ɔrkɪstrə] n. [C] 管弦樂團

▲ My son plays the cello in the orchestra.
我的兒子在管弦樂團中演奏大提琴。

19. **pickle** [`pɪkl] n. [C] 酸黃瓜 (片)

▲ I like to have pickles in the sandwiches.
我喜歡在三明治裡加酸黃瓜。

20. **regulation** [ˌrɛgjə`leʃən] n. [C] 法規，條例

▲ Under safety regulations, all workers have to be trained to operate the machines.
在安全規範下，所有的工人必須受訓才能操作機器。

21. **rejection** [rɪ`dʒɛkʃən] n. [C][U] 拒絕 [同] acceptance

▲ David has applied for five jobs, but so far he has only received rejections.
David 應徵了五個工作，但到目前為止都被拒絕。

22. **sightseeing** [`saɪtˌsiɪŋ] n. [U] 觀光

▲ When I went to London on business, it was a pity that I didn't have much time for sightseeing.

我去倫敦出差的時候，很可惜沒有什麼時間去觀光。

💡 go sightseeing 觀光

---

23. **sway** [swe] n. [U] 支配

▲ Arthur is under the sway of his ambitious mother.
Arthur 受到野心勃勃的母親支配。

sway [swe] v. 搖擺，搖動 [同] wave

▲ We marveled at the small yellow flowers swaying in
the breeze. 我們對在微風中搖曳的小黃花發出讚嘆。

---

24. **translate** [`trænslet] v. 翻譯 <from, into>

▲ Jim translated the book from German into Chinese.
Jim 把這本書從德文翻譯成中文。

---

25. **translation** [træns`leʃən] n. [C][U] 翻譯，譯本

▲ I bought a Chinese translation of a novel by Edgar
Allan Poe. 我買了一本艾德格愛倫坡的小說中譯本。

Unit 30

1. **addict** [`ædɪkt] n. [C] 入迷的人 [同] fan

▲ John is a television addict. John 是個電視迷。

addict [ə`dɪkt] v. 使沉迷 <to>

▲ My younger brother is addicted to reading science
fiction. 我弟弟沉迷於閱讀科幻小說。

addictive [ə`dɪktɪv] adj. 使人上癮的

▲ Don't you think that video games are highly
addictive?

你不認為電動遊戲很容易上癮嗎？

2. **await** [ə`wet] **v.** 等候 [同] wait

▲ I stayed at the airport and awaited my sister's arrival.
我待在機場，等待我妹妹的到來。

3. **blink** [blɪŋk] **v.** 眨眼睛

▲ The girl kept blinking in the bright sunshine.
這女孩在耀眼的陽光下一直眨眼。

blink [blɪŋk] **n.** [sing.] 眨眼睛

▲ Some incredible things happened in the blink of an eye. 一些不可思議的事情在一眨眼間就發生了。

💡 on the blink 出毛病，故障

4. **chew** [tʃu] **v.** 咀嚼，嚼碎

▲ Chewing food well helps digestion and weight loss.
細嚼慢嚥有助於消化和減肥。

💡 chew sth over 仔細思考

chew [tʃu] **n.** [C] 咀嚼

▲ Would you like to have a chew of gum?
你要嚼口香糖嗎？

5. **congress** [`kɑŋgrəs] **n.** [C] 代表大會

▲ The two doctors met at a medical congress.
這兩位醫生是在醫學代表大會上認識的。

congressional [kən`grɛʃənl] **adj.** 會議的

▲ Before starting a war, the president needs to gain congressional approval.

在開戰前，總統必須取得國會的同意。

6. **cottage** [`kɑtɪdʒ] n. [C] 小屋
   ▲ To escape the bustle of the city, we stay in our country cottage during the weekends.
   為了逃離城市的喧囂，我們週末待在鄉村小屋。

7. **diagram** [`daɪə͵græm] n. [C] 圖解
   ▲ Alex drew a diagram of the new machine.
   Alex 畫了一張新式機器的圖解。

   diagram [`daɪə͵græm] v. 圖解
   ▲ The teacher diagramed this new word on the blackboard. 老師在黑板上圖解這新字彙。

8. **disappoint** [͵dɪsə`pɔɪnt] v. 使失望 [同] let down
   ▲ The actress disappointed her fans with her sudden retirement.
   這個女演員突然退休使她的影迷大失所望。

   disappointment [͵dɪsə`pɔɪntmənt] n. [U] 失望
   ▲ To our disappointment, the baseball game was canceled because of the heavy rain.
   讓我們失望的是，棒球賽因為大雨而被取消了。

   disappointed [͵dɪsə`pɔɪntɪd] adj. 失望的 <at, about>
   ▲ Having been a golf coach all my life, I am disappointed at not meeting any talented player.
   當了一輩子高爾夫球教練，我很失望未曾遇見有天分的選手。

   disappointing [͵dɪsə`pɔɪntɪŋ] adj. 令人失望的

▲ It is disappointing that the shirt I like is out of stock.
我喜歡的襯衫賣完了很令人失望。

9. **fatal** [ˋfetl] adj. 致命的 [同] deadly

▲ A bee sting can be fatal if the victim is allergic.
如果傷患過敏的話，蜜蜂螫傷可能會致命。

10. **favorable** [ˋfevrəbl] adj. 贊成的

▲ We are applying for a loan and hope for a favorable reply. 我們正在申請貸款，希望能獲得同意。

11. **giggle** [ˋgɪgl] n. [C] 咯咯笑

▲ On seeing my sister's strange hairstyle, I got the giggles. 一看到我妹妹奇怪的髮型，我咯咯笑不停。
giggle [ˋgɪgl] v. 咯咯地笑 <at> [同] laugh

▲ The girls were giggling at the boy's jokes.
這些女孩子對於男孩的笑話咯咯地笑。

12. **haste** [hest] n. [U] 急忙 [同] hurry

▲ Our father prepared our breakfast in haste.
我們的父親急忙地準備我們的早餐。

♥ More haste, less speed. 【諺】欲速則不達。 | Haste makes waste. 【諺】忙中有錯。

13. **housework** [ˋhaʊsˏwɝk] n. [U] 家事，家務

▲ My mother was exhausted because she spent the whole afternoon doing housework.
我母親很疲累，因為她整個下午都在做家事。

14. **intend** [ɪnˋtɛnd] v. 打算 <to>

▲ I intended to finish the job tonight.
我打算今晚完成工作。

intended [ɪnˋtɛndɪd] adj. 為…打算的 <for>

▲ These cookies are intended for tonight's party.
這些餅乾是為了今晚的派對準備的。

---

15. **logical** [ˋlɑdʒɪkl] adj. 合理的，合乎邏輯的 [反] illogical

▲ To be persuasive, you have to offer logical arguments. 你必須提出合理的論點才能說服人。

---

16. **mechanic** [məˋkænɪk] n. [C] 機械工，修理工

▲ My car broke down, so I will have a car mechanic fix it tomorrow.
我的車子故障了，所以我明天要找汽車修理工修理它。

mechanics [məˋkænɪks] n. [pl.] 方法，手段 (the ～)

▲ Kevin knows nothing about the mechanics of running a business. Kevin 對經營企業的方法完全不知。

---

17. **nutritious** [njuˋtrɪʃəs] adj. 有營養的 [同] nourishing

▲ A nutritious and balanced diet is essential for everyone.
有營養且平衡的飲食對每個人是非常重要的。

---

18. **panel** [ˋpænl] n. [C] 專家小組 <of>

▲ A panel of experts was asked to give advice about the financial problem.
一組專家被請求對此財務問題給予建議。

---

19. **pioneer** [ˌpaɪə`nɪr] n. [C] 拓荒者 [同] trailblazer

▲ In the 19th century, many American pioneers immigrated to the west to develop new areas.
在十九世紀時，許多美國拓荒者移居西部來開墾新地。

pioneer [ˌpaɪə`nɪr] v. 成為先驅

▲ The Wright brothers pioneered the development of airplanes. 萊特兄弟是發展飛機的先驅。

20. **relaxation** [ˌrilæks`eʃən] n. [U] 放鬆

▲ Relaxation plays an important role in doing yoga.
放鬆在做瑜伽上扮演著重要的角色。

21. **relevant** [`rɛləvənt] adj. 有關的 <to> [反] irrelevant

▲ The key to a successful commercial is to make it relevant to the audience.
成功商業廣告的關鍵就是讓它與觀眾相連結。

22. **sincerity** [sɪn`sɛrətɪ] n. [U] 真誠，誠意 [反] insincerity

▲ The candidate's sincerity has deeply impressed me.
這位候選人的真誠令我印象深刻。

23. **systematic** [ˌsɪstə`mætɪk] adj. 有系統的 [同] organized [反] unsystematic

▲ A systematic method will help you work more efficiently. 有系統的方法可以幫助你工作更有效率。

24. **translator** [træns`letɚ] n. [C] (筆譯) 譯者

▲ The publisher is looking for an experienced translator to translate this best-seller into Spanish.
這家出版商正在尋找有經驗的譯者來將這本暢銷書翻譯為西班牙文。

25. **tumble** [ˋtʌmbl̩] v. 跌落，跌倒 <down> [同] fall
▲ Rebecca lost her balance and tumbled down the stairs. Rebecca 失去平衡而從樓梯上跌下來。
tumble [ˋtʌmbl̩] n. [C] 跌倒
▲ Nelson took a tumble and broke one of his legs.
Nelson 跌倒並摔斷一條腿。

Unit 31

1. **allowance** [əˋlauəns] n. [C] 零用錢 [同] pocket money
▲ Alex received a weekly allowance from his father.
Alex 從父親那裡得到每週的零用錢。

2. **bald** [bɔld] adj. 禿頭的
▲ The man went bald at the age of thirty.
這名男子三十歲就禿頭了。

3. **blossom** [ˋblɑsəm] n. [C][U] 花朵
▲ The white lily blossom symbolizes purity.
白色的百合花象徵純潔。
💡 in blossom 開花
blossom [ˋblɑsəm] v. 開花；(關係) 深入發展 <into>

▲ When the roses blossom, the garden is filled with fragrance. 玫瑰開時，花園充滿香氣。

---

4. **choke** [tʃok] v. 噎住，窒息 <on>

▲ Eve choked on a fish bone and was sent to the hospital. Eve 被一根魚刺噎住而被送醫。

🔘 choke sth back 抑制…

choke [tʃok] n. [C] 嗆到 (聲音)

▲ With his hand over his mouth, the little boy let out a choke of laughter.
一手遮住嘴，這小男孩發出一陣笑聲。

---

5. **constitute** [ˋkɑnstə͵tjut] v. 構成

▲ Teachers constitute about 30% of the committee.
老師占委員會中約 30%。

---

6. **coward** [ˋkaʊɚd] n. [C] 懦夫，膽小鬼

▲ Only a coward runs away from the enemy.
只有懦夫才不敢面對敵人。

---

7. **diploma** [dɪˋplomə] n. [C] 學位證書，文憑 <in> (pl. diplomas)

▲ Vanessa has got a diploma in hotel management.
Vanessa 已取得飯店管理的文憑。

---

8. **discourage** [dɪsˋkɝɪdʒ] v. 使沮喪 [同] dishearten [反] encourage

▲ Failing the math exam discouraged Chris.
數學考不及格令 Chris 沮喪。

discouragement [dɪs`kɝɪdʒmənt] n. [U] 沮喪，氣餒

▲ At times of discouragement, many people turn to religion for comfort.

在沮喪的時候，許多人向宗教尋求慰藉。

discouraged [dɪs`kɝɪdʒd] adj. 感覺沮喪的 [同] demoralized [反] encouraged

▲ Jane felt discouraged after hearing the news that her colleague had quit.

Jane 聽到她同事辭職的消息，感到沮喪。

discouraging [dɪs`kɝɪdʒɪŋ] adj. 令人沮喪的 [反] encouraging

▲ The rejection letter from the college is very discouraging to Ken. 大學的回絕信讓 Ken 十分沮喪。

---

9. **fax** [fæks] n. [C][U] 傳真機

▲ We just received an order form by fax.

我們剛從傳真機收到了一張訂單。

fax [fæks] v. 傳真 <to>

▲ You can order our products online or fax the order form to us.

你可用網路訂購我們的產品或傳真訂購單給我們。

---

10. **ferry** [`fɛrɪ] n. [C] (尤指定期的) 渡船 (pl. ferries)

▲ They took the ferry across the bay.

他們乘渡船橫渡海灣。

ferry [`fɛrɪ] v. (尤指定期的) 渡運，運送

▲ The boatman ferried the passengers across the river.

船夫渡運乘客過河。

11. **ginger** [ˋdʒɪndʒɚ] n. [U] 薑
   ▲ You can get rid of the fishy smell of shrimps with a few slices of ginger.
   你可以加幾片薑來去除蝦子的腥味。

12. **hasten** [ˋhesn̩] v. 催促
   ▲ Helen hastened her younger brother to get ready.
   Helen 催促她的弟弟快點準備好。

13. **humidity** [hjuˋmɪdətɪ] n. [U] 溼度
   ▲ Coastal areas usually have higher humidity than inland areas. 沿海地區溼度通常比內陸地區高。

14. **intermediate** [ˌɪntɚˋmidɪət] adj. 中級程度的
   ▲ Sam is taking the intermediate course in English.
   Sam 在上中級英語課程。
   intermediate [ˌɪntɚˋmidɪət] n. [C] 中級學生
   ▲ This Japanese class is for intermediates.
   這堂日文課是給中級學生的。
   intermediate [ˌɪntɚˋmidɪˌet] v. 調解，調停
   ▲ The coach intermediated between the two players.
   教練為這兩名球員調解。

15. **loosen** [ˋlusn̩] v. 鬆開 [同] slacken
   ▲ You can loosen the screw by turning counterclockwise. 你將螺絲逆時針轉就會鬆開了。

16. **memorable** [ˋmɛmərəbl̩] adj. 令人難忘的 [同] unforgettable

▲ We spent a memorable week camping by the river.
我們在河邊露營，度過難忘的一星期。

17. **obedience** [oˋbidɪəns] n. [U] 服從，遵從 [反] disobedience

▲ Absolute obedience is required in the army.
軍中要求絕對的服從。

18. **perfection** [pɚˋfɛkʃən] n. [U] 完美

▲ In order to achieve perfection, Ted made numerous revisions to his writing.
為了達到完美，Ted 反覆修改文章。

♥ to perfection 完美地

19. **plentiful** [ˋplɛntɪfəl] adj. 豐富的，充足的 [同] abundant

▲ Mangoes are plentiful in the summer. 夏天芒果很多。

20. **remark** [rɪˋmɑrk] n. [C] 評論 [同] comment

▲ Susie's colleague hurt her feelings by making rude remarks. Susie 的同事用無禮的批評傷害她。

remark [rɪˋmɑrk] v. 說起，談論

▲ The girl turned down the role after remarking that she wasn't prepared to be an actress.
這女孩說她尚未準備好要當演員後，拒絕了這個角色。

21. **resignation** [ˌrɛzɪgˋneʃən] n. [C] 辭職信； [C][U] 辭職 [同] leaving

▲ Shelly handed in her resignation this morning.
今早 Shelly 遞交了辭職信。

---

22. **slogan** [ˋslogən] n. [C] 口號，標語 [同] tag line
▲ The slogan of that political party is "From the cradle to the grave." 那個政黨的口號是：「照顧你的一生」。

---

23. **technological** [͵tɛknəˋlɑdʒɪkl̩] adj. 科技的
▲ The technological development in the past decade has totally changed the way people communicate.
過去十年的科技發展完全改變了人們溝通的方式。

---

24. **troublesome** [ˋtrʌbl̩səm] adj. 令人討厭的，棘手的 [同] annoying
▲ The troublesome boy from the house next door almost drove us crazy.
隔壁家那位討人厭的男孩快把我們逼瘋了。

---

25. **vegetarian** [͵vɛdʒəˋtɛrɪən] n. [C] 素食者
▲ Betty chose to be a vegetarian for the sake of her health as well as the environment. Betty 選擇做素食者是為了自己的健康和自然環境著想。

Unit 32

1. **ambiguous** [æmˋbɪgjʊəs] adj. 模稜兩可的
▲ The ambiguous statement caused misunderstanding.

這個模稜兩可的聲明造成誤解。

2. **ballet** [bæ`le] n. [U] 芭蕾舞
   ▲ The audience was fascinated by the graceful movements of the ballet dancer.
   觀眾被這位芭蕾舞者的優雅動作所吸引。

3. **bounce** [baʊns] v. 彈起，彈跳
   ▲ The ball bounced over the wall. 球彈出牆外。
   bounce [baʊns] n. [C] 彈跳 (pl. bounces)
   ▲ The infielder tried to catch the ball on the first bounce. 內野手試著要在球第一次跳起時接住。

4. **circulate** [`sɝkjə,let] v. 循環 <through> [同] flow
   ▲ Exercise helps to get blood circulating through the body. 運動幫助血液在體內循環。

5. **convenience** [kən`vinjəns] n. [U] 便利，方便
   ▲ The convenience of online shopping makes it possible for us to buy anything without going out.
   網路購物的便利性使我們不用外出就能買東西。
   💡 convenience store 便利商店

6. **creep** [krip] v. 緩慢行進，悄悄移動 (crept | crept | creeping)
   ▲ A thief crept into the hospital and stole valuable belongings from several patients. 一個小偷躡手躡腳地從醫院裡偷走了幾個病人的貴重物品。

7. **disadvantage** [ˌdɪsəd`væntɪdʒ] n. [C][U] 劣勢，不利因素 [反] advantage

▲ It is a disadvantage to be unable to speak English nowadays. 現今不會說英語很吃虧。

disadvantage [ˌdɪsəd`væntɪdʒ] v. 使處於劣勢，使處於不利地位

▲ It is said this rule could disadvantage the indigenous people. 據說這項條例可能使原住民處於不利地位。

8. **divine** [dɪ`vaɪn] adj. 神的，神聖的 (diviner | divinest)

▲ The fan regards her idol as a divine being.
這位粉絲把她的偶像神化了。

9. **feast** [fist] n. [C] 盛宴 [同] banquet

▲ All the family members got together and had a feast to celebrate their parents' 50th wedding anniversary.
所有家庭成員團聚享用大餐來慶祝父母五十週年結婚紀念日。

feast [fist] v. 盡情享用 <on>

▲ We feasted on food and wine on Chinese New Year's Eve. 我們在除夕夜盡情享用食物和酒。

10. **finance** [`faɪnæns] n. [C][U] 財務，財源

▲ Illness and unemployment cause unbearable strain on Bill's finances.
生病和失業造成 Bill 難以承擔的財務壓力。

finance [`faɪnæns] v. 提供資金 [同] fund

▲ The boy was grateful that his grandfather financed his education.

這位男孩非常感謝他的祖父資助他教育經費。

11. **glorious** [ˋglorɪəs] adj. 光榮的
   ▲ After the athlete won a gold medal in the Olympic Games, he returned home with a glorious victory.
   在贏得奧運金牌後，這名運動員帶著光榮的勝利返鄉。

12. **herd** [hɝd] n. [C] 獸群
   ▲ In the video, a herd of elephants is crossing the river.
   在這影片中有一群大象正在過河。

   herd [hɝd] v. 放牧，將⋯趕成一群
   ▲ It's amazing that the shepherd dog can herd the sheep. 這牧羊犬能趕羊真是令人驚奇。

13. **hurricane** [ˋhɝɪˌken] n. [C] (尤指大西洋的) 颶風
   ▲ A hurricane is a destructive storm which forms in the Atlantic Ocean.
   颶風是在大西洋形成的具有破壞力的暴風。

14. **interruption** [ˌɪntəˋrʌpʃən] n. [C][U] 中斷，打斷
   ▲ The president spoke for 30 minutes without interruption at the opening ceremony.
   總裁在開幕式中不間斷地講了三十分鐘的話。

15. **loyalty** [ˋlɔɪəltɪ] n. [U] 忠誠，忠實 <to>
   ▲ The admiral's loyalty to his country has never been doubted.

這位海軍上將對國家的忠誠從來都是無庸置疑。

16. **memorize** [ˋmɛmə͵raɪz] v. 熟記
   ▲ The teacher told the students to memorize the new words in class.
   在課堂上，老師請學生把新單字背起來。

17. **obedient** [oˋbidɪənt] adj. 服從的 <to> [反] disobedient
   ▲ The students are supposed to be obedient to their teachers. 學生應該服從師長。

   obediently [oˋbidɪəntlɪ] adv. 服從地
   ▲ The dog obeyed its master's orders obediently.
   這隻狗馴服地聽從主人的命令。

18. **persuasion** [pəˋsweʒən] n. [U] 說服，勸服
   ▲ It took a lot of persuasion to make Nelson change his mind. 花了好大的功夫來說服 Nelson 改變心意。

19. **plum** [plʌm] n. [C] 李子；梅子
   ▲ Mike grows a plum tree. Mike 種了一棵李子樹。

20. **repetition** [͵rɛpɪˋtɪʃən] n. [C][U] 重複
   ▲ The teacher asked Justin to revise his essay because of some unnecessary repetition.
   老師要 Justin 修改他的文章，因為一些不必要的重複。

21. **respectful** [rɪˋspɛktfəl] adj. 恭敬的 <to, of> [反] disrespectful
   ▲ Tony is respectful to his elders. Tony 尊敬長輩。

respectfully [rɪ`spɛktfəlɪ] adv. 恭敬地

▲ Simon talked respectfully to the great scholar.
　Simon 恭敬地和那位偉大的學者說話。

---

22. **socket** [`sɑkɪt] n. [C] (電源) 插座 [同] outlet

▲ The mother warned her children not to put their
　fingers into electric sockets.
　這位母親警告她的孩子們不要把手指伸進電插座中。

---

23. **telescope** [`tɛlə,skop] n. [C] 望遠鏡

▲ Amber looked at Halley's Comet through a
　telescope. Amber 用望遠鏡來觀看哈雷彗星。

---

24. **twig** [twɪg] n. [C] 細枝 [同] branch, stick

▲ The campers collected some dry twigs to make a fire.
　露營者撿一些乾的細枝來生火。

---

25. **vital** [`vaɪtl] adj. 重要的 <to> [同] crucial；維生的

▲ Your help is vital to the program.
　你的幫助對這個計畫極為重要。

Unit 33

1. **ambitious** [æm`bɪʃəs] adj. 野心勃勃的，有抱負的 <for>

▲ The ambitious young man wants to establish his own
　business. 那位有雄心的年輕人想要建立自己的事業。

---

2. **bandage** [`bændɪdʒ] n. [C][U] 繃帶 <on, around>

▲ The nurse wrapped a bandage around my injured arm. 護士在我受傷的手臂上纏上繃帶。

bandage [ˈbændɪdʒ] v. 用繃帶包紮

▲ Teresa cleaned the wound and bandaged it up.
Teresa 清潔傷口，並用繃帶包紮。

---

3. **calculate** [ˈkælkjəˌlet] v. 計算 [同] work out

▲ I am calculating how much tax I should pay this year.
我正在計算我今年要繳多少稅金。

---

4. **clash** [klæʃ] n. [C] 衝突，打鬥 [同] fight

▲ There were violent clashes between the police and the protesters today.
今天警方跟抗議者之間發生了嚴重的衝突。

clash [klæʃ] v. 衝突，打鬥 <with> [同] fight

▲ The residents clashed with the police over whether to tear down the old church.
居民為了是否拆除舊教堂而與警方起衝突。

---

5. **converse** [kənˈvɝs] v. 交談，談話 <with> [同] talk

▲ Louis speaks French only, and I speak English only, so it is difficult for me to converse with him. Louis 只會說法文而我只會說英文，因此我很難跟他交談。

---

6. **critic** [ˈkrɪtɪk] n. [C] 評論家 [同] reviewer

▲ The movie was praised by the film critics.
這部影片頗受影評家讚賞。

---

7. **disgust** [dɪs`gʌst] n. [U] 反感，厭惡 <at> [同] dislike

   ▲ People expressed their disgust at the government's new tax policy. 人們對政府的新稅法表示反感。

   disgust [dɪs`gʌst] v. 使作嘔，使厭惡

   ▲ The thought of people spitting on the sidewalk disgusted me.

   一想到人們在人行道上吐痰就令我作嘔。

   disgusted [dɪs`gʌstɪd] adj. 厭惡的，反感的 <with>

   ▲ I was disgusted with Helen's behavior.

   我非常不喜歡 Helen 的行為。

   disgusting [dɪs`gʌstɪŋ] adj. 令人作嘔的 [同] revolting

   ▲ Terry's room is disgusting. There are dirty clothes and used tissues everywhere. Terry 的房間令人作嘔，到處都是髒衣服和用過的衛生紙。

8. **divorce** [dɪ`vors] n. [C][U] 離婚

   ▲ To avoid paying for her husband's debts, the wife filed for a divorce.

   為了避免替她丈夫還債，這名妻子訴請離婚。

   💡 get a divorce 獲准離婚 | divorce rate 離婚率

   divorce [dɪ`vors] v. 和⋯離婚

   ▲ Sunny decided to divorce her husband.

   Sunny 決定和她的丈夫離婚。

9. **fertile** [`fɝtl] adj. 肥沃的 [反] infertile

   ▲ In this country, most fertile farmland, which produces the majority of crops, is located in the west.

在這國家，大部分肥沃的田地都位於西部，生產大多數的穀物。

---

10. **flee** [fli] v. 逃跑 ， 逃離 <from> [同] escape, run away
(fled | fled | fleeing)
▲ The criminal tried to flee the country but was stopped at the harbor.
那罪犯試圖逃亡到海外，但在港口被攔下。

---

11. **gown** [gaʊn] n. [C] 禮服；長袍 [同] robe
▲ The bride wore a beautiful wedding gown.
新娘穿了件漂亮的結婚禮服。

---

12. **hook** [hʊk] n. [C] 掛鉤
▲ Hang your coat on the hook behind the door.
把你的大衣掛在門後的掛鉤上。
hook [hʊk] v. (用鉤子) 鉤住
▲ Luckily, the fisherman hooked a big salmon within an hour. 幸運地，這漁夫一小時內就釣到一條大鮭魚。
hooked [hʊkt] adj. 著迷的 <on>
▲ Tom is completely hooked on video games.
Tom 沉迷於電玩。

---

13. **hush** [hʌʃ] n. [sing.] (突然的) 寂靜
▲ A hush descended over the classroom when the students saw their teacher.
當學生看到老師時，教室頓時變得鴉雀無聲。
hush [hʌʃ] v. 使安靜

▲ The tired mother was trying to hush her crying baby but in vain. 這疲累的母親試著哄啼哭的嬰孩安靜下來，但卻徒勞無功。

14. **isolate** [ˋaɪsḷˌet] v. 使隔離 <from>

▲ The child with an infectious disease was isolated from other people.
這個患有傳染病的孩童與其他人隔離開來。

isolated [ˋaɪsḷˌetɪd] adj. 孤立的，孤獨的

▲ Peter leads an isolated life.
Peter 過著與世隔絕的生活。

15. **luxury** [ˋlʌkʃərɪ] n. [U] 奢侈，奢華 [同] extravagance

▲ The wealthy man lives in luxury in the mansion.
這位富人在豪宅裡過著奢華的生活。

16. **mercy** [ˋmɝsɪ] n. [U] 仁慈，寬恕 <on> [同] humanity

▲ Sandy asked the judge to have mercy on her father.
Sandy 請法官對她的父親給予寬恕。

💡 at the mercy of... 任由⋯擺布 | without mercy 毫無憐憫心地

17. **obstacle** [ˋɑbstəkḷ] n. [C] 阻礙 <to> [同] hindrance

▲ Leo's fear of water is his major obstacle to becoming a sailor. Leo 對水的恐懼是他當船員的最大阻礙。

18. **pest** [pɛst] n. [C] 害蟲

▲ Flies and rats are common pests.
蒼蠅和老鼠是常見的害蟲。

pesticide [ˋpɛstə͵saɪd] n. [C][U] 殺蟲劑

▲ The overuse of pesticide will pollute the environment. 過度使用殺蟲劑會汙染環境。

19. **plumber** [ˋplʌmɚ] n. [C] 水管工人

▲ The toilet is out of order. I'm going to have a plumber fix it.

這馬桶故障了。我要找個水管工人來維修。

20. **rescue** [ˋrɛskju] n. [C][U] 救援

▲ The rescue of the surviving passengers in the plane crash started immediately.

救援墜機存活乘客的行動即刻開始。

🕯 come to sb's rescue 解救…

rescue [ˋrɛskju] v. 拯救，救出 <from> [同] save

▲ The firefighters rescued the baby from the burning building. 消防隊員把嬰兒從失火的大樓中救出來。

21. **restore** [rɪˋstor] v. 恢復

▲ The mayor is trying to restore people's confidence in the city government.

市長正設法恢復民眾對市政府的信心。

22. **spade** [sped] n. [C] 鏟子

▲ The child is digging in the sand with a spade.

這孩童用鏟子在挖沙。

23. **thorough** [ˋθɝo] adj. 徹底的，完全的

▲ The detective is making a thorough search of the house. 這名偵探正在對房子做徹底的搜查。

thoroughly [`θɜ·olɪ] adv. 徹底地

▲ We've cleaned our house thoroughly this afternoon. 今天下午我們徹底地清掃了我們的房子。

---

24. **vain** [ven] adj. 徒勞的，白費的 [同] useless

▲ The butterfly made a vain attempt to escape from the spider web. 那隻蝴蝶嘗試從蜘蛛網逃走，但失敗了。

♥ in vain 徒勞無功

---

25. **voyage** [`vɔɪɪdʒ] n. [C] 航海，航行

▲ The pirates made a voyage from Ireland to Iceland. 海盜們從愛爾蘭航海至冰島。

♥ bon voyage 一路順風

voyage [`vɔɪɪdʒ] v. 航行

▲ The adventurer planned to voyage through the Atlantic Ocean. 這位冒險家計劃航行穿越大西洋。

Unit 34

1. **amuse** [ə`mjuz] v. 使開心，逗人笑 [同] entertain

▲ The teacher's funny joke amused all his students. 老師好笑的笑話讓所有學生都笑了。

amusement [ə`mjuzmənt] n. [U] 快樂，開心 <in, with>

▲ These children are playing with amusement in the park. 這些小孩在公園裡快樂地玩著。

💡 to sb's amusement 令⋯感到好笑的是

amused [əˋmjuzd] adj. 逗樂的，覺得好笑的 <at, by>

▲ Iris was amused at Billy's idea in class.

在課堂上，Iris 被 Billy 的想法逗笑了。

amusing [əˋmjuzɪŋ] adj. 引人發笑的，好笑的

▲ Peter made us laugh with an amusing joke.

Peter 用好笑的笑話逗我們笑。

---

2. **basin** [ˋbesṇ] n. [C] 洗臉盆；一盆 (的量)

▲ The bathroom is equipped with a basin, a shower, and a toilet. 這間浴室備有洗臉盆、淋浴間和馬桶。

---

3. **calculation** [͵kælkjəˋleʃən] n. [C][U] 計算

▲ Leo made some rapid calculations and told the clerk the bill was wrong.

Leo 很快做了計算，然後告訴店員帳單是錯誤的。

---

4. **classify** [ˋklæsə͵faɪ] v. 把⋯分類

▲ The books on the shelves are classified according to subject. 書架上的書是根據學科分類的。

---

5. **correspond** [͵kɔrəˋspand] v. 相當於 <to> [同] agree, tally；通信 <with>

▲ The British prime minister, who corresponds to the president of the United States, is chosen by a general election. 英國總理，相當於美國總統，是由普選產生。

---

6. **crunchy** [ˋkrʌntʃɪ] adj. 鬆脆的，鮮脆的 (crunchier | crunchiest)

▲ The mixed salad is fresh and crunchy.

這什錦沙拉新鮮又鬆脆。

crunch [krʌntʃ] v. (發出嘎吱聲地) 咀嚼 <on> [同] munch, chomp

▲ The dog is crunching on the bone we gave him.

這隻狗正嘎吱嘎吱地啃著我們給牠的骨頭。

crunch [krʌntʃ] n. [C] (咀嚼、踩踏發出的) 嘎吱聲 (usu. sing.)

▲ I heard the crunch of my feet on the gravel trail.

我聽到我踩在碎石小徑上發出的嘎吱聲。

---

7. **disturb** [dɪˋstɝb] v. 打擾，干擾

▲ I could not concentrate because the loud music kept disturbing me.

我無法專注，因為那震耳欲聾的音樂一直打擾到我。

---

8. **dodge** [dɑdʒ] v. 閃躲；躲避 [同] evade

▲ The boxer dodged the blow swiftly.

拳擊手快速地閃開了這一拳。

dodge [dɑdʒ] n. [C] 逃避的妙招

▲ The company keeps investing in real estate as a tax dodge. 這間公司持續投資房地產來避稅。

💡 dodge ball 躲避球；躲避球遊戲

---

9. **fierce** [fɪrs] adj. 凶猛的 [同] ferocious (fiercer | fiercest)

▲ The gladiator had a bitter fight with a fierce lion.

這個角鬥士和一頭凶猛的獅子有一場苦戰。

fiercely [ˋfɪrslɪ] adv. 激烈地

▲ The competition is fiercely competitive.

這場比賽競爭激烈。

10. **fluent** [ˈfluənt] adj. (語言) 流利的 <in>

▲ Brian has a talent for language and is fluent in six languages.

Brian 有語言天分，能把六種語言說得很流利。

fluently [ˈfluəntlɪ] adv. 流利地

▲ People who speak more than one language fluently process information more easily than those who know only one language. 能夠流利地說一種以上語言的人比那些只會說一種語言的人更容易處理資訊。

11. **graceful** [ˈgresfəl] adj. 優雅的 [同] elegant

▲ The ballerina amazes people with her graceful dance. 這位芭蕾舞者優雅的舞姿讓大家驚豔。

12. **hydrogen** [ˈhaɪdrədʒən] n. [U] 氫

▲ In chemistry, water is a compound of hydrogen and oxygen. 就化學而言，水是氫氧化合物。

13. **illustration** [ˌɪləsˈtreʃən] n. [C] 例子 [同] example, instance；插圖 [同] picture

▲ The tide is an illustration of how the earth and the moon interact. 潮汐是地球與月球互動的例子。

💡 by way of illustration 透過例證

14. **jealousy** [ˈdʒɛləsɪ] n. [C][U] 嫉妒 [同] envy (pl. jealousies)

▲ Kevin broke his younger brother's toy on purpose out of jealousy.

Kevin 出於嫉妒而故意弄壞弟弟的玩具。

15. **mechanical** [mə`kænɪkl] adj. 機械的

▲ The plane crash was caused by a mechanical problem. 這架飛機墜毀是起因於機械問題。

mechanically [mə`kænɪkəlɪ] adv. 機械化地，習慣性地

▲ The workers mechanically completed their tasks.

工作人員機械化地完成了他們的任務。

16. **mere** [mɪr] adj. 僅僅的

▲ Mere words won't work. It's time for action!

光說不練沒有用。該採取行動了！

merely [`mɪrlɪ] adv. 僅僅，只 [同] only

▲ Tommy merely wanted to please his wife.

Tommy 只是想讓他的妻子高興。

17. **offend** [ə`fɛnd] v. 冒犯，得罪

▲ I am sorry if I have offended you.

如有冒犯之處，尚請見諒。

18. **physician** [fə`zɪʃən] n. [C] (尤指內科) 醫師

▲ The alternative therapy is recommended by a physician. 這項替代性療法由一位醫師推薦。

19. **poisonous** [`pɔɪzənəs] adj. 有毒的 [同] toxic

▲ The farmer was bitten by a poisonous snake on the calf.

這個農夫被毒蛇咬到小腿。

20. **resolve** [rɪ`zɑlv] v. 決定，決心；解決 [同] solve, settle
   ▲ After careful consideration, the witness resolved to tell the truth. 仔細考慮後，這位證人決定說實話。
   resolve [rɪ`zɑlv] n. [U] 決心 [同] resolution
   ▲ These challenges strengthened Lisa's resolve to realize her dream.
   這些挑戰讓 Lisa 更加堅定去實現夢想。

21. **retire** [rɪ`taɪr] v. 退休
   ▲ Alex is going to retire at the age of sixty.
   Alex 將在六十歲退休。
   retirement [rɪ`taɪrmənt] n. [C][U] 退休
   ▲ After his retirement, Sam will devote himself to gardening. 退休後，Sam 將全心蒔花養卉。
   retired [rɪ`taɪrd] adj. 退休的
   ▲ William is a retired captain. He now has an easy life.
   William 是一位退休的船長。他現在過著安逸舒適的生活。

22. **sprinkle** [`sprɪŋkl] v. 撒，灑 <on, over>
   ▲ The waiter sprinkled some cheese on the pizza.
   服務生在披薩上撒了些起司。
   sprinkle [`sprɪŋkl] n. [sing.] 少量
   ▲ I like to put a sprinkle of cinnamon on my latte.
   我喜歡在我的拿鐵上撒少量肉桂。
   sprinkler [`sprɪŋklə] n. [C] 灑水器

▲ The sprinkler doesn't work. We need someone to fix it. 灑水器壞了。我們需要有人修理它。

---

23. **thoughtful** [ˋθɔtfəl] adj. 體貼的 [同] considerate, kind

▲ It was thoughtful of you to give me a ride home.
你載我回家真是體貼。

---

24. **virtue** [ˋvɝtʃʊ] n. [C][U] 美德 [反] vice ；優點 [同] advantage, merit

▲ Honesty is one of my younger sister's virtues.
誠實是我妹妹的美德之一。

♥ Virtue is its own reward. 【諺】為善最樂。

---

25. **witness** [ˋwɪtnɪs] n. [C] 目擊者 <to>

▲ The only witness to the accident was taken to the police station to make a statement about what had happened. 那起事故的唯一目擊者被帶到警察局做筆錄，說明發生了什麼事。

witness [ˋwɪtnɪs] v. 目睹

▲ We have witnessed remarkable advances in technology over the last fifty years.
近五十年來我們目睹了科技卓越的發展。

Unit 35

1. **annoy** [əˋnɔɪ] v. 使惱怒 [同] irritate

▲ What annoyed Sandy most was that no one showed respect for her. 最惹惱 Sandy 的是沒有人尊重她。

annoying [ə`nɔɪɪŋ] adj. 使惱怒的 [同] irritating

▲ It's annoying that my neighbor keeps making a lot of noise late at night.
我的鄰居在深夜持續製造許多噪音，令人很惱火。

---

2. **beggar** [`bɛgɚ] n. [C] 乞丐

▲ Owing to the recession, the number of beggars on the streets is increasing.
由於經濟衰退，流落街道的乞丐人數不斷增加。

---

3. **calorie** [`kælərɪ] n. [C] 卡路里 (pl. calories)

▲ Counting calories is a good way to lose weight.
計算卡路里是減重的一種好方法。

---

4. **claw** [klɔ] n. [C] 爪；螯

▲ The cat is sharpening its claws on the carpet.
貓正在地毯上磨爪子。

claw [klɔ] v. 用爪子抓

▲ The puppy clawed at the toy. 小狗用爪子抓玩具。

---

5. **costume** [`kɑstjum] n. [C][U] (尤指娛樂活動的) 服裝

▲ Lily's witch costume caught many people's attention.
Lily 的巫婆服裝吸引了很多人的注意。

---

6. **crush** [krʌʃ] n. [C] (短暫的) 迷戀 <on>

▲ Peter has a crush on Rita, the most beautiful girl at school. Peter 迷戀全校最漂亮的女生 Rita。

crush [krʌʃ] v. 壓碎，壓扁

▲ The car accident not only crushed my legs but also my dream of becoming a dancer. 這起車禍不只壓碎我的腿，也讓我成為舞者的夢想破滅。

7. **dominate** [`dɑmə,net] v. 主宰，支配

▲ The aggressive basketball team almost dominates every game.
這支志在必得的籃球隊幾乎主宰每一場球賽。

8. **draft** [dræft] n. [C] 草稿

▲ Emily has made the first draft of her thesis.
Emily 擬了一份論文的初稿。

draft [dræft] v. 打草稿

▲ The secretary is drafting a speech for the company's president. 祕書正在為公司的董事長擬演講稿。

9. **fireplace** [`faɪr,ples] n. [C] 壁爐

▲ Howard didn't turn on the light, and the living room was only lit by a warm glow from the fireplace.
Howard 沒有開燈，客廳裡只有壁爐發出的溫暖柔和光線。

10. **fortunate** [`fɔrtʃənɪt] adj. 好運的 [同] lucky [反] unfortunate

▲ I am fortunate enough to have good health and a steady job. 我很幸運有好的健康和穩定的工作。

fortunately [`fɔrtʃənɪtlɪ] adv. 幸運地 [同] luckily [反] unfortunately

▲ Fortunately, the weather cleared up.
幸好天氣轉晴了。

11. **gracious** [ˈgreʃəs] adj. 親切的

▲ The mayor was gracious enough to attend our garden party. 市長非常親切地參與我們的園遊會。

12. **identification** [aɪˌdɛntəfəˈkeʃən] n. [U] 辨認 (abbr. ID)

▲ Without the aid of DNA testing, the identification of the crash victims would be extremely difficult.
沒有去氧核醣核酸 (DNA) 檢驗的幫助，辨認墜機意外傷亡者會相當困難。

13. **imitate** [ˈɪməˌtet] v. 模仿 [同] mimic

▲ Nelson likes to imitate the teacher to make his classmates laugh. Nelson 常模仿老師來引同學發笑。

14. **kettle** [ˈkɛtl] n. [C] 水壺

▲ Ethan put the kettle on as soon as he got home.
Ethan 一到家就馬上燒開水。

15. **merchant** [ˈmɝtʃənt] n. [C] 商人

▲ The merchant made a fortune by selling antiques.
這位商人藉由販賣古董發財。

16. **messy** [ˈmɛsɪ] adj. 凌亂的 [同] chaotic；棘手的 (messier | messiest)

▲ Iris spent the whole weekend tidying up the messy room. Iris 花了整個週末來清理這個凌亂的房間。

17. **offensive** [əˋfɛnsɪv] adj. 冒犯的，令人不愉快的 [反] inoffensive

▲ Teresa was angry about Jack's offensive remarks.
Teresa 對 Jack 冒犯的言詞感到生氣。

offensively [əˋfɛnsɪvlɪ] adv. 無禮地

▲ Edison spoke offensively about his family yesterday.
Edison 昨天無禮地談論他的家人。

---

18. **physics** [ˋfɪzɪks] n. [U] 物理學

▲ Since I am greatly interested in science, I will major in physics at college.
因為我對科學有強烈的興趣，我將在大學主修物理學。

---

19. **prediction** [prɪˋdɪkʃən] n. [C][U] 預測

▲ The experts made a prediction that the economy will improve next year. 專家預測明年經濟會好轉。

---

20. **respectable** [rɪˋspɛktəbl] adj. 可敬的，值得尊敬的

▲ Although the priest is very poor, he is a respectable person. 雖然這位牧師很窮，但他是個可敬的人。

respectably [rɪˋspɛktəblɪ] adv. 得體地

▲ A public figure must behave respectably in public.
一位公眾人物在大庭廣眾下必須行為得體。

---

21. **revolutionary** [͵rɛvəˋluʃən͵ɛrɪ] adj. 革命性的

▲ The computer was a revolutionary invention in the 20th century. 電腦是二十世紀一項革命性的發明。

revolutionary [ˌrɛvəˈluʃənˌɛrɪ] n. [C] 革命者 (pl. revolutionaries)

▲ Bill is a radical revolutionary in the country.
　Bill 是這國家激進的革命者。

22. **statistic** [stəˈtɪstɪk] n. [C] (一項) 統計數據；[pl.] 統計資料 (~s)

▲ The most shocking statistic is the high crime rate in the city.
　最讓人震驚的統計數據是這座城市的高犯罪率。

💡 become a statistic 成為交通事故的數據 (死於交通事故)

23. **tolerance** [ˈtɑlərəns] n. [U] 容忍 <of, toward> [反] intolerance

▲ Tolerance of different opinions should be encouraged in a democratic country.
　在民主國家中，應該鼓勵大家包容不同的意見。

24. **waken** [ˈwekən] v. 喚醒，弄醒

▲ All of us were wakened by the earthquake.
　我們全被地震給弄醒了。

25. **workplace** [ˈwɝkˌples] n. [sing.] 工作場所 (the ~)

▲ Earning a good profit this year, the boss promised to improve the facilities in the workplace. 由於今年的獲利不錯，老闆承諾要改善工作場所的設施。

Unit 36

1. **accompany** [ə`kʌmpənɪ] **v.** 陪同 [同] go with；伴隨
   ▲ Dora is accompanied by her grandmother to go to school every day. Dora 每天由她的祖母陪同去上學。

2. **apology** [ə`pɑlədʒɪ] **n.** [C][U] 道歉 <to, for> (pl. apologies)
   ▲ The manager made a sincere apology to the customers for the inconvenience.
   經理為造成不便而向顧客誠摯道歉。

3. **bin** [bɪn] **n.** [C] 垃圾桶
   ▲ Please help me throw it in the bin.
   請幫我把它扔進垃圾桶。

4. **candidate** [`kændə,det] **n.** [C] 候選人 <for>
   ▲ Gloria is one of the leading candidates for the mayor.
   Gloria 是競選市長的主要候選人之一。

5. **commander** [kə`mændɚ] **n.** [C] 指揮官
   ▲ Jennifer was a flight commander when she was 40 years old. Jennifer 四十歲時是飛行指揮官。

6. **counter** [`kauntɚ] **n.** [C] 櫃臺
   ▲ The customer put his items on the counter and waited patiently for the cashier to scan them. 這位顧客把物品放在櫃臺上，並耐心等待收銀員掃描它們。

💡 over the counter (尤指買藥時) 不憑處方箋 | under the counter 祕密地，暗地裡

counter [ˋkaʊntɚ] v. 反駁

▲ Grace's brother accused her of breaking the window, but she countered that he was the one to blame.
Grace 的弟弟指控她打破窗戶，但她反駁說該受責備的是他。

counter [ˋkaʊntɚ] adj. 相反的

counter [ˋkaʊntɚ] adv. 相反地 <to>

▲ David's action runs counter to his words.
David 的言行不一。

---

7. **cube** [kjub] n. [C] 立方體，立方形的東西

▲ Sam cut a box of tofu into eight cubes and then deep-fried them in the wok.
Sam 把一盒豆腐切成八塊，然後放進鍋內油炸。

💡 ice/sugar cube 冰塊 / 方糖

cube [kjub] v. 將 (食物) 切丁

▲ The first step in making the soup is to cube the potatoes and carrots.
做這道湯的第一步就是把馬鈴薯和胡蘿蔔切丁。

---

8. **dread** [drɛd] n. [U] 害怕，恐懼 [同] fear

▲ The thought of catching a flight fills me with dread.
想到要搭飛機就讓我非常地恐懼。

dread [drɛd] v. 害怕，恐懼 [同] fear

▲ Most people dread making speeches in public.

大部分的人害怕公開演講。

---

9. **drift** [drɪft] v. 漂流；無意間發生 <into>

▲ The boat drifted quickly downstream.
船快速地順流而下。

drift [drɪft] n. [C][U] 水流

▲ The drift of this current is to the east.
這道海流流向東方。

---

10. **flatter** [ˈflætɚ] v. 奉承，諂媚

▲ Ken flattered Linda by praising her beautiful face.
Ken 誇獎 Linda 漂亮的臉蛋來奉承她。

♥ flatter oneself 自命不凡，自視甚高 | feel flattered 感到榮幸

flattery [ˈflætərɪ] n. [U] 奉承

▲ There must be something underneath Nina's flattery.
Nina 的恭維話裡一定藏有某些用意。

---

11. **frustrate** [ˈfrʌstret] v. 使灰心，使氣餒

▲ It frustrated me that I was rejected by the university.
我沒被這所大學錄取讓我很氣餒。

frustrated [ˈfrʌstretɪd] adj. 受挫的，沮喪的 <at, with>

▲ Ian was frustrated at his colleague's refusal to help him with the project.
Ian 對於他同事拒絕幫助他做這個企劃案而感到受挫。

frustrating [ˈfrʌstretɪŋ] adj. 令人氣餒的

▲ It's frustrating to talk to Stanley because he never listens.

跟 Stanley 說話令人氣餒，因為他從來都聽不進去。

---

12. **greeting** [ˋgritɪŋ] n. [C][U] 問候，招呼；[pl.] 祝詞 (～s)

▲ Jack and Mary exchanged greetings and had lunch together. Jack 和 Mary 互相致意後一起吃午餐。

---

13. **idiom** [ˋɪdɪəm] n. [C] 慣用語，成語

▲ An English idiom may mean something different from the words that make up the idiom. 英文的慣用語可能和組成該慣用語的字面意思有所不同。

---

14. **imply** [ɪmˋplaɪ] v. 暗示 [同] hint

▲ John's repeated absences from work implied that he didn't like his job.
John 屢次曠職暗示了他不喜歡他的工作。

---

15. **kneel** [nil] v. 跪下 <down> (knelt, kneeled | knelt, kneeled | kneeling)

▲ Facing the Wailing Wall in Jerusalem, people knelt down and started to say their prayers.
面向耶路撒冷的哭牆，人們跪下開始禱告。

---

16. **microscope** [ˋmaɪkrə͵skop] n. [C] 顯微鏡 <under>

▲ The scientist examined the blood samples under the microscope. 這位科學家用顯微鏡來檢視血液樣本。

---

17. **millionaire** [͵mɪljəˋnɛr] n. [C] 百萬富翁

▲ The author's first book became a bestseller and made him a millionaire. 這位作者的第一本書成為暢銷書，

並使他成為百萬富翁。

18. **orientation** [ˌorɪənˈteʃən] **n.** [C][U] (價值觀等) 取向；[U] (新工作或新活動的) 培訓，訓練
   ▲ The company employs their employees without regard to their political or religious orientation. 這間公司僱用員工不會考量到他們的政治或宗教取向。

19. **postage** [ˈpostɪdʒ] **n.** [U] 郵資
   ▲ How much postage should I pay for this parcel? 這件包裹我應該付多少郵資？

20. **pregnancy** [ˈprɛgnənsɪ] **n.** [C][U] 懷 孕 (pl. pregnancies)
   ▲ Fiona suffered sickness during her first months of pregnancy. Fiona 在懷孕初期感到噁心。

21. **reunion** [riˈjunjən] **n.** [C] 團聚，聚會
   ▲ We usually have a family reunion on Chinese New Year's Eve. 我們通常在除夕會全家團聚。

22. **romance** [roˈmæns] **n.** [C] 戀愛史，羅曼史
   ▲ The writer's romances with his lovers inspired him to create those great novels. 這位作家與他的愛人們的羅曼史激發他寫出那些偉大的小說。

23. **stereo** [ˈstɛrɪo] **n.** [C] 立體音響 (pl. stereos)
   ▲ Tom spent a lot of money on the stereo so he could enjoy high-quality music at home.

Tom 花了許多錢買立體音響，以便在家欣賞高品質的音樂。

---

24. **tolerate** [ˈtɑləˌret] v. 容忍 [同] stand, bear

▲ Sometimes we have to tolerate some inconvenience while traveling in a foreign country.

當在國外旅行時，我們有時候必須容忍一些不便。

---

25. **wink** [wɪŋk] n. [C] 眨眼

▲ Irene's father gave her a wink and put a thumb up to show his praise.

Irene 的父親向她眨眼睛並對她豎起大拇指表示讚美。

wink [wɪŋk] v. 眨眼 <at> [同] blink

▲ As I looked at the sky, the stars seemed to wink at me mysteriously.

當我看著天空，星星似乎神祕地對我眨眼睛。

Unit 37

1. **admirable** [ˈædmərəbḷ] adj. 值 得 讚 賞 的 [同] commendable

▲ Teresa's contribution to this community was admirable. Teresa 對這社區的貢獻是值得讚賞的。

2. **applicant** [ˈæpləkənt] n. [C] 申請者 <for>

▲ Clare was selected from over 150 applicants for the job. Clare 在超過一百五十名職務申請者中被選中。

---

3. **biography** [baɪˈɑgrəfɪ] n. [C][U] 傳記 <of> (pl. biographies)

▲ As a classical music lover, the writer spent years gathering information and then writing a biography of Mozart. 身為古典樂愛好者，這位作家花很多年收集資料並寫了莫札特的傳記。

4. **cease** [sis] v. 停止

▲ The little boy did not cease crying until his mother returned. 這小男孩直到他的母親回來才停止哭泣。

cease [sis] n. [U] 停止

▲ It looked as if we had walked for days without cease. 我們似乎不停地走了好幾天。

5. **competitor** [kəmˈpɛtətɚ] n. [C] 參賽者 [同] challenger

▲ Over 800 competitors took part in the race. 有超過八百位選手參加賽跑。

6. **courageous** [kəˈredʒəs] adj. 勇敢的 [同] brave

▲ Harry is the most courageous person that I have ever met. Harry 是我見過最勇敢的人。

7. **cue** [kju] n. [C] 提示，暗示

▲ Our boss's arrival was the cue for us to get down to work. 老闆的到來暗示我們要開始工作。

● right on cue 正好在此時 | take sb's cue from sb/sth 照…的樣子做…

cue [kju] v. 給予暗示

▲ The conductor cued the pianist with a nod of his head. 這位指揮家向鋼琴家點頭示意。

---

8. **drowsy** [ˋdraʊzɪ] adj. 昏昏欲睡的 [同] sleepy (drowsier | drowsiest)

▲ The drugs for allergies normally make patients drowsy. 這些治過敏的藥通常讓病人昏昏欲睡。

---

9. **dusty** [ˋdʌstɪ] adj. 滿是灰塵的 (dustier | dustiest)

▲ The house is now dusty. Tony needs to make the time to clean up.
屋子現在滿是灰塵。Tony 需要騰出時間打掃乾淨。

---

10. **flea** [fli] n. [C] 跳蚤

▲ Stray cats and dogs usually have fleas.
流浪貓狗的身上通常有跳蚤。

♥ flea market 跳蚤市場

---

11. **frustration** [frʌsˋtreʃən] n. [C][U] 挫折，沮喪

▲ Tom felt a sense of frustration when he knew that he had not been promoted.
當 Tom 知道自己沒有獲得升遷時，他覺得有挫折感。

---

12. **grief** [grif] n. [C][U] 悲傷，悲痛

▲ Hearing the bad news, the victim's parents were overwhelmed with grief.
得知這個壞消息，這名受害者的父母悲痛欲絕。

---

13. **idle** [ˈaɪdl] adj. 懈怠的 [同] lazy；(機器、工廠) 閒置的
   (idler | idlest)
   ▲ The idle student played the computer games all day
   long and left his homework undone.
   這個懶散的學生打了一整天的電動，把功課擱在一邊。
   idle [ˈaɪdl] v. 虛度時間 <away>
   ▲ Tina idled her time away on the Internet.
   Tina 上網虛度光陰。

14. **indication** [ˌɪndəˈkeʃən] n. [C][U] 指示，暗示 <of>
   ▲ I gave Rosa some flowers as an indication of my
   gratitude. 我送一些花給 Rosa 表示我的感激。

15. **lag** [læg] n. [C] 延遲，落差
   ▲ There is always a time lag between order and
   delivery. 訂貨和送貨之間總是有時間的落差。
   💡 jet lag 時差
   lag [læg] v. 落後 <behind> (lagged | lagged | lagging)
   ▲ After several hours of walking, Edward began to lag
   behind us.
   走了幾個小時之後，Edward 開始落在我們的後面。

16. **mill** [mɪl] n. [C] 磨坊；工廠 [同] factory
   ▲ There is a mill in the village. 這個村莊裡有一間磨坊。
   💡 steel mill 造鋼廠 | windmill 風車 | go through the
   mill 經歷許多困難
   mill [mɪl] v. 磨成粉

▲ The farmer milled wheat into flour.

農夫把小麥磨成麵粉。

miller [ˈmɪlɚ] n. [C] 磨坊主人

▲ My grandfather used to be a miller in his town.

我的祖父在城鎮裡曾經是一位磨坊主人。

---

17. ministry [ˈmɪnɪstrɪ] n. [C] (政府的) 部 (pl. ministries)

▲ The Ministry of Foreign Affairs deals with international relationship between our nation and other countries.

外交部是處理我們國家與其他國家之間的國際關係。

♥ the Ministry of Education 教育部

---

18. orphan [ˈɔrfən] n. [C] 孤兒

▲ The war destroyed thousands of families and left numerous orphans.

這場戰爭摧毀了數千個家庭，留下無數孤兒。

orphan [ˈɔrfən] v. 使成為孤兒

▲ Wendy was orphaned after her parents were killed in a car accident.

Wendy 在她父母死於車禍後成為孤兒。

---

19. pregnant [ˈprɛgnənt] adj. 懷孕的

▲ My wife is five months pregnant.

我的妻子懷孕五個月。

---

20. presentation [ˌprɛznˈteʃən] n. [C] 報告，演講 <on>；[U] 外觀，呈現方式

▲ The sales manager is giving a brief presentation on the product he is promoting.

這業務經理正在為他促銷的產品做簡報。

---

21. **revenge** [rɪ`vɛndʒ] n. [U] 復仇，報復

▲ Henry finally took his revenge on the people who had murdered his father.

Henry 最後向這些人報了殺父之仇。

💡 in revenge for sth 為…復仇

revenge [rɪ`vɛndʒ] v. 復仇，報復

▲ James revenged himself on his neighbor for the insult. James 為他所受的侮辱向他的鄰居報復。

---

22. **sacrifice** [`sækrə,faɪs] n. [C][U] 犧牲

▲ Parents often make sacrifices to give their children better lives.

父母經常為了給子女好一點的生活而做犧牲。

sacrifice [`sækrə,faɪs] v. 犧牲 <for>

▲ Many people sacrificed their lives for their country in the war. 許多人在戰爭中為他們的國家犧牲性命。

---

23. **stripe** [straɪp] n. [C] 條紋

▲ Zebras have black and white stripes.

斑馬身上有黑白條紋。

💡 horizontal/vertical stripe 橫 / 直條紋

striped [straɪpt] adj. 有條紋的

▲ Sam wore a green and white striped shirt for his friend's party.

Sam 穿著綠白條紋襯衫參加他朋友的派對。

24. **torture** [ˋtɔrtʃɚ] **n.** [C][U] 折磨；拷打 <under>

▲ Looking at a table full of sweets can be torture for one with a toothache.

對一個牙痛的人來說，看著滿桌甜點可以是一種折磨。

torture [ˋtɔrtʃɚ] **v.** 使痛苦 <with, by> [同] torment；拷問

▲ John was tortured by his memories of the war.

戰爭的記憶使 John 很痛苦。

25. **wit** [wɪt] **n.** [U] 幽默風趣；[pl.] 頭腦，機智 (～s)

▲ Ted is a man of wit, and thus he is very popular in the office.

Ted 是個幽默風趣的人，因此他在辦公室很受歡迎。

💡 at sb's wits' end 束手無策 | frighten/scare sb out of sb's wits 把…嚇得魂不附體

Unit 38

1. **admiration** [ˌædməˋreʃən] **n.** [U] 讚賞，欽佩 <for>

▲ The director has great admiration for this actor.

導演非常讚賞這名演員。

2. **arch** [ɑrtʃ] **n.** [C] 拱門

▲ Walking through the arch, you will see a beautiful garden. 穿越拱門，你就會看到一座美麗的花園。

arch [artʃ] v. 拱起

▲ When cats get angry, they arch their backs and lift up their tails.

當貓生氣時，牠們會拱起背，且豎起牠們的尾巴。

---

3. **bloom** [blum] n. [C] 花 <in>

▲ The roses in our garden are in full bloom.

我們花園裡的玫瑰花盛開了。

🔮 come into bloom 開始開花

bloom [blum] v. 開花

▲ The lilies are blooming early this year.

今年百合花開得早。

---

4. **chamber** [ˋtʃembɚ] n. [C] 房間

▲ The witch lives in an underground chamber.

巫婆住在一個地底的房間裡。

---

5. **complicate** [ˋkɑmplə͵ket] v. 使複雜化

▲ The language barrier between the employee and employer complicated the situation.

僱員和僱主之間的語言障礙使事情更複雜。

🔮 To complicate matters further... 讓事情更複雜的是…

complicated [ˋkɑmplə͵ketɪd] adj. 複雜的

▲ The rules are so complicated that I can only remember a few.

這些規定如此複雜以致於我只能記得少數。

---

6. **courtesy** [ˋkɝ·təsɪ] n. [U] 禮貌，禮節 [同] politeness [反] discourtesy

▲ I couldn't believe that Carol didn't have the courtesy to call me to cancel our appointment. 我不敢相信 Carol 連打電話取消我們約會的禮貌都沒有。

🔆 courtesy of sb/sth 承蒙⋯的允許

7. **cunning** [ˋkʌnɪŋ] adj. 狡猾的，奸詐的 [同] crafty, wily

▲ Steve is very cunning and good at deceiving others. Steve 非常狡猾，很會欺騙人。

🔆 as cunning as a fox 像狐狸一樣狡猾

cunning [ˋkʌnɪŋ] n. [U] 狡猾，詭詐

▲ David used some cunning to get what he wanted. David 用一些狡猾的手段來獲取他想要得到的東西。

8. **dye** [daɪ] n. [C][U] 染料

▲ These eggs are being boiled in bright red dye to make them red.

這些蛋正在亮紅色的染料中煮好變成紅色。

dye [daɪ] v. 給⋯染色

▲ Alex dyed his hair green. Alex 將頭髮染成綠色。

9. **economical** [ˌɛkəˋnɑmɪkl] adj. 節儉的，節約的 <of, with> [同] frugal [反] uneconomical

▲ My father is economical with his money.
我父親對金錢很節儉。

10. **flush** [flʌʃ] v. 沖馬桶；臉紅 [同] blush

▲ Don't forget to flush the toilet after you use it.
上完廁所後別忘了沖馬桶。

flush [flʌʃ] **n.** [C] 紅暈 [同] blush

▲ A flush colored Judy's cheeks when Allan asked her out. 當 Allan 約她外出時，Judy 的雙頰泛出紅暈。

11. **funeral** [ˈfjunərəl] **n.** [C] 葬禮

▲ When the famous singer died, many of his fans attended his funeral.
那位知名歌手辭世時，許多歌迷都去參加他的葬禮。

12. **guardian** [ˈɡɑrdɪən] **n.** [C] 保護者 [同] custodian；監護人

▲ The United Nations should be a guardian of world peace. 聯合國應該是世界和平的守護者。

13. **idol** [ˈaɪdl] **n.** [C] 偶像

▲ Young people tend to worship and imitate their idols.
年輕人往往崇拜偶像並模仿他們。

14. **inflation** [ɪnˈfleʃən] **n.** [U] 通貨膨脹

▲ When inflation occurs, people have to pay more for things, but get less in return. 當通貨膨脹發生時，人們買東西必須付更多錢，但得到的反而還變少。

15. **landmark** [ˈlændˌmɑrk] **n.** [C] 地標

▲ The Sydney Opera House is one of Australia's most famous landmarks.
雪梨歌劇院是澳洲最著名的地標之一。

16. **miner** [ˈmaɪnɚ] n. [C] 礦工

▲ Three miners have been trapped underground for a week. 有三名礦工已經被困在地底下一個星期了。

17. **mischief** [ˈmɪstʃɪf] n. [U] 惡作劇，淘氣

▲ The teacher will not allow any mischief in her class. 這位老師不允許課堂上發生任何惡作劇的行為。

💡 make mischief 挑撥離間 | get into mischief 調皮搗蛋 | keep sb out of mischief 阻止⋯搗蛋

18. **oval** [ˈovl] adj. 橢圓形的，卵形的

▲ There is an oval mirror on the wall. 牆上有面橢圓形的鏡子。

oval [ˈovl] n. [C] 橢圓形

▲ We found several rocks in the shape of ovals on the beach. 我們在海灘上找到了幾顆橢圓形的石子。

19. **preservation** [ˌprɛzɚˈveʃən] n. [U] 維護，保護

▲ The local government is in charge of the preservation of the old temple. 地方政府負責維護這座古廟。

20. **priority** [praɪˈɔrətɪ] n. [C][U] 優先事項 (pl. priorities)

▲ Some people think that environmental protection should take priority over economic development. 有些人認為環境保護應較經濟發展為優先。

💡 take priority over... 優先於⋯

21. **revision** [rɪˈvɪʒən] n. [C][U] 修訂，修改 <to>

▲ Greg stayed up to make some revisions to his dissertation. Greg 熬夜修改他的論文。

22. **seize** [siz] v. 抓住 [同] grab；沒收
   ▲ The police officer seized the thief by the arm when he tried to run away.
   當小偷要逃跑時，警察抓住他的手臂。
   💡 seize the opportunity 抓住機會 | seize the day 把握現在

23. **summarize** [ˋsʌməˏraɪz] v. 概述
   ▲ In the introduction, the author summarizes what will be included in the book.
   在序言中，作者概述這本書中所包括的內容。

24. **tremendous** [trɪˋmɛndəs] adj. 巨大的 [同] huge；極好的 [同] remarkable
   ▲ The boss praised Simon for the tremendous effort he had made to accomplish the project. 老闆因 Simon 投注相當多的心力來完成此企劃案而稱讚他。

25. **witch** [wɪtʃ] n. [C] 巫婆，女巫 (pl. witches)
   ▲ The witch turned the prince into a frog.
   這巫婆把王子變成青蛙。
   wizard [ˋwɪzəd] n. [C] 巫師，男巫
   ▲ The wizard performed magic tricks with his magic wand. 這巫師以魔杖施魔法。

Unit 39

1. **agreeable** [əˋgriəbl̩] **adj.** 令人愉快的 [同] pleasant [反] disagreeable；欣然同意的 <to>
   ▲ We had an agreeable picnic in the park today.
   我們今天在公園有個愉快的野餐。

2. **arise** [əˋraɪz] **v.** 出現，產生 <from> (arose | arisen | arising)
   ▲ Accidents often arise from carelessness.
   事故常常因疏忽而起。

3. **boast** [bost] **v.** 誇耀 <about, of>
   ▲ The mother boasted about her child's achievements.
   這母親誇耀她孩子的成就。
   boast [bost] **n.** [C] 誇耀
   ▲ Mark made a boast that he could beat me at chess.
   Mark 誇耀他下西洋棋會贏我。

4. **championship** [ˋtʃæmpɪənˏʃɪp] **n.** [C] 錦標賽，冠軍賽；冠軍地位
   ▲ The tennis player finally won the world championship, which he had been dreaming about for years. 這位網球選手終於贏了他多年來夢寐以求的世界錦標賽。

5. **conductor** [kənˋdʌktɚ] **n.** [C] (樂隊、合唱團的) 指揮；列車長 [同] guard

▲ The orchestra conductor bowed to the audience.

這管弦樂團的指揮向觀眾鞠躬。

6. **crack** [kræk] n. [C] 裂縫;爆裂聲

▲ Lily looked through the crack in the door to see if anyone was in the room.

Lily 從門上的裂縫往裡面看,看看是否有人在房間裡。

crack [kræk] v. 使破裂;(非法侵入) 電腦系統

▲ The glass cracked when boiling water was being poured into it. 熱水正倒入玻璃杯時,杯子裂開了。

7. **curl** [kɜl] n. [C][U] 捲髮

▲ Melody has blond curls. Melody 有一頭金色的捲髮。

curl [kɜl] v. 蜷曲

▲ The dog curled itself into a ball.

這隻狗把身體蜷縮成球狀。

8. **earphone** [ˈɪrˌfon] n. [C] 耳機

▲ I usually use earphones to listen to music.

我通常用耳機聽音樂。

9. **elegant** [ˈɛləgənt] adj. 優雅的,高雅的 [同] stylish

▲ Nina tried hard to make herself look elegant in the presence of her date.

Nina 盡力讓自己在約會對象面前看起來優雅。

elegance [ˈɛləgəns] n. [U] 優雅

▲ The prom queen danced with elegance.

這名舞會女王優雅地跳舞。

10. **foam** [fom] n. [U] 泡沫 [同] froth

   ▲ When I poured the Coke into the glass, foam rose to the surface.

   當我把可樂倒進杯子時，泡沫浮到表面上。

   foam [fom] v. 起泡沫 [同] froth

   ▲ Sam applied some soap to his wet hands and rubbed them until it began to foam.

   Sam 抹些肥皂在溼手上，然後磨擦雙手直到起泡沫。

   💡 foam at the mouth (因生病而) 口吐白沫

---

11. **gifted** [`gɪftɪd] adj. 有天賦的 [同] talented

   ▲ As a gifted artist, Nelson can depict human feelings and emotions through his creations.

   身為一位有天賦的藝術家，Nelson 能夠用他的作品刻劃出人的感情和情緒。

---

12. **guilt** [gɪlt] n. [U] 犯罪

   ▲ It takes courage to admit guilt. 認罪需要勇氣。

---

13. **ignorant** [`ɪgnərənt] adj. 無知的 <of, about>

   ▲ Thomas was ignorant of the local custom and thus offended the local people.

   Thomas 對地方的習俗無知，因此冒犯了當地人。

---

14. **innocence** [`ɪnəsn̩s] n. [U] 無罪，清白 [反] guilt；天真，純真

   ▲ The suspect tried to prove his innocence.

   這名嫌犯試著證明自己的清白。

---

15. **lawful** [ˈlɔfəl] adj. 合法的 [同] legal
   ▲ It's not lawful to smoke marijuana in this country.
   在這國家抽大麻是不合法的。

16. **mineral** [ˈmɪnərəl] n. [C] 礦物；礦物質
   ▲ Indonesia has long been known as a country rich in
   mineral resources. 印尼長久以來以礦產豐富聞名。
   mineral [ˈmɪnərəl] adj. 礦物的
   💡 mineral water 礦泉水

17. **motivate** [ˈmotəˌvet] v. 激勵，激發 <to>
   ▲ Teachers must know how to motivate their students
   to learn. 老師必須要知道如何激勵他們的學生學習。

18. **overcoat** [ˈovɚˌkot] n. [C] 大衣
   ▲ After Jack put on a woolen scarf and a thick
   overcoat, he went out.
   Jack 圍上羊毛圍巾並穿上厚大衣後就出門了。

19. **proceed** [prəˈsid] v. 繼續做 <with>；接著做 <to>
   ▲ Emily asked her father to proceed with the bedtime
   story. Emily 要求她的父親繼續說睡前故事。

20. **pronunciation** [prəˌnʌnsɪˈeʃən] n. [C][U] 發音
   ▲ The pronunciation of the word might vary a little in
   different areas.
   這個字在不同地區的發音可能有點不同。

21. **rhyme** [raɪm] n. [C] 押韻詩

▲ The book contains a collection of famous children's rhymes. 這本書集結一些有名的兒歌。

rhyme [raɪm] v. 押韻 <with>

▲ "Run" rhymes with "son." run 和 son 押同韻。

22. **shameful** [ˈʃemfəl] adj. 可恥的，丟臉的 [同] disgraceful

▲ The cruel way this person treated the stray dog was shameful. 這人對待流浪狗的殘忍方式實在太可恥了。

23. **surgeon** [ˈsɝdʒən] n. [C] 外科醫生

▲ Two surgeons are performing emergency surgery on the man suffering multiple fractures. 兩位外科醫生正在幫多重性骨折的男子執行緊急手術。

24. **urge** [ɝdʒ] n. [C] 衝動 <to>

▲ Though I am on a diet, I cannot stand the urge to have some desserts.

雖然我在節食，我仍無法忍受吃甜食的衝動。

urge [ɝdʒ] v. 力勸，督促

▲ The police urged drivers not to take the highway because of the traffic accident.

因為車禍，警察力勸駕駛不要上這條高速公路。

💡 urge sb on 激勵…

25. **workout** [ˈwɝkˌaʊt] n. [C] 運動，鍛鍊

▲ Abby usually has a workout in the gym after work.

Abby 通常在下班後到健身房運動。

Unit 40 🎓

1. **amateur** [ˋæmə͵tʃʊr] adj. 業餘的 [反] professional
   ▲ To the coach's surprise, the amateur player plays basketball better than a professional one. 令教練驚訝的是，這名業餘選手籃球打得比職業選手好。
   amateur [ˋæmə͵tʃʊr] n. [C] 業餘者 [反] professional
   ▲ The photographer won the photo contest when he was still an amateur.
   這位攝影師仍為業餘者時即贏得攝影比賽。

2. **aspirin** [ˋæspərɪn] n. [C][U] 阿斯匹靈 (pl. aspirin, aspirins)
   ▲ Iris took two aspirins for her headache.
   Iris 因頭痛而吃了兩片阿斯匹靈。

3. **bracelet** [ˋbreslɪt] n. [C] 手鐲，手鍊
   ▲ Nina's silver bracelet shone in the sunshine with every movement.
   Nina 的銀手鐲隨著擺動在陽光下閃閃發光。

4. **characteristic** [͵kærɪktəˋrɪstɪk] n. [C] 特徵 <of>
   ▲ One of the characteristics of Byron's poems is passion. 拜倫詩作的一個特點就是熱情。
   characteristic [͵kærɪktəˋrɪstɪk] adj. 特有的，典型的 [反] uncharacteristic
   ▲ Being hospitable is characteristic of Taiwanese people.

好客是臺灣人的特色。

---

5. **confess** [kənˋfɛs] v. 承認 (錯誤、罪行) [同] admit

▲ The man confessed that he had stolen three cars this year. 那個男子坦承今年他偷了三輛車。

---

6. **craft** [kræft] n. [C][U] 手工藝

▲ The school provides lots of courses for those who are interested in crafts.
這學校提供許多課程給對手工藝有興趣的人。

---

7. **economist** [ɪˋkɑnəmɪst] n. [C] 經濟學家

▲ The economist claimed that the unemployment rate would rise this year.
這位經濟學家宣稱今年失業率會上升。

---

8. **embarrass** [ɪmˋbærəs] v. 使尷尬

▲ The boy embarrassed the girl by laughing at her appearance. 這男孩嘲笑女孩的外表，讓她覺得尷尬。

embarrassment [ɪmˋbærəsmənt] n. [U] 尷尬

▲ To her embarrassment, the lawyer forgot her client's name. 令這律師尷尬的是，她忘記客戶的名字。

embarrassed [ɪmˋbærəst] adj. 尷尬的 <at, about>

▲ Emily was embarrassed about her messy room.
Emily 對自己髒亂的房間感到尷尬。

embarrassing [ɪmˋbærəsɪŋ] adj. 令人尷尬的

▲ I wish Ted could stop asking me embarrassing questions. 但願 Ted 不要再問我尷尬的問題。

---

9. **forbid** [fɚˋbɪd] v. 禁止 <from, to> [反] allow, permit
(forbade | forbidden | forbidding)

▲ My father forbade me to drive his car.
我父親不准我開他的車。

forbidden [fɚˋbɪdn̩] adj. 被禁止的

▲ Be careful. Chewing gum is forbidden in Singapore.
小心點。口香糖在新加坡是被禁止的。

10. **glimpse** [glɪmps] n. [C] 一瞥

▲ Ariel caught a glimpse of a figure in the dark.
Ariel 在黑暗中瞥見一個人影。

glimpse [glɪmps] v. 瞥見

▲ I glimpsed my former teacher in the crowd.
我在人群中瞥見我以前的老師。

11. **hardware** [ˋhɑrdˏwɛr] n. [U] 五金製品；(電腦) 硬體

▲ You can find hammers and nails in this hardware
store. 你可以在這家五金店找到鐵鎚和釘子。

12. **imaginary** [ɪˋmædʒəˏnɛrɪ] adj. 虛構的，想像的

▲ The unicorn is an imaginary creature that looks like a
horse. 獨角獸是長得像馬的虛構生物。

13. **input** [ˋɪnˏput] n. [C][U] 投入 <into> [反] output

▲ I want to thank all my team members, whose input
into the project made it a success. 我要感謝我的所有
團隊成員，他們的投入使得這個企劃得以成功。

input [ˋɪn͵pʊt] v. (將資訊) 輸入 <into> [反] output
(input, inputted | input, inputted | inputting)

▲ Olivia's job is to input data into the computer.
Olivia 的工作是將資料輸入到電腦裡。

---

14. **lean** [lin] v. 傾斜，向一側歪斜

▲ All the audience leaned forward and listened
carefully because the speaker's microphone was
dead.

所有的聽眾傾身仔細聆聽，因為講者的麥克風壞了。

💡 lean against sth 斜靠著 | lean on sb/sth 依靠…

lean [lin] adj. (肉) 瘦的

▲ There is a healthy trend to use lean meat for
hamburgers. 有一種健康的趨勢就是用瘦肉來做漢堡。

---

15. **misfortune** [mɪsˋfɔrtʃən] n. [C][U] 不幸

▲ Linda had the misfortune to lose her parents at an
early age. Linda 幼年時就不幸失去雙親。

---

16. **mountainous** [ˋmaʊntn̩əs] adj. 多山的

▲ The mountainous area is not suitable for agriculture
for lack of fertile soil.

這個山區因缺乏肥沃的土壤，不適合農業。

---

17. **parachute** [ˋpærə͵ʃut] n. [C] 降落傘

▲ Jumping from the helicopter, the pilot was landed by
a parachute. 飛行員跳出直升機，用降落傘降落。

parachute [ˋpærə͵ʃut] v. 跳傘

▲ The soldiers were ordered to parachute into the town.
士兵們奉命跳傘進入小鎮。

---

18. **prosper** [`prɑspɚ] v. 繁榮，興盛 [同] thrive

▲ In spite of the depression, the company has continued to prosper. 雖然經濟不景氣，這家公司生意仍舊興隆。

---

19. **prosperity** [prɑs`pɛrətɪ] n. [U] 繁榮，昌盛

▲ Some people said that the prosperity of a country depends on its educational system.
有些人說一個國家的繁榮取決於其教育體制。

---

20. **riddle** [`rɪdl] n. [C] 謎語 [同] puzzle；奧祕，費解的事 [同] mystery

▲ I was unable to guess the answer to the riddle.
我猜不出這個謎語的答案。

---

21. **shift** [ʃɪft] n. [C] 改變 <in>；輪班

▲ The doctor recommended a shift in my diet.
醫生建議我做飲食改變。

shift [ʃɪft] v. 移動；推卸 (責任) <onto>

▲ The boy shifted uneasily in the chair when he was asked whether he had taken the money. 當被問及是否拿了錢時，那男孩不安地在椅子上動來動去。

💡 shift sb's ground 改變立場 | shift attention/focus/emphasis 轉移焦點

---

22. **surrender** [sə`rɛndɚ] v. 投降 <to> [同] give in；放棄 [同] relinquish

▲ We will never surrender to the terrorists.

我們絕不向恐怖分子投降。

surrender [sə`rɛndɚ] n. [U] 放棄

▲ The surrender of the city was a turning point in the war. 這個城市的棄守是這場戰爭的轉捩點。

23. **usage** [`jusɪdʒ] n. [C][U] (語言的) 用法

▲ The first usage of the word was recorded in the 17th century. 這個字最初的使用紀錄是在十七世紀。

24. **wreck** [rɛk] n. [C] 毀損的交通工具；沉船 [同] shipwreck

▲ After the car crash, the wrecks of the two cars were towed away. 車禍之後，這兩輛車的殘骸被拖走了。

wreck [rɛk] v. 破壞，毀壞 [同] ruin

▲ A serious knee injury wrecked this basketball player's career. 嚴重的膝傷毀了這位籃球選手的事業。

25. **yawn** [jɔn] n. [C] 呵欠

▲ My younger brother read a book with a yawn.

我弟弟邊看書邊打呵欠。

yawn [jɔn] v. 打呵欠

▲ Helen was so tired that she couldn't stop yawning. Helen 是如此疲累以致於她不停在打呵欠。

26. **youthful** [`juθfəl] adj. 年輕的，青春的 [同] young

▲ Looking at these old pictures brings back my memories of those youthful days.

看著這些舊照片讓我回憶起年輕的歲月。

Unit 1

1. **abuse** [ə`bjus] n. [U] 虐待；濫用 [同] misuse

▲ Reports of domestic abuse cases often increase during economic downturns.

在景氣低迷時，家暴案件的通報數量通常會增加。

💡 sexual/physical/mental abuse 性 / 肉體 / 精神虐待

abuse [ə`bjuz] v. 濫用；辱罵

▲ The manager abused his power to such an extent that no one wanted to work for him anymore.

經理濫用他的職權，以致於沒有人想再為他工作。

abusive [ə`bjusɪv] adj. 暴力的

▲ Mr. Wang's cruel and abusive son yelled at him last night. 昨晚王先生那殘忍且暴力的兒子對他吼叫。

---

2. **alien** [`eljən] adj. 外國的 [同] foreign；截然不同的

▲ It's hard for Jason to adjust to the alien culture.

適應這外國的文化對 Jason 來說很難。

alien [`eljən] n. [C] 外國人 [同] non-citizen；外星人

▲ Although John is an alien in Japan, he can speak fluent Japanese.

雖然 John 在日本是外國人，但他會說流利的日文。

---

3. **boost** [bust] v. 舉起；增加

▲ The man boosted the little boy up onto the pony.

男子把小男孩舉起來放到小馬上。

💡 boost sb's ego 增加…的自信心

boost [bust] n. [C] 增加；鼓舞

▲ Owing to the typhoon, there was a boost in the prices of vegetables. 因為颱風來襲，蔬菜價格上漲。

4. **certificate** [sə`tɪfəkɪt] n. [C] 證明書 (abbr. cert.) [同] certification

▲ People are required to have a teaching certificate to be a qualified teacher.

人們須有教師證書才能成為一個合格教師。

💡 birth/marriage/death certificate 出生 / 結婚 / 死亡證明

certificate [sə`tɪfəket] v. 用證書證明

▲ The elderly couple's marriage is certificated.

這對老夫妻的婚姻可以用證書證明。

certificated [sə`tɪfəˌketɪd] adj. 合格的

▲ Only a certificated doctor is allowed to practice medicine. 只有合格的醫生才能開業。

5. **chubby** [`tʃʌbɪ] adj. 圓嘟嘟的，豐滿的 (chubbier | chubbiest)

▲ The baby with chubby cheeks and blond hair is my nephew.

那個有著圓嘟嘟臉蛋和金髮的小嬰兒是我姪子。

6. **clause** [klɔz] n. [C] (法律等的) 條款；子句

▲ The lawyer is explaining the contract to the client clause by clause. 律師正在為其委託人逐條解釋合約。

7. **contend** [kən`tɛnd] v. 爭取 <for>；奮鬥 <with>；辯稱 <that> [同] insist

▲ Three contestants are contending for the prize.
有三位參賽者爭取這個獎項。

8. **drought** [draʊt] n. [C][U] 乾旱

▲ Water supplies were rationed during the drought.
乾旱期間水的供給採配給制。

9. **equation** [ɪˋkweʒən] n. [C] 方程式；[U] 同等看待

▲ It took me hours to solve this equation.
我花了好幾小時來解這個方程式。

10. **equivalent** [ɪˋkwɪvələnt] n. [sing.] 同等的事物

▲ The winner of this contest will get a trip to France or its equivalent in tickets to any other place. 本次比賽的獲勝者將獲得法國之旅或是任何同等票價的地方。

equivalent [ɪˋkwɪvələnt] adj. 同等的 <to>

▲ The billionaire's assets are equivalent to those of a small country.
這名億萬富翁的資產等同於一個小國的價值。

11. **excessive** [ɪkˋsɛsɪv] adj. 過度的

▲ Excessive drinking can cause health problems.
過度的飲酒會造成健康問題。

12. **incorporate** [ɪnˋkɔrpəˌret] v. 包含 <in, into>

▲ The singer's new album incorporates music genres of jazz and hip-hop.
這名歌手新專輯的音樂風格包含爵士和嘻哈。

13. **intent** [ɪn`tɛnt] n. [U] 意圖，目的 [同] intention

▲ The talk spoiled everything, despite the fact that its intent was to bring peace between the two countries. 這場會談搞砸了一切，儘管它的意圖是要為這兩個國家帶來和平。

intent [ɪn`tɛnt] adj. 熱切的，專注的

▲ From his intent gaze, I know Bob really likes the gift. 從他熱切的眼神，我知道 Bob 真的很喜歡這份禮物。

14. **loop** [lup] n. [C] 圈，環

▲ Do you know how to tie a loop in a rope? 你會不會用繩子打結做個繩圈？

💡 knock/throw sb for a loop 使很吃驚 | in/on a loop 迴圈方式

loop [lup] v. 纏繞

▲ The man looped a tie around his neck. 那男人在脖子上纏繞領帶。

💡 loop the loop 盤旋

15. **olive** [`ɑlɪv] adj. 橄欖綠的

▲ The Greek girl in an olive sweater has beautiful olive skin.

這個身穿橄欖綠毛衣的希臘女孩有漂亮的淺褐膚色。

olive [`ɑlɪv] n. [C] 橄欖

▲ To cook healthy spaghetti, Jackson replaced the butter in the recipe with olive oil. 為了煮出健康的義大利麵，Jackson 用橄欖油取代了食譜裡的奶油。

16. **overtake** [ˌovəˈtek] v. 超過；突然遭遇 (overtook | overtaken | overtaking)

▲ Our car soon overtook Jane's.
我們的車很快就超過 Jane 的車。

17. **pension** [ˈpɛnʃən] n. [C] 退休金

▲ The old couple lived on a small pension.
這對老夫婦靠微薄的退休金過生活。

pension [ˈpɛnʃən] v. 給退休金使其退休 <off>

▲ Most employees in our company are pensioned off at the age of sixty-five. 我們公司在大部分員工六十五歲時會給退休金讓他們退休。

18. **provision** [prəˈvɪʒən] n. [C][U] 準備；[pl.] 糧食 (~s)

▲ You shouldn't spend all your money, but make provision for the future.
你不應該花掉所有的錢，而要為未來做準備。

19. **sequence** [ˈsikwəns] n. [C][U] 一連串的事物 <of>；順序

▲ A sequence of tragedies led up to her suicide.
一連串的悲劇導致她自殺。

sequence [ˈsikwəns] v. 安排⋯的順序

▲ The organizers will sequence the contestants, putting the youngest first. 活動的籌備人員將安排參賽者的順序，把最年輕的排在第一位。

20. **skull** [skʌl] n. [C] 頭顱

▲ The skull protects the brain from physical harm.
頭顱保護大腦不受到傷害。

💡 get sth into/through your thick skull 弄明白… (用於生氣並覺得對方很愚笨時) | skull and crossbones 骷髏圖

21. **sneak** [snik] **v.** 偷偷地溜走 [同] creep (sneaked, snuck | sneaked, snuck | sneaking)

▲ The pickpocket sneaked away when he saw the police coming.
當扒手看到警察來的時候就偷偷地溜掉。

💡 sneak a look/glance at... 偷偷看… | sneak up on 不知不覺地來到

sneak [snik] **n.** [C] 告密者 [同] snitch

▲ No one likes the boy because he is a sneak.
沒有人喜歡男孩，因為他是個告密者。

22. **storage** [`stɔrɪdʒ] **n.** [U] 貯藏；儲存

▲ To preserve fish, we should put it in cold storage.
為了保持魚的新鮮，我們應該把牠冷藏。

💡 in storage 存放著

23. **theoretical** [θiə`rɛtɪkḷ] **adj.** 理論上的

▲ This method is merely theoretical.
這個方法只是理論上的。

theoretically [ˌθiə`rɛtɪkḷɪ] **adv.** 理論上地

▲ Theoretically speaking, it's difficult to put these proposals into practice.

理論上來說，很難將這些建議付諸實踐。

---

24. **volcano** [vɑl`keno] n. [C] 火山 (pl. volcanoes, volcanos)

▲ The dormant volcano erupted again and sent a large amount of dust and ash into the air. 這座休眠火山又再度噴發，夾帶大量塵土和灰燼到空氣中。

volcanic [vɑl`kænɪk] adj. 火山的

▲ There has been constant volcanic activity around that area. 那區域附近火山活動很頻繁。

---

25. **worthy** [`wɝ·ðɪ] adj. 值得的 <of> (worthier | worthiest)

▲ The passerby's brave action is worthy of a medal.
路人勇敢的行為值得頒給勳章。

Unit 2

1. **acknowledge** [ək`nɑlɪdʒ] v. 承認

▲ The organization finally acknowledged that there was still room for improvement.
該組織終於承認仍有改進的餘地。

acknowledgement [ək`nɑlɪdʒmənt] n. [C][U] 感謝 (also acknowledgment)

▲ Our organization gave the man a medal in acknowledgement of his help.
我們的組織贈送男子一個獎牌以感謝他的幫忙。

---

2. **alliance** [ə`laɪəns] n. [C] 同盟

▲ Switzerland is a neutral country which does not belong to any military alliance.
瑞士是一個不屬於任何軍事同盟的中立國。

---

3. **carbon** [`kɑrbən] n. [C] 副本；[U] 碳

▲ Besides the original, Nancy also kept a carbon.
Nancy 在正本之外還保留了副本。

💡 carbon copy 副本；酷似的東西 | carbon paper 複寫紙

---

4. **chaos** [`keɑs] n. [U] 大混亂

▲ After the earthquake, the whole country was in complete chaos. 地震過後，全國一片混亂。

chaotic [ke`ɑtɪk] adj. 混亂的

▲ Societies would be chaotic without laws.
沒有法律規章，社會就會一團混亂。

---

5. **cling** [klɪŋ] v. 緊貼；緊抓；依附；堅守 <to> (clung | clung | clinging)

▲ The wet clothes clung to her body.
溼衣服緊貼在她的身上。

---

6. **compassion** [kəm`pæʃən] n. [U] 同情 <for>

▲ Out of compassion, people voluntarily donated money to the flood victims.
出於同情心，人們主動捐錢給水災災民。

---

7. **conviction** [kən`vɪkʃən] n. [C][U] 定罪 <for> [反] acquittal；[C] 信念 <that>；[U] 堅定，堅信

▲ The thief had several previous convictions for theft.

小偷先前有好幾次被定罪竊盜。

---

8. **ecology** [iˋkɑlədʒɪ] n. [U] 生態
▲ Industrial development has brought us convenience. However, it has also damaged the ecology of Earth.
工業發展為我們帶來便利。然而，也傷害了地球的生態。

ecologist [iˋkɑlədʒɪst] n. [C] 生態學家
▲ The ecologists estimate that hundreds of animals have been affected by the tsunami.
生態學家估計大量動物在海嘯中受到了影響。

---

9. **errand** [ˋɛrənd] n. [C] 跑腿，差事
▲ Tom was sent on an errand to the store.
Tom 被派到那家店跑腿。
🔆 go on/run errands 跑腿 | errand of mercy 雪中送炭

---

10. **exceptional** [ɪkˋsɛpʃənḷ] adj. 特殊的 [反] unexceptional；優異的 [同] outstanding
▲ The students are allowed to eat in class in exceptional circumstances.
學生被允許在特殊情況下可於課堂上吃東西。

---

11. **executive** [ɪgˋzɛkjutɪv] n. [C] 主管級人員
▲ The executive showed her resolution to extend the business overseas. 主管展現其擴展海外生意的決心。
🔆 the executive (政府的) 行政部門
executive [ɪgˋzɛkjutɪv] adj. 執行的，行政的

▲ A chief executive officer is the leader of a company.
執行長是公司的領導者。

---

12. **infect** [ɪn`fɛkt] v. 感染 <with>
▲ The inhabitants were infected with malaria.
居民感染了瘧疾。

---

13. **interference** [ˌɪntə`fɪrəns] n. [U] 干涉 <in>
▲ The government stated that they won't tolerate any kind of interference in the domestic affairs from other countries. 該政府聲明他們不允許來自他國任何形式的內政干涉。

---

14. **maintenance** [`mentənəns] n. [U] 保養，維修
▲ The historic building is closed for regular maintenance.
這棟具有歷史意義的建築物因定期保養而暫停開放。

---

15. **marine** [mə`rin] adj. 海洋的
▲ The damage of oil pollution to the marine environment is very huge.
油汙對海洋環境造成的傷害是非常大的。
● marine law/court 海事法 / 法庭 | marine life 海洋生物 | marine transportation 海運
marine [mə`rin] n. [C] 海軍陸戰隊員
▲ Committing a disciplinary offense, the marine was held in confinement.
該名海軍陸戰隊員因違反紀律而被關禁閉。

💡 the Marine Corps 海軍陸戰隊

16. **overturn** [ˌovɚˋtɝn] v. 翻倒；推翻

▲ John overturned every piece of the furniture in his room looking for his homework. 為了要找他的回家作業，John 翻倒他房間的每一個家具。

17. **personnel** [ˌpɝsnˋɛl] n. [pl.] 人員

▲ The security personnel in the technology company are all experienced.
這間科技公司的保安人員都經驗老到。

💡 recruit/increase/reduce personnel 招募 / 增加 / 減少職員

18. **qualify** [ˋkwɑləˌfaɪ] v. 有資格 <for, to>

▲ Jack didn't qualify for the competition.
Jack 沒有參加比賽的資格。

qualified [ˋkwɑləˌfaɪd] adj. 有資格的

▲ Dan is now a qualified lawyer.
Dan 現在是一位合格的律師。

19. **shortage** [ˋʃɔrtɪdʒ] n. [C][U] 短缺

▲ Tainan Blood Center reported a shortage of blood and appealed for blood donation yesterday.
昨日臺南捐血中心報告血液短缺並呼籲捐血。

💡 coal/fuel/water/food shortage 煤 / 燃料 / 水 / 食物的短缺

20. **slap** [slæp] n. [C] 拍擊

▲ When Tom scored a basket, his teammate gave him a slap on the back.

Tom 投籃得分，他的隊友拍拍他的背表示讚許。

💡 receive/get a slap 挨耳光 | slap on the wrist 溫和的警告 | slap in the face 侮辱

slap [slæp] v. 打耳光 [同] smack；(生氣的) 隨意扔放 (slapped | slapped | slapping)

▲ The lady slapped her boyfriend on the face.

這位女士打她男友耳光。

slap [slæp] adv. 猛然地

▲ Mr. Wang ran slap into the wall.

王先生猛然地撞上牆壁。

---

21. **sober** [`sobɚ] adj. 清醒的 (soberer | soberest)

▲ Drunk or sober, he is a gloomy man.

無論酒醉或清醒，他總是愁容滿面。

💡 stay sober 保持清醒，冷靜

sober [`sobɚ] v. 醒酒 <up>

▲ A cup of coffee will sober you up.

喝杯咖啡可以幫你醒醒酒。

---

22. **thrive** [θraɪv] v. 繁榮；茂盛 (throve | thriven | thriving)

▲ Our company is thriving in the new market.

我們公司在這新的市場裡蓬勃發展。

💡 thrive on... 享受…；善於…

---

23. **version** [ˋvɝʒən] n. [C] 版本；說法 <of>

▲ Have you ever read the French version of *The Little Prince*? 你有讀過法文版的《小王子》嗎？

---

24. **worship** [ˋwɝʃɪp] n. [U] 崇拜；敬拜

▲ The young lady's worship of money disgusts me. 年輕女人對於金錢的崇拜讓我厭惡。

worship [ˋwɝʃɪp] v. 崇拜；敬拜

▲ Steve worshipped his father. Steve 崇拜他的父親。

---

25. **yield** [jild] v. 屈服，讓步 <to> [同] give way；產出

▲ Many countries state that they won't yield to terrorism. 多國聲明他們不會屈服於恐怖主義。

yield [jild] n. [C] 產量，利潤

▲ There is a huge reduction in milk yield because of the hot weather. 因為天氣炎熱，牛奶產量大減。

● ━━━━━━━━━━━━━━ ◆ ━━━━━━━━━━━━━━ ●

Unit 3

1. **abnormal** [æbˋnɔrml] adj. 異常的 [反] normal

▲ Environmental pollution is causing abnormal weather conditions. 環境汙染造成天氣異常。

2. **abolish** [əˋbɑlɪʃ] v. 廢除

▲ A rising number of countries have abolished the death penalty. 有越來越多國家廢除死刑。

abolition [͵æbəˋlɪʃən] n. [U] 廢除 <of>

▲ Many organizations work for the abolition of child labor. 許多組織爭取廢除童工。

---

3. **adolescent** [ˌædl`ɛsn̩t] adj. 青春期的

▲ Parents sometimes cannot understand their adolescent children.
父母有時無法了解他們正值青春期的孩子。

adolescent [ˌædl`ɛsn̩t] n. [C] 青少年

▲ Acne bothers a lot of adolescents.
青春痘困擾許多青少年。

---

4. **allocate** [`ælə,ket] v. 分配；撥出 <to, for>

▲ As a group leader, you should allocate jobs to your members. 身為組長，你應分配工作給你的組員。

allocation [ˌælə`keʃən] n. [C] 分配額

▲ The charity made an allocation of funds for the orphanage. 慈善機構撥了一筆資金分配額給孤兒院。

---

5. **browse** [brauz] v. 瀏覽 <through>

▲ Jenny browsed through all the websites related to "ancient wonders."
Jenny 瀏覽所有與「古代奇觀」相關的網站。

browse [brauz] n. [C] 瀏覽

▲ Kevin had a quick browse through all the books on the shelf. Kevin 很快地瀏覽架上所有的書。

---

6. **celebrity** [sə`lɛbrətɪ] n. [C] 名人 [同] star；[U] 名聲 [同] fame (pl. celebrities)

▲ Lots of celebrities showed up at the opening of the Cannes Film Festival.

許多名人出現在坎城影展的開幕式。

7. choir [ˋkwaɪr] n. [C] 合唱團，唱詩班
▲ The famous actress sang in a school choir when she was in high school.

這位知名的女演員中學時是學校合唱團成員。

8. colonial [kəˋlonɪəl] adj. 殖民的
▲ The country gained independence from British colonial rule in the 20th century.

這個國家在二十世紀從英國的殖民統治下獲得獨立。

colonial [kəˋlonɪəl] n. [C] 殖民地居民
▲ The term "Wansei" refers to the Japanese colonials born in Taiwan.

「灣生」這個詞指的是在臺灣出生的日裔殖民地居民。

9. compromise [ˋkɑmprə͵maɪz] n. [C][U] 妥協
▲ After a long discussion, we finally reached a compromise over the issue.

經過長時間的討論，我們終於對此議題達成協議。

💡 make/reach a compromise 達成妥協

compromise [ˋkɑmprə͵maɪz] v. 妥協 <with>
▲ They finally compromised with each other over the amount of the compensation.

他們終於就賠償的金額達成協議。

10. **coordinate** [koˋɔrdˏnet] v. 協調
  ▲ The company needs Mr. Liu to coordinate the whole conference. 公司需要劉先生協調整個會議。
  coordinate [koˋɔrdnɪt] n. [C] 坐標
  ▲ The injured mountain climber gave the coordinate by radio so that the search and rescue team could find out where she was. 這名受傷的登山者利用無線電發射坐標，以便讓搜救隊找到她。
  coordinate [koˋɔrdˏnet] adj. 對等的
  ▲ "And," "but," and "or" are coordinate conjunctions. and、but 和 or 是對等連接詞。
  coordination [koˏɔrdn̩ˋeʃən] n. [U] 協調 <between, of>
  ▲ Ray and Anne are responsible for the coordination between different departments.
  Ray 和 Anne 負責各部門間的協調。
  coordinator [koˋɔrdn̩ˏetɚ] n. [C] 協調者
  ▲ Mr. Lee was appointed to be the coordinator to the project. 李先生被指定擔任此計畫的協調者。

---

11. **elaborate** [ɪˋlæbərət] adj. 精細的 [同] intricate
  ▲ Collecting elaborate miniatures is one of Wendy's hobbies. 蒐集精細的袖珍品是 Wendy 的嗜好之一。
  elaborate [ɪˋlæbəˏret] v. 詳述 <on, upon> [同] enlarge
  ▲ The dean elaborated on the new policy for college applications. 教務主任詳述申請大學的新政策。

---

12. **eternal** [ɪˋtɝnl̩] adj. 永恆的

▲ Mary seems to be an eternal optimist.

Mary 似乎是個永遠的樂觀主義者。

💡 hope springs eternal 希望常在

eternally [ɪˋtɝnḷɪ] adv. 總是 [同] constantly

▲ The teacher is angry because the students are eternally chatting in class.

老師在生氣因為學生們總是在上課時閒扯。

---

13. **exotic** [ɪgˋzɑtɪk] adj. 外來的，異國風味的

▲ John enjoys tasting various exotic foods.

John 很享受有異國風味的多樣美食。

exotic [ɪgˋzɑtɪk] n. [C] 外來種

▲ The living space of some native species is threatened by exotics.

有些本土物種的生存空間受到外來種威脅。

---

14. **extraordinary** [ɪkˋstrɔrdṇˏɛrɪ] adj. 意想不到的 [同] incredible

▲ It was extraordinary that I bumped into my childhood sweetheart in London yesterday. 我昨天在倫敦巧遇我青梅竹馬的戀人，真是意想不到。

---

15. **flip** [flɪp] v. 快速翻動 <over> (flipped | flipped | flipping)

▲ The cook skillfully flipped the egg over in the pan.

廚師很有技巧地將鍋裡的蛋翻面。

💡 flip out/flip your lid 勃然大怒 | flip through sth 快速翻閱

flip [flɪp] n. [C] 輕輕一彈

▲ The woman removed the ash from her cigarette with a flip of her forefinger.
女人食指輕輕一彈，把香菸上的菸灰弄掉。

---

16. **infinite** [ˋɪnfənɪt] adj. 無限的 [反] finite

▲ Natural resources are not infinite; they are exhaustible.
天然資源並非無限的；它們是會被用盡的。

🌑 in sb's infinite wisdom 以…無比的智慧

---

17. **kidnap** [ˋkɪdnæp] v. 綁架 [同] abduct, seize

▲ Three men kidnaped a student on his way home.
三名男子綁架了一名在回家路上的學生。

kidnapper [ˋkɪdnæpɚ] n. [C] 綁架者 (also kidnaper)

▲ The kidnapper demanded a ransom of one million dollars. 綁匪要求一百萬美元的贖金。

---

18. **medication** [ˌmɛdɪˋkeʃən] n. [C][U] 藥物 <for>

▲ My sister takes medication for her allergies.
我妹妹服用抗過敏的藥物。

🌑 on medication 服藥中

---

19. **parallel** [ˋpærəˌlɛl] adj. 平行的 <with, to>

▲ The road runs parallel with the stream.
這條路與河流平行。

parallel [ˋpærəˌlɛl] n. [C] 平行線；相似點

▲ Draw a parallel to the first line.

畫一條與第一條平行的線。

parallel [ˋpærə͵lɛl] v. 與…相對應

▲ The student's theories parallel those of the professor.
這名學生的理論與那位教授的相對應。

---

20. **plead** [plid] v. 懇求 <with> [同] beg (pleaded, pled │ pleaded, pled │ pleading)

▲ Nick pleaded with his boss to reconsider his proposition. Nick 懇求上司再次考慮他的提案。

pleading [ˋplidɪŋ] adj. 哀求的

▲ In a pleading voice, the man asked his boss for his job back.
這個男子以哀求的語氣向他的老闆請求復職。

pleadingly [ˋplidɪŋlɪ] adv. 哀求地

▲ The girl is looking at her father pleadingly, hoping he will buy her the toy.
小女孩哀求地看著她的父親，希望他買這個玩具給她。

---

21. **quest** [kwɛst] n. [C] 追求 <for>

▲ Their quest for treasures was in vain.
他們對寶藏的追求是徒勞無功。

---

22. **skeleton** [ˋskɛlətn̩] n. [C] 骨骼；骨架 <of>

▲ The old man is merely a walking skeleton.
老人只是一副行走的骨骼。

♥ skeleton in the/your closet 醜事

---

23. **slavery** [ˋslevərɪ] n. [U] 奴隸 [反] freedom

▲ In ancient China, girls from poor families were often sold into slavery.
在中國古代，窮困人家的女孩常被販賣為奴隸。

24. **statistical** [stə`tɪstɪkl̩] adj. 統計上的
   ▲ The report contains a lot of statistical information.
   這份報告包括了很多統計上的資料。

25. **toll** [tol] n. [C] 通行費；鳴鐘
   ▲ We have to pay a toll when we cross the bridge.
   過那座橋時，必須繳通行費。
   🕯 take a/its toll (on sb/sth) (對⋯) 造成損害
   toll [tol] v. 鳴鐘
   ▲ The bells were tolling for the dead.
   哀悼死者的鳴鐘聲響起。

Unit 4

1. **abortion** [ə`bɔrʃən] n. [C][U] 墮胎 [同] termination
   ▲ The doctor warns the woman about the dangers of abortion. 醫生告誡這名女人墮胎的危險。
   🕯 have/get an abortion 墮胎 | support/oppose abortion
   支持 / 反對墮胎

2. **accommodate** [ə`kɑmə͵det] v. 能容納；適應 <to>
   ▲ The hotel can accommodate 500 guests.
   這家旅館能容納五百名旅客。

3. **advocate** [ˈædvəkət] n. [C] 擁護者 <of>

▲ Ms. Lin is an enthusiastic advocate of women's liberation. 林女士是婦女解放運動的積極擁護者。

advocate [ˈædvəˌket] v. 主張

▲ Some people advocate the abolition of the death penalty. 有些人主張廢除死刑。

advocacy [ˈædvəkəsɪ] n. [U] 提倡

▲ Dr. King is known for his advocacy of the rights of the black. 金恩博士以提倡黑人人權著名。

---

4. **ally** [ˈælaɪ] n. [C] 同盟國 (pl. allies)

▲ Germany and Turkey, then called the Ottoman Empire, were allies in World War I. 德國和土耳其，那時稱作鄂圖曼帝國，在第一次世界大戰時結盟。

ally [ˈælaɪ] v. 結盟 <with, to>

▲ The small company will ally with the large company to make more money.
這間小公司將會和大公司結盟來賺更多錢。

---

5. **ceremony** [ˈsɛrəˌmonɪ] n. [C] 儀式 (pl. ceremonies)

▲ Students held back their tears during the graduation ceremony. 學生在畢業典禮強忍淚水。

---

6. **circuit** [ˈsɝkət] n. [C] 繞行一周 <of>；巡迴

▲ The earth completes its circuit of the sun in one year.
地球一年繞行太陽公轉一周。

---

7. **commitment** [kəˈmɪtmənt] n. [C] 承諾；[U] 致力

▲ Joe is afraid to make a commitment in a relationship.
Joe 害怕在一段感情中做出承諾。

8. **conceal** [kən`sil] v. 隱瞞 <from>；藏

▲ My husband concealed nothing from me.
我丈夫對我毫無隱瞞。

9. **confidential** [ˌkɑnfə`dɛnʃəl] adj. 機密的

▲ Don't reveal the confidential information to anyone else. 別跟任何人透露這條機密消息。

10. **consumption** [kən`sʌmpʃən] n. [U] 消耗

▲ To conserve natural resources, we have to reduce the consumption of paper and gasoline. 為了維護天然資源，我們必須減少紙張及汽油的消耗量。

11. **corporate** [`kɔrpərɪt] adj. 公司的

▲ Those computers are corporate property, so you can't take them home.
那些電腦是公司的財產，所以你不能帶回家。

12. **evolve** [ɪ`vɑlv] v. 進化；發展 <from, into>

▲ According to Darwin's theory of evolution, humans evolved from apes.
根據達爾文的進化論，人類由人猿進化的。

13. **extensive** [ɪk`stɛnsɪv] adj. 大面積的

▲ After the typhoon, the government had to deal with the extensive damage.

颱風過後，政府需要處理大面積的損害。

---

14. **graphic** [ˋɡræfɪk] adj. 生動的 [同] vivid
   ▲ The man gave a graphic account of the disastrous earthquake. 男人生動的描述這場損失慘重的大地震。
   graphic [ˋɡræfɪk] n. [C] 圖像
   ▲ There are simple graphics on the doors of restrooms, indicating whether they are for men or women.
   廁所門上有簡單的圖像顯示是男廁還是女廁。

---

15. **grim** [ɡrɪm] adj. 嚴肅的；憂愁的 (grimmer | grimmest)
   ▲ The judge walked into the court with a grim face.
   法官一臉嚴肅的走進法庭。

---

16. **interior** [ɪnˋtɪrɪɚ] adj. 內部的 [反] exterior
   ▲ The landlord painted all the interior walls creamy white. 房東把內部的牆都漆成米白色。
   interior [ɪnˋtɪrɪɚ] n. [C] 內部 <of> [反] exterior
   ▲ The interior of the private jet is luxurious and far beyond our imagination. 該私人噴射機的內裝是如此奢華，遠遠超乎我們所想像。

---

17. **legendary** [ˋlɛdʒəndˌɛrɪ] adj. 傳說的；有名的
   ▲ The cave is the home of a legendary dragon.
   這個洞穴是傳說中龍的家。

---

18. **metaphor** [ˋmɛtəfɚ] n. [C] 暗喻
   ▲ The snake is often a metaphor for evil.
   蛇常作為邪惡的暗喻。

metaphorical [ˌmɛtə`fɔrɪkl] adj. 暗喻的

▲ The writer used several metaphorical terms in his novel. 作家在他的小說裡用了幾個暗喻的字眼。

---

19. **participant** [pə`tɪsəpənt] n. [C] 參加者 <in>

▲ All the participants in the game are under the age of 20. 所有參賽者的年齡都在二十歲以下。

---

20. **portfolio** [port`folɪˌo] n. [C] 資料夾，公事包；作品集 (pl. portfolios)

▲ Jimmy screwed up the meeting because he left his portfolio in the taxi.

Jimmy 搞砸了會議，因為他將資料夾留在計程車裡。

---

21. **ragged** [`rægɪd] adj. 破爛的；凹凸不平的

▲ The refugees are in ragged clothes.
難民穿著破爛的衣服。

---

22. **soak** [sok] v. 泡；溼透

▲ My mom likes to soak in a hot bath when she is tired. 我媽累的時候喜歡泡熱水澡。

🔮 soak up sth 吸收…(液體或資訊)；盡情享受…(氣氛)；耗盡…(金錢)

soak [sok] n. [C] 浸泡 <in>

▲ Follow the recipe and leave the peeled soft-boiled eggs to soak in the sauce for one night. 照著食譜的作法並將剝殼的半熟蛋浸泡在醬汁中一個晚上。

23. **spicy** [ˋspaɪsɪ] adj. 辛辣的 (spicier | spiciest)

▲ This Mexican dish is quite spicy.
這道墨西哥菜相當辛辣。

---

24. **stimulate** [ˋstɪmjə‚let] v. 促進；激發

▲ Physical exercise stimulates the body's circulation.
運動促進身體血液循環。

---

25. **torment** [ˋtɔrmɛnt] n. [U] (精神上的) 折磨 <in> [同]
anguish

▲ The abused woman was in torment.
這個受虐的婦女備受折磨。

torment [tɔrˋmɛnt] v. 折磨 [同] torture

▲ The man was condemned for tormenting dogs.
男子因為虐狗被譴責。

Unit 5

1. **abrupt** [əˋbrʌpt] adj. 突然的；唐突的

▲ The car came to an abrupt stop. 車子緊急剎車。

abruptly [əˋbrʌptlɪ] adv. 突然地；陡峭地

▲ When Mom came in, they stopped talking abruptly.
媽媽進來時，他們突然停止說話。

---

2. **acute** [əˋkjut] adj. 敏感的；劇烈的；急性的 (acuter |
acutest)

▲ Dogs have an acute sense of smell. 狗的嗅覺敏銳。

3. **affection** [əˋfɛkʃən] n. [C][U] 喜愛 [同] fondness；感情 <for>

▲ Some people feel no affection for children.
有些人不喜愛小孩。

💡 win sb's affections 贏得⋯的愛

---

4. **alongside** [əˋlɔŋˋsaɪd] prep. 在旁邊；並排

▲ The bus driver pulled his car alongside the road to take a rest. 公車司機把車停在路旁邊休息。

alongside [əˋlɔŋˋsaɪd] adv. 與⋯一起

▲ Every evening Julia goes jogging and her dog runs alongside. 每天傍晚 Julia 會與她的狗一起慢跑。

---

5. **clarity** [ˋklærətɪ] n. [U] 清楚；清澈

▲ My colleague explained the problem with great clarity. 我同事將問題解釋得很清楚。

---

6. **comparable** [ˋkɑmpərəbl] adj. 可相比的；可比擬的 <to, with>

▲ John's weekly income is comparable to my monthly salary. John 一星期的收入與我一個月的薪水差不多。

---

7. **consent** [kənˋsɛnt] n. [U] 同意 <to>

▲ My parents reluctantly gave their consent to my marriage to an actor. 我的父母勉強同意我和演員結婚。

💡 give sb's consent to... ⋯的同意 |
without sb's consent 未經⋯的同意 |
by common consent 大多數人同意

consent [kən`sɛnt] v. 同意 <to>

▲ My boss consented to finance our project.
我老闆同意資助我們的企劃。

8. **convert** [kən`vɝt] v. 轉變；換算；改信仰 <to, into>

▲ The panel can convert solar energy to electricity.
這板子可將太陽能轉變成電力。

9. **corporation** [ˌkɔrpə`reʃən] n. [C] 大公司 (abbr. Corp.)

▲ It has been Darren's dream to work for a multinational corporation.
在跨國大公司工作一直是 Darren 的夢想。

10. **discrimination** [dɪˌskrɪmə`neʃən] n. [U] 歧視

▲ All people are created equal, so there should be no discrimination in employment because of sex, age, race, or any other form.
人人平等，因此在就業這方面，不應該因為性別、年紀、種族或其他形式而遭到歧視。

💡 racial/sex/age discrimination 種族 / 性別 / 年齡歧視

11. **exaggeration** [ɪgˌzædʒə`reʃən] n. [U] 誇張，誇大

▲ It's no exaggeration to say that a school is a miniature society. 說學校是小型社會一點也不誇張。

12. **external** [ɪk`stɝnl] adj. 外面的 [反] internal

▲ The wound is in the external part of her ear and won't influence her hearing.
傷口在耳朵外面，並不影響她的聽力。

externals [ɪk`stɝnḷz] n. [pl.] 外表

▲ My parents always tell me not to be misled by externals. 我父母總是告訴我不要被事物的外表誤導。

---

13. **hence** [hɛns] adv. 因此 [同] therefore

▲ The chorus sings well; hence they got the name "Angel's Voices."
這個合唱團歌聲美妙，因此有「天使之音」之稱。

---

14. **indifferent** [ɪn`dɪfərənt] adj. 漠不關心的 <to>

▲ Most people are indifferent to politics.
多數人對政治漠不關心。

---

15. **interpretation** [ɪn,tɝprɪ`teʃən] n. [C][U] 詮釋 <of>

▲ Works of literature are open to interpretation.
文學作品可以有各種不同的詮釋。

---

16. **mammal** [`mæmḷ] n. [C] 哺乳類動物

▲ Human beings, dogs, cats, and whales are all mammals. 人類、狗、貓和鯨魚全都是哺乳類動物。

---

17. **nonprofit** [nɑn`prɑfɪt] adj. 非營利的

▲ This is a nonprofit organization, whose aim is not to make money but to provide shelter for battered men and women. 這是非營利的組織，目的不是賺錢而是為受暴的男性及女性提供庇護。

---

18. **passionate** [`pæʃənɪt] adj. 熱中的 <about>

▲ Sara has always been passionate about playing volleyball. Sara 一直熱中於打排球。

passionately [`pæʃənɪtlɪ] adv. 熱烈地

▲ The graduates talked passionately about their future plans. 畢業生們熱烈地談論他們未來的計畫。

19. **premature** [ˌprimə`tjʊr] adj. 過早的

▲ Dr. Kim thinks it is still premature for us to make judgments. 金博士認為現在下判斷為時過早。

prematurely [ˌprimə`tjʊrlɪ] adv. 過早地

▲ My little sister was born prematurely and lived in an incubator for a long time.

我妹妹過早出生並且在保溫箱裡住了很長一段時間。

20. **rear** [rɪr] adj. 後面的 [反] front

▲ The rear part of the car was badly damaged.

車子後面的部分損壞嚴重。

rear [rɪr] n. [U] 後面 (the ～) <of>

▲ The parking lot is at the rear of the restaurant.

停車場在餐廳的後方。

🔆 bring up the rear 走在最後面，殿後

rear [rɪr] v. 撫養 [同] raise

▲ The woman reared her son alone after she divorced her husband.

這位婦女跟丈夫離婚後就獨自撫養兒子。

🔆 rear its (ugly) head (令人不開心的事) 發生

21. **series** [ˋsɪrɪz] n. [C] 一連串 <of> (pl. series)
   ▲ Every seemingly small decision can spark off a series of major events in your life. 每一個看似不重要的決定都可能引發人生中一連串重大的事件。

22. **sophisticated** [səˋfɪstɪˏketɪd] adj. 世故老練的；精密的
   ▲ Clare became sophisticated after working overseas for many years.
   在海外工作多年之後，Clare 變得世故老練。

23. **sponge** [spʌndʒ] n. [C] 海綿
   ▲ Wipe up the water with a sponge. 用海綿把水擦乾。
   sponge [spʌndʒ] v. 用海綿擦洗；吸
   ▲ David sponged down the car.
   David 用海綿擦洗車子。

24. **strap** [stræp] n. [C] …帶
   ▲ The watch strap needs to be fixed.
   這條錶帶需要修補。
   strap [stræp] v. 用帶子繫 (strapped | strapped | strapping)
   ▲ The flight attendant reminds me to strap myself in before the plane takes off.
   空服員提醒我在飛機起飛前繫好安全帶。
   💡 strap sb in 為…繫好安全帶 | strap sth up 包紮

25. **transformation** [ˏtrænsfɚˋmeʃən] n. [U] 變化 ；(生物) 蛻變，型態改變

478 Level 5–1 Unit 5

▲ Helen was surprised at the transformation of the city's public transportation.

Helen 對這座城市大眾運輸的改變感到驚訝。

Unit 6

1. **absurd** [əb`sɜˈd] adj. 荒謬的 [同] ridiculous

▲ The idea that the number 13 brings bad luck is absurd. 十三這個數字會帶來不幸的想法是可笑的。

absurdity [əb`sɜˈdətɪ] n. [C] 荒謬之事；[U] 荒謬 (pl. absurdities)

▲ There are a lot of absurdities in the movie.

這部電影有許多荒謬之處。

absurdly [əb`sɜˈdlɪ] adv. 荒謬地 [同] ridiculously

▲ Don't behave absurdly. 別做出荒謬的舉動。

---

2. **administration** [əd͵mɪnə`streʃən] n. [C] 政府；[U] 行政，管理

▲ Ann's thrust at the administration upset many people.

Ann 對政府的猛烈批評讓很多人不滿。

---

3. **agricultural** [͵ægrɪ`kʌltʃərəl] adj. 農業的 [同] farming

▲ Agricultural land is shrinking fast in the country.

國家的農地快速縮減。

---

4. **alternate** [`ɔltəˈnɪt] adj. 交替的

▲ Your birthday cake consists of alternate layers of sponge and custard.

你的生日蛋糕是由一層層海綿蛋糕和卡士達醬交疊而成。

alternate [ˋɔltɚˌnet] v. 使交替 <between, with>

▲ Her emotions alternated between anger and despair.
她的情緒交錯著憤怒與絕望。

alternate [ˋɔltɚnɪt] n. [C] 替代者 [同] substitute

▲ Jane couldn't attend the meeting, so Lily served as her alternate.

Jane 無法參加會議，所以 Lily 作為她的替代者參加。

alternately [ˋɔltɚnɪtlɪ] adv. 交替地

▲ This country alternately suffered from flood and drought. 這國家接連遭受水災及旱災之苦。

alternation [ˌɔltɚˋneʃən] n. [C][U] 交替

▲ The rapid alternation of low and high temperature makes it hard for me to decide what to wear.
溫差變化太快讓我難以決定穿著。

---

5. **architecture** [ˋɑrkəˌtɛktʃɚ] n. [U] 建築學；建築物

▲ Robert majors in architecture and minors in economics. Robert 主修建築學且副修經濟學。

---

6. **cocaine** [koˋken] n. [U] 古柯鹼

▲ Shelly smuggled cocaine into the country.
Shelly 走私古柯鹼進入這個國家。

---

7. **compensate** [ˋkɑmpənˌset] v. 彌補 <for> [同] make up for；賠償 <for>

▲ Nothing can compensate for the loss of a loved one.

失去所愛的人是無法彌補的。

---

8. **conservation** [ˌkɑnsə`veʃən] n. [U] (資源) 保存；(自然) 保護

▲ I go to work by bicycle for the purpose of energy conservation. 為了節約能源，我騎腳踏車上班。

💡 conservation of water/fuel 節約用水 / 燃料

---

9. **copyright** [`kɑpɪˌraɪt] n. [C][U] 版權 <on, in>

▲ The author who holds the copyright on this article allows me to quote from his work.
擁有文章版權的這名作者同意我引用他的作品。

💡 hold/own a copyright 持有版權

copyright [`kɑpɪˌraɪt] v. 獲得版權

▲ You should copyright your design, or others may steal your idea. 你應該為你的設計註冊版權，不然其他人有可能偷用你的點子。

---

10. **correspondent** [ˌkɔrə`spɑndənt] n. [C] 記者

▲ Our war correspondent in Iraq sent this report.
我們在伊拉克的戰地記者傳送來這則消息。

correspondent [ˌkɔrə`spɑndənt] adj. 相符的 <with, to>
[同] equivalent

▲ Jenny's improvement was correspondent with her efforts. Jenny 的進步和努力相應。

---

11. **epidemic** [ˌɛpə`dɛmɪk] n. [C] 流行病

▲ A flu epidemic broke out in the village last week.

上週流感在村裡爆發。

epidemic [ˌɛpəˈdɛmɪk] adj. 流行的

▲ Air pollution has reached epidemic proportions in the recent years. 近幾年來，空氣汙染問題肆虐。

---

12. **exceed** [ɪkˈsid] v. 超越 (法律或命令的) 限制

▲ Don't exceed the speed limit. 開車時不要超速。

---

13. **facilitate** [fəˈsɪləˌtet] v. 促使

▲ Computers have facilitated the work of complicated calculation. 電腦使繁雜的計算工作變得容易多了。

---

14. **immune** [ɪˈmjun] adj. 有免疫力的 <to>；不受影響的 <to>；免於⋯的 <from>

▲ Once you have had measles, you are probably immune to it for the rest of your life.

一旦你出過麻疹，或許終生都對此病具有免疫力。

💡 immune system 免疫系統

immunity [ɪˈmjunətɪ] n. [U] 免疫力

▲ The scientists say that this vaccine can give us immunity against the disease.

科學家說這疫苗可以讓我們對這種疾病有免疫力。

---

15. **juvenile** [ˈdʒuvənḷ] adj. 少年的；不成熟的 [同] childish

▲ The case of an 11-year-old boy charged with forgery has been moved to juvenile court. 十一歲男童依偽造文書罪被起訴的案件已移送少年法庭。

💡 juvenile crime 少年犯罪

juvenile [ˈdʒuvən!] n. [C] 未成年人

▲ Juveniles are prohibited from drinking alcohol.
未成年人禁止飲酒。

---

16. **manipulate** [məˈnɪpjəˌlet] v. (熟練地) 操作；操縱

▲ Bill skillfully manipulated the puppet.
Bill 靈巧地操作木偶。

manipulation [məˌnɪpjəˈleʃən] n. [C][U] 操縱

▲ Anna and John engaged in stock market manipulations. Anna 和 John 參與股市操縱。

manipulative [məˈnɪpjəˌletɪv] adj. 有控制慾的

▲ My boss is manipulative, and that is why so many people quit.
我的老闆很有控制慾，這就是為什麼很多人離職。

manipulator [məˈnɪpjəˌletə] n. [C] 操縱者

▲ It is widely known that Sam is a political manipulator. 眾所皆知，Sam 是一個政治操縱者。

---

17. **mock** [mɑk] adj. 假的 [同] sham

▲ "Oh, it's amazing," Zoe said with mock surprise.
Zoe 故作驚訝地說：「喔，太棒了。」

mock [mɑk] v. 嘲弄

▲ It is impolite of you to mock Frank's accent.
你嘲弄 Frank 的口音真是無禮。

mock [mɑk] n. [C] 模擬考試

▲ Do you know when we are going to have mocks？
你知道我們何時模擬考試嗎？

mockery [ˋmɑkərɪ] n. [U] 嘲弄

▲ Tony couldn't stand any more of Natasha's mockery. He decided to fight back. Tony 無法再忍受 Natasha 任何的嘲弄。他決定要反擊。

♥ make a mockery of 嘲弄

---

18. **peasant** [ˋpɛzn̩t] n. [C] 農民

▲ The peasants revolted against the high taxes. 農民起來反抗高額的稅收。

---

19. **penetrate** [ˋpɛnəˏtret] v. 穿透

▲ The beam from the lighthouse penetrates the heavy fog. 燈塔的光線穿過濃霧。

penetrating [ˋpɛnəˏtretɪŋ] adj. 刺耳的 [同] piercing；銳利的

▲ We were frightened by the penetrating scream from next door. 我們被隔壁傳來的刺耳尖叫聲所驚嚇。

penetration [ˏpɛnəˋtreʃən] n. [U] 滲入；洞察力

▲ The worker covered the machine to prevent water penetration. 這位工人將機器蓋住以防止水滲入。

---

20. **prescription** [prɪˋskrɪpʃən] n. [C] 處方箋

▲ Peter got his prescription filled at the pharmacy on the way to work.
Peter 於上班途中在藥房依照處方箋拿藥。

---

21. **recommendation** [ˏrɛkəmɛnˋdeʃən] n. [C][U] 推薦；[C] 建議

▲ Leo ordered the salmon on the waitress'
recommendation.
Leo 依據女服務生的推薦，點了鮭魚。

---

22. **souvenir** [ˌsuvəˈnɪr] n. [C] 紀念品

▲ I bought this key ring at a souvenir shop in Paris.
我在巴黎的紀念品店買了這個鑰匙圈。

---

23. **stumble** [ˈstʌmbl] v. 絆倒 [同] trip；結巴地說

▲ Kevin stumbled and fell down the stairs.
Kevin 絆倒從樓梯上跌下來。

stumble [ˈstʌmbl] n. [C] 絆倒

▲ Helen felt so frustrated after a few stumbles.
在幾次絆倒後，Helen 感到很沮喪。

---

24. **subtle** [ˈsʌtl] adj. 微妙的；巧妙的 (subtler | subtlest)

▲ There was a subtle change in his attitude.
他的態度有微妙的變化。

---

25. **trauma** [ˈtraʊmə] n. [C][U] 精神創傷 (pl. traumas,
traumata)

▲ Lily could not recover from the trauma of losing her
child. Lily 無法從失去小孩的創痛中恢復。

traumatic [trɔˈmætɪk] adj. 衝擊性的

▲ The death of a pet can be traumatic for a child.
寵物的死亡對小孩來說可能會造成衝擊。

Unit 7

1. **accelerate** [æk`sɛlə,ret] v. 促進
   ▲ Farmers use fertilizers to accelerate the growth of crops. 農夫使用肥料來促進作物生長。

   acceleration [æk,sɛlə`reʃən] n. [U] 加速
   ▲ Acceleration of tooth decay is caused by lack of care and cleanness. 加速蛀牙的原因是缺乏照顧和清潔。

2. **alcoholic** [,ælkə`hɔlɪk] adj. 酒精的 [反] nonalcoholic
   ▲ This restaurant doesn't serve alcoholic beverages.
   這家餐廳不賣含有酒精的飲料。

   alcoholic [,ælkə`hɔlɪk] n. [C] 酗酒者
   ▲ Sam had such a drinking problem that people thought him to be an alcoholic. Sam 有如此嚴重的酗酒問題，以致於人們都認為他是個酒鬼。

3. **allergy** [`ælə-dʒɪ] n. [C][U] 過敏 <to> (pl. allergies)
   ▲ Peter has an allergy to dog hair. Peter 對狗毛過敏。

4. **amend** [ə`mɛnd] v. 修正
   ▲ The majority of committee members agreed that this resolution should be amended.
   大多數的委員會會員同意這項決議應該修正。

5. **coffin** [`kɔfɪn] n. [C] 棺材
   ▲ They stood around Vicky's coffin and mourned her death. 他們站在棺材周圍，並為 Vicky 的去世悲傷。

💡 the final nail in the coffin 致命打擊，導致失敗的事件

6. **complexity** [kəm`plɛksətɪ] n. [C] 複雜的事物；[U] 複雜 (pl. complexities)
   ▲ There are a lot of complexities surrounding the new policy. 這個新政策牽涉到很多複雜的事物。

7. **considerate** [kən`sɪdərɪt] adj. 體貼的，周到的 [同] thoughtful [反] inconsiderate
   ▲ It is considerate of you to prepare the gifts for the visitors. 你為訪客準備了禮物，真是周到。

8. **courteous** [`kɝtɪəs] adj. 禮貌的 [反] discourteous
   ▲ We all like Danny because he is very courteous all the time.
   我們都很喜歡 Danny，因為他總是很有禮貌。

9. **cuisine** [kwɪ`zin] n. [C][U] 菜肴，烹飪
   ▲ I don't like vegetarian cuisine, but this one is amazing. 我不喜歡素菜，但這道很讓人驚豔。

10. **descriptive** [dɪ`skrɪptɪv] adj. 描述的
    ▲ The descriptive parts in the novel are superior to the parts with dialogue.
    這本小說的敘述部分優於對話部分。

11. **expedition** [ˌɛkspɪ`dɪʃən] n. [C] 探險，遠征
    ▲ They dreamed of going on an expedition to Mars.
    他們夢想到火星探險。

12. **fatigue** [fə`tig] n. [U] 疲憊，疲勞 [同] exhaustion

▲ Mary was suffering from physical and mental fatigue. Mary 感受到身心靈的疲憊。

fatigue [fə`tig] v. 使疲倦

▲ My parents were fatigued with work.
我的父母因工作而疲倦。

13. **heritage** [`hɛrətɪdʒ] n. [C][U] (文化) 遺產

▲ Irene was fascinated by the country's cultural heritage. Irene 對這國家的文化遺產著迷。

14. **innovative** [`ɪnə,vetɪv] adj. 創新的

▲ Sandy is full of innovative ideas.
Sandy 有許多新點子。

15. **legislation** [,lɛdʒɪs`leʃən] n. [U] 立法，法規

▲ Although the new piece of legislation on the tax rates raised a lot of disputes, it will still be introduced next year. 雖然關於稅制的新立法引起很多反彈，但仍會在明年推行。

16. **mechanism** [`mɛkə,nɪzəm] n. [C] 機件，機械零件

▲ The mechanism on this new device runs very well. It makes the device work more effectively. 這機件在新裝置上運作很好。它讓裝置更有效率地運作。

17. **monopoly** [mə`nɑplɪ] n. [C] 壟斷 <on> (pl. monopolies)

▲ The party has a monopoly on the media.

這個政黨壟斷媒體。

---

18. **perceive** [pɚˋsiv] v. 察覺，注意到
   ▲ Although Peggy had a smile on her face, I perceived a note of sadness in her voice. 雖然 Peggy 臉上掛著笑容，但是我從她的聲音中察覺到一絲悲傷。

---

19. **perception** [pɚˋsɛpʃən] n. [C] 看法 <of>；[U] 洞察力
   ▲ What are the public's perceptions of the president? 民眾對總統的看法是什麼？

   perceptive [pɚˋsɛptɪv] adj. 敏銳的，有洞察力的
   ▲ William gave a perceptive comment on the election. 對於選戰 William 給了一番敏銳的評論。

   perceptible [pɚˋsɛptəbl] adj. 可察覺的 [同] noticeable [反] imperceptible
   ▲ The change of Wendy's attitude was perceptible. Wendy 態度的改變是可察覺的。

---

20. **presidency** [ˋprɛzədənsɪ] n. [C] 總統任期，總統職位 (pl. presidencies)
   ▲ The economy of the country has revived during his presidency. 在他的總統任期期間，國家經濟已復甦。

---

21. **rehearsal** [rɪˋhɝsl] n. [C][U] 排演，排練，預演
   ▲ The play, currently in rehearsal, will be performed next month. 目前在排練的這齣戲下個月會上演。

---

22. **specialist** [ˋspɛʃəlɪst] n. [C] 專家 <in> [同] expert
   ▲ Anna is a specialist in international law.

Anna 是國際法的專家。

---

23. **substitute** [ˈsʌbstəˌtjut] n. [C] 替代品 <for>
▲ Since Frank was injured, the coach found a substitute for him. 由於 Frank 受傷，教練找一個人代替他。
substitute [ˈsʌbstəˌtjut] v. 代替 <for> [同] replace
▲ The doctor suggests olive oil should be substituted for lard when you cook.
這位醫生建議你在烹調時應該用橄欖油代替豬油。
substitution [ˌsʌbstəˈtjuʃən] n. [C][U] 代替
▲ In my experience, the substitution of gum chewing for smoking doesn't work.
就我的經驗來說，以嚼口香糖來取代吸菸不可行。

---

24. **superb** [suˈpɝb] adj. 極好的 [同] excellent
▲ The sweater is more expensive because it's of superb quality. 這件毛衣比較貴是因為它的品質極為上等。

---

25. **ultimate** [ˈʌltəmɪt] adj. 最終的 [同] final；根本的，基本的 [同] basic, fundamental
▲ Our ultimate goal is to establish world peace.
我們最終的目標是達成世界和平。
ultimate [ˈʌltəmɪt] n. [U] 極品
▲ The hotel is the ultimate in luxury.
這間飯店極盡奢華。

Unit 8 📚

1. **accommodation** [ə͵kɑmə`deʃən] n. [C][U] 和解，調節；
   [pl.] 住宿 (~s)
   ▲ The two parties finally came to an accommodation.
   這兩黨最後終於達成和解。
   🔎 reach an accommodation with sb 和…達成和解

2. **allergic** [ə`lɜdʒɪk] adj. 過敏的 <to>
   ▲ Carl is allergic to pollen. Carl 對花粉過敏。

3. **ample** [`æmpl] adj. 寬敞的，足夠的 [同] sufficient,
   plenty；豐富的 (ampler | amplest)
   ▲ There's ample space in the attic. 閣樓有寬敞的空間。

4. **applause** [ə`plɔz] n. [U] 鼓掌
   ▲ Let's have a round of applause for our host today.
   讓我們掌聲歡迎今天的主持人。

5. **commission** [kə`mɪʃən] n. [C][U] 委任；佣金
   ▲ The artist was given the commission to paint the
   king's portrait.
   這位藝術家被委任替國王畫肖像的任務。
   commission [kə`mɪʃən] v. 委任
   ▲ I was commissioned to translate this treaty into
   Chinese. 我受託將這項條約譯為中文。

6. **contagious** [kən`tedʒəs] adj. (疾病) 接觸性傳染的；(情
   緒等) 易感染的

▲ Don't use other people's towels in order to avoid catching contagious diseases.

別使用他人的毛巾以免得到傳染疾病。

7. **curriculum** [kə`rɪkjələm] n. [C] 課程 (pl. curriculums, curricula)

▲ Learning a second language is in the curriculum.

學習第二外語已經納入課程中。

8. **debris** [də`bri] n. [U] 碎片，殘骸

▲ After the earthquake, rescuers searched the area to see if there were any survivors under the debris. 地震過後，搜救人員搜尋此地區看是否在碎片下有生還者。

9. **essence** [`ɛsn̩s] n. [U] 本質 <of>

▲ In my opinion, the theories developed by the two scientists are almost the same in essence. 就我看來，這兩位科學家所提出的理論在本質上幾乎是相同的。

10. **expertise** [ˌɛkspɚ`tiz] n. [U] 專門技能，專門知識 <in>

▲ The job requires expertise in computer programming.

這項工作需要專業的電腦程式設計能力。

11. **format** [`fɔrmæt] n. [C][U] (整體的) 安排

▲ The format of the meeting has proved very successful. 會議的整體安排是很成功的。

format [`fɔrmæt] v. 格式化

▲ Format the flash drive before using it.

使用隨身碟前，先格式化。

12. **indispensable** [ˌɪndɪ`spɛnsəbl] adj. 不可或缺的 <to, for> [同] essential, necessary [反] dispensable
   ▲ Katherine did her job extremely well and made herself indispensable to the company. Katherine 工作表現卓越，成為這家公司不可或缺的一分子。
   indispensably [ˌɪndɪ`spɛnsəblɪ] adv. 不可或缺地

13. **layer** [`leɚ] n. [C] 層
   ▲ There is a thick layer of dust under the bed.
   床底下有厚厚一層灰。
   layer [`leɚ] v. 分層放置
   ▲ A cook is teaching on TV how to layer a mille crepe cake with crepe and whipped cream.
   一位廚師正在電視上教如何用法式薄餅和打發的鮮奶油分層排放製成法式千層蛋糕。

14. **lest** [lɛst] conj. 以免
   ▲ Be careful lest you should slip on the icy road.
   小心點，以免在結冰的道路上滑倒。

15. **milestone** [`maɪlˌston] n. [C] 里程碑 [同] landmark
   ▲ Graduating from college is an important milestone in his life. 大學畢業是他人生中一個重要的里程碑。

16. **persist** [pɚ`sɪst] v. 堅持 <in, with>
   ▲ Brian persists in walking to work every day.

Brian 堅持每天走路去上班。

17. **preference** [ˈprɛfrəns] n. [C][U] 偏好 <for>

▲ Shelly has a preference for spicy and sweet food.
Shelly 喜歡又辣又甜的食物。

18. **productivity** [ˌprodʌkˈtɪvətɪ] n. [U] 生產力

▲ The manager comes up with ways to increase the productivity of the office.
經理想出能增進辦公室生產力的方法。

19. **profile** [ˈprofaɪl] n. [C] 簡介

▲ The author of the novel has her picture and profile in the book.
這本小說的作者在書中放了她的照片和簡介。

💡 in profile 側面地｜keep a high/low profile 保持高調 / 低調

profile [ˈprofaɪl] v. 簡介

▲ The latest school newsletter profiled the new principal. 最近一期的校刊簡介新任的校長。

20. **purchase** [ˈpɝtʃəs] n. [C][U] 購買

▲ The eggs were broken on day of purchase.
這些雞蛋在購買當天就被打破了。

purchase [ˈpɝtʃəs] v. 購買 <from>

▲ Anna uses a coupon when she purchases household commodities at the store so she can save more money.

Anna 用折價券在那家店購買家庭用品，所以她可以省更多錢。

21. **reminder** [rɪ`maɪndɚ] n. [C] 提醒人的事物 <to>
▲ Grandmother got from her granddaughter a reminder to take medicine regularly.
祖母拿到一張孫女要她定時吃藥的提醒。

22. **specialty** [`spɛʃəltɪ] n. [C] 專長；特產 (pl. specialties)
▲ The painter's specialty is portraits.
這個畫家的專長是肖像畫。

23. **surveillance** [sɚ`veləns] n. [C] 監視
▲ The nightclub has been kept under surveillance because of suspected illegal activities.
這家夜店因涉嫌非法活動而被監視。

24. **therapy** [`θɛrəpɪ] n. [C][U] 療法 (pl. therapies)
▲ I am getting therapy to conquer my acrophobia.
我正在接受懼高症的治療。

25. **undermine** [ˌʌndɚ`maɪn] v. 侵蝕…的底部；逐漸損害
▲ The sea has undermined the pier.
海水侵蝕了碼頭的底部。

Unit 9

1. **accord** [ə`kɔrd] n. [C][U] 符合，一致

▲ It's a shame that things didn't happen in accord with expectations. 真遺憾事情未符合期望。

💡 with one accord 一致地

accord [ə`kɔrd] v. 一致 <with>；給予

▲ His account of the accident accords with yours. 他對事故的描述跟你的說法一致。

---

2. **analyst** [`ænlɪst] n. [C] 分析家

▲ You can see a number of financial analysts on TV making predictions about the stock market. 你可在電視上看到一些財務分析師在對股市做預測。

---

3. **appliance** [ə`plaɪəns] n. [C] (家用) 電器 [同] device (pl. appliances)

▲ Televisions and refrigerators are household appliances. 電視和冰箱是家用電器。

---

4. **arouse** [ə`raʊs] v. 喚醒 [同] awake；引起

▲ The noise aroused me from my sleep. 喧鬧聲把我從睡夢中吵醒。

---

5. **commodity** [kə`madətɪ] n. [C] 貨物，商品 (pl. commodities)

▲ The commodity prices are getting higher and higher. 物價越來越高。

---

6. **controversial** [ˌkɑntrə`vɝ.ʃəl] adj. 引起爭議的

▲ The same-sex marriage has been a controversial issue in the society.

同性結婚一直是社會上有爭議的議題。

7. **decent** [`disn̩t] adj. 合理的，像樣的
▲ My son gets a decent salary in the city.
我兒子在城市的收入相當不錯。

8. **ecological** [ˌikə`lɑdʒɪkəl] adj. 生態的
▲ Rachel warned us of the upcoming ecological catastrophe.
Rachel 警告我們即將來臨的生態大災難。

9. **execute** [`ɛksɪˌkjut] v. (依法) 處死；實行
▲ The person was executed for murder.
這人因殺人罪被處死。

10. **explicit** [ɪk`splɪsɪt] adj. 明白清楚的
▲ Can you be a little more explicit about your needs?
能否把你的需要說得再清楚一些？

11. **foul** [faʊl] adj. 骯髒惡臭的 [同] disgusting；充滿髒話的 [同] offensive
▲ Where does that foul smell come from?
惡臭味是從哪裡傳來的？
foul [faʊl] n. [C] 犯規
▲ The player committed three fouls.
這個選手犯規三次。
foul [faʊl] v. 弄髒
▲ The oil spill fouled the ocean. 漏油汙染了海洋。

foul [faʊl] adv. 違反規則地

---

12. **genetic** [dʒəˋnɛtɪk] adj. 基因的，遺傳學的

   ▲ Due to genetic defects, the boy has only one arm and one leg.

   男孩因為基因的缺陷而只有一隻手臂和一隻腳。

   💡 genetic engineering 基因工程

   genetically [dʒəˋnɛtɪklɪ] adv. 基因地，遺傳學地

   ▲ These soybeans are not genetically modified.

   這些大豆未經基因改造。

   geneticist [dʒəˋnɛtɪsɪst] n. [C] 遺傳學者

---

13. **likelihood** [ˋlaɪklɪˌhʊd] n. [U] 可能性

   ▲ In all likelihood, the candidate will win the election.

   這名候選人極可能在選舉中獲勝。

---

14. **manifest** [ˋmænəˌfɛst] v. 證明，顯示 <in>

   ▲ The fact manifests his innocence.

   事實證明他是清白的。

   manifest [ˋmænəˌfɛst] adj. 顯而易見的 <in> [同] clear

   ▲ Fear was manifest in the child's face.

   這個孩子的臉上明顯地露出恐懼。

   manifestation [ˌmænəfɛsˋteʃən] n. [C][U] 表示，表明 <of>

   ▲ Nelson made no manifestation of his disappointment.

   Nelson 沒有表現出失望的神情。

---

15. **miniature** [ˈmɪnɪətʃɚ] adj. 小型的

▲ Fiona has a whole set of miniature furniture for her dolls. Fiona 有娃娃專用的整套迷你家具。

miniature [ˈmɪnɪətʃɚ] n. [C] 小畫像

▲ Gloria always wears a locket that contains a miniature of her husband.
Gloria 總是戴著含有她丈夫小畫像的項鍊。

♥ in miniature 縮小的

16. **muscular** [ˈmʌskjəlɚ] adj. 肌肉的

▲ Tony lifts weights to develop his muscular strength.
Tony 舉重以鍛鍊肌力。

17. **petition** [pəˈtɪʃən] n. [C] 請願書

▲ We asked Leo to sign the petition, but he refused.
我們要求 Leo 簽署請願書，但他拒絕。

18. **provoke** [prəˈvok] v. 激怒 [同] goad；引起

▲ Iris was provoked to shout at him.
Iris 被激怒才對他大吼。

19. **pulse** [pʌls] n. [C] 脈搏

▲ The nurse is taking his father's pulse.
護士正在量他父親的脈搏。

pulse [pʌls] v. 搏動，跳動 [同] throb

▲ Simon could feel the blood pulsing through his veins when he was jogging. 當 Simon 慢跑的時候，他能感覺到血液在他的血管裡翻騰。

20. **radical** [`rædɪkl̩] adj. 激進的
   ▲ Olivia has very radical ideas about social reforms.
   Olivia 對社會改革抱持激進的看法。
   radical [`rædɪkl̩] n. [C] 激進分子
   ▲ Some political radicals staged a protest on the street.
   一些政治激進分子在街上發起抗議。
   radically [`rædɪklɪ] adv. 徹底地
   ▲ Diana believes that our educational system needs to
   be changed radically.
   Diana 認為教育制度需要徹底改革。

21. **removal** [rɪ`muvl̩] n. [U] 去除
   ▲ Stain removal may not be as difficult as you think
   once you learn some scientific tips. 一旦學會一些科
   學小妙招，去除汙漬或許不像想像中困難。

22. **specimen** [`spɛsəmən] n. [C] 樣本 <of> [同] sample；標
   本 <of>
   ▲ Please show me some specimens of your work.
   請讓我看看你作品的一些樣本。

23. **tactic** [`tæktɪk] n. [C] 手段；[pl.] 戰術 (~s)
   ▲ Violent tactics are unlikely to help.
   暴力的手段於事無補。
   tactical [`tæktɪkl̩] adj. 策略上的 [同] strategic
   ▲ We need a tactical plan to win the election.
   我們需要策略上的計畫去贏得選舉。

24. **unprecedented** [ʌn`prɛsə͵dɛntɪd] adj. 空前的，史無前例的

▲This company has created one unprecedented invention this year. 今年公司已創造一個空前的發明。

---

25. **vacuum** [`vækjʊəm] n. [C] 真空 (pl. vacuums, vacua)

▲Sound doesn't travel in a vacuum.
聲音在真空狀態無法傳送。

vacuum [`vækjʊəm] v. 用吸塵器清掃

▲Please vacuum the room. 請用吸塵器把房間吸一吸。

Unit 10

1. **accounting** [ə`kaʊntɪŋ] n. [U] 會計

▲My younger brother majored in accounting in college. 我弟弟大學時主修會計。

2. **anonymous** [ə`nɑnəməs] adj. 不知名的，匿名的

▲The poem was written by an anonymous poet.
這首詩是一位不知名的詩人所寫的。

anonymously [ə`nɑnəməslɪ] adv. 不知名地，匿名地

▲A large amount of money was donated anonymously.
無名氏捐贈了一大筆錢。

3. **array** [ə`re] n. [C] 大批，大量

▲There was a dazzling array of movie stars attending the ceremony. 有大批耀眼的電影明星參加典禮。

4. **asset** [ˋæsɛt] n. [C] 資產

▲ Some of the company's assets were sold to pay off debts. 這間公司部分的資產被變賣以還債。

---

5. **communism** [ˋkɑmjuˏnɪzəm] n. [U] 共產主義

▲ The goal of communism is to establish a shared society. 共產主義的目標是建立共享的社會。

---

6. **core** [kor] n. [C] 核心

▲ The commentator got straight to the core of the problem. 那位時事評論者直指問題的核心。

💡 to the core 徹底的

---

7. **declaration** [ˏdɛkləˋreʃən] n. [C][U] 宣布

▲ The US made a declaration of war to Japan after the Japanese bombed Pearl Harbor.
日本轟炸珍珠港後，美國對日本宣戰。

---

8. **ecosystem** [ˋikoˏsɪstəm] n. [C] 生態系統

▲ Environmental pollution can have a destructive influence on the ecosystem.
環境汙染可能帶給生態系統破壞性的影響。

---

9. **extinct** [ɪkˋstɪŋkt] adj. 絕種的

▲ Many animals became extinct after their habitats were destroyed. 很多動物在棲息地遭到破壞後滅種。

extinction [ɪkˋstɪŋkʃən] n. [U] 絕種

▲ We should save whales from extinction.

我們應該保護鯨魚，免於滅種。

10. **gathering** [ˋgæðərɪŋ] n. [C] 聚會 <of>

▲ The couple met and fell in love in a social gathering.
這對情侶在社交聚會上相遇與相愛。

11. **highlight** [ˋhaɪˏlaɪt] v. 強調

▲ You should highlight your strengths and skills.
你應強調你的長處和技能。

highlight [ˋhaɪˏlaɪt] n. [C] 最精采的部分

▲ The highlight of the activity was the fireworks
display. 活動中最精采的部分是施放煙火。

12. **mainstream** [ˋmenˏstrim] n. [C] 主流 (the ~)

▲ The government's policy should conform to the
mainstream of public opinion.
政府的政策應順應主流民意。

mainstream [ˋmenˏstrim] adj. 主流的

▲ Playing in the mainstream movie brought fame to the
actor. 演出主流電影讓這演員成名。

mainstream [ˋmenˏstrim] v. 為大眾所接受

▲ The concept of gender equality has been
mainstreamed. 性別平等概念已被大眾接受。

13. **massive** [ˋmæsɪv] adj. 巨大的 [同] huge, big

▲ Lucas didn't know why many people loved the
massive sculpture.
Lucas 不明白為什麼許多人喜愛那個巨大的雕像。

massively [ˈmæsɪvlɪ] adv. (程度、量等) 龐大地，非常

▲ We are doing a massively complicated task in the company. 我們正在公司裡進行一個極為複雜的任務。

---

14. **modify** [ˈmɑdəˌfaɪ] v. 修改，調整 [同] adapt

▲ My mother modified the recipe in order to suit my family's taste.

母親調整了這份食譜以符合我們家人的胃口。

modification [ˌmɑdəfəˈkeʃən] n. [C][U] 修改，調整 <to> [同] adaptation

▲ The boss requested that Bill make some modifications to the new project.

老闆要求 Bill 在新企劃上做一些調整。

---

15. **opposition** [ˌɑpəˈzɪʃən] n. [U] 反對

▲ The new policy met with strong opposition from the rival party. 新政策遭到了反對黨的強烈反對。

---

16. **overall** [ˌovəˈɔl] adj. 全面的

▲ My overall impression of that city is still favorable although my wallet was stolen there. 雖然我的錢包遭竊，但我對那個城市的總體印象仍很不錯。

overall [ˌovəˈɔl] adv. 大致上

▲ There were minor mistakes, but overall the fund-raising campaign was successful.

雖然有些小錯誤，但整體而言募款活動很成功。

overall [ˈovəˌɔl] n. [C] 工作服

▲ Mina put on a white overall and went into the laboratory. Mina 穿上白色的工作服走進實驗室。

---

17. **pitcher** [ˋpɪtʃɚ] n. [C] 投手
   ▲ Carl will be the pitcher in the game.
   Carl 將在比賽中擔任投手。

---

18. **pyramid** [ˋpɪrəmɪd] n. [C] 金字塔
   ▲ We visited the pyramids and Sphinx in Egypt.
   我們去埃及參觀金字塔和獅身人面像。

---

19. **rail** [rel] n. [C] 圍欄
   ▲ My son leaned on the rail and watched the cows grazing. 我的兒子倚在圍欄上看著牛吃草。
   railing [ˋrelɪŋ] n. [C] 柵欄
   ▲ Alan had a good view from his perch on the railing.
   Alan 坐在高高的柵欄上，視野很好。

---

20. **regardless** [rɪˋgɑrdlɪs] adj. 不管 <of>
   ▲ Helen will do anything, regardless of the consequences. Helen 不顧後果，什麼事都做得出來。
   regardless [rɪˋgɑrdlɪs] adv. 無論如何
   ▲ Her family are against the idea of her quitting the job, but she'll probably go ahead and do it regardless.
   她的家人反對她辭職，但是不管怎樣她都可能這樣做。

---

21. **reservoir** [ˋrɛzɚˏvɔr] n. [C] 蓄水池
   ▲ The capital's water is supplied by this reservoir.

首都的水是由這個蓄水池提供的。

---

22. **spectacular** [spɛk`tækjələ] adj. 精采的
   ▲ The race ended in a spectacular finish.
   那場比賽以精采的收場結束。

   spectacular [spɛk`tækjələ] n. [C] 精采的演出 [同] show
   ▲ My family and I enjoyed a TV spectacular together after the Thanksgiving dinner. 我和我的家人在感恩節晚餐後一起看電視精采的節目。

---

23. **terminal** [`tɝmənl] n. [C] 終點站
   ▲ Amy and I decided to meet up at the bus terminal.
   Amy 和我決定在公車終點站碰面。

   terminal [`tɝmənl] adj. (疾病) 末期的
   ▲ The patient is diagnosed with terminal cancer.
   這名病患被診斷出癌症末期。

---

24. **update** [`ʌp,det] n. [C] 最新消息 <on>
   ▲ The chief of police will provide an update on the hostage crisis.
   警察首長將會提供人質危機的最新消息。

   update [ʌp`det] v. 更新
   ▲ Don't forget to update the computer before you leave. 你離開前別忘了更新電腦。

---

25. **verbal** [`vɝbl] adj. 言語的
   ▲ Having good verbal skills is one of the basic requirements to be an anchor.

具備良好語言表達技巧是成為主播的基本條件之一。

💡 verbal abuse 語言攻擊

verbal [ˋvɝbl̩] n. [C][U] 從動詞衍生出來的動名詞、不定詞及分詞等

Unit 11

1. **acquaint** [əˋkwent] v. 使熟悉 <with>

▲ It is Laura's job to acquaint newcomers with the rules of the office.

Laura 的職責是使新進員工熟悉辦公室的規定。

---

2. **anticipate** [ænˋtɪsə͵pet] v. 預期 <that>；期待 [同] look forward to

▲ The patient recovered faster than anticipated.

這名病人比預期的更快康復。

---

3. **arrogant** [ˋærəgənt] adj. 傲慢的

▲ The arrogant official refused to answer any questions about her scandals.

這名傲慢的官員拒絕回答關於她醜聞的任何問題。

arrogance [ˋærəgəns] n. [U] 傲慢

▲ Paul's friends all left him because they could not put up with his arrogance. Paul 的朋友全部都離他遠去，因為他們無法忍受他的傲慢。

---

4. **athletics** [æθˋlɛtɪks] n. [U] 體育運動

▲ Wendy was praised for her impressive performance in school athletics.

Wendy 因為在學校體育運動表現優異而受到表揚。

---

5. **awe** [ɔ] n. [U] 敬畏 <with, in>

▲ The sights of Taroko National Park filled me with awe. 太魯閣國家公園的景色使我敬畏不已。

💡 be/stand in awe of sb 對…心存敬畏

awe [ɔ] v. 使敬畏

▲ All the tourists were awed by the majestic view.

壯麗的景色令所有遊客嘆為觀止。

---

6. **communist** [ˋkɑmjʊ͵nɪst] adj. 共產主義的

▲ North Korea is a communist country.

北韓是一個共產國家。

💡 the Communist Party 共產黨

communist [ˋkɑmjʊ͵nɪst] n. [C] 共產主義者

▲ Mark is a communist; he wants to create a society where everyone is equal. Mark 是一位共產主義者；他想要創造一個人人平等的社會。

---

7. **coverage** [ˋkʌvərɪdʒ] n. [U] 新聞報導；保險 (範圍) <for>

▲ The newscaster is giving live coverage of the election campaign.

這名新聞報導者正在實況報導選舉活動。

💡 media/press coverage 媒體報導 | medical coverage 醫療保險

---

8. **deficit** [ˋdɛfəsɪt] n. [C] 赤字，虧損 <of, in>

▲ The startup tried to reduce its budget deficit by cutting spending.

這家新創公司嘗試藉由削減開支減少預算赤字。

💡 trade deficit 貿易逆差

---

9. **extension** [ɪkˋstɛnʃən] n. [C][U] 延伸，擴大 <of>；[C] 延期；分機

▲ The research is an extension of the topic Dr. Lin introduced in the book.

這份研究是林醫生在書中所介紹的主題的延伸。

---

10. **federal** [ˋfɛdərəl] adj. 聯邦政府的

▲ The federal government is criticized for being slow to react to the disastrous impacts of the hurricane.

聯邦政府被批評太慢回應颶風所帶來的災難性影響。

💡 federal laws 聯邦法

federation [ˏfɛdəˋreʃən] n. [C] 聯邦

▲ Moscow is the capital of the Russian Federation.

莫斯科是俄羅斯聯邦的首都。

---

11. **generate** [ˋdʒɛnəˏret] v. 產生，引起

▲ The house mainly relies on solar panels to generate electricity. 這間房子主要仰賴太陽能面板發電。

💡 generate interest/income 產生興趣 / 收入

---

12. **hostile** [ˋhɑstl̩] adj. 有敵意的 <to, toward>；反對的 <to>；艱苦惡劣的；敵軍的

▲ Clara is hostile to the new classmate for no reason.
Clara 無緣無故對新同學有敵意。

---

13. **mansion** [ˋmænʃən] n. [C] 豪宅

▲ Jessie spent all her savings on the purchase of a lavish mansion.
Jessie 花費她所有的積蓄購買一棟豪宅。

---

14. **mount** [maʊnt] n. [C] 山 (abbr. Mt)

▲ The mountain climbers overcame all the difficulties and got to the top of Mount Everest.
登山客克服所有困難，登上聖母峰頂端。

mount [maʊnt] v. 增加；準備發起；攀登 [同] ascend

▲ The students' pressure is mounting as the exam draws nearer.
隨著考試越來越近，學生們的壓力也增加了。

---

15. **performer** [pɚˋfɔrmɚ] n. [C] 表演者

▲ Amy's dream is to become a brilliant performer.
Amy 的夢想是成為一名傑出的表演者。

---

16. **plea** [pli] n. [C] 懇求 <for, to>

▲ Doris made a plea to the police to look for her missing son. Doris 懇求警方找尋她失蹤的兒子。

---

17. **questionnaire** [ˌkwɛstʃənˋɛr] n. [C] 問卷

▲ Participants were asked to fill in the questionnaires after the workshop.

參加者被要求在研討會結束後填寫問卷。

---

18. **recite** [rɪ`saɪt] v. 背誦，朗誦

▲ At the request of the audience, the poet recited several poems she had written.

應聽眾要求，這位詩人朗誦了幾首她寫的詩。

recital [rɪ`saɪtl] n. [C] 獨奏會

▲ Venus is going to give a violin recital at the cultural center. Venus 即將在文化中心舉辦小提琴獨奏會。

---

19. **revenue** [`rɛvə‚nju] n. [C][U] 收入，收益

▲ Ten percent of the company's revenue will be spent on charity. 公司收益的 10% 將用在慈善活動上。

---

20. **sponsor** [`spɑnsɚ] n. [C] 保證人；贊助者

▲ Before signing the contract, you need to find a sponsor. 在簽合約之前，你需要找到一位保證人。

sponsor [`spɑnsɚ] v. 贊助

▲ The road running race is sponsored by a bank.

這場路跑比賽是由一家銀行所贊助。

---

21. **stock** [stɑk] n. [C][U] 存貨；股票，股份

▲ Emily always keeps a good stock of cosmetics.

Emily 總是囤積大量化妝品。

💡 in/out of stock 有 / 沒有庫存 ｜ stock exchange 股票 (或證券) 交易所

22. **texture** [ˈtɛkstʃɚ] n. [C][U] 質地；口感
   ▲ This lotion can give your skin a silky texture.
   這乳液能使你的皮膚摸起來光滑如絲。
   texture [ˈtɛkstʃɚ] v. 使具有特別的質地

23. **tribute** [ˈtrɪbjut] n. [C][U] 表尊敬的行為；貢品，禮物
   ▲ The president paid tribute to the soldiers who fought
   bravely in the battle.
   總統對那些在戰爭中勇於奮戰的士兵們表示敬意。
   ● be a tribute to sb/sth 顯示…(價值、長處) 的證據

24. **vague** [veg] adj. 粗略的 <about>；模糊的 [同] indistinct
   (vaguer | vaguest)
   ▲ The politician only made vague promises to abolish
   nuclear power.
   這位政治家對廢除核能的承諾言辭含混。
   ● have a vague impression of sth 對…印象模糊
   vaguely [ˈveglɪ] adv. 模糊地 [反] clearly
   ▲ The girl's face looked vaguely familiar but I couldn't
   remember where we had met. 這女孩的臉孔似曾相
   識，但我忘記我們曾經在哪裡見過。

25. **wildlife** [ˈwaɪldˌlaɪf] n. [U] 野生生物
   ▲ Construction of highways is very likely to endanger
   wildlife. 公路建設很有可能會危及野生生物。
   ● wildlife conservation 野生生物保育

Unit 12

1. **accessible** [æk`sɛsəbl] adj. 易接近的，易得到的 <to, by>
   ▲ The village is only accessible by air. There is no other way to reach it. 這個村莊只有搭飛機才能到達。沒有其他的方式可以到達。

2. **acquisition** [ˌækwə`zɪʃən] n. [U] 獲得 <of>；[C] 收購品
   ▲ Amy's acquisition of writing skills is mainly through continuous practice.
   Amy 寫作技巧的獲得主要來自於不斷的練習。
   💡 language acquisition 語言習得

3. **antique** [æn`tik] adj. 年代久遠的，古董的
   ▲ The antique china is worth millions of dollars.
   這個古董瓷器價值數百萬元。
   antique [æn`tik] n. [C] 古董
   ▲ Kathy has a fine collection of antiques.
   Kathy 有精緻的古董收藏品。

4. **assess** [ə`sɛs] v. 評估 [同] judge；估計 <at>
   ▲ Some experts are invited to assess if the seaside resort meets the requirements of environmental protection. 一些專家受邀評估濱海渡假村是否符合環境保護要求。
   assessment [ə`sɛsmənt] n. [C][U] 評估；估算
   ▲ Greg made a careful assessment before investing in the property market.

Greg 在投資房地產市場前做了仔細評估。

💡 risk assessment 風險評估

5. **ban** [bæn] n. [C] 禁止 <on>

▲ Some argued that the total ban on smoking violates human rights. 有些人爭論全面禁菸違反人權。

💡 impose/lift a ban 頒布 / 解除禁令

ban [bæn] v. 禁止 <from> [同] prohibit [反] allow (banned | banned | banning)

▲ Caught drunk driving, Bill was banned from driving for one year. 酒駕被抓，Bill 被禁止駕駛一年。

6. **commute** [kə`mjut] v. 通勤 <to, from, between>

▲ Carrie commutes between Taipei and Keelung by intercity bus every day.

Carrie 每天搭客運通勤於臺北和基隆之間。

7. **contemporary** [kən`tɛmpə͵rɛrɪ] adj. 當代的 [同] modern；同時代的

▲ The use of electronic sounds is one characteristic of contemporary music.

電音的使用是當代音樂的特色之一。

contemporary [kən`tɛmpə͵rɛrɪ] n. [C] 同時代的人 <of> (pl. contemporaries)

▲ Tang Xianzu was a contemporary of Shakespeare. 湯顯祖和莎士比亞是同時代的人。

8. **cruise** [kruz] n. [C] 乘船遊覽

▲ The newlyweds went on a 10-day Mediterranean cruise. 這對新婚夫婦參加十天的地中海乘船遊覽。

cruise [kruz] v. 乘船遊覽

▲ Maria cruised around the Caribbean for 5 days.
Maria 乘船遊覽環繞加勒比海五天。

---

9. **depict** [dɪ`pɪkt] v. 描繪，描寫

▲ The painting vividly depicts what a church was like 100 years ago.

這幅畫生動描繪出一百年前教堂的模樣。

💡 depict sb/sth as 將⋯描繪成

depiction [dɪ`pɪkʃən] n. [C][U] 描繪，描寫 <of>

▲ The bloody depiction of the war on TV disgusted the viewers.

電視中關於戰爭的血腥描繪讓觀眾感到反感。

---

10. **fabric** [`fæbrɪk] n. [C][U] 布料 [同] material；[sing.] 結構 <of>

▲ You can find various kinds of fabrics in that fabric market. 你可以在布市找到各式各樣的布料。

💡 cotton/wool/silk fabric 棉 / 羊毛 / 絲布料 | the fabric of society 社會結構

---

11. **flexibility** [ˌflɛksə`bɪlətɪ] n. [U] 易曲性；柔軟度

▲ Because of its flexibility, rubber is used for tires.
由於橡膠是可彎曲的材質，因此被用來做輪胎。

---

12. **genre** [ˋʒɑnrə] n. [C] 體裁，類型

▲ The novels on Molly's bookshelf are arranged according to the genres.

Molly 書架上的小說依據不同體裁排列。

---

13. **howl** [haʊl] n. [C] (狼、狗) 嗥叫聲 <of>；怒吼 <of> (usu. pl.)

▲ The howl of dogs made me toss and turn all night.

狗的嗥叫聲讓我整晚輾轉反側。

🥭 the howl of the wind 風的呼嘯聲

howl [haʊl] v. (狼、狗) 嗥叫；怒吼 <for>

▲ Wolves howl to call the pack together.

狼嗥叫來集結狼群。

---

14. **midst** [mɪdst] n. [U] 中間；期間 <of> [同] middle

▲ A school in the midst of the city doesn't usually have a large campus.

在市中心的學校通常沒有很大的校園。

midst [mɪdst] prep. 在⋯之間

▲ A swarm of bees fly midst the flowers.

一大群蜜蜂在花間飛舞。

---

15. **nasty** [ˋnæstɪ] adj. 惡意的 <to> [同] mean；粗魯的 (nastier | nastiest)

▲ Don't be so nasty to those who care about you.

別對那些關心你的人那麼壞。

nastily [ˋnæstəlɪ] adv. 不友善地

▲ The violent criminal smiled nastily at the police.
殘暴的罪犯不友善地對著警方微笑。

---

16. **pledge** [plɛdʒ] n. [C] 誓言，諾言 <to> [同] commitment；
擔保品 <of>

▲ Will made a pledge to take his kids to the aquarium.
Will 承諾要帶他的孩子去水族館。

pledge [plɛdʒ] v. 發誓，承諾 <to>

▲ The government pledged to rebuild the bridge ruined
by the typhoon as soon as possible.
政府承諾會盡快重建被颱風破壞的橋。

---

17. **prey** [pre] n. [sing.] 獵物 [反] predator；受害者，受騙者

▲ Spiders use their webs to catch their prey.
蜘蛛利用牠們的網來捕抓獵物。

💡 be/fall prey to sb/sth 受⋯捕食；受⋯所害

prey [pre] v. 捕食 <on, upon>；坑騙 <on, upon>

▲ Sparrows prey on worms and fruits.
麻雀捕食蟲子及果實。

---

18. **random** [ˋrændəm] adj. 任意的，隨機的

▲ The survey used a random sample of 500 students
throughout the town.
這調查採隨機抽這座小鎮上五百名學生為樣本。

💡 at random 任意地，隨意地

randomly [ˋrændəmlɪ] adv. 任意地，隨意地

▲The magician asked the little girl to pick a card randomly. 魔術師要求小女孩任意抽取一張卡片。

19. **refuge** [ˋrɛfjudʒ] n. [U] 避難，庇護 <from>；[C] 避難所，庇護所 <from>

▲A thunderstorm forced the passers-by to take refuge from the rain in the arcade.
這場雷陣雨迫使行人們在騎樓尋求庇護以躲雨。

20. **reverse** [rɪˋvɝs] v. 使反轉

▲It will take some time to reverse the economic decline. 扭轉經濟衰退的局勢會花上一些時間。

reverse [rɪˋvɝs] adj. 相反的

▲The FBI agent says one way to spot liars is to ask them to tell their stories in reverse order.
聯邦調查局人員說，要看出說謊者的方法之一是要求他們以倒敘的方式來描述事情。

reverse [rɪˋvɝs] n. [C][U] 相反

▲Many of Julia's friends think Julia is outgoing; however, the reverse is true. 許多 Julia 的朋友認為 Julia 是個外向的人，然而，事實上情況正好相反。

💡 put sth in(to) reverse 使出現逆轉

reversal [rɪˋvɝs!] n. [C][U] 逆轉 <of, in>

▲The clothing factory experienced a reversal of fortune, but now it's getting better. 這間成衣工廠曾經經歷過命運逆轉，但是現在發展越來越好。

21. **strain** [stren] n. [C][U] 緊張；[sing.] 負擔 <on>
▲ Thomas is learning to cope with the stresses and strains of his studies. Thomas 正在學習處理課業所帶來的壓力與緊張情緒。

strain [stren] v. 使緊繃，竭力；弄傷 (身體、肌肉)
▲ Without subtitles, Vicky needs to strain her ears to catch the conversations in the movie.
沒有了字幕，Vicky 需要豎起耳朵去聽電影裡的對話。

strained [strend] adj. 緊張的，緊繃的 [同] tense
▲ Relations between the Soviet Union and the United States were strained during the Cold War.
在冷戰時期，蘇聯和美國關係緊張。

22. **toxic** [ˋtɑksɪk] adj. 有毒的 [同] poisonous
▲ The factory was caught releasing toxic chemicals into the river. 工廠被發現在河裡排放有毒化學物質。
💡 toxic fumes/gases/substances 有毒的煙霧 / 氣體 / 物質

23. **transaction** [trænsˋækʃən] n. [C][U] 交易
▲ Remember to get a receipt after the transaction.
交易完畢後，請記得索取收據。

24. **vendor** [ˋvɛndɚ] n. [C] 小販
▲ Jacob bought a hot dog from a street vendor on the sidewalk.
Jacob 向人行道上的街頭攤販買了一支熱狗。

25. **via** [ˋvaɪə] prep. 經由;藉由

▲ Sophia flew to Taiwan from London via Bangkok.
Sophia 從倫敦經由曼谷飛往臺灣。

Unit 13

1. **abundant** [əˋbʌndənt] adj. 豐富的 [同] plentiful [反] scarce

▲ There will be abundant supplies of food and medicine sent to the refuge.
會有充足的食物和藥物資源送到難民區。

---

2. **activist** [ˋæktɪvɪst] n. [C] 積極分子

▲ The environmental activists organized a protest against the planned new factory. 環境保護積極分子組織抗議活動抗議計劃建造的新工廠。

💡 animal rights activist 保護動物權益的積極分子

---

3. **administrative** [ədˋmɪnəˏstretɪv] adj. 行政的,管理的

▲ Molly had worked for many years as an administrative assistant before she was promoted to manager.
在 Molly 晉升為經理前,她已任職行政助理多年。

💡 administrative duty 行政責任

---

4. **apt** [æpt] adj. 適切的 <for> [同] appropriate;有…傾向的 <to>

▲ Both reward and punishment should be apt for students' behavior.

獎懲皆應該適切於學生的行為表現。

aptitude [ˈæptəˌtjud] n. [C][U] 天賦，才能 <for> [同] talent

▲ Leslie has a natural aptitude for music. No wonder she plays the piano so well.

Leslie 在音樂方面很有天賦。難怪她鋼琴彈得很好。

---

5. **barren** [ˈbærən] adj. 貧瘠的 [同] infertilc；無成果的

▲ Nothing can grow in this barren soil.

這貧瘠的土壤什麼東西都長不出來。

---

6. **beloved** [bɪˈlʌvd] adj. 摯愛的 <by, of>

▲ The accident took the life of Ken's beloved daughter.

這場意外奪走了 Ken 摯愛的女兒。

beloved [bɪˈlʌvd] n. [C] 所愛的人

▲ Dan sent a bunch of red roses to his beloved on Valentine's Day.

情人節當天 Dan 送了一束紅玫瑰給他的摯愛。

---

7. **compatible** [kəmˈpætəbl] adj. (尤指電器、軟體等) 相容的 <with>；投緣的 <with>

▲ This software is not compatible with my computer.

這個軟體與我的電腦不相容。

---

8. **density** [ˈdɛnsətɪ] n. [U] 密度

▲ The city has the high density of convenience stores.

這座城市的便利商店密度很高。

💡 population density 人口密度

---

9. **derive** [dəˋraɪv] v. 起源於 <from>；得到 (樂趣 等) <from>

▲ Many English words are originally derived from Latin. 許多英文字起源於拉丁語。

---

10. **fiber** [ˋfaɪbɚ] n. [C][U] (衣服) 纖維；[U] (食物) 纖維素 [同] roughage

▲ Vivian has very sensitive skin, so she only buys clothes made of natural fibers.
Vivian 有敏感性肌膚，因此只買天然纖維做的衣服。

💡 artificial fiber 人造纖維 | high-/low-fiber diet 高 / 低 纖飲食

---

11. **fluid** [ˋfluɪd] n. [C][U] 流質

▲ After the operation, the patient was asked to drink fluids only. 手術過後，病人被要求只能喝流質的東西。

fluid [ˋfluɪd] adj. 流暢的 [同] flow；不穩定的

▲ The ballet dancer was dancing with graceful and fluid movements.
這位芭蕾舞者以優美和流暢的動作跳著舞。

---

12. **glare** [glɛr] n. [C] 怒視

▲ Leo's teacher gave him an angry glare.
Leo 的老師憤怒地瞪他一眼。

glare [glɛr] v. 怒視 <at> [同] glower

▲ Sharon glared at Gary and walked out of the kitchen.
Sharon 怒視 Gary 並離開廚房。

---

13. **legitimate** [lɪˋdʒɪtəmɪt] adj. 合法的 [同] legal [反]
illegitimate；合理的 [同] justifiable, valid

▲ All of Robert's property went to his daughter as she
was the only legitimate heir. Robert 所有的財產都由
他的女兒繼承，因為她是唯一的合法繼承人。

legitimate [lɪˋdʒɪtə‚met] v. 使合法 [同] legitimize

▲ Some victims of sexual assault hoped to legitimate
abortion. 一些性侵受害者期盼能讓墮胎合法化。

---

14. **migration** [maɪˋgreʃən] n. [C][U] 遷移，移居

▲ The biologists are studying the seasonal migration of
the birds. 生物學家們正在研究這種鳥的季節性遷移。

migrate [ˋmaɪgret] v. 遷移 <to>

▲ Swallows migrate to the south in autumn.
燕子秋天遷移至南方。

---

15. **neutral** [ˋnjutrəl] adj. 中立的 [同] impartial, unbiased

▲ Ivan takes a neutral stand in the argument between
his parents. Ivan 在雙親之間的爭執中持中立態度。

💡 remain/stay neutral 保持中立

neutral [ˋnjutrəl] n. [C] 中立國 ；[U] (汽車) 空檔 <in,
into>

▲ Switzerland was a neutral throughout the Second
World War.

瑞士在第二次世界大戰自始至終是個中立國。

---

16. **plunge** [plʌndʒ] n. [C] (某人或某物) 突然落下 <into>；
暴跌 <in>

▲ One witness recorded the helicopter's plunge into the valley. 一位目擊者錄下直升機墜落山谷畫面。

💡 take the plunge (深思後) 毅然決定

plunge [plʌndʒ] v. 突然墜落 <over, off, into>；暴跌 <to>

▲ The tour bus was hit by the falling rock and plunged over the cliff. 遊覽車被落石擊中墜落懸崖。

---

17. **prior** [ˈpraɪɚ] adj. 較早的，先前的 [同] previous

▲ The fire broke out without any prior warning.
這場火災毫無預警的發生。

💡 prior to sth 在…之前

prior [ˈpraɪɚ] adv. 在先，事先

prior [ˈpraɪɚ] n. [C] 小修道院院長

---

18. **residence** [ˈrɛzədəns] n. [C] 住所；[U] 定居 [同] residency

▲ The White House is the residence of the president of the United States. 白宮是美國總統的住所。

---

19. **ridiculous** [rɪˈdɪkjələs] adj. 可笑的，荒唐的 [同] absurd

▲ Whenever Brian got drunk, he would unknowingly do something ridiculous.
每當 Brian 酒醉的時候，他會不自覺做些可笑的事情。

ridicule [`rɪdɪ,kjul] n. [U] 嘲笑，嘲弄 [同] mockery

▲ Fiona became an object of ridicule since her skirt was inside out.

Fiona 因為裙子穿反而成了眾人的笑柄。

ridicule [`rɪdɪ,kjul] v. 嘲笑，嘲弄 [同] mock

▲ Grace was upset when her hairstyle was ridiculed by her classmates.

Grace 因為被同學嘲笑髮型而感到沮喪。

---

20. **saint** [sent] n. [C] 聖人，聖徒 (abbr. St, St.)；至善之人

▲ St Paul's Cathedral is one of the most popular tourist attractions in London.

聖保羅大教堂是倫敦最熱門的觀光景點之一。

saint [sent] v. 指定…為聖徒

---

21. **scent** [sɛnt] n. [C] 香味 <of> [同] fragrance；氣味

▲ Some can't stand the scent of durian.

有些人無法忍受榴槤的香氣。

scent [sɛnt] v. 使有香味；(動物) 嗅出

▲ The incense scents the air in the temple.

線香使寺廟充滿香氣。

---

22. **suburban** [sə`bɝbən] adj. 郊區的

▲ The newlyweds are looking for a suburban house at an affordable price.

這對新婚夫婦正在尋找在郊區可負擔得起的房子。

---

23. **trait** [tret] n. [C] 特徵，特質

▲ Honesty is one of Ann's most admirable traits.

誠實是 Ann 最令人讚賞的特質之一。

💡 personality/character trait 人格特質

24. **transparent** [træns`pɛrənt] adj. 透明的 [同] clear；易懂的

▲ Rays can go through transparent glass.

光線可以穿過透明玻璃。

25. **viable** [`vaɪəbl] adj. 可行的

▲ Honestly speaking, we don't think your plan is viable. 老實說，我們並不認為你的計畫可行。

Unit 14

1. **administrator** [əd`mɪnə,stretɚ] n. [C] 管理者

▲ Due to the political scandal, the administrator made a public apology and decided to resign.

由於政治醜聞，管理者公開道歉並決定辭職。

2. **alter** [`ɔltɚ] v. 改變

▲ One small thought may alter your life.

一個小小的念頭可以改變你的一生。

alteration [,ɔltə`reʃən] n. [C][U] 改變 <to>

▲ Emma made some alterations to her old apartment.

Emma 對她的舊公寓做了一些改變。

3. **arena** [ə`rinə] n. [C] (運動) 競技場；界

▲ A boxing match was held in the arena.
一場拳擊賽在競技場舉行。

4. **behalf** [bɪˋhæf] n. [C] 代表…；為了幫助…
  ▲ Lily will receive the award on behalf of her class.
   Lily 將代表全班領獎。

5. **belongings** [bəˋlɔŋɪŋz] n. [pl.] 所有物 [同] possession
  ▲ Hank ran away from home with only a few personal belongings.
   Hank 只帶了一些私人物品就離家出走了。

6. **beware** [bɪˋwɛr] v. 當心，注意 <of>
  ▲ Beware of falling asleep when sunbathing! Otherwise, you might get sunburned.
   在曬日光浴時當心別睡著了！否則，你可能會曬傷。

7. **caution** [ˋkɔʃən] n. [U] 謹慎 <with>；[C][U] 告誡
  ▲ We must proceed with caution, or it will add insult to injury. 我們須謹慎行事，否則只會雪上加霜。
  💡 throw/cast caution to the winds 不顧風險，魯莽行事
  caution [ˋkɔʃən] v. 告誡 <against>
  ▲ The locals cautioned me against walking alone in the forest. 當地人告誡我不要單獨在森林行走。

8. **competence** [ˋkɑmpətəns] n. [U] 能力 <in, of>
  ▲ The software company is looking for those who have a high level of competence in Japanese.

這家軟體公司正在尋找日文能力強的人。

9. **destination** [ˌdɛstəˈneʃən] n. [C] 目的地
   ▲ Due to the storm, only half of the sailors have reached their destination.
   因為暴風雨，只有一半的水手抵達目的地。
   ♥ holiday/tourist destination 渡假勝地

10. **destructive** [dɪˈstrʌktɪv] adj. 破壞性的 <to>
    ▲ It concerns teachers that bullying can have a destructive effect on students.
    老師們擔心霸凌會帶給學生不良的影響。

11. **forge** [fɔrdʒ] v. 偽造
    ▲ The man was under arrest for forging bills.
    這個男人因為偽造鈔票而被逮捕。

12. **immense** [ɪˈmɛns] adj. 極大的 [同] enormous
    ▲ Mastering a language requires an immense effort.
    學好一個語言需要極大的努力。
    immensely [ɪˈmɛnslɪ] adv. 非常 [同] enormously, extremely
    ▲ Belinda is an immensely talented ballet dancer.
    Belinda 是個才華洋溢的芭蕾舞者。

13. **implement** [ˈɪmpləˌmɛnt] v. 實施 (計畫等)
    ▲ The new tax policy is scheduled to be implemented next month. 新的稅務政策預計下個月開始實施。
    implement [ˈɪmpləmənt] n. [C] 工具，器具

▲ Adam put all of the agricultural implements in the warehouse. Adam 將所有的農具放在倉庫裡。

14. **likewise** [ˋlaɪk‚waɪz] adv. 同樣地 [同] similarly

▲ Jacob took a vacation to Dubai and his uncle did likewise. Jacob 去杜拜渡假，而他的叔叔也是。

15. **naive** [nɑˋiv] adj. 天真無知的 (naiver | naivest)

▲ It's naive to think that catching all the criminals would bring peace.

認為抓走所有罪犯就能帶來和平是很天真的想法。

naively [nɑˋivlɪ] adv. 天真無知地

▲ Tina naively believed every word the stranger said and gave him her mobile number. Tina 天真地相信陌生人所說的話，並且給對方她的手機號碼。

16. **norm** [nɔrm] n. [C] 準則 (usu. pl.)；常態 (the ～)

▲ People who stay away from social norms are often described as odd.

遠離社會準則的人常被說成是古怪的。

17. **poetic** [poˋɛtɪk] adj. 詩的；詩意的

▲ Wilson has a collection of Emily Dickinson's poetic works. Wilson 有一套艾蜜莉狄金生的詩集。

poetically [poˋɛtɪklɪ] adv. 富有詩意地

▲ The musician composed the symphony poetically.

作曲家把這個交響曲寫得富有詩意。

18. **resort** [rɪˋzɔrt] n. [C] 遊覽地；[C][U] 手段

▲ Lucy and her family stayed in a ski resort while they were taking a vacation in Hokkaido.

Lucy 與她的家人在北海道渡假時停留在滑雪勝地。

resort [rɪ`zɔrt] v. 訴諸於… <to>

▲ The company resorted to the law to settle the dispute.

公司訴諸法律來解決爭端。

---

19. **rigid** [`rɪdʒɪd] adj. 僵硬的 ；嚴格的 [同] inflexible [反] flexible

▲ The girl was rigid with fear at the sight of the snake.

女孩一看到蛇就被嚇得無法動彈。

rigidly [`rɪdʒɪdlɪ] adv. 嚴格地

▲ In order to lose weight, Hannah sticks rigidly to her diet plan. 為了減肥，Hannah 嚴格遵守她的節食計畫。

---

20. **setting** [`sɛtɪŋ] n. [C] 環境 <for>；背景

▲ Alex thought this restaurant would be the perfect setting for the first date.

Alex 認為這家餐廳會是第一次約會的理想環境。

---

21. **sow** [so] v. 播種；引起 (sowed | sown, sowed | sowing)

▲ We sowed the tulip seeds in November. They are expected to blossom in March.

我們在十一月播種鬱金香。它們預計三月會開花。

sow [so] n. [C] 母豬

▲ There are some sows in the pigpen.

豬圈裡有一些母豬。

---

22. **sturdy** [ˋstɝdɪ] adj. 結實的，堅固的 (sturdier | sturdiest)

▲ The shelf is not sturdy enough for the encyclopedia.
那個架子不夠堅固，無法承受那套百科全書的重量。

23. **superstition** [ˌsupɚˋstɪʃən] n. [C][U] 迷信

▲ It is a superstition that giving a friend a fan as a gift
will destroy the relationship with him or her.
送朋友扇子當禮物會毀了與他或她的情誼是個迷信。

24. **trigger** [ˋtrɪgɚ] n. [C] 扳機;(引起反應的) 一件事或情況
<for>

▲ The soldier aimed at his target and pulled the trigger.
士兵瞄準他的目標並扣下扳機。

trigger [ˋtrɪgɚ] v. 引發 <off>

▲ The smell of the cuisine triggered a fond memory of
Susie's childhood.
這道菜的味道讓 Susie 想起美好的童年回憶。

25. **vicious** [ˋvɪʃəs] adj. 惡意的 [同] malicious ; 殘暴的 [同]
violent

▲ Those boys made some vicious remarks about Bill.
那群男孩說著 Bill 的壞話。

💡 vicious circle 惡性循環

Unit 15

1. **adore** [əˋdor] v. 熱愛，崇拜

▲ Chloe adores Snoopy and all of its products.

Chloe 熱愛史努比和它所有的商品。

adoration [ˌædəˈreʃən] n. [U] 熱愛，崇拜

▲ Those devoted fans looked at their idol with adoration.

那些狂熱的粉絲以崇拜的眼光看著他們的偶像。

adorable [əˈdorəbl] adj. 可愛的，討人喜歡的

▲ Blaire's parents gave her an adorable puppy on her birthday.

Blaire 的父母在她生日的時候給她一隻可愛的小狗。

2. **articulate** [ɑrˈtɪkjəˌlet] v. 清楚表達

▲ Nancy could articulate her feelings in French.

Nancy 能用法文清楚表達她的感受。

articulate [ɑrˈtɪkjəlɪt] adj. 能清楚表達的

▲ It's difficult to imagine that Jimmy is illiterate after listening to his creative and articulate storytelling.

在聽完 Jimmy 有創意且清楚表達的述說故事後，很難想像他是個文盲。

articulation [ɑrˌtɪkjəˈleʃən] n. [U] 表達

▲ Sandy is a good lecturer with clear articulation.

Sandy 是一位表達清楚的好講師。

3. **attribute** [əˈtrɪbjut] v. 把⋯歸因於⋯ <to>

▲ The champion attributed her success to her coach's support. 冠軍把她的勝利歸功於她教練的支持。

4. **beneficial** [ˌbɛnəˈfɪʃəl] adj. 有益的 <to, for>

▲ The new policy will be beneficial to all citizens.
新政策將有益於所有市民。

beneficially [ˌbɛnəˋfɪʃəlɪ] adv. 有益地

▲ A balanced diet will beneficially affect the patient's health. 均衡的飲食將有益地影響病人的健康。

beneficiary [ˌbɛnəˋfɪʃərɪ] n. [C] 受益人 <of> (pl. beneficiaries)

▲ David was the chief beneficiary of the business deal. David 是這場商業交易的主要受益人。

---

5. **biological** [ˌbaɪəˋlɑdʒɪkl] adj. 生物的

▲ Sleeping and eating are human biological necessities. 睡與吃是人類的生理需求。

💡 biological diversity 生物多樣性 | biological parents 親生父母

---

6. **bodyguard** [ˋbɑdɪˌɡɑrd] n. [C] 保鏢

▲ The movie star hired a team of bodyguards to protect her. 這名影星僱用一群保鏢保護她。

---

7. **component** [kəmˋponənt] n. [C] 構成要素，成分 <of> [同] constituent

▲ The scientists are analyzing the components of the substance. 科學家正在分析這物質的成分。

component [kəmˋponənt] adj. 構成的，組成的 [同] constituent

▲ Laura put the component parts together into a model plane by herself.

Laura 自己組裝零件做了架模型飛機。

8. **compound** [ˋkɑmpaʊnd] n. [C] 化合物 <of>

▲ Carbon dioxide is the compound of carbon and oxygen. 二氧化碳是碳和氧氣的化合物。

compound [kəmˋpaʊnd] v. 使惡化；混和 <with>

▲ Andy's depression was compounded when his marriage broke up.

Andy 的婚姻破局使他的憂鬱症惡化了。

compound [ˋkɑmpaʊnd] adj. 合成的，複合的

▲ "Doghouse" is an example of compound words.

「狗屋」是複合字的例子之一。

9. **crucial** [ˋkruʃəl] adj. 極重要的 <to> [同] vital, critical, essential

▲ Mike's home run was crucial to our victory.

Mike 的全壘打是我們勝利的關鍵。

10. **diagnosis** [ˌdaɪəgˋnosɪs] n. [C][U] 診斷 <of> (pl. diagnoses)

▲ The doctor gave Cleo a diagnosis and then prescribed her some painkillers.

醫生替 Cleo 做診斷，然後開些止痛藥給她。

💡 initial diagnosis 初步診斷

11. **discriminate** [dɪˋskrɪməˌnet] v. 歧視 <against>；辨別，區分 <from, between> [同] differentiate

▲ The technology company discriminates against females and in favor of male job applicants.
這間科技公司歧視女性，偏好男性應徵者。

---

12. **gross** [gros] adj. 總共的；嚴重的

▲ The shipping fee is based on the gross weight.
運費以總重量計價。

💡 gross income 總收入

gross [gros] v. 獲得…總收入

▲ The trading company grossed about $10 million last year. 這間貿易公司去年總收入大約十億美元。

gross [gros] n. [sing.] 總收入 ；[C] 籮 (12 打，144 個) (pl. gross)

▲ Serena donated half of her gross to the animal shelter. Serena 捐了她一半的收入給動物收容所。

---

13. **incentive** [ɪnˋsɛntɪv] n. [C][U] 刺激，誘因 <to>

▲ Julia gave her daughter a dress as an incentive to complete the report on time. Julia 送她女兒一件洋裝，作為把報告準時完成的誘因。

incentive [ɪnˋsɛntɪv] adj. 激勵的

▲ The company provides incentive pay for hard-working employees.
這間公司提供獎勵性薪資給勤奮的員工。

---

14. **indigenous** [ɪnˋdɪdʒənəs] adj. 本地的，本土的 <to> [同] native

▲ Koalas are indigenous to Australia.

無尾熊是澳洲本土的動物。

💡 indigenous species 本土物種

---

15. **mint** [mɪnt] n. [C][U] 薄荷；[C] 鑄幣廠

▲ Steve likes to decorate the cake with a sprig of mint.
Steve 喜歡以薄荷枝點綴蛋糕。

---

16. **nowhere** [`no͵hwɛr] adv. 任何地方都沒…

▲ Nowhere else could you find such a good car.
你在任何地方都無法找到一臺這麼好的車。

💡 go/get/head nowhere 一無所成 | nowhere near 絕非

nowhere [`no͵hwɛr] pron. [U] 無處

▲ There was nowhere for the earthquake victims to go.
地震災民無處可去。

---

17. **offering** [`ɔfərɪŋ] n. [C] 供品

▲ Doris often makes offerings of fruit to the gods.
Doris 時常給神明供奉水果。

---

18. **precaution** [prɪ`kɔʃən] n. [C] 預防措施 <against>

▲ As a precaution, you should keep the copy of the contract. 為防萬一，你該保留合約影本。

💡 safety precautions 安全防範措施 | take the precaution of V-ing 做…來當預防措施

---

19. **riot** [`raɪət] n. [C] 暴動

▲ Many students were injured in the street riot last night. 許多學生在昨晚的街頭暴動中受傷。

💡 provoke/spark a riot 引起暴動

riot [`raɪət] v. 暴動

▲ The staff rioted when they learned about the pay cuts. 當員工得知減薪時開始暴動。

riotous [`raɪətəs] adj. 狂歡的 [同] wild；暴亂的

▲ After the riotous party, all the guests said their farewell to the host.

狂歡的派對後，所有賓客和主人道別。

---

20. **ritual** [`rɪtʃʊəl] n. [C][U] 儀式；慣例

▲ Many animals have rituals for mating.
許多動物有求偶儀式。

ritual [`rɪtʃʊəl] adj. 慣例的

▲ Every morning, Daniel makes ritual visits to the bakery for fresh bread.

Daniel 每天早上習慣去麵包店買新鮮麵包。

---

21. **straightforward** [,stret`fɔrwəd] adj. 直率的 ；明白的 [同] easy [反] complicated

▲ Sean is straightforward; he never beats around the bush. Sean 很直率，他從不拐彎抹角。

22. **subsequent** [`sʌbsɪ,kwɛnt] adj. 隨後的 ，接下來的 <to> [反] previous

▲ The political observer's subsequent statement cleared up the confusion.

政治評論家接下來的說明解開了疑惑。

subsequently [`sʌbsɪ,kwɛntlɪ] adv. 隨後 [反] previously

▲ The missing child was found and was subsequently sent to the police station.
失蹤小孩被找到，隨後被送進警局。

23. **supervisor** [ˌsupɚˈvaɪzɚ] n. [C] 監督者，主管
▲ A good supervisor requires the ability to communicate effectively and confidently.
一位好的主管要有能力進行有效而自信的溝通。

24. **trivial** [ˈtrɪvɪəl] adj. 微不足道的
▲ Let's not waste our time talking about trivial matters.
我們不要浪費時間在談論小事上。

25. **vulnerable** [ˈvʌlnərəbl] adj. 脆弱的，易受攻擊的 <to>
[反] invulnerable
▲ Regina is vulnerable to stress; she easily becomes frustrated. Regina 抗壓能力較差，她容易變得沮喪。

Unit 16

1. **adverse** [ədˈvɝs] adj. 不利的
▲ The baseball team successfully won the game in spite of adverse conditions.
儘管在不利的情況下，棒球隊成功贏得比賽。

2. **ass** [æs] n. [C] 傻瓜 [同] fool
▲ Harry made an ass of himself at the party.

Harry 在舞會上大出洋相。

---

3. **bid** [bɪd] n. [C] 招標 <for>；競爭

▲ The government invited bids for the construction of the museum. 政府招標博物館建築工程。

🔥 make a bid for... 對…出價 | win/lose a bid 得標 / 未得標

bid [bɪd] v. 出價 <for> (bid | bid | bidding)

▲ Kevin bids ten dollars for the old stove.

Kevin 出價十美元買這個舊爐子。

🔥 bid up sth 抬高…的價格 ; 競出高價購買… | bid against sb 與…爭相出高價競標

---

4. **blast** [blæst] n. [C] 一陣強風；爆炸

▲ A blast of wind shook the window.

一陣強風搖晃著窗戶。

🔥 blast from the past 舊物，故人 | full blast 最響亮地

blast [blæst] v. 爆破；發出刺耳聲

▲ The miners tried to blast a tunnel through the mountains. 礦工試著爆破出一條穿山隧道。

---

5. **bound** [baʊnd] v. 與…接界 <by>；彈跳

▲ Canada is bounded in the south by the U.S.

加拿大南端與美國接界。

bound [baʊnd] n. [C] 跳躍；[pl.] 限定區域 (～s) <of>

▲ The horse jumped over the fence with one bound.

這匹馬一個跳躍跳過了圍籬。

🔥 by/in leaps and bounds 非常迅速地

bound [baʊnd] adj. 一定會 <to>

▲ It's bound to snow tomorrow. 明天一定會下雪。

♦ bound and determined 一定要 | bound up 緊密相關的

---

6. **cognitive** [ˋkɑgnətɪv] adj. 認知的

▲ Is Mr. Lin still in the field of cognitive science?
林先生是否還在認知科學領域？

---

7. **comprehend** [ˌkɑmprɪˋhɛnd] v. 理解 [同] understand,
grasp

▲ The police still can't comprehend how the murder
was committed. 警察仍無法理解凶案是如何發生的。

---

8. **comprehension** [ˌkɑmprɪˋhɛnʃən] n. [U] 理解力 [同]
understanding

▲ Tina's crazy idea is far beyond our comprehension.
Tina 的瘋狂點子遠超乎我們的理解力。

comprehensible [ˌkɑmprɪˋhɛnsəbl] adj. 可理解的 <to>
[同] understandable [反] incomprehensible

▲ This postmodern movie is not comprehensible to me.
我看不懂這部後現代電影。

---

9. **dilemma** [dəˋlɛmə] n. [C] 進退兩難

▲ Fiona is in a dilemma about whether she should tell
the truth. Fiona 進退兩難，不知是否該說實話。

♦ caught in a dilemma 處於兩難的情況 |
confronted/faced with a dilemma 面對進退兩難的情
況 | moral/ethical dilemma 道德 / 倫理兩難

---

10. **distinction** [dɪ`stɪŋkʃən] n. [C][U] 區別，差異
<between>

▲ Make a clear distinction between good and evil.
明確的區別善與惡。

11. **franchise** [`fræntʃaɪz] n. [C] 特許經營權；[sing.] 選舉權
(the ～)

▲ You need to pay a lot to become a franchise holder
of this company.
你需要付很多錢才能成為這家公司的特許經營者。

12. **habitat** [`hæbə,tæt] n. [C][U] (動物的) 棲息地

▲ Many animals are losing their natural habitats
because of the area's urbanization. 許多動物正因這
個地區的都市化而失去牠們的天然棲息地。

13. **index** [`ɪndɛks] n. [C] 索引 (pl. indexes, indices)

▲ It's easy for you to find your friend's name with the
help of the index.
在索引的協助下，你可以很輕鬆地找到你朋友的名字。

● index finger 食指

index [`ɪndɛks] v. 編索引

▲ Wendy needs me to help her index all the subjects in
this book.
Wendy 需要我幫她索引這本書裡所有的主題。

14. **infrastructure** [`ɪnfrə,strʌktʃɚ] n. [C] 基礎建設 (usu.
sing.)

▲ The government will invest 100 million in the city's infrastructure.

政府將會投資一億在該城市的基礎建設上。

---

15. **noticeable** [`notɪsəbḷ] adj. 明顯的

▲ There is a noticeable improvement in your work in such a short time.

你的工作表現在短時間內有非常明顯的進步。

noticeably [`notɪsəblɪ] adv. 明顯地

▲ After the New Year's Eve celebration, the streets were noticeably dirtier than usual.

跨年晚會過後，街道明顯比平常更髒亂。

---

16. **obligation** [,ɑblə`geʃən] n. [C] 義務 <to>

▲ Every citizen has an obligation to vote.

每一個市民都有投票的義務。

obligatory [ə`blɪgə,torɪ] adj. 必須做的 [同] compulsory, mandatory [反] optional

▲ The wearing of a uniform is obligatory.

依照規定穿制服是大家都必須做的。

---

17. **opponent** [ə`ponənt] n. [C] 對手 [同] adversary；反對者 <of>

▲ Even though I defeated you this time, I must admit that you are a worthy opponent.

雖然這次打敗了你，但我必須承認你是個可敬的對手。

---

18. **prejudice** [`prɛdʒədɪs] n. [C][U] 偏見 <against, for>

▲ The woman has a strong prejudice against homosexuals. 這位女子對同性戀者有強烈的偏見。

💡 eliminate/dispel the prejudice 摒除偏見 | racial/sexual prejudice 種族 / 性別偏見

prejudice [ˋprɛdʒədɪs] v. 使有偏見 <against>

▲ The TV station tried to prejudice people against the candidate.
這電視臺試圖使人們對這位候選人產生偏見。

prejudiced [ˋprɛdʒədɪst] adj. 有偏見的 <against>

▲ Nick has always been prejudiced against domestic wine. Nick 對國產酒一直有偏見。

---

19. **rival** [ˋraɪvl̩] adj. 競爭的

▲ Our company's losses come from the largest customers changing to our rival company.
我們公司的損失來自於最大的客戶轉向競爭公司。

rival [ˋraɪvl̩] n. [C] 對手 <for> [同] competitor

▲ The athlete is Ken's main rival for the swimming competition.
這名運動員是 Ken 在游泳比賽中最主要的對手。

rival [ˋraɪvl̩] v. 與⋯相匹敵 <in, for>

▲ My aunt can rival the celebrity in beauty.
我阿姨的美貌可以和這明星相匹敵。

---

20. **salon** [səˋlɑn] n. [C] 美髮廳，美髮沙龍

▲ Wendy went to the hair salon yesterday and had her hair cut. Wendy 昨天去美髮廳剪頭髮了。

21. **striking** [ˈstraɪkɪŋ] adj. 驚人的 [同] marked
   ▲ These two paintings have striking similarities.
   這兩幅畫作有著驚人的相似處。
   💡 striking contrast/similarity 驚人的對比 / 相似

22. **supposedly** [səˈpozɪdlɪ] adv. 大概
   ▲ This was supposedly the place where da Vinci painted his famous painting.
   這大概是達文西畫他著名畫作的地方。

23. **transmission** [trænsˈmɪʃən] n. [U] 傳播 <of> [同] transfer
   ▲ Mosquito bites open an avenue to the transmission of dengue fever.
   蚊子的叮咬替登革熱的傳播開啟了一條途徑。

24. **undergo** [ˌʌndəˈgo] v. 經歷；接受 (underwent | undergone | undergoing)
   ▲ The country has undergone great changes in recent years. 這個國家近幾年來經歷了很大的變化。

25. **whatsoever** [ˌhwɑtsoˈɛvə] pron. 無論什麼
   whatsoever [ˌhwɑtsoˈɛvə] adj. 無論什麼的

Unit 17

1. **agenda** [əˈdʒɛndə] n. [C] 議題 <on>

▲ How to improve our economy is the first item on today's agenda.

如何改善我們的經濟是今天的第一個議題。

💡 on the agenda 在議程上｜set the agenda 制定議程

---

2. **assault** [ə`sɔlt] n. [C][U] 襲擊 <on>

▲ Assaults on police officers have greatly increased over the past five years.

襲擊警察的事件在過去五年大幅增加。

💡 sexual/indecent assault 性侵害／猥褻行為｜assault and battery 暴力毆打｜make an assault on sb/sth 攻擊…；抨擊…

assault [ə`sɔlt] v. 攻擊；擾人

▲ It is reported that a crazy man assaulted passengers at random at the airport.

據報導指出，有名瘋狂男子在機場隨機攻擊旅客。

---

3. **boom** [bum] n. [C] (商業) 繁榮 <in> (usu. sing.)；熱潮

▲ No one could have foreseen a financial crisis would follow the boom in real estate. 沒有人能預料到房地產的突然繁榮之後是一場金融危機。

boom [bum] v. 發出轟鳴聲 <out>；迅速發展

▲ A voice suddenly boomed out from the speakers in the office and surprised the staff.

辦公室的喇叭突然發出轟鳴聲驚嚇到所有員工。

---

4. **boxer** [`bɑksɚ] n. [C] 拳擊手

▲ The boxer is in strict training for his next fight.

這名拳擊手為了他下一次的搏鬥正進行嚴格的訓練。

---

5. **breakthrough** [`brek,θru] n. [C] 突破 <in>

▲ The discovery of penicillin was a major breakthrough in medicine. 盤尼西林的發現是醫學上的重大突破。

---

6. **conduct** [kən`dʌkt] v. 實行，安排

▲ The protesters called on cosmetic industries to stop conducting experiments on animals.
抗議者呼籲美妝產業停止實行動物實驗。

💡 conduct oneself …舉止表現

conduct [`kandʌkt] n. [U] 舉止

▲ The customer was driven out for his violent conduct.
這名客人因其暴力舉止被趕出去。

---

7. **conform** [kən`fɔrm] v. 順從 (規範) <to>；符合 <to, with>

▲ Every student is required to conform to the school regulations. 每個學生均必須順從校規的規範。

---

8. **confrontation** [,kanfrən`teʃən] n. [C] 衝突 <with, between>

▲ Violent confrontations between the employees and the employer were reported.
員工與僱主的暴力衝突被報導出來。

---

9. **diminish** [də`mınıʃ] v. 減少，縮小 [同] reduce

▲ Our food supplies are diminishing rapidly.
我們的糧食供應正迅速減少中。

💡 diminish sb's resolution 削弱…的決心 | diminish in value 價值滑落

---

10. **distract** [dɪ`strækt] v. 使分心 <from> [同] divert
  ▲ Don't let the noise outside distract you from your reading. 別讓外面的噪音分散你閱讀的注意力。
  distracted [dɪ`stræktɪd] adj. 心煩意亂的 <by>
  ▲ Danny was distracted by the devastating news. Danny 因那噩耗而心煩意亂。

---

11. **horizontal** [,hɔrə`zɑntl̩] adj. 水平的
  ▲ The company's new logo consists of horizontal and vertical lines.
  這個公司的新標誌包含水平和垂直的線。
  horizontal [,hɔrə`zɑntl̩] n. [sing.] 水平線 (the ～)
  ▲ It's difficult to stand at an angle of 45 degrees to the horizontal without any external assistance. 在沒有外力幫助下很難以與水平線成四十五度的角度站立。

---

12. **initiate** [ɪ`nɪʃɪ,et] v. 發起
  ▲ The government initiated a series of economic reforms. 政府發起一連串的經濟改革。
  initiate [ɪ`nɪʃɪ,et] adj. 新加入的
  initiate [ɪ`nɪʃɪ,et] n. [C] 新進者
  ▲ Jerry is an initiate of this religious group.
  Jerry 是這個宗教團體的新進者。
  initiation [ɪ,nɪʃɪ`eʃən] n. [U] (正式的) 開始 <of>

▲ This detective fiction was the initiation of Joanne's writing career.

這本偵探小說是 Joanne 寫作生涯的開始。

---

13. **institute** [ˈɪnstəˌtjut] n. [C] 研究機構 <of, for>

▲ Scott is eager to enter the prestigious institute for space studies.

Scott 渴望進入這個享負盛名的太空研究機構。

institute [ˈɪnstəˌtjut] v. 制定，建立

▲ The local government had no choice but to institute policies to improve the quality of tourism.

當地政府不得不制定政策來改善旅遊品質。

---

14. **obscure** [əbˈskjʊr] adj. 模糊不清的；偏僻的

▲ When the police inquired about his missing wife, the man gave an obscure explanation.

當警方詢問他失蹤妻子的下落，男子的解釋很含糊。

obscure [əbˈskjʊr] v. 掩蔽

▲ A thick mist obscured the path. 濃霧遮蔽了道路。

obscurity [əbˈskjʊrətɪ] n. [U] 模糊；默默無聞

▲ The obscurity of the passage puzzled the scholar.

這個語意模糊的段落令這學者困惑。

---

15. **opt** [ɑpt] v. 選擇 <for, to>

▲ Allen opted for a trip to Tokyo rather than to Thailand. Allen 選擇去東京旅行而不是泰國。

---

16. **preliminary** [prɪˈlɪməˌnɛrɪ] adj. 初步的 [同] initial

▲Taiwan has begun preliminary talks with Japan on a wide range of issues.

臺灣已和日本展開關於各種的問題的初步對談。

preliminary [prɪ`lɪməˌnɛrɪ] n. [C] 預賽 (usu. pl.) (pl. preliminaries)

▲Those who win the preliminaries will go on to the final competition. 預賽中的獲勝者將進入決賽。

17. **prospect** [`prɑspɛkt] n. [C][U] 可能性；前景 (usu. pl.)

▲After having a fight with Helen, Tom found that there was no prospect of making it up with her in a short time. 與 Helen 爭吵後，Tom 發現短期內沒有與她和好的機會。

💡 career/job/business prospects 事業 / 工作 / 商業前景 | in prospect 即將到來的

prospect [`prɑspɛkt] v. 探勘 <for>

▲The oil company has prospected for oil in Africa for fourteen years.

這家石油公司花了十四年在非洲探勘石油。

18. **recession** [rɪ`sɛʃən] n. [C][U] 經濟蕭條

▲The hardest-hit country is now in a deep recession.

這個受災最嚴重的國家正經歷嚴重的經濟蕭條。

19. **sandal** [`sændl] n. [C] 涼鞋

▲Wearing a pair of sandals in summer is quite comfortable. 夏天穿涼鞋還蠻舒服的。

20. **scheme** [skim] n. [C] 計畫，方案 <for, to> [同] program

▲ More and more universities now start schemes to strengthen the links between schools and the industries. 越來越多大學開始執行計畫以強化學校和業界之間的連結。

scheme [skim] v. 密謀 <against, to> [同] plot

▲ The military leader is scheming against the present government. 該軍事領袖密謀策反現任政府。

21. **structural** [ˋstrʌktʃərəl] adj. 結構上的

▲ The monument doesn't suffer from any structural damage. 這座古蹟沒有遭到任何結構上的損壞。

💡 structural damage/changes/defects 結構上的損害 / 改變 / 缺陷

22. **sustain** [səˋsten] v. 維持 (生命) [同] maintain

▲ The planet which was recently discovered is unable to sustain animal or plant life for its lack of water resources. 這個最近發現的星球因為缺乏水資源而無法維持動植物的生命。

23. **undoubtedly** [ʌnˋdautɪdlɪ] adv. 確實地，無疑地

▲ While working hard doesn't guarantee to make progress, making progress undoubtedly requires working hard.
雖然努力並不保證進步，但是要進步無疑需要努力。

24. **venture** [ˋvɛntʃɚ] n. [C] (有風險的) 企業

▲ My husband invested in a joint venture.
我丈夫投資一項合資企業。

venture [ˋvɛntʃɚ] v. 冒險去；冒昧地說 <to>

▲ Owen ventured into the Amazon jungle.
Owen 冒險進入亞馬遜叢林。

---

25. **whereabouts** [ˋwɛrəˌbaʊts] n. [pl.] (某人或某物的) 行蹤 <of>

▲ The police don't have a clue to the suspect's whereabouts. 警方不知嫌犯的行蹤。

whereabouts [ˌwɛrəˋbaʊts] adv. (詢問) 在哪

▲ Whereabouts are they filming the documentary?
他們在哪裡拍攝紀錄片？

Unit 18

1. **aggression** [əˋgrɛʃən] n. [U] 攻擊

▲ The September 11 attacks could be considered an act of aggression. 九一一攻擊事件可說是攻擊的行為。

---

2. **assert** [əˋsɝt] v. 宣稱；堅持

▲ The counsel asserted the accused to be innocent.
辯護律師宣稱被告是清白的。

💡 assert oneself 堅持己見 | assert sb's rights/independence/superiority 堅持…權利 / 獨立 / 優勢

assertion [əˋsɝʃən] n. [C][U] 主張 <that> [同] claim

▲Nobody agrees with his assertion that women are inferior to men. 沒有人贊同他男尊女卑的主張。

assertive [əˋsɝtɪv] adj. 自信的 [反] submissive

▲Kelly speaks in such an assertive way that everyone listens to her.

Kelly 說話十分有自信所以大家都聽從她。

3. **bruise** [bruz] n. [C] 瘀傷；(水果) 碰傷

▲Lewis was so lucky that he just got a few cuts and bruises in the car accident. Lewis 是如此幸運而在這場車禍中只有些傷口和瘀傷。

bruise [bruz] v. 使出現傷痕，碰傷

▲Cindy fell down the stairs and bruised her arms. Cindy 從樓梯上跌落，擦傷了她的手臂。

4. **bully** [ˋbʊlɪ] n. [C] 欺負弱小的人 (pl. bullies)

▲Sam is very strong, but he never plays the bully. Sam 很強壯，但他從不欺負弱小的人。

♥ bully for sb (表諷刺)⋯太棒了

bully [ˋbʊlɪ] v. 欺負；強迫

▲Ben was big for his age and used to bully his classmates. 就 Ben 的年齡來說，他身材高大，因此常欺負班上同學。

♥ bully sb into/out of 強迫人去做 / 停止做⋯

5. **bureau** [ˋbjʊro] n. [C] 局 (pl. bureaus, bureaux)

▲The Tourism Bureau provides useful information and suggestions on travel in Taiwan.

觀光局提供在臺灣旅遊的實用資訊及建議。

6. **consecutive** [kən`sɛkjətɪv] adj. 連續的
   ▲ Winning three consecutive basketball games was a major triumph for our school team. 連續獲得三場籃球賽的勝利是我們校隊的一大勝利。

7. **currency** [`kɝ·ənsɪ] n. [C][U] 貨幣 (pl. currencies)
   ▲ Bitcoin is a digital currency that can be used to pay for goods and services.
   比特幣是一種可以用來支付商品和服務的數位貨幣。

8. **devotion** [dɪ`voʃən] n. [U] 致力於 <to>
   ▲ Mr. Liu's devotion to the study of English history is well-known.
   劉先生致力於英國史的研究是眾所皆知的。

9. **dissolve** [dɪ`zɑlv] v. 融化 <in>；結束
   ▲ Salt dissolves quickly in water. 鹽在水中會迅速融化。
   💡 dissolve into tears/laughter 情不自禁哭了 / 笑了

10. **distinctive** [dɪ`stɪŋktɪv] adj. 獨特的 [同] characteristic
    ▲ A wombat has a distinctive pouch, which opens toward its bottom rather than its head. 袋熊有獨特的育兒袋，它的開口朝向牠的臀部而非頭部。
    💡 distinctive smell/taste 獨特的氣味 / 味道

11. **dreadful** [`drɛdfəl] adj. 討厭的，糟透的 [同] terrible
    ▲ Not until this moment did Ben realize that he made a dreadful mistake.

直到此刻 Ben 才意識到他犯了很糟的錯誤。

12. **housing** [ˋhaʊzɪŋ] n. [U] 住宅；住宅供給
   ▲ The policy is aimed at providing affordable housing for all citizens.
   這項政策的目的在於提供所有市民負擔得起的住宅。

13. **insight** [ˋɪn͵saɪt] n. [C][U] 理解，洞察力 <into>
   ▲ The book gave me an insight into life in medieval Europe. 這本書使我清楚地了解中世紀的歐洲生活。

14. **journalist** [ˋdʒɝnlɪst] n. [C] 新聞記者
   ▲ Cathy is a journalist with *The Times*.
   Cathy 是《泰晤士報》的新聞記者。

15. **optional** [ˋɑpʃənl] adj. 可選擇的
   ▲ Some courses are compulsory, while others are optional. 有些課程是必修，有些是選修。

16. **organism** [ˋɔrgən͵ɪzəm] n. [C] 有機體，生物
   ▲ The doctors are trying to identify the organism that caused the infection.
   醫生正試著找出導致感染的有機體。

17. **presumably** [prɪˋzuməblɪ] adv. 可能，大概
   ▲ Presumably my boyfriend was busy and forgot our date. 可能我男友很忙忘記了我們的約會。

18. **ratio** [ˋreʃo] n. [C] 比率 (pl. ratios)

▲ The ratio of male to female births in this country is approximately six to five.

這個國家的男女出生比率約為六比五。

---

19. **scandal** [`skændl] n. [C][U] 醜聞；恥辱

▲ The politician resigned his post because of the sex scandal. 政治家因性醜聞而下臺。

♥ sex/political/financial scandal 性 / 政治 / 金融醜聞 | cause/create a scandal 變成醜聞 | scandal broke 醜聞曝光

scandalous [`skændələs] adj. 誹謗性的

▲ It is really a scandalous rumor. 這真是誹謗性的流言。

---

20. **segment** [`sɛgmənt] n. [C] 部分 <of>

▲ A large segment of the laborers were laid off because of the economic recession.

一大部分的勞工因經濟不景氣而被解僱。

segment [`sɛgmənt] v. 分割 <into>

▲ The cake was segmented into 12 pieces.

蛋糕被分割為十二塊。

---

21. **supervision** [ˌsupə`vɪʒən] n. [U] 監督

▲ The project was conducted under the supervision of the manager. 企劃案在經理的監督下進行。

♥ under sb's supervision 在…的監督下

---

22. **symbolic** [sɪm`bɑlɪk] adj. 象徵性的 <of>

▲ The dove is symbolic of peace. 鴿子是象徵和平。

23. **valid** [ˋvælɪd] adj. 正當的；有效的

▲ Tommy had a valid reason for being absent.
Tommy 有正當的理由缺席。

validity [vəˋlɪdətɪ] n. [U] 正當性；效力

▲ The validity of the law is questionable.
這條法律的正當性令人質疑。

---

24. **wheelchair** [ˋwilˋtʃɛr] n. [C] 輪椅

▲ After a car accident, the man was confined to a
wheelchair. 男子車禍後就離不開輪椅了。

---

25. **whereas** [hwɛrˋæz] conj. 然而

▲ The rich enjoy luxuries whereas the poor struggle for
survival.
有錢人享受奢華，然而窮人必須掙扎奮鬥才得以生存。

Unit 19

1. **agony** [ˋægənɪ] n. [C][U] (精神或肉體上) 極大的痛苦
<in> (pl. agonies)

▲ The abandoned baby was crying in agony when
found on the park bench.
棄嬰在公園的長椅上被發現時正痛苦地哭泣。

agonize [ˋægənaɪz] v. 苦惱 <over, about>

▲ The man agonized for weeks about whether he
should marry the demanding woman. 男人花了好幾
個星期苦惱是否該和那苛刻的女人結婚。

2. **assumption** [ə`sʌmpʃən] n. [C][U] 假定

▲ Many people make the assumption that going to college can help them find a better job.

許多人假定上大學可以幫助他們找到較好的工作。

💡 on the assumption that... 在假定…的情況下

3. **burial** [`bɛrɪəl] n. [C][U] 葬禮

▲ Last Friday, my family went to Tainan for my grandfather's burial.

上週五，我家人去臺南參加祖父的葬禮。

4. **calcium** [`kælsɪəm] n. [U] 鈣

▲ Soy milk has a lot of calcium content.

豆漿有豐富的鈣含量。

5. **cathedral** [kə`θidrəl] n. [C] 大教堂

▲ Heavy moisture slowly rotted the sculpture in the cathedral. 濃厚的溼氣慢慢腐蝕了大教堂的雕塑。

6. **contaminate** [kən`tæmə͵net] v. (毒物、輻射等) 汙染 <with>

▲ Some people are concerned that food from Japan may have been contaminated with radiation.

有些人擔心日本來的食物可能遭到輻射汙染。

contamination [kən͵tæmə`neʃən] n. [U] 汙染

▲ Hundreds of people were poisoned owing to the contamination of the water supply.

供水系統的汙染造成數百人中毒。

7. **deadly** [ˋdɛdlɪ] adj. 致命的 [同] lethal；死一般的；極度的 (deadlier | deadliest)

▲ The policeman received a deadly wound in gun fights with a heavily armed bandit.
在與重武裝匪徒的槍戰中警察受了致命的傷。

deadly [ˋdɛdlɪ] adv. 極度地

▲ The lecture was deadly dull.
這場演講極度地枯燥乏味。

8. **document** [ˋdɑkjə‚mənt] n. [C] 文件

▲ Lily has stored tons of documents in the cloud.
Lily 已經將很多文件儲存在雲端。

document [ˋdɑkjə‚mənt] v. 記錄

▲ The film documents the beauty of Taiwan.
這部電影記錄了臺灣的美。

9. **donation** [doˋneʃən] n. [C][U] 捐贈

▲ The victims of the earthquake need donations of food and other daily necessities.
地震災民需要食物和其他的日常用品的捐贈。

10. **eloquent** [ˋɛləkwənt] adj. 有說服力的

▲ The lawyer made an eloquent plea to the judge.
這個律師有說服力的向法官申訴。

eloquently [ˋɛləkwəntlɪ] adv. 口才好地

▲ The politician speaks eloquently on the issue of human rights. 這位政治家口才好地談論人權議題。

11. **hypothesis** [haɪˋpɑθəsɪs] n. [C] 假設 [同] theory (pl. hypotheses)

▲ Although nobody trusted the woman's hypothesis, she still held her ground. 雖然沒有人相信女人的假設，她仍然堅持自己的立場。

12. **institution** [ˌɪnstəˋtjuʃən] n. [C] 機構

▲ The charitable institution is raising a fund for the homeless. 這間慈善機構正為無家可歸的人們募款。

13. **justify** [ˋdʒʌstəˌfaɪ] v. 證明…合理

▲ How can you justify borrowing to invest? 你如何能證明貸款去投資是合理的？

14. **nutrition** [njuˋtrɪʃən] n. [U] 營養

▲ Good nutrition is essential to a child's growth and development.
良好的營養對孩子的成長與發育是必要的。

15. **output** [ˋaʊtˌpʊt] n. [U] 生產量

▲ Last year, manufacturing output increased by 20%.
去年的工業生產量增加了 20%。

output [ˋaʊtˌpʊt] v. 生產 (output, outputted | output, outputted | outputting)

▲ The machine can output the products in a short time.
這臺機器可以在短時間內生產商品。

16. **partly** [ˋpɑrtlɪ] adv. 部分地

▲It is partly because of the high tuition that Amy decided not to go to university.

部分是因為高學費，所以 Amy 決定不讀大學。

---

17. **progressive** [prə`grɛsɪv] adj. 進步的

▲People are pressing for a more progressive social policy. 人民要求更進步的社會政策。

progressive [prə`grɛsɪv] n. [C] 革新主義者

▲Progressives are supporting new ideas, in contrast with reactionaries.

與保守分子相比，革新主義者支持新的想法。

---

18. **recommend** [ˌrɛkə`mɛnd] v. 推薦 <for>

▲Vicky was recommended for a promotion by her superior. Vicky 被她的上司推薦升職。

---

19. **sensation** [sɛn`seʃən] n. [C][U] 知覺；[sing.] 轟動

▲The man lost his sensation in his leg after the car accident. 在車禍之後，男人的腿失去了知覺。

sensational [sɛn`seʃnl] adj. 轟動的

▲There has been much sensational reporting of the president's assassination.

有很多轟動的報導關於總統遇刺案。

---

20. **sentiment** [`sɛntəmənt] n. [C][U] 觀點；[U] 傷感

▲Clara agreed with my sentiment about the war.

Clara 同意我對這場戰爭的觀點。

---

21. **syndrome** [`sɪnˌdrom] n. [C] 綜合症

▲ People over forty should have regular checkups to see if they have any syndromes closely associated with cancer. 四十歲以上的人需要定期健康檢查，確認是否有與癌症密切相關的綜合症。

22. **theft** [θɛft] n. [C][U] 盜竊 <of>
▲ Mr. Lin was accused of car theft.
林先生被控盜竊車輛。

23. **variation** [ˌvɛrɪ`eʃən] n. [C][U] 變動 <on, in>；[C] 變奏曲
▲ There is little variation in the temperature here all year round. 這裡的氣溫一年四季幾乎沒有什麼變化。

24. **widespread** [`waɪdˌsprɛd] adj. 廣泛的
▲ The widespread use of plastic products causes serious damage to not only the environment but the human body. 廣泛使用塑膠製品不只對環境也對人體造成嚴重傷害。

25. **witty** [`wɪtɪ] adj. 機智的 (wittier | wittiest)
▲ The actress made a witty reply to the interviewer's question.
這位女演員對於訪問者的問題做了機智的回答。

Unit 20

1. **aisle** [aɪl] n. [C] 走道

▲ Can I have an aisle seat in the non-smoking section?
我可以選在禁菸區的靠走道座位嗎？

💡 go/walk down the aisle 結婚

2. **architect** [`ɑrkə,tɛkt] n. [C] 建築師
▲ The architect will be present at the groundbreaking ceremony. 這位建築師會來參加動土典禮。

3. **astonish** [ə`stɑnɪʃ] v. 使驚訝 [同] amaze
▲ The violinist's brilliant performance astonished the audience. 小提琴家精采的演出使觀眾很驚訝。

astonishment [ə`stɑnɪʃmənt] n. [U] 驚訝 <in> [同] amazement
▲ Gary stared at his wife in astonishment.
Gary 驚訝地看著他妻子。

astonished [ə`stɑnɪʃt] adj. 驚訝的 <to, at> [同] amazed
▲ The man was astonished to hear what had happened.
聽到所發生的事讓男子感到驚訝。

astonishing [ə`stɑnɪʃɪŋ] adj. 令人驚訝的 [同] amazing
▲ Rita has made astonishing progress in English recently. 最近 Rita 在英文方面已有令人驚訝的進步。

4. **capability** [,kepə`bɪlətɪ] n. [C][U] 能力 <of, to> (pl. capabilities)
▲ Owen's capability of making a fortune became evident. Owen 賺錢的能力都顯露出來了。

5. **cautious** [`kɔʃəs] adj. 謹慎的 <about>

▲ The government promised to take the most cautious approach to the forest exploitation.

政府承諾會以最謹慎態度面對森林開發。

💡 cautious optimism 謹慎的樂觀態度

---

6. **chef** [ʃɛf] n. [C] 主廚 (pl. chefs)

▲ Paul is determined to be the best chef in the world.
Paul 立志要當世界上最棒的主廚。

---

7. **contemplate** [ˋkɑntəmˌplet] v. 考慮；深思 [同] consider

▲ The man contemplated quitting his current job and pursuing his dream.

這男子考慮離開現職去追求他的夢想。

contemplation [ˌkɑntəmˋpleʃən] n [U] 沉思

▲ Looking at the old photos, Emma seemed lost in contemplation. 看著舊照片，Emma 似乎陷入沉思。

---

8. **decline** [dɪˋklaɪn] n. [sing.] 下降 <in> ；衰退 (the ~) <in>

▲ There has been a gradual decline in that aging singer's popularity. 那位年老歌手的聲望逐漸下滑。

decline [dɪˋklaɪn] v. 下降；衰退

▲ The birth rate is rapidly declining in this country.
該國的出生率正在迅速下降當中。

---

9. **eligible** [ˋɛlɪdʒəbl̩] adj. 有資格的 <to, for>

▲ Anyone over twenty is eligible to vote.
二十歲以上者有資格投票。

💡 eligible for membership 有資格成為會員

10. **embrace** [ɪm`bres] **v.** 擁抱 [同] hug
    ▲ When my parents saw me at the airport, they embraced me warmly.
    當我父母在機場見到我，他們熱情地擁抱我。

    embrace [ɪm`bres] **n.** [C] 擁抱
    ▲ Penny held me in a tight embrace.
    Penny 緊緊的擁抱我。

11. **evolution** [͵ɛvə`luʃən] **n.** [U] 進化；發展
    ▲ According to Darwin's theory of evolution, humans evolved from apes.
    根據達爾文進化論的說法，人類從猿猴進化而來。

12. **impulse** [`ɪmpʌls] **n.** [C] 衝動 <to> [同] urge
    ▲ Ian feels an impulse to run out of here and run to the beach for a swim.
    Ian 有股衝動想逃離這裡去海灘游泳。

    💡 on impulse 衝動地

    impulsive [ɪm`pʌlsɪv] **adj.** 衝動的 [同] impetuous, rash
    ▲ Tim is an impulsive person; we never know what he will do next.
    Tim 是個衝動的人，我們從不知道他下一步會做什麼。

    impulsively [ɪm`pʌlsɪvlɪ] **adv.** 衝動地
    ▲ Linda bought the tablet impulsively.
    Linda 衝動地買了這臺平板電腦。

13. **intact** [ɪnˋtækt] adj. 未受損的 [同] undamaged

▲ The building remained intact after the earthquake.
這棟建築物在經歷地震後仍未受損。

---

14. **lawsuit** [ˋlɔ͵sut] n. [C] 訴訟 [同] suit

▲ The former employee filed a lawsuit against her former employer.
這位前員工對她的前僱主提出訴訟。

---

15. **oversee** [͵ovɚˋsi] v. 監督 [同] supervise (oversaw │ overseen │ overseeing)

▲ James was assigned to oversee the branch in Taiwan.
James 被指派監督在臺灣的分公司。

---

16. **patrol** [pəˋtrol] n. [C][U] 巡邏 <on>

▲ After a series of robberies, more and more police officers are on patrol.
在接二連三的搶案之後，有越來越多警察在巡邏。

💡 patrol car/boat 巡邏車 / 艇

patrol [pəˋtrol] v. 巡邏 (patrolled │ patrolled │ patrolling)

▲ A body was found while the police patrolled along the riverbank. 警方在沿河岸巡邏時發現一具遺體。

---

17. **presidential** [͵prɛzəˋdɛnʃəl] adj. 總統的

▲ In America, presidential elections are held every four years. 在美國，總統選舉每四年會舉行一次。

---

18. **prolong** [prəˋlɔŋ] v. 延長 [同] lengthen, extend

▲ The improvement of medicine has prolonged human life. 醫學進步延長了人類的壽命。

prolonged [prə`lɔŋd] adj. 長時間的

▲ After a prolonged discussion, they finally made a decision. 在長時間的討論之後,他們終於做了決定。

---

19. **risky** [`rɪskɪ] adj. 危險的 [同] dangerous (riskier | riskiest)

▲ The patient is going to undergo a risky operation this week. 這個病人這星期將接受一項危險的手術。

---

20. **sensitivity** [ˌsɛnsə`tɪvətɪ] n. [U] 敏感 <to>

▲ Antony was shut out by his colleagues because of his sensitivity to criticism.

Antony 對批評過於敏感,讓他被同事排擠。

---

21. **shed** [ʃɛd] v. 掉下;擺脫 (shed | shed | shedding)

▲ Mina shed tears while listening to the moving story.

Mina 聽動人的故事時掉下眼淚。

💡 shed light on... 照亮⋯;為⋯提供解釋 | shed blood 流血

shed [ʃɛd] n. [C] 車棚

▲ There is a bicycle shed behind the building.

這棟大樓後面有個腳踏車車棚。

---

22. **temptation** [tɛmp`teʃən] n. [C] 誘惑物;[U] 誘惑

▲ A big city provides many temptations.

大城市有許多誘惑的事物。

---

23. **virtual** [ˋvɝtʃʊəl] adj. 實質上的；(透過電腦) 虛擬的

▲ The plan is a virtual impossibility.

這計畫實際上是不可行的。

virtually [ˋvɝtʃʊəlɪ] adv. 實質上地

▲ Ted virtually runs the shop when the boss is away.

當老闆外出時，Ted 實質上是這間店的管理者。

24. **vocal** [ˋvokl] adj. 直言不諱的 <about> [同] outspoken

▲ The city's mayor was extremely vocal about the danger of nuclear plants.

該市市長非常直言不諱地表達核能電廠的危險性。

💡 vocal critic 直言不諱的批評

vocal [ˋvokl] n. [C] 人聲演唱 (usu. pl.)

▲ Who sang the vocals on that track?

那張唱片人聲部分的演唱者是誰？

25. **workshop** [ˋwɝk͵ʃɑp] n. [C] 工作坊

▲ The city government actively holds a series of workshops for migrant workers.

該市政府積極為外籍移工舉辦一系列工作坊。

單字索引

Index

單字索引

單字索引

單字索引

單字索引

單字索引

單字索引

單字索引

單字索引

單字索引

單字索引

單字索引

單字索引

單字索引

單字索引

單字索引

國家圖書館出版品預行編目資料

核心英文字彙力2001~4500隨身讀／三民英語編輯小
組彙整.——修訂三版一刷.——臺北市: 三民, 2023
面;　公分.——(英語Make Me High系列)

ISBN 978-957-14-7708-4 (平裝)
1. 英語 2. 詞彙

805.12   112015956

英語 *Make Me High* 系列

核心英文字彙力 2001~4500 隨身讀

彙　　　整	三民英語編輯小組
發 行 人	劉振強
出 版 者	三民書局股份有限公司
地　　　址	臺北市復興北路 386 號 (復北門市)
	臺北市重慶南路一段 61 號 (重南門市)
電　　　話	(02)25006600
網　　　址	三民網路書店 https://www.sanmin.com.tw
出 版 日 期	初版一刷 2021 年 10 月
	二版一刷 2022 年 9 月
	修訂三版一刷 2023 年 10 月
書 籍 編 號	S871570
I S B N	978-957-14-7708-4